Those Beneath

Almedia Ryan

Part One

Veil

prologue

She ran, the cold biting at her feet which had long ago turned a disturbing shade of blue. Though she normally preferred her feet bare, this was a tactic to keep her trapped within the confines of her dismal new home, a home she had been forced to choose. A home she could never escape.

"You really shouldn't run from me." Her captor's taunts echoed off the bleak corridor's frozen stones. "I warn you—patience is not a virtue I possess."

She pushed herself harder. The massive, black iron doors, upon which hung the undesirables who had failed their masters, were only a few feet away. The puca and trolls dangled, their skin searing from the iron and covered in oozing blisters. She tried to block out their agonizing screams, but the shrill noise pierced her ears. Their suffering filled her chest with a vicious knot as if it were her own. It clamped down on her kind heart like a vice. Her eyes glistened, the subtle brimming moisture transforming to frosted crystals. True tears threatened to escape if she didn't avert her gaze—if she had any left to spill.

"There you are." He growled. His breath touched the back of her neck. She ran faster. This was the farthest she had ever made it and the pain was already beginning to fester in her left arm. It would spiral its way up to encompass her entire body, consuming her to her last breath. This was the misery of a broken vow. She would suffer and freely welcome death rather than stay a moment longer. "Where do you think you are going, hmm?" His laughter grew louder as each step brought him closer. "You know you can't leave."

Just as her hand grazed the large hoop handle, blinding pain struck her chest. It was enough to drop her to her knees, where her delicate skin met the freezing hard floor. A strangled cry escaped her mouth. Her captor laughed, his slowing footsteps telling of his mockery. She pushed through the agony to reach for the handle, tugging on it with all her might. It took all her effort, but the heavy door creaked open, and the arctic winds hit her face, feathering her eyelashes with delicate snow. She smiled. It was right there—freedom. Freedom from the horrors she had witnessed. Freedom from all the heartbreak. Freedom from everything she had endured since that dreadful day in the woods. She only had to walk through the door.

She was stuck. The tender skin of her hand had fused to the frostbitten handle. She panicked, pulling until her hand was released with a sickening rip. She stared in shock at what was left of her palm. Most of her skin remained on the handle. Blood trickled from her hand in ribbons, dripping from her elbow to the floor, painting it a bright crimson. A numbness set in and the only pain that remained was that of the broken vow. She moved in slow motion, forcing herself to take one more sluggish step. Her heart stuttered as the tips of her toes met the icy threshold. A wispy fog escaped her mouth in what she prayed would be her last breath. Before it could dissipate, harsh hands grabbed her from behind, bruising the tender flesh of her arms.

"I told you." He sneered. "You are mine." He jerked her back inside, slamming the door behind them. On the brink of death and too weak to fight back, she crumbled. He pulled her up by her curls and dragged her back to the hell that was her life.

The room she had been gifted was haughtily beautiful and disturbingly heinous. The exquisite bed, draped in a blue so deep it reminded her of the night sky, kept a strong watch near the enormous gothic windows—windows that were frozen shut. Nefarious histories glared at her from every angle, woven into the tapestries that covered her walls. A small section remained bare to accommodate a set of aged shackles. Below them rested a carved trough saturated with many years' worth of stains. She had been held captive within the Cold Valley for weeks. In that time she had been forced to watch countless humans brutalized within those chains, some of which still held pieces of their decaying flesh. In all her seasons, she had never before witnessed such monstrosities.

"I'm starting to think you don't like it here." He tutted, tossing her inside the room. "That's the sixth time you've fled. So very rude on your part—I thought you had been raised better. Guess I'll need to teach you some manners." He hauled her up from the floor, dragging her by the hair once again. She focused all the energy she had left on getting away, clawing at his arms and twisting her body, but he easily maintained his control over her. He shoved her hard against the wall, knocking the breath from her lungs. He clasped the heavy shackles around her wrists and stood back, flashing a sinister grin she had become all too familiar with. "There, that's better," he said. He took his time studying his most prized possession, his eyes sliding over her form. "You know, growing up I was always told how special you were. You are our key back into Heaven. If not that, then back into the good graces of the horned beast, at least. Father says it's better to walk in flames than to fizzle into nothingness." His hungry eyes landed on the length of her elegant neck, following the trail of blood left behind by her injured hand. "Oh, look what you've done." His long fingers floated over her fair skin, the tips dipping into the blood and gliding down her plunging neckline. The emerald green fabric of her dress halted his course. "I'm supposed to wait. Father's rather insistent on it. Something about decorum and ceremony…" He lifted his red-smeared fingers to his nose and inhaled her essence, his eyelids fluttering. "But would a small taste really hurt?"

1. chapter

"Maeve," Jack said, sounding defeated, "please try and understand, will you?" The hellish wind gusted out of nowhere before Maeve could answer. It whipped across the beautiful valley floor, causing their powder blue car to weave from one side of the road to the other. A sudden surge jerked the wheel from Jack's hands, his muffled curse breaking through the gale. Maeve gripped her seatbelt while Jack fought a courageous battle against the wind. She sat back, relieved, when he was finally able to keep a good hold, though she could see by the moonlight that the wind still played havoc on the poor valley outside her window. Usually the picture of peace, the valley was made up of grassy hills that bordered large mountains, crystal clear lakes, and beautiful pockets of the greenest woods Maeve had ever seen. The scenic route was not for the skittish though; the narrow roadways could be hazardous on the best of days, and this was not the best of days. "Maeve," Jack continued, "did you hear me?"

Maeve's tongue had turned to lead, and she squeezed her eyes shut to hold back her tears. Jack waited patiently. The simple fact was that she couldn't understand, no matter how hard she tried. Jack had decided to leave. He had decided to abandon their family, their farm, their small way of life...and her. Jack claimed he was only going to university, yet so many others had been lured away permanently by big city prospects. That's what left her mouth dry and her heart pounding—*he may never come back.* The weight of dread lay squarely on Maeve's chest, leaving her fighting for air. She pressed her forehead against the ice cold glass, desperately searching for some kind of relief.

Maeve let out a small puff of air, allowing the warmth of her breath to fog up the window. She was half tempted to let her fingertips trace the smiley face they had drawn so many times when they were younger, but the happy memory was tainted with what lay ahead. The trip was not nearly long enough, and she was out of time. As the imaginary clock ticked its way down, she looked up at the boy who was technically her older brother—though, the truth was, they often passed for twins. Maeve smiled meekly at his matching dark, unruly hair and knew those eyes that were so focused on the road were the same shade as her own. They had the same tall stature and healthy frame, shaped by years of farm chores and a steady supply of home-cooked meals. Unfortunately for their parents, they also shared the same unyielding curiosity, which got them into trouble more often than not. Maeve took her time studying all their shared traits, fearing that this may be the last she was able to.

"I, for one, would love to know what's going on in that pretty little head of yours, dear sister." Jack's eyes met Maeve's for a fraction of a second before focusing back on the dark roadway. It was enough for her to realize the real reason she was so scared—he was not just her brother; he was her most trusted friend. He would do anything for her, even stay if she asked. But she wouldn't. After all, he would never ask her to give up her dreams if their roles were reversed. He would try harder to understand. How she would find the strength to let him go, she had no idea.

"For you, Jacky, I'll try." Jack's response to Maeve's whispered words was his trademark slanted smirk and a playful pinch above her knee. Just like that, they were back on their journey, the cab filling with their usual sibling snipes.

"I tell you, Maeve, this rust bucket is dodgy! We'll be needing the luck of the leprechauns to make it in this brutal weather." Jack's voice carried a teasing tone, but his posture was rigid with concern. The wind had gained momentum, and a cold rain peppered the windshield.

"The birds up at uni are going to know you're a mental from the bog if you keep spouting out like that. Besides, you shouldn't poke fun at that."

Jack laughed heartily. "At what, little sister? Fairytale rubbish and old superstition? Who's the bogger now?" Maeve's answer was an attempted slap to Jack's arm, which he dodged. Then she crossed her arms and muttered "arse" in his direction. His laughter only grew more obnoxious. Jack could be insufferable at times, but Maeve couldn't stay angry with him for long. He had a knack for talking his way out of almost anything. Their father had told them on many occasions that the men in their family had a healthy knack for finding mischief and the charm to talk their way out of it. "Oh, you know I love it when you make that face. You look like a wee babe," Jack mocked, reaching out to pinch Maeve's cheek.

"Oh stuff it, you. And get your grubby hands away from my face and back on the steering wheel, will you?"

"*Ohhhhh*, come on, Maeve. You know you can't stay mad at your favorite brother."

"You're my only brother, you git," she grumbled.

"Exactly! So now we have that all straightened out, let's work on fixing that pretty little face of yours." He poked at Maeve's ticklish ribs with his long fingers, and it wasn't long before she was laughing right along with him. Jubilant as they were, in the midst of all their roughhousing they'd almost forgotten about the treacherous conditions outside. There was a loud pop, and suddenly the old car was spiraling down the slippery, wet road. The car skidded to a stop in the ditch. Maeve turned to Jack with eyes so wide she resembled an owl. Jack gripped the steering wheel with both hands, his knuckles white.

"You all right?" she asked, her heart racing.

"Mum and Da are gonna be right pissed off." Normally, Maeve would agree, but her thoughts about their parents' reaction faded away as she gazed out the windshield. The forceful winds and heavy rains had strangely stopped.

"I think we're in a heap." Jack groaned, kicking the shredded tire. Maeve stood beside him, gripping the torch as though it was her anchor. She was terrified of the dark, a phobia Jack often teased her for. He could tease her all he liked; she wasn't letting go of their only light.

"We have a spare, don't—" Maeve asked, but Jack's pained expression answered her question before the words had fully left her mouth.

"I took the spare out of the boot to make room for my things." Jack turned away from her, scrubbing his face with his hands. "Look, we'll walk a ways up the road and try to catch a car to Killarney for a phone, okay?" Jack turned back to see Maeve's disbelieving face. "Oi! Don't look at me like that, Mae. Besides, you've got a mighty fine grip on that magic torch of yours. No puca will be messing with you, I can guarantee you that." He finished by pinching the right side of her face, yet again.

Maeve didn't have time to think of a proper comeback as Jack's laughter disappeared with him up the road. No longer caring about his ridiculous plan and not wanting to be left alone, she sprinted after him without a rational thought. When she caught up to him, "eejit" was all she could wheeze out. She doubled over, pulling deep breaths into her lungs. Jack's body shook with laughter; he was obviously well aware that he had won this round.

"You know, I think I'll quite miss Evelyn," Jack said, jumping over a puddle. "Fine thing, that one. Ouch! What, Mae? She is! Stop abusing me, will you?" He snickered, rubbing his chest.

"You keep your thoughts clean about my best mate," Maeve warned. She gave him her best threatening expression, squinting her eyes and tensing her jaw. Jack wrapped his arms around his middle, howling with laughter.

"You look about as frightening as a lazy barn cat." He gasped. He did, however, also raise his hands in surrender. Maeve decided she would accept it—*for now.*

They walked for some time without seeing another car. Maeve sighed. Her once bright white shoes were coated in mud, and her socks were drenched. Her feet ached from the cold.

"Maeve, you could come with me, you know, after you graduate? You only have a few months left. You could come live a little before settling down." Maeve remained quiet, pushing her empty hand into the front pocket of her bell bottom jeans. Jack would already know her answer. Her heart was with their farm, their home. Jack wanted to see new things, to experience life away from the tractors and dirt. But Maeve... Her eyes glowed at the idea of a beautiful, simple life.

"I want to be home, Jack, you know that," Maeve whispered, turning away from him. She wasn't ashamed of her decision. Their parents had been busy trying to fill Jack's place on the farm. Even though he had put off leaving to give them as much time as possible, deep down they were still not prepared. They would need Maeve more than ever, but she couldn't wait to help out more.

Jack wrapped his arm around her shoulders and tilted his head onto hers. A sudden movement up the roadway caught Maeve's attention. Frightened, she stepped out of Jack's arms and raised the torch, scanning the area, her eyes squinting into the darkness.

"Did you see that?" Maeve glanced back at her brother. Jack just stood there, his attention fixed on the large hill to their left and the thick line of trees that grew on top. She returned to stand in front of him, staring up at his puzzled expression, but he didn't meet her eyes. He didn't even acknowledge her when she shined her light into his face. She pointed the torch toward the trees.

"What is it, then?" she asked. Jack didn't answer. "Jack?"

"Do you hear it?" His voice was so soft his words barely made their way to her ears. His eyes searched the tree line.

Maeve looked at the trees again. "Hear what, Jack? There's nothing there."

"The music," he slurred. "It's pretty." Before Maeve could blink, Jack was off, quick as lightning up the hill. He vanished into the darkness, leaving her speechless along the deserted roadside. Maeve only hesitated a moment before following him into the woods, but all that awaited her was an unnatural silence.

"*Jaaaccck! Jaaaccck!*" she screamed, her voice breaking. "Please, Jack! You answer me!" More haunting silence was her answer. Maeve had no choice but to continue deeper into the woods.

Maeve's light did little good. She tripped over gnarled roots hidden in the moss-covered floor, drenching herself in wet grime and losing her torch. She shivered, her skin prickling with goosebumps from the cold winter air. Her throat was raw from screaming, and her tears had dried into salty tracks down her dirty, freckled cheeks. Fatigue set in. Maeve had been going for hours. She was lost. She had almost given up when her cold, exhausted body stumbled out of the denser growth and landed in a clearing. The moonlight reached more of the forest floor there, but somehow the darkness still overwhelmed her. *So much for luck.*

Maeve tried to find her bearings, blindly reaching out for anything to help guide her way. A weariness like she had never before experienced began to creep over her. Her body was heavy, like solid stone. She was dizzy, her head filling with dense fog, and soon her mind was laced with warped, distorted voices. She shook her head to clear whatever had taken hold of her, but the more she tried, the thicker the fog became. The voices, however, became clearer.

"Everything is all right," they whispered. "Jack is fine. Jack left." *That's right. Jack was supposed to leave...isn't that right?*

"That's right, you remember. Jack left and he's happy...so happy." The voices were hypnotic, their reassurances chasing away her fear. Her body slumped as she gave herself over to them. She didn't mind when two icy fingers grabbed her chin and twisted it back and forth appraisingly. Two impossibly vivid eyes penetrated the fog.

"Oh, you poor thing. Get lost, did you? What a pity. I think I'll keep this one."

"Do not be a fool, Darragh, you know the fit Mother will have."

"All the more reason then, yes?" Maeve's icy keeper flashed a puckish grin. The strange man never let his piercing eyes leave hers. They held something within them. *Danger!* her mind screamed. Her thoughts were stamped down again by the comforting voices within her head.

"And how will your future intended feel about this, dear brother?" Darragh's grip tightened on Maeve's chin and his intense eyes finally left hers as he cut a murderous glare toward the hidden stranger.

"Since when have my feelings ever been taken into consideration?" he asked. "Besides, nothing has been signed yet, has it?"

Maeve pulled against the hand that grasped her face, trying to see the person on the receiving end of Darragh's irritation. His eyes snapped back to hers in an instant. His grip had loosened, but his other hand had made its way into her hair, keeping her in place while he studied her. "I like her looks—they're unique. It's refreshing, don't you think?"

"I'd say she looks more manky at the moment—disgusting,

really. You know, I didn't throw such a tantrum with my betrothal."

"And we all see how happy you are, Faelan." Maeve caught the playful wink Darragh shot over her shoulder at his brother. By his tone, Faelan didn't think it was cute.

"It is your war to wage with them all," Faelan answered. "Now hurry up, they'll wonder why I haven't brought you back yet. I'm rather bored of all this nonsense, and the wretched smell of dirt coming off this one is burning my nose."

"All right, all right, calm yourself," Darragh said. "You want the other one? They look like a set."

"Let the forest have him. Hard lessons learned, yes?" Darragh agreed with a subtle nod.

"What is your name, girl?" Darragh asked, pulling her face even closer to his. His pupils grew larger, covering the shimmering blue of his irises and drawing her further in.

"Maeve," she said.

Darragh flashed her a toothy smile, repeating her name in his deep, sensual voice. "Maeve. Seems fitting, doesn't it?" Maeve didn't respond. She was lost in the darkness of Darragh's eyes... Wasn't she afraid of the dark? "Come along, Maeve," he crooned.

As Maeve's feet started to move, her mind tried to push something forward. Something—*someone* she had forgotten. She could hear his tortured screams echoing through the woods. Her muscles tightened with the need to run to him, but all she could force herself to do was whimper, "*Jacky*."

The name had barely left her lips when she was once again drawn into the black abyss of Darragh's eyes. "Stubborn, this one. Jack is gone, little one."

The voices came again. This time their words melted into harmony, the musical tones too beautiful to resist as they bounced around her skull. The last thought she had before everything went dark was exactly how right Jack had been. It was indeed *pretty*.

2. chapter

Scattered ivy crawled across the earthen floor, tickling her tiny, bare feet. Bell-like giggles echoed down the empty hall, bouncing off the massive stone walls to create an enchanting yet deceptive melody. The girl knew she was not allowed to wander. She was never allowed out alone, but she had heard *the noise*. The noise was not new, she heard it from time to time. Her door being left unlocked and slightly ajar, however, was new, and her curiosity could not be tamed. She tiptoed along in her faded green nightdress which caught the flickering of the glowworm beetles. The tunneled halls were a maze of twists and turns. She followed this path and that, discovering each unique hallway, intrigued by their moss floors, sculpted stone walls, and climbing wood trellises. When she reached the end of one such hall, she stopped. The hall opened into an enormous circular room. Her eyes widened; the extravagance was almost too much to take in. She stepped forward as though beckoned.

Ancient tree roots and sturdy stones made archaic archways, linking the shimmering walls and creating entries for the numerous halls that connected to the room. Large slab tables sat empty, each with its own set of carvings etched deeply into the stone. They told stories the girl didn't know and depicted creatures the girl had never seen. She ventured deeper and came upon a strange raised pool. The barrier walls were made of quartz stone, all different in shape and color, though the gold ones were by far the most vast. She studied the walls and noticed tiny markings, inked in black, which she also couldn't understand. She ventured closer, rising up on the tips of her toes, and was surprised to see water behind the mysterious barrier. But the girl had never seen water like this. It was beyond dark, almost like pitch in color. Unable to resist, she reached over to dip her fingers in, but was distracted by the reflection of the glowing moon on the dark surface. Her eyes traveled upward, following the fragrant blooms that climbed the walls. The air was heavy with their sweet scent. The high ceiling was made completely of glass pieced together like a puzzle, which allowed the moon to shine in and dance across the water. The girl's senses were so captured by the magical sight that she didn't realize what stirred beneath the water's surface, nor what would have happened if she had not wandered over to a large stone platform at the other end of the circular room.

On the left side of the platform rested a harp. She smiled brightly; she had one of her own in her room. But this harp wasn't exactly like hers. It was a glossy black and she could *feel* it. Somehow she knew it wanted to be touched, that it wanted to be played. She ran her hand across the ebony, tracing the intricate patterns carved into its surface. Her small hands had just started to graze the strings when she heard her name called. She was familiar with the voice and its tone—she was in serious trouble. The girl fumbled before darting behind one of several large ornate chairs sharing the platform. The only sound that escaped was her ragged breath.

"Oh, that girl!"

"Have you found her yet, Dara?" The girl knew that voice as well. Her father had arrived.

"No... I locked her door—I know I did," Dara answered, stomping her foot. "Someone wanted her to get out."

"Oh, I'm sure we know who to thank, Dara," Darragh said. "I can't prove it, but I know this was Moira's doing. The evil creature has been harping on incessantly about 'proper place' and how it is beyond time for her to learn hers."

"Moira's idea of teaching is what scares me, Darragh," Dara replied.

"I know. We need to get her back. Now. Keep Looking."

The girl listened as their footsteps retreated. She knew that she should have spoken up. After taking a moment to prepare for what trouble may come, she opened her mouth to call them back. Before she could get out so much as a squeak, she heard the noise again. *Such a strange sound*.

She left her hiding place, forgetting all about Dara and her father. She tried to determine what direction the noise came from—a near impossible task in the echoing labyrinth. She followed the sound from one hall to another. Eventually, the girl lost her patience, throwing her arms up and letting out a frustrated sigh. As if sensing her turmoil, the lights in a nearby hall began to dance wildly. She approached the empty hallway, giggling at the playful patterns. As she stood outside the looming archway, the lights returned to their normal steady gleam. She frowned. She had so liked their dancing.

She didn't dwell on the loss for too long, for she soon heard the noise again, louder than ever.

The girl traveled the hall for what seemed an eternity, marveling at the wonders around her. She passed large driftwood sculptures of beasts she did not recognize, monstrous flowers with petals that glowed as bright as the glowworms, and thick, barren vines that creepily clung to the tunnel walls. Her mind was so consumed with it all that she didn't notice she had reached the end of the hallway until she barreled face first into a great set of doors. She wasn't hurt but still rubbed at her tiny nose while she studied them. The doors appeared heavy and were engraved with intricate, curving symbols. Though the girl could not understand their meaning, she could sense something was wrong. Her tiny body vibrated as the noise that had sounded so far off now bellowed from behind the doors.

The doors creaked open, and the noise stopped. Her inquisitive nature got the better of her sense of caution, and she stepped into the darkness. The room was dreary. It made her feel sad, empty, and lost. It was filled with an overwhelmingly wretched smell, a decaying stench that made her eyes water and her stomach turn sour. Still, she pressed on until she came upon more sculptures, which were not like those from the hall. These appeared to be people, twisted and petrified. Some were manipulated into odd angles, crawling along the walls, while others were curled up on the floor in agony. She couldn't stand to look at them. Their gruesome forms called for her queasy stomach to rebel, the acid burning her throat as she fought to keep the mutinous liquid down. She turned and raced toward the exit, stumbling blindly in the low light with her desperate need to escape.

In her haste to get away, the girl slipped, landing hard on all fours. A sticky wetness began to soak into her nightdress, turning the pretty green an ugly mucky color. She lifted both of her small hands to her face to see...*red*. The deep red stained her hands and dripped down her thin arms. She felt a drop hit the top of her head and trickle down into her curly hair. She cautiously looked up and flinched as more drops hit her face. Frozen figures covered the ceiling, blood cascading down their bodies in thick red streams. The girl screamed at the sight of their tortured faces; their eyes still held a dimming flicker of life. She scrambled away, her bare feet skidding in the sticky red mess. She reached the heavy doors only to have them slam shut, trapping her in the dark with the damned. Her blood-curdling cries echoed off the walls and soon blended with the woeful wailing of the petrified creatures. And the noise that had guided her into this hellish place once again filled the darkness.

Veil sat up from her pillows, her forehead wet and her heart pounding. She lifted her shaking hands to her face. Thankfully, pale, bloodless palms met her eyes. With a deep breath, she pulled her knees up and rested her forehead on them, allowing her hair to fall in a thick curtain around her. She clenched her tired eyes shut, trying to force the terrifying images from her mind.

The nightmare was always the same. No one knew how long she had been trapped in that room. Those sentenced to that terrifying place were tormented, their lifeforce drained from them slowly, leaving plenty of time for them to contemplate their dishonorable actions. It was a horrible tomb. Its name, the Saeculum, was rather fitting since most who entered it would never leave. She was beyond hysterical by the time her father found her that fateful night. He hadn't seen any alternative at the time but to listen to the others, committing a deed he had regretted from the moment he set his hard eyes into her own, and one he had not allowed anyone to repeat since. The hurt and confusion remained fresh in her mind for many years, but with experience and tutoring, she eventually learned how grateful she should be for the protection he provided.

Allure, compulsion, glamor—the act had many names, but to her kind it was known as clouding. No matter the name, the result was always the same—the loss of one's free will. To become a slave trapped within her own mind was Veil's biggest fear, and she was reminded often of how easily it could happen. Unfortunately, she learned early on that most of her kind considered her beneath them, which made her a constant target.

Over the initial shock of her nightmare, Veil made her way to her most treasured possession—her harp. She drew her fingers in featherlight patterns over the rustic wood until she reached the silver strings. Music was a gift that had been given to her to fill the lonely hours, encouraged by not only Dara and her father but, strangely, by her entire family. Another lesson she learned early on was that her family's praise was rare and never free; there was always a hefty price.

She vividly remembered how beautiful the ebony harp had been and the strange way it seemed to connect with her. She didn't think twice when her family led her back to where it rested, only this time the grand circular room was filled with joyful guests, all dressed in bright attire. Laughter spilled from their mouths, their exuberance so inviting that Veil didn't notice the tension on Dara's face or how tightly she held Veil's hand. It was the first time she had been allowed to attend one of their celebrations. She was so caught up in the magic filling the room, that all she did was smile when her hand was taken from Dara's. Such a simple thing, holding a child's hand, but a touch from anyone other than Dara or her father was a foreign thing to her, and she thirsted for affection. *I should have known better.*

Her grandmother, with head held high, escorted her through the throng of guests to the platform where the harp sat. She gave Veil a pointed look and left her with the instrument to sit regally upon the most ornate of the chairs on the platform. Thrilled with the chance to impress, Veil touched the shimmering strings. That one touch was all it took.

Veil shook her head, burying her morose thoughts deep before sitting on the worn wooden stool that matched her harp. It took many seasons and countless reassurances from her father that her harp was safe before she would allow its return into her room, but eventually she fell back in love with it. She never played a specific song after her nightmares, only tried to clear her mind and let instinct guide her hands. Soon her voice joined in with a soft hum, and she relaxed into the rhythm. It wasn't long before she felt a presence within her room, but she was not afraid; she had known her visitor would come, just like always.

"Keeping me up at all hours of the night again, girl? And this hair! It's shameful, really."

"All is as it should be then, Dara?"

"Watch your cheekiness, girl," Dara said, her words holding no heat and making Veil snicker. Dara tried to work her fingers through the knots in Veil's wild waves. It was a futile act. Still, Dara tried because the motions helped soothe.

Dara's hand slowed and Veil smiled. "Lost cause, is it?" Dara paused her combing and raised an eyebrow, taking the time to make a full appraisal. Veil did her best to hold in her amusement, but she knew what would be coming next; they had played this game many times.

"Completely, girl," Dara answered dryly. "Not worth the

effort, at all." Veil shook with quiet laughter, and it wasn't long before Dara's eyes were dancing too.

Dara was old...*very old*. Though she, like the others, didn't have to worry about her appearance betraying her true age. Her dark brown skin was flawless, and her silvery white hair was still long and full, though she tended to keep it in a plait and pinned. She was neither brittle nor frail, but she often complained that she was not as strong as she once had been. She came across stern most of the time, but behind her rough exterior lay a kind heart. Dara was the one whom Veil relied upon for her basic needs.

"Hair just like your mother, girl."

At the mention of her mother, Veil lowered her eyes. Dara didn't speak often of the woman who had birthed Veil; her father didn't speak of her at all. Dara had once told her that sometimes sadness can surround a memory so completely it drowns. Some things were better left in the past. Still, Veil found her mind wandering to thoughts of her mother more often the older she got.

"Nessa says it's the color of mud. Filthy, like my lineage."

"That girl's heart is as cold as her mother's. Pure poison, just like Moira, I tell you." Dara didn't mind her tongue when it came to her opinions of Veil's half-sister and stepmother. "Besides, girl, I'd say it's more like dirt," Dara said, pausing her tirade. "Funny thing about dirt, most try to be rid of it, never realizing how important it really is. Without dirt, life wouldn't stand a chance."

Veil's younger eyes met Dara's wiser ones, understanding taking hold. True feelings were discouraged among their kind. Emotions made you vulnerable, and that weakness would be shamelessly exploited. Veil accepted Dara's camouflaged affection and held her gaze a moment longer, until Dara reverted back to her coarse self.

"All right, enough of this nonsense. Get dressed. We might as well go and gather—can't let stock get low, now can we?" Veil's mood lifted, her bad dreams forgotten.

Dara had become knowledgeable about many things throughout her lifetime and developed many talents. But her true gifts lay with healing. She used the bounty the forest provided to craft remarkable powders, salves, and teas as the healers before her had since the beginning of time. Even creatures in this realm were susceptible to injury or death, making healers like her indispensable. Dara gathered most of her own supplies, which meant they had to leave the underground halls of the barrows—they had to go outside.

Veil dropped onto the wooden bench of her vanity and rushed to find her useless hairbrush. She caught Dara's amused reflection in the mirror and chose to ignore the urge to poke her tongue out in retaliation.

"You know what day the sun brings, girl?" Dara asked.

Veil paused. She *did* know the day. "Yes...it's May Eve, I believe," she answered, attempting to keep her voice steady.

"Indeed it is. A rough one, I know. Still, you'll have to be on your best behavior, yes?" Dara's voice was kind, yet the warning was clear. Veil nodded and continued on in hopes of forgetting a little while longer, her frantic movements now more languishing as she searched for something suitable to wear. Her wardrobe was filled with lavish gowns that were good for one thing, and that was to bring scarlet to her cheeks.

Her father's people were well-known for their attractiveness and most were not bashful or coy. Clothing suitable for digging plants or climbing trees was normally reserved for servants. Although the majority of her family refused to claim her as their equal, they also wouldn't permit her to dress like those in the lower class. Veil was openly berated for her simple taste and shy demeanor; it was bad breeding, and she would have to learn.

Bad breeding or not, Veil preferred to be comfortable and barefoot, and with that in mind, she reached for her deep blue dress, a beloved gift from Dara. The material was soft, and the embroidered pattern reminded Veil of autumn leaves.

Dara smirked, her eyes sparkling with mischief. "The sun hasn't risen, yet—a little trouble won't hurt, I guess. Come along then, girl." Veil rushed to follow, still adjusting her gown as she went. She didn't need to be told twice.

3. chapter

Veil looked up from her task, letting the wonders of the barrows distract her. She found the deep underground mazes to be suffocating, but out here she could breathe and pretend her life was her own. The sun painted the sky in a kaleidoscope of colors, the woods greedily soaking it in. All the dancing shades of green hypnotized, and the smell of lavender and honeysuckle was intoxicating. Everything was so vibrant in the nature surrounding their home; Veil understood how it could overwhelm the senses. Most outsiders wouldn't stand a chance once they entered this realm, a place the Sidhe called the In Between.

Pushed into the side of a grassy mound, not far from Dara and Veil, was a large oak tree. For those who couldn't truly see, it appeared to be just one of many trees. Veil remembered the first time she stepped through the small hollow into the open air, letting her hand run over the rough bark, fearful and fascinated for what was to come. Dara had convinced Veil's father long ago that she would be safer outside with Dara than inside with her family. So Dara began taking Veil along on some of her outdoor pursuits. Teaching Veil how to identify and collect useful plants was just a small part of it; Dara also told her about the many beings that called the In Between home. Every life and creature had a purpose, even if that purpose wasn't understood or agreed upon. Veil was privileged with so little time away from her room that she didn't question much of what Dara said. She was thankful for the knowledge and effort Dara invested in her and for these short moments of freedom.

"Is that bog moss going to put itself in the basket, then?" Dara asked, trying to pull up a stubborn plant. Veil cringed. She had been caught lost in her daydreams...*again*. She gave Dara her sweetest smile, but it earned nothing more than a pointed look toward her pitiful, nearly empty basket. Veil laughed and resumed digging up the pretty green plant that spread across the forest floor. According to Dara, bog moss was abundant across the Isle and should be one to remember because it was useful when tending to wounds. It was not Veil's favorite subject, but Dara continued. "If you are ever in a bind and cannot get the bleeding to stop, the moss—though usually overlooked—could save your life. It grows far and wide, so always look toward your feet. That is good advice for all things, girl. When you are in need, what's beneath your feet will provide."

Veil, remembering Dara's teachings, mused over how far the world stretched. Every once in a while, Dara left the In Between in search of the few items that didn't grow within their realm, but Veil was strictly forbidden from tagging along. Veil looked toward the border. The translucent wall was like a living entity, expanding and contracting as if it were breathing. Its iridescent colors caught the light, creating a dance which left the images on the other side distorted. For Veil, the eerie unknown was both frightening and intriguing. She knew of at least one thing that came from the other side.

"Can they see it, Dara? Would they see us if they were near?"

"As curious as your mother," Dara grumbled. "Only those who want to see past it will—most do not. To them, we're just lore and legends now." Dara returned to her work and Veil's curiosity changed to concern. Her mother's name and memory had been all but buried with her after she died, but Dara had been mentioning the woman more and more as of late. Veil turned back toward the border, and her worry grew.

"Dara, will you tell me what is wrong?" Dara shook her head, her remarkable silver eyes refusing to meet Veil's questioning gaze.

Dara and Veil moved to a field nearer to the tree hollow, gathering comfrey roots. As Veil went to place the roots into her basket, a yellow butterfly landed on the handle, surprising her.

"Nothing to fear, girl," Dara said, rising to her feet. "Butterflies are messengers of good things to come. All except the dark-winged ones, mind you. Nothing but sadness rides their wings. You stay clear, you hear?" Veil nodded, sighing as she stood. Their baskets were nearly full, and with the sun's light stretching across the forest floor, she knew their time was coming to an end. Her posture slumped, her shoulders heavy with the weight of what the day offered. She turned to find Dara quietly studying her. Veil's face surely revealed what she had been struggling to keep hidden. "Come on, girl," Dara said, walking past her. "Let us see if the deer have gotten into the rowan trees." Veil both needed and was grateful for the extra time. The deer, however, was not thrilled with the rude disruption of his breakfast. "Blasted deer! Always nibbling this and that!" Dara marched toward the unfazed deer, fists waving. Tired of Dara's screeching voice, the stubborn deer relented with a loud huff and disappeared into the dense brush. Veil giggled.

"Beautiful creatures, though." The look Dara sent Veil's way was hysterical. Veil rocked back and forth on her feet, pressing her lips together to keep herself from laughing.

"Well, thanks to that 'beautiful creature,' you'll be getting in some practice, at least. Those trees are desperate, girl." The deer had left behind trees that had seen far better days and certainly could use some help in returning to their full potential. Veil was nervous. She hadn't been granted the luxury of the time needed to develop much skill, but the practice couldn't hurt. She reached out and touched the poor leaves with affection, noticing that most of the berry clusters were now gone. She lowered herself to the ground and sank her hands deep into the dark rich soil. "You have to reach out for it," Dara urged. "Concentrate, girl." Closing her eyes, Veil tried to focus all her energy on her center.

Nothing.

She tried to push further, willing the link to open and accept her. But still, she felt absolutely nothing.

28

Veil and Dara sat in silence—Veil, in frustration, and Dara, in contemplation. The rowans flourished once more thanks to Dara, and Veil felt useless, as always. She had witnessed the miracles Dara was capable of, miracles Veil should also be able to perform, but had yet to. The Sidhe had been blessed with the ability to mentally merge with nature *among other things*. They called it 'the connection.' Veil had learned that its original purpose was to allow the Sidhe to help heal the beauty of the world but, sadly, many used it for more selfish or sinister intentions. Dara and Veil had pondered every possible reason or excuse as to why the gift seemed to have passed her over, but only the hurtful words of Veil's well-bred family offered any explanation.

"Maybe it is my blood, Dara. Maybe it wasn't passed to me because of my mother's line."

"Gibberish, that," Dara replied. "Others with the mix have the knack. You let them get to you, girl—it impairs your thoughts. You may look like your mother, but your father's endowment is strong. Veil nodded but the seed of doubt had been planted long ago. "When you have faith in yourself and the time is right, it will come to you. After all, you never know when the moment will appear that you'll be forced to use it."

"Dara...what's wrong? Please?" Dara remained quiet for a moment, her silence worrisome. She took a deep breath and then told Veil a story she had never told her before.

"I cannot tell you much, girl. I made a promise to your father, and you know the importance of such things to our kind." Veil nodded. A vow was to be held in the highest regard, death meeting those who broke their word. "I was also your father's guardian, and your uncle's for that matter, did you know that?" Dara didn't wait for an answer before continuing. "Yes, Darragh was a mischievous boy, like most—terrorized all the barrows. Faelan was more...stifled.

Spent more time with your grandmother, that one did. Nevertheless, as the two of them grew and became men, our land and people were consumed by a horrible war with the Cold Valley. A dreadful sort, they are. Your uncle and that maddening boy of his are visiting there now."

"Will they be all right?" Veil asked, almost shouting. Dara patted Veil's hand.

"Calm yourself. They'll be fine, girl. The war ended long ago. An agreement was made, but the cost was greater than we ever could have imagined, I'm afraid." Dara appeared lost in thought as she spoke. Still, Veil waited patiently. After all, insight such as this was never freely given to her. She was captivated. "You remember what I told you about our people's origins?"

"Of course, Dara," Veil answered. "The Sidhe were once angels of Heaven, cast out due to their selfish ways. Not evil enough to be banished to the fires of Hell, they were forever exiled to wander the Earth, waiting for death and Judgment Day. The Sidhe, scattered across the world, formed clans, taking refuge in the beautiful In Between with others of the realm." The memorized lesson rolled off her tongue smoothly.

"Yes, that's right," Dara said, her lips almost forming a proud smile. "Now, this was long ago when the earliest fell—long before me, if you can believe it. A heavy toll was paid for their sins. Some even believe the Sidhe lost their souls, making the return to Heaven impossible. We should count ourselves lucky we kept what we did, if you ask me, the extra years and our connection with...well, everything." Dara reached out and cupped Veil's cheek. Dara released a sigh and dropped her hand. "It's not enough for some, though. Greed and jealousy can make creatures of all sorts do ugly things, girl—unforgivable things."

"Like war?" Veil asked.

"Yes, among other things." Dara stood and began to pace,

her hands clasped behind her back. "You see, along with the clans' division came the struggle for more territory, more control—just more. Greed is what it was, and war is what it led to. Deals were made and agreements signed, most of them rubbish to keep those in power right where they wanted to be. Your poor father was made complicit in such an agreement—shame on them for it." She paused long enough to shake her head. "But he wouldn't have ta-taken…We wouldn't have…have you, if not…"

"If not for what? What happened to Father? I don't understand, Dara."

"I know you don't, girl," Dara said, hanging her head. "So much has been kept from you. We sheltered you, protecting you from the darkest of us—or so we thought. Evil is out there, and the prejudices against your mother's kind, your kind, run deeper than you know."

But I do know. The hostile stares and angry whispers she endured because of her so-called 'mongrel' heritage. She knew how appealing her subservient mind could be to those who would abuse the connection; she had witnessed what some of the crueler Sidhe were capable of, and it was not a fate she wanted. Luckily, she had been guarded against it for the most part, having barely been allowed to leave the sanctuary of her room and never again without an escort since that dreadful night she had spent in the Saeculum.

"Dara, what are you actually trying to protect me from?" Dara lowered her face, wringing her hands.

"We didn't think this could ever happen—we planned so carefully. But that blasted boy! I'm sure he had plenty of help in making up his mind." Veil knew what boy from Dara's tone alone.

"Haven? He hasn't even spoken to me in months, Dara, you know this." Dara wasn't making any sense. Veil didn't understand how Haven could have cut off their friendship so abruptly, but none of his behavior seemed logical any more. Nonetheless, she didn't see what part he played in any of what Dara was trying to say. Veil looked into Dara's eyes, and the swirling mix of sadness and fear terrified her.

"You two are in deep trouble."

4. chapter

Veil's maddening cousin, as Dara affectionately called him, stood before them in all his self-proclaimed glory with his blond hair in its usual high knot and a flirty smile Veil had seen far too many swoon for. He was a little impish and more than a little conceited, but he was also one of the few kin that treated Veil kindly.

"Cace!" Veil exclaimed, her feet leaving the ground as he swung her wildly around, laughing at Dara's disapproving face.

"Put her down," Dara said, shaking her finger at him. "A bad influence, you are. Your mother should have put you over her knee long ago, boy."

"You'd have to convince her to return from her never-ending string of holidays first." Cace put Veil down and turned to face Dara. "Besides, I have your gorgeous self to fill the job, yes?" Dara was indifferent to Cace's silver tongue. She readily stood in his absent mother's place, and though she chastised him often, she held a solid position within his heart. Cace couldn't resist teasing her with a big wink. He was not at all deterred when all he got in return was a dramatic roll of the eyes.

"No different than a toddler." Dara scoffed. "Mischievous thing." Unconcerned, Cace placed a loud smacking kiss on her cheek.

"Ooh, you know you love it."

"I merely tolerate it, boy." Dara's voice was serious, but her arms came up to wrap the boy she had helped raise in a warm hug. Their verbal sparring amused Veil. Dara did indeed love it, but she would never admit it out loud.

"As you say, my lady," Cace mocked. "Now, what am I interrupting?"

"Not a thing—just a little gardening." Veil glanced at Dara when the half-truth left her mouth, but she didn't return Veil's gaze. Though not a word passed between them, the message was clear to Veil: their conversation was over, at least in present company. "Why? Wish to get your pretty hands dirty, boy?"

"As appealing as you make it sound, I'm afraid not," Cace answered, his eyes darting from Dara's to Veil's. "I was sent to fetch my beautiful cousin."

"Fetch me? Why?"

"Do you not see how high the sun is?" Cace asked. "You were expected at the morning meal to discuss the importance of today's events. You're late, cousin, and Grandmother is not pleased." Veil lifted her face toward the brightened sky and sucked in a quick breath. She was not only late, she was very late. Dara's eyes filled with regret.

"I'm so sorry, girl. There was so much to say…" Veil knew the blame lay strictly on herself, but regardless of who was at fault, Cace was right—she was in trouble.

Cace looked her up and down. "By the looks of you, I'll be thoroughly entertained this morning." Veil should have been affronted by his repugnant face, but she had to admit that she was a sight. Her hands and feet were covered in muck, and her dress was in a sad state.

"I'm so glad my misery keeps you entertained." Cace laughed, his eyes dancing with mischief.

"Oh, it definitely does."

"Have I mentioned that I can't stand you?" Veil asked, pursing her lips.

"Not yet, but the day has only just begun." Cace's teasing earned another eye roll, this time from Veil, but she wasn't really cross with him. Staying angry with Cace was nearly impossible.

Veil picked at the dried dirt on her hands, fearful once again of what awaited her. Her grandmother did not like tardiness or dirt.

"Have I time to bathe?"

"I'm afraid not. She's rather testy today, even more so than usual. Threatened to come get you herself." Cace wasn't known for his seriousness, so when it appeared, Veil's anxiety peaked. She hung her head in defeat. She had hoped her grandmother would be in a rare and glorious mood, considering the circumstances.

"I'd love to see that," Dara gibed. "It will be a cold day in hell before her Royal Highness strolls outdoors, though the fresh air would probably do her wonders." Veil glanced around nervously. The In Between was full of eyes and ears that would take those words and whisper them to Veil's grandmother, whose tolerance for such things was nonexistent. Veil was familiar with her grandmother's temper, and she would not wish it upon anyone.

"Shhh! Please, Dara." Her begging received only a small nod in return. Veil knew Dara didn't care; she had always been blunt with her opinions.

"Well, shall we, ladies?" Cace asked. "I wasn't kidding when I said she was waiting—pretty impatiently, I might add."

"Of course," Veil answered. "Let me help Dara with these baskets and I'll be right there."

"No, girl. You need to go. Now. I'll take care of this." Dara turned toward Cace. "Will you tend to her?"

"I'll guard her with my life, oh beautiful one." Cace smiled, patting his sword.

"That you better, boy. Today of all days, watch her closely... please?" *Please?* Please was not a word Dara used often, and her sadness had returned. Veil glanced at Cace, silently begging for some kind of explanation, but judging by the perplexed look on his face, he didn't understand Dara's behavior either.

"No worries, Dara, I'll keep her close," Cace reassured. "All right, let us get this day started, cousin." His voice was upbeat, but his body betrayed his thoughts. They were all aware of the wrath awaiting Veil. Veil mustered up her courage—it was time.

"Let us be off, then. I'll see you soon, Dara...yes?"

"Indeed you will, girl." Dara's voice still held the same sadness, her eyes showing a trace of her usual fire...but only a spark.

5. chapter

Veil was glad to have Cace by her side. From the moment they stepped back through the tree hollow, they were assaulted by the boisterous sounds of the barrow which was busy with preparations for the evening's special occasion. Veil could already feel the weight of judgment as a group of Sidhe nobles brushed past. The majority paid no attention to her, and for that, she was grateful.

Veil was regarded with disdain by many of the Sidhe, and a few were brazen enough to openly voice their dislike of her despite her royal lineage. Most of her family took pleasure in cutting her to the bone with their words, and their cruelty had spread throughout the barrows, growing as the years went on. Nessa and Cace didn't face the same prejudice; their blood status gave them free rein of the realm, something Veil was envious of.

The looks Veil could endure, but the underlying thread of *want* scared her. They didn't dare act on their lustful thoughts, thanks to her father, but the desire for control was there. She walked with her head down to avoid all the eyes that didn't hold the same uniqueness as her own—that trace of humanity, a piece of her mother.

Humans of all ages were brought to the barrows for many reasons: slavery, entertainment, and punishment. Breeding was also a motive; Dara said the act was only permitted to keep the bloodlines from intermixing, though the queen's tolerance for such things only extended to those outside the royal family. Veil was a constant reminder of what her grandmother loathed, nothing more than a blemish on her pure bloodline.

"If you do not watch where you are going, you will run one of them over, cousin." Veil looked up just in time to dodge a small blond child, playfully running about.

"Oh! I am so sorry, little one." The girl looked up; her pretty eyes were so different from Veil's own. Human children were, at times, taken from their homes and replaced by creatures that were most definitely not human. Changelings, trolls, and other undesirables that wished to roam the human world were quite keen on this practice. Veil found it barbaric, but Dara had told her it was just the way things were and had always been. It was about control, plain and simple, and control was like ambrosia to most Sidhe. The precious girl didn't say a thing as Veil looked her over, and soon the girl's golden strands were bouncing away, disappearing into the crowded hall. *Poor girl.*

"Try not to think on it, Veil," Cace said. "Trust me, it could be so much worse for them. Not all clans are as merciful as ours. I must say, it is good to be home." Cace had been away since he had come of age the previous summer. His father, Veil's Uncle Faelan, had been adamant he be introduced to the world outside the barrow tunnels.

Though Veil was often worried sick over him, she also found herself jealous imagining all the places he got to explore.

"How were your travels?" she asked.

"Oh, cousin, it was fantastic!" Cace answered. "Father took me past the borders, Veil. There's so much out there. And the humans we did come across didn't even realize we were different from them. Well, some can sense it—small children and such, mostly those open to the possibility. The rest brushed our presence off. Although, naturally, they couldn't help but notice my finer qualities." Cace's chest puffed out proudly.

Veil was not at all surprised by Cace's bragging, but she was shocked by his revelation that he'd left the In Between. It wasn't common for those of high descent to take the risk. She tried to imagine what it was like to be among so many humans who still had their wits about them. All the humans she encountered had been clouded to some degree. The allure of the In Between was enough to keep most of them foggy and compliant. It was their weak constitutions, the same as Veil's own, or so her grandmother claimed. Every once in a while, a human would try to fight the allure, but they would always fall to their conquerors in the end.

Veil had never attempted to reach into another's mind, though Dara had tried to convince her to for the sake of knowing if she could. Veil desperately wanted to feel the connection, but not so badly she would take away someone's free will. Cace, however, would have to bring one of them into submission at some point in his life, Veil was certain of it. With his blood and rank, it would be nearly impossible for him to avoid. She prayed for more time. She didn't want him to be like the others.

"Did you have to...*you know?*" she whispered.

Cace let out a loud sigh before answering. "No, Veil, I give you my word. I have no interest in using my connection for that. Father simply thought it would be best for me to see more of the Isle. I'm fairly sure he believes it will keep me from leaving like Mother did. You know what that did to him." Veil tried to picture Cace's mother. It had been so long since she'd last laid eyes on her. His mother and father, like most of the royal line, had been bound by a forced betrothal in order to produce an adequate heir to continue their pureblood line. Veil appraised Cace, noticing an uneasiness to him.

"I worry for you, Cace." His laugh echoed all around the hall. He teased her, pretending to wipe away an invisible tear.

"Aww, and here I thought you couldn't stand me, cousin." Veil swatted his arm.

"I most definitely cannot, especially when you act so child-ishly. Now, tell me more about the Cold Valley. I was fretful for you and Uncle Faelan when Dara told me you were there."

"Dara told you?" Cace asked, his posture stiffening. "About *them*? What exactly did she say?" His uneasy tone didn't come as a shock to her; Veil was kept within a tight circle, and many things were kept hidden from her.

"Not much," Veil insisted, not wanting to reveal more until she had a chance to finish hearing Dara's story. "Only that there was war between them and us long ago. I assume since you're here looking like your proper self that you were treated well. I can't explain how wonderful it is to have you back."

"Odd thing, that, don't you think?" Cace asked. "Dara telling you anything about what's out there. They usually treat you as if you're this fragile little thing, keeping you locked away like a dark secret, yet the people there knew enough to ask about you."

"They asked about me?"

"Did you know that is where Aunt Moira is from? A ghastly

place but a good fit for her—cold and dark most of the time. It was not a place I wanted to stay long. And I would never leave you to face this day alone, cousin. I'm guessing the coward hasn't come to his senses?"

"You know how things must be, Cace. He has his reasons."

"Ah yes, 'his reasons' being he's scared to death of your sister and the rest of them. I tell you, Nessa has always gone out of her way to make you miserable, but this tops everything. Haven should be ashamed of himself for going along with it." Veil didn't want to discuss it. She had decided she would be there if Haven ever changed his mind, but until then she just wanted to avoid the topic at all cost. Luckily, Cace was easily redirected.

"Do you think Moira told them about me?"

"The Cold Valley? I would assume so. We both know you are not her favorite person, but they didn't seem bitter when asking—I'm sure it's nothing, cousin. We spent most of our time with Lord Lorcan and his son. Father was rather taken with their pets—huge, wolfish creatures—absolutely horrifying." Veil wanted to ask more, but they had arrived at their journey's end, and judging by the arguing coming from behind the door, breakfast was indeed going to be interesting. Cace leaned in closer, pressing his ear against the wood for a moment. She winced as his eyes widened, and he let out a low whistle. Veil steeled herself.

"Marvelous. No sense in putting it off."

"Try not to let it get to you," Cace said. He looked about as excited as Veil felt, but he tried to reassure her by placing his hand gently upon her shoulder. The wink Veil gave was enough to bring out a smile.

"You know I will bear it, cousin, lots of practice and all."

"Dara's right, I am a bad influence on you." He laughed. "Shall we?" His hand was already pulling the door open, whether she was ready or not. The force of Darragh's anger hit them the moment they stepped through.

"I will not allow it, you hear me?" Darragh's entire body shook with rage. Veil's grandmother, Bidalia, was in her usual spot at the head of their massive table.

"Do not be foolish, Darragh," Bidalia mocked. "How do you plan to stop it, hmm? It seems things did not work out how you imagined, did they?" She paused long enough to send him a dagger-like glare. "I still can't fathom how you could choose that abomination over your true heir."

"They are both mine, and you left me with little choice."

"You would do well to remember that I am your queen. You will do as I say on all things, Darragh."

"Have you no heart at all?" Darragh slammed his fist on the table. The yelp Veil let out alerted them to her arrival, and both sets of intense blue eyes landed directly on her. Darragh dropped his gaze at the sight of Veil's terrified face. Bidalia's hard eyes, however, held Veil's as the queen rose from her seat. Bidalia scrutinized Veil from the top of her curls down to the tips of her bare toes, her face purple with anger.

"Are you bound and determined to make a mockery of this family? I swear to the Heavens if I couldn't see your father's eyes when I looked at you, I would never believe that you were his offspring, pathetic thing that you are!" As much as Veil wanted to defend herself, she knew better than to interrupt her grandmother. Veil could tell by the vein pulsing in Bidalia's neck that she was most certainly not done. "I should have known you would try to ruin your sister's day, wretched girl. Well, what do you have to say for yourself?" Bidalia was panting by the end of her tirade. Veil needed to proceed with caution, so she kept her eyes directed toward the floor.

"I apologize, Grandmother. I was out with Dara and lost track of time. I truly meant no offense." The queen, with hair pinned back so tight it pulled her eyebrows into a high arch, twisted and tugged the cloth napkin she gripped, clearly not satisfied with Veil's excuse.

"No offense? Your very existence is an offense."

"That is more than enough, Mother," Darragh ordered. "You will leave her be."

"I will do as I please, Darragh."

"Please, Father, I'm the one at fault." Veil's voice wavered, but she refused to let her grandmother see her cry. Darragh stared at Veil for a moment before dropping his head again. He stood up from the table, and without a word he marched out, slamming the door behind him. Veil watched him leave, hoping he understood why she had spoken out. She only wished to protect him, as he had done for her many times over.

"Some sense for once. You will remember your place as I've graciously allowed you to keep it. Do you hear me?"

"Yes, Grandmother."

"Good," Bidalia said. Her attention strayed to Cace, and Veil knew the worst was over, at least for the time being. "Cace, my dear boy, thank you for seeing to her, though she should be ashamed to have wasted so much of your precious time." Bidalia was a different person when she spoke to him, or to almost everyone other than Veil. It had hurt when Veil was younger, but time had a way of dulling the knife.

"It was my pleasure, Grandmother. You know how much I enjoy time with my family."

Bidalia sneered at Veil. "How fortunate you are to have family that tolerates you. Though it's a pity you lost your only friend once that boy came to his senses. Of course, Haven doesn't have your charisma, Cace, nor the bloodline for that matter. He should count himself blessed to even be considered by one of our own." It hurt Veil to hear her grandmother speak of Haven in such a way.

"Now, since you've already started this day off so poorly, there will be no morning meal for you. Not that it would hurt you to miss a meal or two. You really should take more pride in yourself. I tell you—if it wasn't for Nessa, your father's line would be branded a tragedy..." Bidalia prattled on and on, letting Veil know exactly how much she loathed her, reminding her that she was an outcast.

All Sidhe were extremely strong, and the women were willowy in stature. Most were fair-haired with a light complexion, and Veil's family was no exception. But she took after her mother and was not what her grandmother considered well-built or anything close to willowy. Her skin was freckled and her dark-brown hair unruly. Dara was always quick to point out that their hurtful words were drivel that Veil should let pass in one ear and out the other, but she still felt ugly when she was around her family—they made sure of it.

"Of course, Grandmother," Veil mumbled. "I'll go and prepare myself right away if it pleases you."

"Yes, you shall. We have important guests this evening, and I want you to try to look the part. I will not tolerate any disorder, you hear?"

"Yes, Grandmother," Veil tried to answer, but a menacing laugh cut her off. Moira. *Could this day get any worse?*

"Bidalia, we both know she simply cannot be trusted to make the right decisions when it comes to these matters," Moira said, her silky voice filled with a false sweetness. "Can't place all the blame on her, really. The poor thing never had a proper mother to teach her the ways. I, however, would be thrilled to assist. We can't have her ruining our Nessa's day, now, can we?" Veil started to shiver. Although Moira was Veil's stepmother, she had never taken on a mothering role with Veil. She most certainly had never offered to assist Veil. Veil had good reason to be frightened, but her grandmother was excited by Moira's offer.

"Ah, Moira, what a wonderful idea. Are you sure you can sacrifice the time?"

"Absolutely, Bidalia. Our sweet Nessa will always take precedence, but I am sure I can find the time to help with this...situation. I know just the gown. With my help, I'm sure our little Veil here will be quite the sight."

"Very well, then," Bidalia said. "It would do her good to have some proper guidance since Darragh has been so foolish with his handling of her." Bidalia turned toward Cace and smiled. "Cace, I know you must have better things to do, but do you think you could escort her to her chambers? I trust she can at least bathe herself."

"Anything you wish, Grandmother," Cace answered, bowing at the waist. "She is family, after all." He smiled when Bidalia didn't so much as blink an eye at his words. It was Cace, after all, and he obviously knew he could do little wrong in Bidalia's mind.

"You sweet boy, you are exactly like your father," said Bidalia, beaming proudly. "Too bad Darragh is such a disappointment. I blame your grandfather—he babied him too much and made him weak. Thank the heavens that Faelan was my firstborn and will reign when I'm gone." Bidalia paused long enough to notice Veil was still there. "Well? Get going! You will need all the time possible to make yourself passable."

Cace snatched Veil's arm and led her out the same way they had come, but before he could, Moira called out, "Oh, and Veil, I'll be seeing you *very* soon." Moira's icy eyes were focused on Veil, who could only manage a subtle nod.

Once they were out of earshot Cace spoke. "Good Lord, Veil. They were in rare form, weren't they?"

"You know how they are."

"That I do. I can't believe your father just walked out."

Veil frowned at the mention of her father and turned away. The last thing she had wanted was to disappoint or humiliate him. Her frown deepened. "I don't know, Cace. Father has taken to avoiding me quite a bit while you've been away, ever since Haven and Nessa announced their binding. I don't know what I've done to disappoint him. Dara has been acting odd as well. Something is wrong—I feel it—but no one will tell me anything."

"She does seem a little more uptight than usual. Maybe it's because the barrows are filled with all the extras? This place is packed for May Eve and the ceremony, and she isn't exactly known for her sociability, cousin."

"Hmmm... That's true," Veil agreed. She knew the only reason Dara attended gatherings was to keep an eye on her. "I just can't help but feel like something is off."

"Of course something is off," Cace said. He gave a little shake of his head. "Your sister and your so-called friend are about to be bound. I never saw it coming. I thought he was sweet on you, actually."

"Hush, you. We're only friends...or I thought we were. I don't fault him for it, Cace. I thought we were closer, but you know as well as I do that he's only trying to do what's best for his family."

"You and your forgiving heart, cousin," Cace teased. "Must be a human quality."

"Good thing too, for your sake. We'd never speak to one another if I easily held grudges. Now, where are you taking me? This isn't the way to my room, Cace."

"Oh, I have every intention of getting you to your dungeon eventually, but I think we need a quick stop at the stables to lift both our spirits. What say you, cousin?"

"I'd say you've lost your mind." Veil chuckled. "Besides, you only want to go so that you can try and sweet talk Calla. Don't try to deny it."

"I-I most certainly do not! And even if I did, you know nothing could ever come of it. I merely thought a stroll outside, away from these stuffy halls, would help free our minds for this evening's activities." Veil let out a peal of laughter. She loved visiting the stables, and Cace knew it. Cace, however, was fascinated by more than the horses, and Veil poked fun at him every chance she was given. Though she teased him well, she thought his little crush was cute and decided to give in to him without too much fuss.

"Well, I guess a quick trip wouldn't hurt, but we must be swift," she said, pointing a strict finger at him. "I'm in desperate need of a bath." Veil, emphasizing her point, pulled her finger back and picked at the dried mud that had somehow made it into the ends of her hair. She would be scrubbing for a while.

Cace's whole body vibrated with excitement. "The risk will be worth it, cousin, I swear."

Veil began to laugh again, giving him her most skeptical look. "If you say so, Cace... If you say so."

chapter 6.

The stable itself amazed Veil with its large wooden frame and piles of hay littered about, but it was the horses that were truly special. They were broad with cords of well-defined muscle rippling through their bodies. Their coats shone, and they had wild, flowing hair, much like Veil's own. They were magnificent creatures. She admired much about them, but it was their large, expressive eyes—eyes that didn't lie—that she loved the most.

The Sidhe took tremendous pleasure in horsemanship, with most being splendid riders. Veil wasn't allowed to ride; as with most things, her father claimed it wasn't safe. Veil knew of no one else who was denied the right, but she did not argue.

Calla walked into the stables carrying a large wooden pail of water and wearing her unique quirky smile. "Well, look what we have here," she called out. "Are you lost? Surely, royalty have better things to do than dodge horse mess, do they not?" She bumped Veil's shoulder as she passed by. Cace huffed when Calla ignored him but was fast on her heels to help pour the water into the horse's trough. Calla eyed him as though he was nothing but a thorn in her side. Veil chuckled at her antics.

Calla was like Veil...sort of. She was a halfbreed, her human mother having wandered into the In Between years ago. Calla's father was a Sidhe who happened to be the stable master. They had raised Calla like she was no different than a highbred, something Veil tried her best to not be jealous of.

"Don't be stubborn, woman," Cace whined. "Let me help you." Calla didn't stop performing her chores but did begin to snicker.

"You think you can do better, do you? I doubt those soft hands know much about manual labor, Your Highness."

"My soft hands have many uses, thank you very much." Cace's innuendo wasn't lost on Calla...or Veil, unfortunately.

"I'm sure many maidens within the barrows could attest to that," Calla said. Cace's many conquests at court were no secret.

"Jealous are we, my lady? There's no need. You know you hold my heart."

"Should I be honored, Your Highness?" Calla scoffed. "I doubt your heart has much room for me with so many falling at your feet."

Cace winced at the hurt in Calla's eyes. "They couldn't hold a candle to you, Calla."

"Oh, it hardly matters, now, does it?" she whispered back, before stating in a much louder voice, "I really don't think your delicate frame could handle me anyway." Calla was a lot like Cace—she camouflaged her hurt with humor.

Veil made an obnoxious gagging sound. "All right, my ears can only handle so much. Behave you two."

"You're right. Apologies, cousin." Cace turned back to Calla. "We figured the fresh air might help Veil free her mind of worry. You know how they keep her tied down." Veil rolled her eyes at his attempt to hide the fact that it was he who had wanted to stray to the stables.

Calla only sighed. "That I do. Too bad you're not permitted to ride. That's what I do to release my troubles. It forces us to center ourselves and trust—the horses sense our feelings, did you know that? It's magnified when you're connected." Veil listened while Calla brushed a snow-white mare with affection. She began to feel the ache in her chest that always appeared when the connection was brought up. Calla did not have the same difficulty with the connection as Veil did. In fact, with the support of her parents, Calla was actually quite skilled.

"Yes, well, I don't expect to be given that privilege any time soon," Veil muttered. "Happy May Eve, by the way."

"Is it a happy May Eve? Sounds like those in the barrows are working themselves into a frenzy. Seems a bit much to me, but I guess it's not every day a royal is bound, is it?" Calla shook her head. "Nessa must be pleased as punch—never can have too much attention, that one."

"I suppose she is," Veil answered. "She doesn't tend to share her feelings with me, though."

"That girl doesn't share anything with anyone, cousin." Cace was always quick with the opportunity to bad-mouth his other cousin. Nessa *was* spoiled, though Veil didn't think she knew any other way. Before Veil could come to her defense, she was interrupted by a familiar, nasally voice.

"And why should I? Especially, with the likes of her." They

all turned to see Nessa standing in the stable's open doorway. Worse, she was not alone—Haven stood stiffly at her side. Veil had not seen him up close in some time. Even in passing, he had never stopped to speak with her. His deep auburn hair was shorter than she was used to, and as she studied his face more closely, she was troubled by what she discovered. There was no trace of his carefree nature. His unnaturally blank face disturbed her. Cace was unable to hold his tongue.

"Always taking what doesn't belong to you, aren't you, Ness? I'm surprised you even allowed your new pet to be out."

"Don't you dare call me 'Ness!'" Nessa shrieked. She ran her hands down the skirt of her yellow dress, smoothing the fabric. "And I assure you, he's quite happy. Aren't you, Haven?" Haven focused on the floor as Nessa snaked her hands up his chest.

"Of course, Nessa... Why wouldn't I be?" Smiling sweetly at the others, Nessa wrapped her arms around him and placed a kiss upon his cheek.

Cace's expression showed nothing but disgust. "I would think you were clouded if it were possible. They must have offered you something good for you to abandon your friend so cruelly. Have you no pride?"

When Haven finally looked up, his blue eyes stared right through Veil. "I found my pride when I realized I'd wasted so many years with someone so far below my station. It's something you should consider yourself, Cace, before it's too late."

Veil, in shock, could only stare.

Cace's anger erupted as soon as the hurtful words escaped Haven's lips. "How dare you? You're not part of this family yet. I should—"

"Oh, please." Nessa scoffed. "Enough of this, Cace. She's really not worth the effort." Cace started toward Nessa, but Calla held him back. Veil pleaded silently for him to stop, and soon she felt his body relax. Veil couldn't have Cace getting into trouble on her account, and, lucky for her, Calla stepped in to help defuse the situation.

"Is there something you wanted, Nessa?" she asked politely. "Would you like to ride? I'll prepare your horse."

"No need, Calla. I have a binding ceremony to prepare for, after all. I simply wanted to give my dear sister a message."

"Say it and be on your way," Cace snapped.

"Mother has left your gown on your bed," Nessa continued, unfazed. "She was quite shocked that you weren't in your bedchamber getting ready. She was so worried that she thought it best to inform Grandmother of your absence. I'm sure both will be delighted to learn you're just fine here in the stables, rolling around with the horses." Nessa finished her message with an evil grin.

If Nessa sounded pleased at the thought of Veil getting into more trouble, it was because she most certainly was. Moira had raised Nessa to look down on those with the mix and Veil in particular. Veil had stolen their father's attention, which Nessa believed was hers by right, for she was pureborn. Veil cringed at the myriad of hateful expressions pouring off her. To look at Nessa, most would never perceive her true nature. She had an innocent, doll-like face with large, wide-set eyes, a perfect button nose, and pouty lips, all framed by silky hair that cascaded down her back.

Cace tried to speak once more in Veil's defense, but Veil wouldn't allow it. "I'm sorry," she blurted out. "I'll get back to my room straightaway."

"See that you do," Nessa said. "Honestly, I can smell you from here." Veil nodded her agreement and for once Nessa was satisfied, at least for the time being. Without another word she grabbed Haven's hand and led him out of the stables.

"Yes, follow along coward!" Cace yelled after them. Haven paused at the insult and glanced back at them, stopping on Veil. For a moment, his stoicism was replaced with sadness, then the look left him and he walked away.

"Are you sure you two are related, Veil?" Calla asked.

"Sometimes I wonder, Calla, but Nessa has had different influences than me. She doesn't know any better." Veil wasn't sure why she always felt the need to defend Nessa.

"That's a crock and you know it, cousin," Cace said, certainly still angry. "Nessa is plain evil and Haven is a disgrace."

Cace's mood lifted when he noticed that Calla was still grasping his arm. Veil smiled at how nicely they paired. They gazed at one another with the goofiest of grins, and Veil couldn't resist teasing.

"Cozy are we?" Realizing they had been caught in their intimate moment, they fumbled their way apart. Their sputtering excuses forced Veil to cover her mouth to hide her smile. "Oh, please, don't stop on my account. I think it's adorable, really."

Cace's cheeks turned a rosy shade of pink, but he was fast to recover, as always. "I don't know why you're so surprised, cousin. She obviously cannot resist this." He gestured up and down his entire body, clearly infatuated with himself.

Calla did not show an ounce of being impressed with his peacocking. "Your ego has no limits, does it? I'm surprised you could fit your enormous head through the stable doors."

"All right, you two, as much as I enjoy these lovers' quarrels, I really must go," Veil said, glancing toward the stable doors. "Cace?"

"Yes, I suppose we have caused enough of a ruckus—for the morning, at least. I shouldn't have convinced you to stray. I do not wish ill upon you, cousin."

"It's fine," Veil reassured. "I wanted to come just as badly as you did. Calla, will we see you tonight?"

"Yes, unfortunately." Cace reached out to grab Calla's hand.

"All will be all right, Calla, you'll see," he softly reassured, placing a delicate kiss on the back of her hand. "I look forward to a dance with you, my lady."

Calla allowed him his moment before starting in on him again. "You think you can manage to find the time for me? You always seem to have a long line just waiting to fawn over you."

"I think I can work you in," he said, giving a little wink that got him nothing but a loud snort from her. Unruffled, he dropped her hand and offered his arm to an amused Veil. "Shall we make our way to that dreary place you call a room now?"

Veil smiled, linking her arm with his. "Lead the way, Cace."

chapter 7.

Veil wasted no time in getting ready, heading at once to the bathing room adjoining her chambers. She hurried to undress and shuddered as she dipped her toes into the stone basin. The water, which had obviously been brought in earlier by one of the human servants, was now frigidly cold. She gasped as she submerged the rest of her body. The bright yellow mountain reeds, which had been so carefully placed along the water's surface, jostled in her wake. In a rush to get out of the icy water, she snatched the wildflower soap and scrubbed vigorously. Before long, the once clear water had turned murky. Veil dreaded doing so, but left with no other choice, she dunked her entire head to rinse her hair. She resurfaced to find that she was no longer alone.

"Finally found your way, have you?" Moira asked, her eyes

drilling straight into Veil's. "I was quite concerned, Veil. It would have been a terrible shame if something had happened to you. Especially today."

Veil's heart pounded. She rushed to cross her arms over her bare chest. Moira's top lip curled as she took her time scrutinizing; she truly did loathe Veil.

"Still so shy...You're nothing like us, are you?" she mused. "No matter, though, time to finish up. We have lots to do, after all." Moira turned and walked briskly out of sight, her deep amethyst gown billowing like smoke behind her.

"Of course," Veil mumbled, reaching for her towel. "I'll be right out." Veil knew better than to make Moira wait. Her hair was still damp when she hastily pulled the linen dressing gown over her head and made her way into her room. Moira was the only one there. Veil tried not to panic at the thought of Moira dressing her alone. "Dara should be here soon, Moira. I'm certain she can tend to me. Surely you have Nessa to attend to on such a special day."

"And miss the opportunity to witness your face when you see the gown I've chosen for you? I think not." Moira waved her hand toward the bed. Seeing the gown laying there now, Veil had no idea how she could possibly have missed it. She walked over to the bed, fear threatening to consume her with every step.

Red.

The color was straight from her nightmares, like fresh blood. Veil looked the dreaded thing over more closely, the sheer bodice screaming at her. Moira ran her hand affectionately along the blooming skirt, her deranged smile sickening Veil.

"Well, what do you think? Lovely, isn't it?" Veil trembled and tried to force any words from her mouth, but no sound escaped. Her reaction was exactly what Moira had wanted. "Isn't the color just beautiful? I know red is not customary here, but where I'm from it is a sacred color, worn only for the grandest of celebrations. Someone like you should feel honored to wear it."

'Not customary' was one way to put it, another would be 'intolerable.' To most in the barrows, it was a reminder of death and the judgment day they all feared. The color was avoided at all costs.

Finally finding her voice, Veil asked, "The Cold Valley?"

"Oh, yes, I wasn't born here you see," Moira said. "I was brought here for your father, but the Cold Valley will always be my home. I do quite miss it."

"I'm grateful, Moira. Truly, I am. But I do not wish to offend anyone and draw attention away from Nessa. Perhaps another gown would be more appropriate?" Veil's hands shook as she pleaded.

"Nonsense," Moira replied, her hand finally leaving the red dress. "This is the perfect gown for you." Moira didn't even try to hide the hint of disgust in her voice. Dara would have said it was jealousy. Veil almost looked exactly like her mother, and Moira couldn't stand the constant reminder that Darragh had found a human woman more appealing than her.

"But I—"

"No buts!" Moira shouted, losing her patience. "After all, we wouldn't want you to end up in the Saeculum, now would we?" Memories flashed within Veil's mind—the blood and the horrible wailing. She lowered her eyes and shook her head. Moira would follow through on this threat if Veil was not careful. "Good. Now disrobe," Moira ordered. Veil had no choice but to obey. She undressed silently, accepting the tightness settling within her chest.

Veil sat in front of her vanity and watched Dara pace back and forth in the reflection, ranting and raving.

"I cannot believe this. It is indecent! Moira has lost her mind. There is no way your father approved of this." Veil didn't like to see Dara in such distress, but she also didn't want to disturb her father. He already had enough to handle without her adding to his worries.

"Dara, please, you know it will do little good. Besides, it's not that bad...is it?" Dara let out a sigh before gently placing her hands on Veil's freckled shoulders. She searched Veil's eyes in the mirror and gave her a knowing wink.

"You always look beautiful, girl, even when you are covered in muck," she said. "This is just unexpected. At least these cover most of your bits." Dara cleared her throat, picking at the few strategically placed adornments. A dark ruby thread ran through the gown, resembling thorny vines. The design crawled across Veil's chest and down her arms like ivy before flowing to the bottom of the blooming skirt. Her skin shone through the gossamer fabric. Normally, she preferred to remain unseen at these events, but there was no way she would go unnoticed on this night.

"Thank the heavens that witch didn't touch your hair," Dara muttered. "No telling what she would have done." Veil said a quick prayer in thanks. The way the courtiers presented themselves normally was already over the top. On celebration days, however, they took it to the extreme: glittering faces painted with crushed quartz, flowers of every size and pigment sewn into elaborately teased hair, and the most intricate gowns of *almost* every color. Dara had kept Veil's look light and natural, allowing her hair to pour down over her shoulders. She had worked in the tiniest of braids, twined with gold thread, to sweep the hair out of Veil's face.

Veil allowed herself only a small quirk of the lips. She still looked like herself, for the most part. "Thank you, Dara, for everything."

"You need not thank me for anything, girl. I wish I could have done more for you. Veil, you should know—" An unexpected knock echoed through the stone wall. Her hands tightened their grip on Veil's shoulders. The door opened, revealing a familiar, handsome face, and Dara whispered a curse in aggravation *and* relief.

"My, my. Never have I been blessed with such a sight as this. You both look gor—" Cace stalled as he took in Veil's appearance. He coughed and cleared his throat. "Uh, cousin, that color choice is quite...unexpected, don't you think?"

"We are well aware, boy," Dara answered dryly. "Your aunt has truly outdone herself, hasn't she? This will be a trying night, I'm afraid."

"We'll be cautious, Dara," Cace said. "Uncle Darragh sent me to walk her down. I'll keep her safe." Veil furrowed her brow. *Why would father send another in his place?* He always insisted on being her escort to these things, for he too became anxious when she was put on display.

"It's not that I wouldn't cherish spending my evening with you, Cace, but did Father say why he couldn't come himself?"

"He didn't. He just asked me to keep you close. He probably has more to tend to with the binding. Don't you think, Dara?"

"I don't," Dara said weakly. She turned her head, refusing to look at them. "Now, off with you two. I'll be along shortly." She was already shoving Cace and Veil toward the door before the last word had left her lips. She ignored their confusion and hurriedly made her way down the hall in the opposite direction.

"Do you find this as strange as I do?" Cace asked, his eyes following Dara's fleeing form. "Not that I'm not capable of babysitting you, but they are usually quite possessive. I don't know about you, but I for one cannot wait for this May Eve to pass and take its madness with it." Veil silently agreed, tucking her arm through his before they set off.

Bring on the madness.

8. chapter

Veil had only attended one previous binding. She had just passed her eleventh winter, but she still remembered gazing at the young couple with awe. Witnessed beneath the twinkling stars, the two had promised themselves to one another while standing on a worn, circular patch of grass surrounded by bountiful mushrooms, emerald green shamrocks, and thousands of floating fireflies. The love they had for one another was clear as crystal to Veil from where she sat on an aged wooden bench. Her thoughts were confirmed when the officiant, with gloved hands, wrapped a thin silver rope around their entwined arms from elbow to wrist. The shining thing melted almost effortlessly into their skin, leaving only a thin scar. Veil watched in wonder as the newly bound pair gazed into each other's eyes, the shared scar putting off a lustrous pearlescent glow. It was truly the most beautiful thing she had ever seen.

Veil had grabbed Dara's hand to make sure she saw the magic too. In response, Dara had merely squeezed hers back, smiling. Dara said it was a blessing, adding that not all bindings turned out that way. She gravely explained what could happen if there was any doubt.

"Taking the union vows is not to be treated lightly, girl. The binding rope knows one's heart and will fight against the bond if intentions are not true. It will brand the couple with burning pain, and I can assure you that it takes its sweet time."

"Why do they do it, then?" Veil asked, wide-eyed with disbelief.

"Do not fret, girl," Dara said, pointing to the happy couple. "The risk is worth it because every so often a pair such as them finds each other. They are well suited, you see? When they entered the union and made the sacred vow, the rope knew. You can always tell by the glow—the stronger the glow, the purer the match. My very own mother and father were a match so pure they bore what our kind calls the 'true mark', a special and extremely rare thing."

"Do you think I'll find my true mark someday, Dara?" Veil asked, bouncing in place. "Do you, do you?"

Before Dara could answer, a man on the bench next to theirs sneered. "How foolish you are to think such things, halfling."

"Shut your mouth, you," Dara warned. "She's only a girl."

The man continued. "You know as well as any, Dara—those with the dirty mix cannot bear a true mark—it kills them. The mark is only for the pure, and to let her believe otherwise is repulsive. Even if the girl wasn't tainted, she wouldn't stand a chance—just look at her father. Even with his royal line, he couldn't find a true match—his awful screams were testimony to that. I'd say it serves him right, the human lover."

Veil never again laid eyes on the disgruntled old man after that night, but Dara said he had gotten what he had coming. At the time, Veil didn't understand. As she got older, she tried not to think about what it meant.

Sitting in the exact spot she had watched her first binding ceremony from, Veil took in her second. Unlike the couple from all those years ago, the couple before her now showed no signs of fondness toward one another. Nessa proudly sashayed down the aisle, her sleek silver gown catching the glow of the fireflies while her inflorescent crown filled the air with a wild honey scent. She put on a show, basking in the attention, her smile nothing more than a pretty lie. Haven's face portrayed nothing but regret. The same gloved officiant stood tall before them, his voice carrying over the crowd.

"I ask that you join arms as a symbol of the union you are choosing to make." Haven hesitated, closing his eyes, but Nessa did not. She jerked his arm to hers, locking it in place with her unyielding grip. The officiant sadly shook his head as he secured the silver binding rope around their arms. "Promises made but not kept lead hearts to be broken and tears to be wept. No words are needed for the rope knows your will, if you are both certain, a simple kiss will seal."

Veil turned away. Her father sat rodstraight on a bench closer to the front. He wore his usual attire: a dark, high-necked tunic with long sleeves. Though her father rarely wore a sleeve short enough to show it, Veil knew what lay beneath—his binding marks, the same angry lines Moira displayed with pride. Now Nessa and Haven would have a matching pair. Veil couldn't help but cover her ears, hearing them scream.

"Don't feel bad for them, cousin," Cace said. "The choice was theirs. Now they can live with it."

"I'm sorry," Veil mumbled, her face locked on the ground to hide her misty eyes. "I can't help but feel for both of them."

Cace shook his head. "You and your bleeding heart, Veil. You waste it on the undeserving. The fools could have stopped it at any time. You won't see me tied to another, no you won't." He nervously ran a hand through his hair. Veil could hear the sadness hidden within his stubborn tone.

"Not even with Calla?" she asked. "If she could—"

Cace scoffed. "You know that is impossible. Father would never go against Grandmother, and I do not wish to make Calla's life harder than it already is."

"Maybe things will change. Don't give up, cousin." Even as Veil reassured Cace, the odds of such a union occurring under their grandmother's rule were near zero. The queen was set in her ways and would not approve of one of her kin entering into a union with someone like Calla. The royal line was to remain pure, according to Bidalia.

"I am to be arranged like the rest of them," Cace replied bitterly. "I only mess around with the ladies of the court to hold Grandmother off. If she thinks I'm hunting on my own, she's less likely to get involved, but eventually, she will tire of it. You should thank your lucky stars you will not face the same fate." Veil remained silent. Perhaps she was lucky in this one regard. Cace nudged Veil's shoulder. "This is a celebration, is it not? Come, let us go congratulate the happy couple and enjoy your liberties while you still have them, yes?" Cace's way of bouncing from one emotion to another made

Veil's head spin.

"As you wish," she agreed. The two followed the crowd from the alcove, back down the weaving halls of the barrows, and toward the Great Hall. As Veil had suspected, she had not gone undetected. In a sea of vibrant gold, blue, and green, the red gown brazenly stood out. Veil tried to keep her head held high, but the heated stares turned to angry whispers, so she clung tighter to Cace. Upon realizing the cause of her discomfort, he sent their glares right back at them, daring anyone to approach. His method worked, and they made their way to the room that had dazzled Veil as a child.

Not much had changed since the first time she had stepped foot in the Great Hall all those years ago. The vast stone arches still stood, the stocky roots still winding up to support them. The crafted glass ceiling still let in the night sky, with all the flickering stars surrounding a moon that hung like a silver medallion. Veil and Cace entered, pausing a moment to take it all in. Veil's eyes landed on the ebony harp at once. Its soft calls were indistinguishable at first, merely inviting whispers vying for Veil's focus. Her body stalled long enough for Cace to notice. He cleared his throat and used his elbow to nudge her side.

They weaved their way through the crowd, nearing the merrows who sat along the edge of the raised pool. The males all had stubby bodies with stunted limbs and were covered in deep green scales. Their hideous, squished faces held two bloodshot eyes framed in an impressive mane of coarse, green hair. As horrible as they were, it was the females one needed to be wary of; they were the true hunters. Unlike the males, they had long, glossy hair and the most bewitching features. Nature had gifted them the perfect camouflage, for they resembled their favorite prey—humans. If their beauty alone wasn't enough, they also had the power of song to lure the unsuspecting into their grasp. The mysterious creatures surveyed the room from their perches, their predatory looks landing on Veil.

Cace shivered as another merrow broke the water's surface—a female. The splash from her scaly tail was thrown high into the air. She reached the pool wall and raked her long, pointed nails along the edge. As she pulled herself up, her versicolored scales glimmered in the light, her wet hair barely concealing her nudity. The creature's nose began to work as they passed, and her lifeless onyx eyes focused on Veil. Faded black lips peeled back into a terrifying smile, revealing her razor-sharp teeth. Cace positioned himself firmly between the beast and its chosen prey, trying to lay claim to his cousin and make it known she was off limits. Cace's intensity did nothing but make the merrow laugh, her bewitching giggle tinkling like chimes.

After Veil had almost been dragged into the abyss as a child, Dara had given her a good talking to. "You best watch yourself, girl," she'd warned. "Merrows are cunning creatures. Their deceptive songs are meant to lure in humans, but even those with the mix have something to fear should the music reach their ears." Once entranced by their seductive songs, the merrows would drag you into their inky depths. Veil was grateful that vulnerability to the merrows' song was a human trait she had avoided. While she could feel the appeal the merrows gave off, it wasn't enough to draw her in.

Finally past the merrows, Veil felt Cace's body relax, though the dangers were far from over. The usual trolls, changelings, and puca were all in attendance. They had an alliance with the Sidhe, but Veil had never been allowed to converse with them—with good reason, according to Dara. So Veil only stared at the puca's pointed, fur-covered ears. The shapeshifters could present themselves as a great many things. On this night, they reminded her of the docile rabbits she had once seen hopping around while she and Dara gathered healing herbs. Regardless of their appearance, she had learned long ago never to be fooled. It was these creatures she feared the most. Children were their primary targets, and the puca took immense pleasure in their purpose. Whenever a pair of their yellow eyes met hers, Veil was quick to turn her gaze elsewhere.

The slab tables, which had sat empty and cold when Veil was a child, were now covered in delicious fruit, large floral arrays, and many golden goblets of nectar. It was a glorious display meant to entice and ensnare. Humans of all sorts littered the Great Hall, some having been taken due to their ignorance and others just for the pleasure of doing so. Their dull eyes remained unfocused, proof the clouding was well in place.

A few had already taken part in the festivities. They stuffed their mouths with sticky fingers while guzzling from goblets, allowing the sweet nectar to drip from their chins and dribble down their necks. *They were the first.* Giving in to the temptation carried a life sentence; for their weakness, they would never be allowed to leave. Veil's heart filled with sorrow watching them and she made a silent wish for the others. If they could resist the seduction, they might stand a chance. But most would never make it home. Their families would never know the truth of what had happened to them.

Cace showed no emotion as he led Veil to the platform where the royal chairs and vile harp rested. She took in deep breaths, struggling to keep her eyes from straying over to the dark instrument. Instead, she tried to focus on her father and uncle, who were already seated and appeared to be having a heated discussion.

"What do you think they are arguing about?" Veil whispered. Cace shrugged his shoulders.

"I don't know, cousin. You know they don't see eye to eye on most things. Brothers, you know?" Veil was well aware of how often her father and his brother disagreed, but as she and Cace drew nearer, the frustration on her father's face shifted into rage.

"What are you wearing?" Darragh demanded, his knuckles turning white as he gripped the chair's armrest. "You can't be seen like this, Veil." Veil shrunk back from her father's outburst and hunkered closer to her cousin for comfort.

"Uncle, please," Cace said briskly. "She didn't choose it."

"I did," Moira cut in. "I think she fills it quite nicely, don't you agree? Perfect for tonight." Moira held her head high, ignoring Darragh's glare. She flashed her perfect white teeth and flipped her hair over her shoulder.

Darragh stood and took a threatening step toward his bride. "How could you do this." He snarled. "I know you are angry with me, Moira, but she has done nothing to you. Why do this to her?"

"You know perfectly well why," Moira said, pushing a bony finger into Darragh's chest. "She would too if you had prepared her. Too bad she will pay the price for your poor decisions. Soon Nessa will claim her birthright."

"Stop this now!" Veil and Cace spun around in surprise at the sound of their grandmother's voice. Her withered form was tucked in between Nessa and Haven. "You are causing a scene, Darragh." Bidalia sniffed in contempt, shoving her way past them all and taking her seat at the center of the platform. Moira smiled smugly before scampering to the queen's side. Bidalia ignored her son's pinched face and took a goblet Moira offered. "Moira is right, Darragh, the fault lies with you and you alone. The girl should have been properly educated from the beginning. We'll be lucky if they don't change their minds when they see how she's turned out."

Veil searched each of their faces for an explanation but found none. Veil's eyes wandered to Haven, who had decided to keep his focus on the newly blistering wounds spiraling up his arm. She winced at his apparent pain, but her discomfort was short-lived.

Nessa, who until now had appeared bored, began clapping her hands together while bouncing on her toes like a child. "Mother, look. Grandmother, they're here, they're here! Finally!"

Bidalia and Moira both smiled, but it was Bidalia who answered, rising grandly from her seat. "So they are, my sweet grand-daughter, so they are." A group of Sidhe unfamiliar to Veil made their way toward the royal family, the crowd splitting to give them a wide berth. They were draped from head to toe in the darkest shades of royal blue, but as they grew closer, Veil could see what appeared to be a dusting of snow upon their hair and shoulders. Cace tightened his hold on her.

"Ah, Bidalia," a steely voice drawled. "Your Highness is a vision, as always. And my dear cousin, Moira. It has been too long." The Sidhe nobleman stood proudly at the head of the group he led, his lanky form adorned in crisp layers of the finest velvet and silk.

Veil's eyes moved from him to the rest, noticing the resemblance he shared with a younger man flanking his right. The two had the same fine white hair, wavy from where the snow had melted into it. Their strong jawlines and sharp cheekbones appeared to be carved from stone. Their glittering green eyes were all focused on her.

"Ah, this must be Veil," the strange man said.

"Lord Lorcan, we are honored to host you and your family. Thank you for blessing our Nessa's big day with your attendance," Bidalia said, her words drenched in honey. "Yes, this is the girl."

"She is quite magnificent, as you said, Moira." Lord Lorcan turned to the young man at his side. "Don't you think, son?" Lorcan's son took his time with his appraisal. He scanned her body lustfully, lingering on her strategically placed appliques. A wave of nausea hit

Veil as the unusual man finished his evaluation with a disturbing smile.

"Indeed, Father," he mused. "Her appearance is quite different, but I find I rather enjoy it." Veil could virtually smell the man's arrogance as he lowered himself into a bow, but years of etiquette lessons prevailed. She steadied her breathing, obediently dropped her head, and fell into a deep curtsy.

"I see she has been taught well, Bidalia, impressive indeed," Lorcan said. "My dear Moira, I assume I have you to thank for her enticing appearance this evening?"

Moira flushed under Lorcan's praise. "I'm so happy she is to your liking."

"Oh, she is," Lorcan said, tilting his head toward his son. "Truly brilliant, wouldn't you agree, Colden?" Colden nodded and gave Veil a look that sent chills down her spine. Lorcan squeezed his son's shoulder, pride pouring out of him. The way Colden stared at Veil suggested he was taken with her just as much as Lorcan was. Unsettled more than ever, Veil tried to make sense of the conversation happening around her.

"You will redirect your eyes or I will gouge them from your skull," Darragh threatened. Unperturbed, Colden lazily tore his eyes from Veil. Lorcan stared directly at Darragh, his lip curling.

"Darragh, good to see you. You seem distressed, my friend. This is a splendid occasion, is it not?"

"It is not, Lorcan, and you know it." Darragh growled.

"Pity you feel that way. I would think you would be overjoyed, all things considered. After all, it's such a big day for both of your daughters." Lorcan finished with a flirtatious wink at Veil.

Darragh lunged at Lorcan but was restrained by his brother's strong arms. He foamed at the mouth, struggling as he yelled, "You can't have her!"

The wilder he became, the more Lorcan laughed. "Oh, stop this childish behavior, Darragh. Perhaps some dancing will improve your mood? I hear Veil is quite the talented musician." Lorcan focused his eyes into Veil's. "Will you entertain us, my dear?" Veil felt a tug in her mind and let out a gasp. Cace pulled her behind him. If Lorcan was disturbed by Cace's actions to thwart his hostile attempt, he didn't let it show. "Cace, so good to see you again, and so soon at that," he said. "You left my court in quite the frenzy with your departure. My poor ladies were completely devastated. If I had allowed it, they would all have come, but alas I only brought a few—Oh! And some of my familiars, of course. You remember them, don't you? If my memory serves me correctly, your father was quite fond of them."

Faelan, who still had Veil's father detained, lit up. As he vibrated with open excitement, Cace reached back, gripping Veil's hand. Unable to hold his elation any longer, Faelan blurted, "Excellent, Lorcan. Where are the beasts?" In his excitement he squeezed Darragh too hard.

"Faelan, what are you doing?" Darragh yelped, kicking his legs into the air. "Release me!"

Faelan blew out an irritated breath at Darragh's fit. "Come, Darragh, let us be finished with this mess. What's done is done."

"No, it is not," Darragh barked. "And she'll not be playing that dreadful thing for their entertainment, either!"

"Cace, my son, perhaps it would be best for you to take Veil out onto the floor for a dance," Faelan suggested. "It would seem we have much to resolve here."

"Of course, Father. Will you allow me, cousin?" Though he asked, Cace didn't bother waiting for Veil's assent. He led her to the center of the room, placed his hand on her waist, and gave a nod. The merrows, who had been watching with anticipation, bared their pointed teeth and began their deadly song. As Cace danced with Veil, others filled the floor, surrounding them. Through the crowd, they could hear the chaotic splashing as the first of the weak succumbed to their watery graves. Veil's body went rigid.

"Are you all right?" Cace asked.

"What is going on, Cace? Who are Lord Lorcan and Colden?"

"They're members of the royal line who rule the Cold Valley. Father told me they've not been to the barrows in many years—they like their dark home. Veil, it's not like it is here. I don't know what's going on, but it can't be good."

A freezing hand tapped Veil's bare shoulder. She swiveled around to find Colden standing so close that his nose grazed her own. She flinched back into the safety of her cousin's arms.

"Cace, I have been promised a dance with this beautiful creature," Colden said, ignoring her reaction. "Faelan said you wouldn't be too disappointed to be pulled away, what with all the others awaiting their turns with you. May I, my lady?"

Cace's body was unyielding against Veil's back. She knew where this would lead. She searched the vast room for her father, but he was no longer there. In fact, her entire family, along with Lord Lorcan, had vanished. Not finding any help, she did the only thing she could to keep the peace.

"Cace, it's fine. Please, go and find Calla for that dance you promised her." Cace's eyes flew to Veil's in disbelief. She gently laid a hand on top of his and gave it a squeeze. "I'll be all right, cousin, honest." While Veil's words had not sounded as brave as she had hoped, they did the trick.

"All right," Cace agreed. He turned his stern eyes to Colden. "But you had better behave yourself. This is not your home, understand? We do things much differently here."

"As you wish. You know I can be quite refined when I wish to be." Colden returned his attention to Veil. "Shall we?" Veil allowed him to draw her into position, though he pulled her much closer than Cace had. "Such a pretty thing you are. So different. And I'm told you play the harp beautifully. I would so enjoy hearing it."

Veil's graceful movements stalled at his request. She glanced toward the platform. "Sorry to disappoint, but I do not play *that* harp—especially at gatherings. Is this music not to your liking?" Veil cringed at her sarcastic tone. She wasn't so naïve as to think she wouldn't be punished for offending someone of his stature.

"Such a shame." Colden pouted. "I was looking forward to finally witnessing what you are capable of. It's a rare gift—did they tell you? No, I don't suppose they did, given what I've heard of you."

Veil stayed silent while he finished twirling her around, but her curiosity soon got the better of her. "Rare?"

Colden gave her a big toothy smile. "Oh, yes, so very rare. In the beginning, after the fall, each clan was gifted with a tool to help them survive the new world they had been sentenced to. The gift was a harp made from the blackest ashes—"

"Gifted by whom?" Veil interrupted.

"Oh, I do like your inquisitiveness." Colden paused to clear his throat. "Now, each clan has their own story as to their harp's origins, but the histories all have one thing in common—they portray the giver as a horned beast. Would you like to know the rest, Veil?"

Lost in his story, all Veil could do was nod.

"Of course you do," Colden said, dipping her low. "You see, they say our souls were viciously ripped from us during the fall, taking our immortality with them. Though still strong, our bodies had to adjust to the new possibility of death, and many did not adapt well to the change. Extinction became a real probability. That's when our

73

people began to panic, giving the beast the perfect opportunity to approach with an offer they could not refuse. The original leaders were each bestowed a special harp that would allow the Sidhe to exchange their fates with lesser beings."

"Humans," Veil whispered. "You speak of humans."

"Indeed, I do. Have you figured out the beast's offer yet?" She clenched her eyes shut and shook her head, not because she hadn't figured it out, but because she had. Colden continued. "It's fairly simple to understand, actually—"

"It's enslavement," Veil said, boldly. "It's condemning them to damnation."

"I hear you've had quite the hand in their enslavement, have you not?" he asked, twirling her around once more. Shame filled Veil until she verged on tears.

"Oh, come now, none of that," Colden cooed. "You should be proud. Remember what I said? You're a rare thing. There has never been a covetable who had the mix."

"Covetable?"

"They really didn't teach you any of this? Yes, when the originals accepted the offer, they discovered that not just anyone could play, or even touch, the harp—Heaven's way to even out the odds, my father says. That's why you're such a phenomenon, you see? The covetable are so rare that only a handful have ever been documented. Most of them passed long ago, and none ever held both of the bloodlines. That's why you're such a keepsake, you see? You have blessed blood."

Veil tried to swallow, but the enormous lump forming in her throat choked her. She didn't want to believe him. She couldn't.

Her struggle must have been obvious to Colden, who tutted pityingly. "It's a sad thing to see you so upset over fate. The sooner you accept it, the better."

"No," Veil said, trying to pry herself from his grasp. "My father won't allow it."

"You still don't realize, do you?" He cackled. "You think your father has a say."

"He'll protect me."

"You're no longer his to protect, Veil," Colden replied, pulling her back against him and gripping her chin. Veil again tried to break free. She knew what he had planned, but in the middle of the crowded dance floor, she couldn't find Cace or anyone else willing to help her. "I'm afraid you do lack the discipline I desire, just as Moira claimed. It's all right, I will teach you."

Veil shuddered, and her eyes went wide. "Father!"

Colden shook with laughter. "Oh, you entertain me so. I think we're going to get along perfectly fine. As for your father, he's likely trying to renegotiate the terms. Unlikely that'll happen, though. The agreement was made and signed years ago."

"Let me go!" Veil shouted, struggling to get away.

"All right, now you're making a scene." Colden paused long enough to give her a smirk. "Why don't you look at me when I speak to you, Veil? Your eyes are quite beautiful for a half breed." Colden attempted to infiltrate her mind using his connection. Terror filled her. She tried to fight off his mental attack; beads of sweat formed on her brow from the effort. "Come on now, look at me," he demanded. "We were told you were a stubborn one, but there's no point in trying to fight. We are destined, Veil." Colden's force was so powerful it overtook her, breaking through her will. Her blue eyes were pulled into his green ones, which blackened as his pupils expanded. The familiar feeling of fog soon filled her head, and she couldn't shake it. "That's it. Very good, Veil. All is well, you'll see. Now, will you please play for me? It would please me so." He smiled, effortlessly taking control and working her like a puppet. He escorted her to the platform, placing her on the dark harp's matching stool.

The malicious harp's call was all consuming. Inside her head, a wild war raged. Her body trembled from the intensity of her fight. She clutched at her dress, her nails tearing through the delicate fabric and biting into the palms of her hands. Unable to stop herself, Veil's thin fingers uncurled from her skirt, one by one, leaving crescent-shaped wounds in her palms. Her hands rose of their own accord, her fingers twisting so unnaturally that her bones should have snapped. Her possessed hands reached the harp and rested on its strings which already hummed in anticipation. Its impatience filled Veil's mind and body, suffocating her. It had been too long since the last time its craving had been satisfied. Weak and worn down, she plucked the strings.

With the first resonating sound, powerful vibrations rolled up her arms. The symbols on the ebony harp started to shift, creating swirling dimensions on its surface and releasing a dreary haze that flowed from the pores of the wicked wood. The putrid odor it brought with it, the scent of rotting flesh, stung her eyes and burned her throat as bile clawed its way up from her turned stomach.

"Incredible," Colden hummed, his arm motioning to the scene behind him. "See what you can do? It's remarkable how you can call them with only one musical note. Just look at them—you should be filled with pride." Veil's eyes unwillingly left the harp at Colden's command. She already knew what she would see.

It was the same as the last time she had sat on that stool. The harp was a cursed vessel and its music a spell that beckoned the evil within. The more Veil played, the thicker the haze became until it billowed across the platform, tumbled down the steps, and flooded the Great Hall. Colden had said that humans couldn't resist the harp's silky melody, and he was right. Despite the haze and the eerie atmosphere it created, it continued to lure them in. The more she played, the more they swayed to the ominous rhythm until they filled the clouded dance floor. Veil watched in horror as the haze pooled around their feet, thickening into a dense soupy smog, pulsing with tar-like veins. Wispy tentacles floated up from the entity's surface encircling every human in the room.

At once, every human stilled, their slack bodies held up by Sidhe dance partners who only laughed and carried on without missing a single step. Although the humans' bodies were beyond their own control, tears flowed down their cheeks—evidence of the incredible agony they were forced to endure. Their mouths were pried open perversely wide to let out a high-pitched shriek no mortal could possibly make. The demon, feeding on their misery and woe, grew stronger as the shrieks grew to a deafening pitch.

Even as the glass ceiling began to crack, Veil's music played on. A translucent dust, shimmering and ethereal, was drawn from the humans through their skin. The sparkling matter filled the air and drifted down to the tentacled demon lurking below, which absorbed every speck. As the last particle disappeared, the shrieking stopped, the humans nothing more than hollow shells. Their vitality waned. Their tears turned to bloody rivers that flowed from sunken and faded eyes over their cadaverous skin. They would forever be playthings, the Sidhe taking pleasure in their servitude until their empty bodies surrendered.

Its deed done, the harp forced Veil's hands to slow the tempo, recalling the grisly spirit. The demon returned, bringing with it the bitter and tortured souls it had claimed. The cries of the damned filled Veil's head. Their anguished faces bounced through her mind, threatening to split her head in two.

A set of arms wrapped around Veil, knocking her to the floor. Cace's panic-stricken face stared into hers. His lips were moving, but she couldn't hear his words over the harrowing screams still echoing within her. Ruthless, feral, and unrelenting, they would not stop until they engulfed her.

9. chapter

"I can't believe you allowed this to happen. You were supposed to stay with her, boy!" Dara's shouting woke Veil, though no one seemed to notice straightaway. "And you, Darragh—you must tell her now."

Cace dropped his head in shame, and Darragh pulled at his hair as he said, "I know that, Dara, but did you find anything in the library?"

"We have searched those blasted books numerous times, Darragh," she answered, pressing the palm of her hands against her closed eyes. "Tonight was no different. There is nothing in the books that can help us."

Veil pulled herself onto her elbows. Her father and Cace were standing at the foot of her bed while Dara fidgeted by her side. "Oh, thank the Heavens, girl," Dara said. "You gave us a right scare, you did. Are you all right?"

Veil took a moment to collect her thoughts, her hands twisting in her green blanket. "I think so... What happened?"

"You were clouded by that filth. I can't believe he had the gall to do that to a royal in the middle of the Great Hall," Dara spat. "Shameless, the lot of them. Do you remember anything?"

Veil closed her eyes. "I do," she whispered, "but I wish I did not."

"None of that," Dara insisted. "You couldn't control your actions." Dara's words did little to console Veil. She should have been stronger, and she should have fought harder.

"Will someone please tell me what is going on?" she asked, her eyes begging along with her words. "Father?"

"Darragh, you must tell her." Dara folded her arms stubbornly across her chest, daring him to say no. "It is time."

"So it would seem," Darragh agreed. "Cace, will you please escort Dara out and keep her company? Don't stray too far, though."

Cace made no move to leave.

"Come on, boy," Dara said, tugging on Cace's sleeve. "They have much to talk about." Cace gave one more wary look toward Veil before he gingerly took hold of Dara's arm and left. Veil watched them leave before turning to her father, who had come to sit next to her on the bed.

"I can't tell you how sorry I am, Veil," he said, lowering his eyes. "I have failed you *and* your mother. She would be so ashamed of me."

"Father, don't say such things," Veil replied, reaching for him. Darragh stopped her.

"No," he mumbled. "You must hear this, Veil—all of it. It's

way past due, I'm afraid." Veil, unused to seeing her father struggle, reached out again to take his hand. This time he allowed it.

She gave him an encouraging smile. "It's all right, Father." Darragh took in a deep breath, placing his other hand on top of hers.

"Did I ever tell you that humans used to know us as part of their reality? In the beginning, they all believed in us, not only the few. They worked with us and fought by our side in times of need…"

"What of the harps, the beast, and its offer?" Veil cut in.

"Who told you of such things?" Darragh snapped. Veil, thinking she was in trouble, forced her head down and sealed her lips. Darragh's fingers gently tilted her face back up to his.

"I'm not angry with you, Veil, but I do want to know who told you."

"Cold-Colden," she stuttered. "It was Colden." Darragh's hand left his daughter's face and anxiously rubbed his own.

"What did he say?" he asked.

"He said the harps were gifts, given to the first of the fallen Sidhe, that they used them to build up their worlds and trap humans here. He said the souls of those trapped were the beast's payment… Is it true, Father?"

"That is the history, yes."

Sadness swirled in Veil's eyes and her body sagged, heavy with worry. "He said only some can play the harps. He called them 'covetables.' Am I one of them, Father? Am I evil?" Veil's voice caught in her throat.

Darragh scooped her onto his lap and affectionately rubbed her back. "Oh, my child, I know you don't understand," he answered. "And I'm so sorry you had to hear such things from the likes of him. You could never be evil, Veil. The histories tell us those born with the gift, the covetable, are a blessing. Not because you can touch that dreadful thing, but because you are one of so very few. If anyone could do it, many more humans would have suffered. They would have faced extinction long ago, you see? With only the few able to play the harp, so many have been saved."

"But, why do we do this to them?"

Darragh released a heavy sigh. "Veil, I'm afraid I do not have a good answer for you. I believe our ancestors didn't know what else to do. Banished to a new realm and struggling to adapt, they finally reached a point where all hope was lost. They saw the beast's offer as a way to save themselves—only the harps didn't turn out to be their saving grace with so few able to touch them. So they turned to the other creatures of this realm to help with bringing in the humans. Everyone from the merrows to the puca aligned with us, and together we thrived. That was the way things had to be, until a new covetable was born under the light of a Cold Moon."

"Cold Moon?"

Darragh squeezed Veil a little harder. "I promise I'll tell you, but first I'd like to tell you about your mother." Veil looked at him in shock. There was pain in her father's eyes, proof of how difficult this was for him. She waited with bated breath.

"You know, your mother once told me the eyes are the window to the soul," he said, staring at Veil. "It's a saying used among her kind. I remember thinking how fitting it was, considering the things we're capable of. Remember I told you about how we used to work together with the humans? That camaraderie ended when the offer for the harps was accepted, but I truly believe it would have ended regardless. They began to see us as the soulless creatures we are and our eyes as proof of that. But your dear mother, she saw things differently." He blinked back tears and his voice cracked. "She told me how foolish it was to believe we weren't capable of redemption. I couldn't believe it—after everything that had been done to her, she forgave me. She truly was exceptional." Veil had never heard her father's voice so soft or witnessed him display so much emotion. Clearly his heart was hurt.

"I was taught to use humans, such as your mother, as I saw fit," Darragh admitted. "We were all taught they were beneath us. My mother and father didn't see eye to eye on most things, but this they agreed on. We need humans and compelling them is a whole lot easier than asking. I know how horrible that sounds, Veil, I do, but it's just our way. I can't tell you how much I regret everything you have been exposed to and how I didn't do more to prevent it."

Unable to bear the hurt in Darragh's voice, Veil desperately wrapped her arms around his neck. "No, Father, you've done so much for me."

Darragh held Veil's shaking body to his. He shook his head, squeezing her tighter. "Not nearly enough. I should have stood up and made the choice to do more. You deserved so much better, and so did your mother. Her kindness and wisdom are what changed me, Veil."

Veil smiled, listening to him describe the stranger she wished she could have known, but something crept into her mind as he spoke of her mother. "She wasn't clouded?"

"She chose to love me," Darragh muttered, avoiding Veil's eyes. "I see so much of her in you. All the good in you, you inherited from her. She would disagree if she were here, of course. She would say you are the best of both of us. We were so happy when we found out she was pregnant, even with all the trouble that hung over us. She'd sing soft lullabies and tell you how much she loved you... She would have been so proud of you, Veil."

Veil felt undeserving of his praise after the terrible events of the day. She looked down, nervously picking at the material of her dress. But Darragh wouldn't let her hide for long.

"No doubts, you hear? Even though she never got to meet you, she loved you very much, Veil. From the stories of our world, she knew the border by another name—the 'veil.' You were like the veil to her, the thing tying both of our worlds together. You are the connection—I've just never allowed you to reach your full potential. I should have allowed you to blossom. But after I lost her, I was afraid of losing you too."

"Losing me to what?"

"To *them*, Veil," Darragh answered, his face draining of color. "To the dark in which they thrive... To the Cold Valley."

"Cold Valley? First Dara talks in riddles of that place and now you? Can you just tell me, please?"

Darragh slid her off his lap and back onto the bed. "There is no choice but to tell you," he replied, his voice cracking again. "We can't hide you anymore. I thought I did what had to be done, that it would all work out as planned, but I'm afraid it hasn't—they have seen to that. I never wanted you to be forced into the same arrangement I was. I wanted you to be able to choose, to know love, but Mother coerced me. She threatened to take you away or banish us both. And with all the dangers the In Between harbors, I didn't know how to protect you out there alone."

"They?" Veil repeated, a tightness forming in her chest. "Who are you speaking of?"

"You said Dara has spoken to you?" Darragh asked. Veil nodded. "Did she tell you about the war? The agreement that ended it?"

"She revealed little—said she made a promise to you, one she couldn't tell me."

"Another thing I'm not proud of, but I couldn't risk you asking questions or drawing attention to yourself. It was vital you be as invisible as possible. We had to keep you tucked away, at least until our plan had a chance to unfold. We were so close! I can't prove it, but I know in my gut it was Mother and Moira who encouraged the binding between Nessa and Haven. I'm sure they used his family as leverage to get him to agree—that boy was clearly taken with you. I thought he would take you as his intended and everything would be all right. But it's not, and I don't know how you'll ever forgive me."

"Surely there is nothing so horrible to forgive?"

"Oh, yes, there is," Darragh claimed, balling his hands into fists. "You must try to understand, Veil, that when I chose your mother I made things worse. At first, she was a way for me to rebel against my parents. She was lost in the woods, searching for her brother. She and I developed a fondness for one another, and you were the result. Your mother brought me to life, and she gave me you. When she passed, a part of me died with her." Veil considered her father's words, her stomach sick. She hoped he was finished, but he wasn't.

"I'm afraid the story only gets worse from here," he muttered. "In the beginning, I chose your mother because I was angry. I didn't want my choices taken away from me—ironic, isn't it? The barrows were ravaged by war. Your grandfather was a good man, but he would have agreed to anything to stop it. I was written into a so-called peace agreement with the Cold Valley. Lorcan wanted one of his own to have a place among us—a place of high authority. It was agreed that his cousin would be bound to me in union, and that's how Moira came to be in the barrows. He thought he would have more control over us, and he was right to think so, but then I met your mother. When I brought her here, I did more than just act out—I insulted them. I had carried on with another woman and refused to sign the agreement, and that led to them declaring war once more. You were the changing factor in all this, Veil. When word reached Lorcan of the circumstances of your birth, he wanted to talk again."

"Circumstances? What circumstances?"

"Your birth was not an ordinary one," he answered, stroking her cheek with the back of his hand. "You took your first breath in the winter, under an occurrence that holds great importance—the same occurrence that makes you a covetable. The day of your birth fell on the winter solstice, when the shining Cold Moon was full. When you add that to the fact that you possess both human and Sidhe blood, well...you're unique, Veil."

Her father's words fell flat, and Calla came to mind as she thought about how truly unimpressive she was. Calla had mixed blood and was able to do all things Sidhe. Calla had never ever been clouded. *Her* father had started training her young to keep others out. Veil couldn't even make a connection with a simple plant, much less manipulate nature's other elements such as water, air, and fire. Her mind had been easily conquered and used for evil. Darragh must have been mistaken.

"I'm not—"

"Yes, you are," Darragh stressed, grabbing hold of her arms. "You're so valuable, in fact, that Lorcan wanted you under his roof from the moment he found out about you. I wouldn't have it! But Father passed suddenly, leaving Mother to rule, and she wanted you gone from the moment she learned of your conception. She's only ever been able to see you as a smudge on her perfect bloodline. I knew I couldn't risk her hurting you, so when the agreement was altered, I consented and signed."

"The agreement changed?"

"Yes, and the wretched thing has plagued me since I signed it. Lorcan offered to end the war if I would agree to give up one of my own, someone from my direct line to make up for my past transgressions. He wanted you. At first, I refused, but Mother threatened that if I didn't sign the agreement, she would end you. I knew she meant it, so that's when Dara and I came up with a plan. The agreement didn't name you specifically, and by signing, I would be bound to Moira, thus allowing me to sire another heir."

"Another heir," Veil repeated. Her eyes widened with disbelief when she realized what he meant. "Nessa. You wanted to give them Nessa, didn't you? How could you even think of doing it, Father?"

"You don't understand," Darragh said, his voice laced with anguish. "Lorcan and his people are not like us. The things they do to humans make the barrows seem like a dream. With Nessa's pure blood, she would have been safe with them. But Mother and Moira—I know they convinced Haven to agree to the binding—they ruined everything. We only had another year to go. The agreement is that I have to fulfill my end of the contract by the time the next full moon lights the winter solstice—the next Cold Moon. And this winter, your nineteenth birthday, will be it. Veil, I never wanted you or your sister to pay for my mistakes. I never wanted to give either of you up, but especially not you." In that vulnerable moment, Darragh seemed to age right in front of Veil. Deep lines etched his brow and heavy circles sat under his eyes. She could see how this had affected him.

"I will go," she volunteered. "If it will keep everyone safe, I'll go."

"No, I can't allow it!" Darragh shouted, shaking her arms. "It will be a life of slavery and torture. You'll be made to play their sinister harp, and that is not all—they drink human blood, Veil! As soon as you are bound to Colden, they will draw from you. They think it belongs to them, that you are not worthy of it because of your mother's lineage."

"They want to drink my blood?" She gulped. "Why?"

"They believe it will guarantee their way back into Heaven, and they are not the only clan to believe so. They believe that by consuming the blood of humans, they are taking the soul to replace the one they lost during the fall. They have deranged logic, and I haven't seen any human or halfbreed who has been taken by them make it out alive. That's why it had to be Nessa, her blood guarantees she would not face the same fate as you."

A Sidhe clan that drank blood—Veil had never heard of such a thing. Her heart began to race as she panicked at the thought of the future she faced. "What do I do?"

Darragh pulled her into what must have been the fiercest hug she had ever received. "You will do nothing. I will fix this. I can't tell you how sorry I am."

"It's all right, Father," she mumbled.

"You are as good as your mother," he whispered into her hair. "I was unworthy of her as well. You will stay here with Dara while I tend to this, understand?"

Veil pulled back from Darragh, silently agreeing. He seemed reluctant to release her, but eventually they parted. Darragh had already made it to the door when Veil whispered a question she had never before allowed herself to ask.

"Father, what was my mother's name?"

His hand hovered over the handle and shook as though her question might bring him to his knees. He answered without looking back. "Maeve... Her name was Maeve." He opened the door, calling Dara back in. "Keep her safe, Dara. And put her in something more suitable. I'm going to see Lorcan and Mother."

"And you want me to dress her for that?" she shrieked in response.

"No," Darragh said, his own lethal eyes meeting hers. "I want you to dress her to run."

After Darragh and Cace had gone, Dara ripped the red gown from Veil's body, dumping it to the floor. Veil slipped into a simple black dress with fitted sleeves, which Dara deemed adequate. The new dress gave Veil the freedom to run—to where, she still didn't know. She sat silently on her bed, waiting. Dara had tried to engage her in conversation, but finally gave up when it was clear she didn't want to talk. Her father and Cace were still gone, and it felt as though an eternity had passed. *Where are they?*

"Do you think something happened to them, Dara?" Veil asked, not sure she wanted a truthful answer. Dara crawled onto the bed, her comforting hands combing through Veil's long hair. Veil welcomed the little bit of peace it brought her.

"I'm sure they're all right, girl," Dara said, gently pulling Veil's head to her shoulder. "Try to close your eyes and rest. Have faith—all will happen as it should."

No matter how hard Veil tried, though, sleep would not come.

Suddenly the door was thrown open with a loud bang, startling them both. Cace rushed in, his sword at his hip, and hurried to lock the door behind him. He was alone.

"Get up!" he shouted, his eyes frantically darting from them back to the door. "We have to go now!"

"Where is Darragh?" Dara yelled, jumping up from the bed. Cace turned to Dara, wiping at the sweat beading on his forehead.

"They took him. None of them would listen to what he had to

say, and when he refused to let Veil go, Grandmother stepped in and had him taken to the Saeculum." Cace turned to Veil, his eyes wide. "There were too many—I-I'm so sorry. We don't have any more time. We have to get you out of here."

Dara paced this way and that before her resolve appeared to set in. "So be it. Up, girl. We must run."

"Run where?" Veil asked, her eyes wide. "I can't just leave Father here, Dara. And what about you and Cace? They'll punish you—I can't allow that."

"You must. Now move." Veil stubbornly folded her arms, refusing Dara's instructions for the first time in her life.

"Don't make me drag you, cousin," Cace pleaded, taking a step toward her. "I promise I will help Darragh—once you are safe. I saw the things Lorcan and his clan do. It's not something I would ever want to happen to you, but if we do not leave right now..."

"I can't. Father's life is tied to the agreement, Cace; he will die if it isn't fulfilled."

Dara put her hands firmly on Veil's shoulders. "We have until the winter, girl. Getting you away will give us the time we need to work this out, but you must go now. Darragh will never forgive himself, and neither will I, if you are taken to that dreadful place."

"You honestly believe he'll be safe if I leave?" Cace and Dara looked at each other, appearing to come to an unspoken agreement, then Cace reached out, attempting to twine his arm with Veil's for a formal vow. She jerked away before he could proceed. "Only your word, Cace," she said. "I will not tie your life." His willingness to take the vow was reassurance enough for her.

"As soon as you are safe, I will do everything in my power to get him out. I give you my word." His eyes never left Veil's as he spoke.

Veil nodded before glancing around her room, her eyes landing on her beloved harp one last time. She straightened her posture with resolve.

"I'm ready."

10. chapter

Cace hadn't let go of Veil's hand since they left the sanctuary of her room. Dara led the way as they stepped through the tree hollow, tripping over the roots in their hasty escape. They were lucky the moon was full. It lit up the night sky, proving to be a helpful guide.

Dara stopped. Her eyes darted around the dark forest. "I don't think we were seen," she whispered. "We've been fortunate so far, but once we cross the border, we should step up our pace and stay close together."

"Cross the border?" Veil asked. "But you said—"

"Keep your voice down, girl," Dara warned, her finger flying to her lips. "I know what I told you. The dangers are very much real, but we haven't a choice at the moment. Trust me." Veil did trust Dara. She trusted Dara with her life. Dara stepped over the boundary line first.

"It doesn't hurt, cousin," Cace said, tugging on Veil's arm. Veil nodded before stepping into the wavering iridescence of the border, a slight tingle vibrating over her skin. Cace was right. It didn't hurt, it only tickled. The sensation lasted mere seconds before they were through.

The forest was the same and yet, so different. The In Between held colors too vivid to be gazed upon for long, but the human realm was dark and dull. The leaves were lifeless by comparison, and the moss, which normally dotted the landscape in every shade of green imaginable, was now muted and drab. Somehow dirt was even more cruddy in the human realm, if that were possible. The smell was also different. Veil was so used to the heavy perfumes of her home that she didn't smell much of anything here, except for mold. Even so, the human world felt more real, as though it was the way things were supposed to be.

"Wild feeling, isn't it?" Cace asked, glancing at Veil.

"Get moving, you two," Dara interrupted. "We aren't here to explore. We need to put some distance between us and the barrows before they notice our absence."

It started to rain. As the wind whipped her hair wildly about, Veil strangely felt free. Dara muttered something about cursed emotions bringing on the rain. She turned and started to run faster, forcing Cace and Veil to pick up their pace to keep up with her.

Veil was not as graceful as the others, and running through

the dark proved how little coordination she had. Cace had to catch her repeatedly as she stumbled over moss-covered roots and hidden stumps.

"The dark woods do not suit you, cousin," he said, holding her up by her arms and chuckling.

"So it would seem," Veil answered, her face hot with embarrassment. "I don't know what I'd do withou—" A monstrous howl filled the air. Veil latched onto Cace's sleeve. "What was that?"

"It's their *pets*," Cace said, his complexion growing even paler. "They must know you're gone. Run!" Cace took off after Dara with Veil floundering after him. Wet brush slapped at Veil's face as she ran, stinging her cheeks. Layers of mud, caked on from her numerous falls, weighed down her black dress. The haunted howling closed in.

"They're going to catch us!" Cace exclaimed. "Dara, we have to do something." Dara stopped running and turned around frantically. Cace and Veil skidded to a standstill to keep from plowing over her. "What are you doing, Dara?" Cace asked, his voice panicked. "Go!"

"Hush, boy," Dara ordered, guiding them in another direction. "This way—come on." Soon the dense brush began to thin until a vast valley had opened in front of them. The dark outline of mountains were visible in the distance. Veil turned her eyes toward the sky. With the trees now behind them, millions of brilliant stars shone brightly through the rain. "There's no time for this. Move, girl!" Veil jumped at Dara's command, careening down the steep hill, with Cace helping Dara make her way down at a safer pace. The slippery terrain proved too much for Veil. In her hurry, she stepped on a wet rock. She let out a yell as her foot slipped out from under her and tumbled down the large hill, leaving Cace and Dara far behind.

She came to a stop, landing onto a rough surface. Not even the rain could soothe her stinging palms and raw knees. She strained to push herself up from the ground and discovered a thick white line painted on the surface below. Curious, Veil gently prodded at it, but the line remained, even with the rain pounding down on it.

A rumbling noise unlike anything Veil had ever heard caught her attention. She turned toward it, and something large with two yellow eyes charged right for her. She threw her hands up and screamed. The monster let out a loud squeal and skidded to a shaky stop mere inches from her. The monster's eyes cast a hazy glow through the rain. Veil dared not move.

"Are you okay?" a deep voice shouted. "I'm so sorry, I didn't see you." The voice belonged to what Veil assumed was a man, although with his height and broad shoulders, he could have passed for a giant. He knelt down in front of her, and she could feel the panic rise from within her. "Hey now, don't be scared," he said, his voice soft. "I promise I won't hurt you. Blimey, I can't imagine how that must sound after I almost ran you over with my truck." The man shook his head and rubbed at the back of his neck with one of his large hands.

Veil glanced from the man's rain-covered face to his yellow-eyed beast.

"Truck?" she asked, fascinated. "Is that its name?"

"What?" He was clearly taken aback by her question. He leaned in closer, and she could see the concern in his eyes. They were a deeper shade of blue than her own—the color of stormclouds. *So gentle and...human.*

Finally, he asked, "Are you sure you're okay? What are you doing out here?"

"Veil!" Cace yelled, sliding between them, drawing his sword, and pushing it toward the stranger's neck. "Get away from her, you."

The man cautiously rose to his feet. He backed away with both hands raised. "Whoa, whoa, mate! I didn't mean to hurt her. She was in the middle of the road. I didn't see her until I was right on top of her."

"Cace, don't," Veil insisted, gripping her cousin's arm. "I'm fine." Cace held steady. He lowered his sword at Veil's insistence, but his eyes never left the stranger.

"What the bloody hell is going on? Who are you people?" The man's panic-stricken questions were answered by hellish howls which filled the air once more. "What was that?"

Another round echoed through the darkness before Dara finally reached them.

"Don't you worry about it," she answered.

"Don't worry about it?" the man asked incredulously. "Are you out of your bloody mind? Is that wolves?"

Dara ignored him and studied the tree line. "We can't outrun them," she mumbled. She glanced at the man, whose wide eyes gave away his fear. "Cace, take him now."

Veil didn't hesitate. She placed herself in front of the man, facing her guardian in defiance. "You can't do this, Dara. He has done nothing wrong." Veil worriedly chewed her lip when Dara wasn't moved by her words. She turned to Cace, who was openly struggling with his own indecision. "Please, Cace," she begged. "You gave me your word." Cace lowered his head. Veil believed she had won—until Dara stepped forward.

"He may have, girl, but I did not," she said. "Hold her, boy. We are out of time."

"I'm so sorry, cousin," Cace whispered as he wrapped Veil securely in his arms.

"No!" Veil shouted. "Stop! No, please."

"Let her go!" the man demanded, reaching out to grab Veil's arm.

"Maybe we have found a brave one here," Dara said, raising

an eyebrow. "Good. Now, look at me." Dara pushed her way into his face and focused her shimmering silver eyes on his.

"What?" he asked, still holding onto Veil. "No, you need to let her go—"

"Look at me," Dara repeated, leaning in closer. "That's right... Now, tell me your name, human." The knowledge of one's name gave the Sidhe more power over them. It would make the connection stronger, but Veil knew Dara was strong enough, even without it.

"No, Dara!" Veil yelled, struggling in Cace's strong arms. "Stop this!"

"Hush her up, boy," Dara said, her words rushed and urgent. Cace covered Veil's mouth with his hand, muffling her screams. "Now, your name. What is it?" The man trembled all over, fighting the urge to speak. But like most of his kind, he succumbed.

"Kellan."

"Good, *Kellan*," Dara replied. "Now, hear me. You will take Veil with you and protect her. If *she* feels pain, so will *you*. You will not abandon her, you understand?" Kellan's body still shook but he nodded—just as the wolves let out another hair-raising howl. "Put her in that contraption, Cace, and hurry," Dara ordered. "Come on, Kellan, in with you as well."

Veil fought Cace the entire way, using all her strength to escape his hold. She sunk her fingernails deep into his arm. Even with her fighting him, Cace was able to place her inside the truck and onto a worn leather seat.

"Cace, please," Veil begged, "don't do this. Don't send me off!" Terror swam in her eyes. Cace's face showed the trouble he was having in maintaining his resolve.

"I hope you have a good plan, Dara," he said.

"I do, boy." Dara turned her attention to Veil. "Stop this, now.

Do not be frightened. Stay with this human, and he will watch over you." Dara pulled Veil's shaking body into a gentle hug. "We need you to survive, Veil. Understand?" She pushed Veil farther into the truck then slammed the metal door, trapping her within. Veil peered through the window separating them, pounding her fist on the glass with all her might. Through the window and the rain she could still hear them.

"Cace, you will return and act like you had nothing to do with this," Dara said. "Get Darragh out and find a way to void the agreement. Here is where I leave you, boy." Dara embraced Cace before shoving him back in the direction of the woods. Cace paused long enough to look at Veil, his wet face etched with regret, and then he was gone. Dara appeared on the other side of the glass once again, gently placing her hand against it. Not knowing what else to do, Veil raised hers to match.

"Dara...please."

The woman who had always tried to protect her, who had always tried to be there for her, now tried to say goodbye. Veil had never seen so much raw emotion on Dara's face, and for the first time ever, Veil watched as Dara's eyes filled with tears. Howls bellowed all around them, louder than ever.

Dara's weeping eyes never left Veil's, even as she screamed to Kellan, "Leave! Now!"

The truck rumbled to life beneath them. As they sped away, Veil watched a massive black wave descend upon Dara. The last memory of the only mother Veil had ever known would be filled with the vicious clapping of teeth tearing into Dara's flesh and gnawing on her bones.

"Dara! Dara!" Veil screamed until she was hoarse. Soon the sorrow deep in her chest was too much for her to carry. Tears flowed, leaving trails down her dirt-covered cheeks. She folded herself up as small as possible against the truck's door, putting all the space she could between her and Kellan. Dara was gone, and Veil was alone with a stranger—a human, at that. Her mind ran wild, but it wasn't long before exhaustion overtook her. For once, she welcomed it. *Let the nightmares come.*

11. chapter

When Veil woke, she was no longer in the truck but lying on something soft and plush. She pushed herself up to see she was on some sort of couch, a thinning quilt draped over her. The only source of light was that which poured in from a neighboring room. She stood, and the wooden floorboards creaked beneath her.

She took her time looking around. A large fireplace was set into the wall across from her, its gray stones were weathered and jutted out in places where the mortar had crumbled. She stepped closer to inspect the strange oval and rectangular frames which sat upon the mantel, running her fingers over the smooth glass they held.

Across the room was a set of stairs. Veil peered up but froze at the sound of a chair scraping against the floor. She heard voices coming from the room adjoining hers. Veil leaned forward, hiding in the shadows casted by the wall of the opening. She peeked in to see Kellan at a table with a robed woman sitting at his side.

"You're not making any sense, Kellan," the woman said, folding her hands on the tabletop. "First, you burst into our bedroom in the middle of the night, nearly scaring us to death, then you drag us down the stairs to see some stranger sleeping on our couch. Now, who is that?"

"Mum, I'm telling you, I-I don't know," Kellan stuttered, pulling at his damp hair. "She just appeared in the middle of the road, in the middle of the bloody night. I almost ran her over."

"Don't use that language around your mum, Kellan, and keep your voice down," a man Veil could not see said. "You'll wake Maddy and whoever you've got laying on our couch."

"Sorry, Da. Sorry, Mum," Kellan replied, hanging his head. "I don't know what's happening. She had two more with her, and they were dressed in these strange clothes—one of them even had a sword, for Lord sakes. And the other woman, she did something to me. I couldn't *not* do what she said, Da. And I think there were *wolves*... What sense does that make?"

"Kellan, there haven't been wolves in Ireland for centuries."

"I know that, but I heard them."

"Maybe we should call the gardai, Liam?" Kellan's mother suggested. "They should be able to take the girl."

"No police!" Kellan shouted, jumping up from his chair. "I can't let her leave."

"What do you mean you can't let her leave?" Veil could hear the worry in the woman's voice.

"I'm so sorry, Mum, but I can't send her away," Kellan answered. He sounded confused by his own words. "I have to know she's safe."

Dara's compulsion was definitely in full force; Kellan couldn't help his words or his actions. Veil knew his torment was all because of her. He would be a prisoner to this mental entrapment until another Sidhe set him free.

Veil moved in closer to hear them better. A small tap on her shoulder scared the life out of her. A girl, shorter than Veil, now stood at the bottom of the stairs. She was pretty, with her sandy hair and round face.

"Who are you?" the girl asked, rattling off more questions before Veil could answer. "Are you Kellan's new girlfriend? You're a right mess, you know? Why are you covered in mud? And *what* are you wearing?"

The girl reached out to touch Veil's dress. Startled, Veil swiftly backed away and into the center of attention as she unknowingly entered the lit room. The girl followed Veil in and continued to examine her as if she were a strange riddle the girl was determined to solve.

"Maddy, get away from her," Kellan said, his voice filled with concern. He moved fast, placing himself between his sister and the oddity he had found.

Kellan was angry, but the girl he'd called Maddy didn't seem to care. She continued to gaze at Veil's terrified face.

"Kellan, would you stop? You're scaring her."

"You don't understand, Maddy. She's dangerous." Maddy rolled her eyes at her brother and stood with her hands on her hips.

"Dangerous? *Her*?" she asked doubtfully. "Why'd you bring her here, then?"

Kellan grabbed his head, violently pulling at his hair once again. "I don't know!" He turned his hate-filled eyes on Veil. "What have you done to me?" Veil backed away until she bumped into something hard and extremely warm.

"You need to calm down, Kellan. Your sister is right, the poor thing is scared." Veil turned to the woman reprimanding Kellan. Her mahogany hair was braided off to one side. Next to her stood another man. Veil glanced from him, to Kellan, to the young girl they'd called Maddy. The resemblance was uncanny.

Kellan's mother took a small step toward Veil.

"Mum, don't go near her!" Kellan shouted. He barreled toward them. Veil tried to steady herself but fell to the floor, sweeping against something piping hot as she dropped. Whatever it was, she had knocked it over, and it hit the floor with a loud clang, spraying scalding liquid across her arm. She screamed and cradled her injured arm protectively against her chest. Angry red blisters began to form. Kellan also held his arm, though his blisters were nowhere near as severe.

"Oh, the kettle!" Kellan's mother hollered, running over to them. "Are you both all right?"

"It didn't even touch me, Mum... It's her," Kellan hissed.

"That's not possible, Kellan. The water must have hit you both."

"I'm telling you, Mum," Kellan argued. "It's because of her, because of what *they* did to me." Veil could tell he desperately wanted someone to believe him.

"Enough of this, Kellan. You need to calm down—I mean it. The poor girl is terrified." Kellan listened in disbelief, but he held his tongue. The look he sent his mother's way was enough for Veil to know exactly what he was thinking. Ignoring Kellan's scowl, his mother asked, "Can I see it?" She pointed at Veil's wounded arm and started to approach again. Instinctively, Veil pulled her arm tighter to her chest and scooted as far away as possible, wedging herself in a corner. At Veil's reaction, the woman tried a different tactic. She spoke calmly and said, "I'm Aileen, and this is my husband, Liam. The girl who should be up in bed is Maddy, and I think you already know Kellan. I promise we raised him with better manners." Kellan huffed and crossed his arms across his broad chest.

"Will you tell us your name?" Aileen gently asked.

Veil tilted her head to study Kellan's mother, Aileen. She was beautiful. Her dark eyes held the same softness as Calla's mother, especially when they were directed at her daughter. Veil was astonished to see Aileen looking at her with the same kindness.

"Veil," she answered softly.

"Veil," Aileen repeated, a small smile brightening her face. "That's pretty. Well, Veil, I'd really like to take a look at your arm, it may need tending to. Come, let's get you off this old floor and away from the stove." Kellan's face twisted with disbelief. It was enough to make Veil agree to going with Aileen. She wanted to get away from Kellan just as badly as he wanted to get away from her. Still ignoring her son's heated stares, Aileen offered, "Let's go upstairs to the bathroom and get you all cleaned up, okay?" She gave Veil another kind smile and moved cautiously like one would coax out a wild animal. "All right. The rest of you clean up this mess. Maddy, get back to bed. Remember, you have to help out at Shannon's in the morning. Kellan and Liam, you should both get some rest as well. Dawn comes early, and the animals don't care if you're tired come feeding time. I'm going to help our guest get settled," she instructed with enough authority that they all did as she said, including Veil.

She tugged on Veil's uninjured arm, guiding her up the stairs and into the oddest bath chamber Veil had ever seen. Aileen closed the door, but not before Veil heard Kellan and Liam.

"I can't believe you're allowing Mum to go up there with her, alone at that," Kellan complained. "I'm telling you—something is wrong with her, Da.”

"Enough for tonight, son. I think we all need some sleep like your mum said. She's usually right—don't you dare tell her I said that, though.”

"Ooh, I'm so telling her," Maddy teased.

"Maddy, to bed, girl," Liam said, sounding exasperated. Maddy's laughter rang throughout the house, followed by her footsteps as she raced up the stairs. "I tell you, son, that girl is making me gray.”

Veil lay wide awake in the strange room, wearing a borrowed plaid night dress that Aileen had called 'pajamas.' Aileen had taken Veil's black dress away, pinching it between two fingers and mumbling about how a washing would do it little good. She had been gracious in allowing Veil to wash away the mud, even showing Veil how to operate the silver spout that poured water directly into the claw-foot tub.

It had been most awkward when Aileen explained the purpose of something she'd called a 'toilet.' Its complexity was far beyond the chamber pots Veil was used to and much louder, too. Aileen was patient the entire time, yet Veil could sense an underlying concern. Veil's lack of knowledge, of what surely every *human* should be familiar with, would get her into trouble. Veil sighed heavily. She had no idea how she was going to get through this.

"Are you comfortable, Veil?" Aileen asked. She cringed when Veil jumped at the sound of her voice. Aileen stood in the doorway, quietly watching the unusual girl her son had brought home. "I'm sorry, dear. Didn't mean to sneak up on you." She must have taken Veil's silence as forgiveness, for she placed herself on the edge of the bed. She began to readjust the navy-blue blanket, tucking Veil in. "You look exhausted. You should try to sleep. I promise you will be safe here."

Aileen's sincerity took Veil by surprise. She was as much a stranger to the kind woman as Aileen was to her, but still she cared for Veil and allowed her to stay. At least for the night.

Aileen let out a worried sigh.

"Everything will look better in the morning, dear, you'll see." She gently placed her hand on Veil's damp hair. "Now, try to get some rest. We're just in the next room if you need anything." Aileen walked out of the room, leaving Veil alone. She had insisted Veil sleep, and sleep did eventually find her, though it was far from restful.

12. chapter

Veil woke with the sun. It poured through the gauzy curtains covering the one lonely window. She lay in bed and watched the rays bounce around, illuminating every corner of the tidy room. *It wasn't a dream.*

The room was small, with no furniture but a wooden desk and chair and the bed she had slept in. Her tired eyes made their way around and finally settled on the open door. *No use putting it off.* She pulled back the blanket, shivering as the crisp air hit her, and rose from the plush bed. She mustered all the courage she could and tiptoed her way across the floor until a loud clang alerted her that someone else was awake. She eased her way to the door, hearing the noise again. It came from downstairs.

Aileen stood in her leafy green kitchen, whisking a pot on the stove. Veil winced at the obnoxious noise the pot made when Aileen moved it aside to cool. Focused on her task and singing a humming melody, Aileen didn't hear the quiet guest until it was too late.

"Good Lord!" she hollered, clutching at her chest. "You scared me to death, Veil."

Veil shrank back. "I'm so sorry—that wasn't my intention."

Aileen gathered her bearings and gave Veil a tender little smile. "No worries, dear," she said. "I get lost sometimes while baking. How did you sleep? Is your arm any better?" She glanced at Veil's bandaged arm. Veil, having almost forgotten about her arm, twisted it around and noticed it was remarkably less painful.

"Yes, thank you," she answered. "Are you a healer?"

"A *healer*?" Aileen asked, scrunching her brows. "Do you mean a doctor? No, I'm afraid not. Just a mum of two boys—I had a lot of practice with those two. Maddy is an angel compared to them. Are you hungry? The rest of them have already eaten breakfast, so there won't be a need to fight for your own." The smell of Aileen's cooking filled the room. The scent of warm spices made Veil's mouth water. She didn't want to be a bother, but she was hungry.

"I am," she said shyly. "Thank you."

"Grand! Come and wash up at the sink. The muffins are still warm." Aileen smiled and gestured toward a basin with a tall silver spout. Veil twisted one of the knobs and marveled at the cool water that flowed over her hands. Aileen ushered her over to one of the many mismatched chairs that surrounded a large wooden table, worn from what must have been many years of use. It was homey and comfortable, exactly like the rest of the house. Aileen happily placed a small plate of food and a dainty porcelain cup in front of her.

Veil looked at the dark, steaming liquid the cup held. Her curiosity was lost, however, when she tore off a small piece of what

Aileen had called a muffin and placed it in her mouth. She let out a moan when the taste hit her tongue—its airy, buttery, and crumbly goodness was nothing like the bread back home. These were fluffy and sweet, filled with apples, and unlike anything Veil had ever tasted.

"You make these?" Veil asked, eagerly grabbing another.

"Oh, I'm so glad you like it," Aileen said, her eyes bright. "I bake often. We even bake for some of the local bed and breakfasts in town. The extra money helps around here, with the farm and such."

"Farm?"

"Yes," Aileen answered with a confused expression. "There are quite a few farms around here... Veil, can I ask you something?"

Veil reluctantly placed the muffin back onto the plate and sighed. She didn't wish to offend Aileen, but she couldn't possibly answer her questions. Dara and her father had said that most humans stopped believing in the Sidhe ages ago. Cace had confirmed this to Veil after his recent travels.

Shaking her head sadly, she whispered, "I'm sorry, I can't answer much. You've been so kind, and I can't lie to you."

Aileen furrowed her brow at Veil's words. "Fair enough. Okay, will you tell me where you're from?"

Veil smiled triumphantly. "The woods," she answered. That was sure to be a safe answer. Dara had told Veil that the woods and what they provided were vital to her kind's survival. So Veil assumed humans also had to live near them. *How would they survive if not?*

"The woods?" Aileen asked. "You mean you live in the woods? Kellan said he found you near Killarney—those woods?"

"Killarney? I don't know that name, but yes, I grew up in the woods."

The undeniably troubled look plastering Aileen's face told Veil her answer was not what it should have been. "With your family?

They must be worried sick about you, Veil. Your poor mum and da. I would be going out of my mind with worry."

"My mother passed giving birth to me. And my guardian, Dara... She's gone too." Veil looked at her feet. "And my father, well...I'm not sure."

Grief was what Veil felt, though she didn't know how to express it. She could hear Dara saying, *"Keep check of your emotions, girl, for they can be used against you."* But the pain in her heart was so heavy, and the thought of her father still buried within the cold of the Saeculum, or worse, flooded her with dread. She hoped Cace was able to get to him.

Aileen reached out to squeeze Veil's hand, her face changing from a look of worry to one of compassion. "Oh, you poor girl. I'm so sorry. It's okay, we will work it all out."

A door that Veil hadn't noticed earlier was suddenly thrown open, and she jerked her hand away from Aileen's. The tall man that Aileen had called Liam stood in the doorway with the blinding sunlight pouring in from behind him.

"Sorry for the scare, ladies. Don't know my own strength," Liam bragged, flexing his arms.

"Oh, stop with your silliness, Liam," Aileen said. "You just about gave poor Veil here a heart attack. I can't imagine what she must be thinking of us between last night and now you parading about like a teenager."

"Sorry, lass," Liam said. "This house stays loud, I'm afraid, but you'll soon get used to it. Love, has Kellan come in from the field yet? I need his help in the barn—those horses have made quite the mess."

Veil couldn't contain her excitement after Liam had finally mentioned something that was familiar to her. "You have horses?"

"Aye, we do, along with a zoo of other critters. Do you like the ornery beasts? Can you ride?"

"I cannot," Veil admitted, "but I do enjoy their company."

Liam clapped his hands and all but yelled, "Well, get the lass dressed, Aileen. I can't have her parading around the barn in her pajamas—she'll distract all the help." Liam looked her up and down, laughing, and Veil felt her cheeks warm. She had forgotten she was still in her borrowed bedclothes.

"All right, all right, Liam," Aileen answered, shaking her head. "Hush up, now. Remember, she's not Maddy or the boys—she isn't used to your so-called jokes."

"I am wounded, woman. You know all my jokes are brilliant. It's how I got you, after all." Liam finished with a quick, sweet kiss on Aileen's lips. Their open affection with one another fascinated Veil as it was not something she had often witnessed. They clearly adored each other and that made her smile.

"Get off me with your scruff, you." Aileen laughed, already moving toward the stairs. "Now, make yourself useful and take the next batch out of the oven. Veil, come along and we'll find you something to wear." Aileen suddenly stopped, as if she had considered who she had left in her kitchen, and peeked back over her shoulder. "And Liam. Don't you dare eat all those."

Liam's mouth was already so full that he couldn't answer. Veil laughed as he threw his hand up to his chest like he was insulted by the very notion. Aileen gave him a stern point of her finger before turning to continue up the stairs. Liam's crumb-coated grin followed his wife before he sent Veil off with a quick wink.

Veil was, once again, sitting on her borrowed bed when Aileen returned, carrying a rather large box. Aileen's braid had loosened, clinging to her flushed face. Veil rushed to help her with the box, which was much heavier than it appeared.

"Thank you, dear," Aileen said, brushing the loose hair away from her face. "I tell you, that attic is a mess. I've been on those boys to clean it out for years." A puff of dust burst into the air as Aileen and Veil set the box on the bed, giving proof to Aileen's claim. "You can see it's been up there for quite some time, but I think we should be able to find you some things to wear until we make a trip to town. These might be a little dated for you, but your dress was beyond help, I'm afraid." Intrigued, Veil watched as Aileen blew the rest of the dust off the lid and opened the box. The clothing inside appeared aged and fragile. The box held knitted and lace tops, wool trousers, and plenty of dresses.

Aileen picked up a pretty shirt laying on top and gently rubbed the jade green material between her fingers. "These belonged to Liam's mum, Anna," Aileen said, running her hand over the shirt in Veil's hands. "She died when he was just a wee lad. His poor da raised him as best he could and took care of the farm. That's something we all have in common, dear—we lost our loved ones far too soon. But enough of the heavy. I think this should fit you nicely. His mum held a nice shape as well." Veil blushed at Aileen's words. She had never been good at receiving compliments when the rare one was offered. When Aileen noticed the color of Veil's cheeks, she reached out and placed a tender hand on Veil's face. "You're a shy one, aren't you?" Aileen asked. "Trust me, dear, you have nothing to be embarrassed of. Now, do you think you can manage, or would you like some help?"

Veil peered into the box with trepidation. It wasn't as though she was unable to dress herself, but the style was so different from what she was accustomed to. She reached into the seemingly endless box, feeling all the different textures. *What if I pick wrong?* She glanced at Aileen's knitted top and brown pants.

"Will you show me what is considered appropriate?"

"Appropriate?" Aileen echoed with a giggle. "Dear, this stuff is as old fashioned as they come, most of it hand-me-downs and home-made. I doubt we will find anything inappropriate. Just pick things you like and, more importantly, that are comfortable. You'll want to be able to move freely about. I'm afraid your interest in the horses has Liam chomping at the bit to get you out there—pun unintended." Permission to be comfortable was a rare thing for Veil, and her awed look sent Aileen into another fit of giggles. Finally able to regain her composure, Aileen said, "Okay. Get on with it, then. I'll only be able to keep him at bay for so long. We'll be downstairs when you're ready." Aileen left the room, and Veil reached back into the box, pulling out the first item her fingers touched. The lavender blouse was cotton soft.

She took a deep breath and mumbled, "I can do this." The top, with its sash around the middle, was almost a perfect fit. Having never worn pants before, she almost shied away from them, but then she remembered the brown pair Aileen had been wearing. She decided to be brave and slid on a long, dark pair that hugged her from her waist to her ankles. Her grandmother would most definitely not approve, but Veil had never felt more at ease.

Aileen was right—most of the clothing in the box was simple and modest. The dresses all appeared as though they would reach her knees or lower and almost all had long sleeves. She ran her hands through her unmanageable hair in an attempt to make it more presentable but soon gave up; it would have to do.

Veil found Aileen and Liam sitting in the same room she had awoken in the night before. She interrupted what seemed to be a deep, whispered discussion between the two. Liam was the first to notice her. He jumped up from the couch and clapped his hands.

"Ah, there she is! I must say this look does suit you beautifully, lass."

"Thank you," Veil said graciously before adding, "for the clothes and, well, just for everything. I'm so sorry for my intrusion, sir."

"Nonsense. Aileen has explained a little. I hope you don't mind—we don't keep secrets from each other. And, it's Liam, yes?"

A life without secrets. "Of course, Liam. I'm sorry. As I have said to Aileen, I wish I could explain more about myself."

"Oh, lass, don't you fret on it. I'm sure we will get it sorted in time. Until then, the least we can do is be good hosts. I'd love to show you around."

"I'd like that," Veil replied, a small smile forming. "Is that all right, Aileen?"

"Sure, dear, you don't need my permission to go. You are grown, after all... Wait—Veil, how old are you?"

"I'll have seen nineteen winters this season," she answered. Liam and Aileen looked at her as though she had spoken another language. Liam gave an odd glance to Aileen, and Veil did not miss Aileen's '*I told you so*' look in return.

"Nineteen winters?" Liam repeated. "Are you saying you will be nineteen this year? Your birthday falls during the wintertime?"

114

Veil was not accustomed to worrying about time or days. Dara had said their connection with nature reminded them of the seasons and when it was time for celebration and ceremony. They could feel it in the air as the leaves changed their colors, when the first snow began to fall, and when the early spring flowers bloomed. And they trusted that magic.

Humans were not capable of the connection as far as Veil knew, which was evident in the peculiar way Liam and Aileen stared at her.

"Yes, near the winter solstice, my father said," she explained.

"Winter Solstice?" Liam asked slowly. "So late December, then?" Liam seemed to be having a difficult time trying to understand Veil, and the same could be said about her toward him. She shrugged her shoulders.

Liam went to speak again, but Aileen touched his arm and said, "Didn't you want to show Veil the horses, dear? We can continue this later, I think."

"Yes, of course!" Liam said. "Well, what do you say, lass? Fancy a stroll through the barn?" Liam's smile stretched across his face and soon Veil's matched. He accepted her excited nod as an answer. "All right, then. Put some shoes on those feet and let's go!"

13. chapter

"Those are your stables?" Veil asked.

"That's a fancy way of putting it, but yes," Liam answered. "We usually just call it the barn. We like to keep it simple around here. What do you think?"

From the moment Liam had opened the kitchen door, Veil had been blown away. The wide, lush, green fields were endless, scattered with violet blooms more gorgeous than anything she had ever seen before. The air smelled fresh, and the cool breeze fanned her hair away from her face. In the near distance, the large stone structure Liam had called 'the barn' sat nicely on a small hill.

"It's beautiful," Veil said. "How far does it go?"

"We have a small one, only about eighty acres. Enough for the crops and a few animals." He pointed toward the barn. "See, the cows are over there, and the sheep are just there. There are several hostile chickens looking after their chicks around here also, so mind yourself."

"Am I allowed to go out there?" Veil asked, her wary eyes focused on the animals. "Are they dangerous?"

"Dangerous? The farm animals? No, you're safe and sound. Although, one of the sheep gets after Rory every now and then. I think it's the bright red hair, honestly. You should be just fine, though. I assumed since you like horses so much, your family must have a little farm of their own. I know Aileen said you lived in the woods—"

"I've only ever seen stables filled with horses," she interrupted. "But I was kept indoors most of the time. You allow your children to wander out there alone?"

Liam removed his hat to scratch his head. "Well, I guess I do. They help run the place—and a good help they are. They're not really children anymore, though. Maddy will be eighteen come September, bless her. And all the boys are twenty-one. Kellan moved back from uni a few months ago, and you see the blue house?" He pointed to a house on the next hill. "That's Connor's place. That's whose old bed you're sleeping in. Now he lives there, has a wife and child of his own. But even when they were younger, we let them roam about and explore. Let them learn, you know?"

Veil didn't know. Her life was arranged and planned for, but that was not what she replied. "What do you call this place?" she asked instead.

Liam waved his arm dramatically. "Welcome to McGrath Farm, Veil!" he exclaimed. "Now, come on. Let me give you the grand tour." Veil found Liam's exuberance contagious, and she happily followed him, a skip in both their steps.

Liam showed Veil a great many things on the 'grand tour,' as he'd called it. The cows and sheep came in many different colors, ranging from brown to black and white. Some had long hair, some had short. Some had no markings, and some had spots. They didn't appear at all bothered by Liam and Veil's presence. They kept eating the abundant grass, ignoring their spectators as they walked by. The chickens, however, were a different matter. *Such strange and finicky things.*

Liam had chuckled at her flabbergasted face. "I don't understand how someone could have gone nearly nineteen years and not seen a cow, sheep, or chicken."

Veil's face lit up with each new discovery, until they neared the barn.

"What's wrong?" Liam asked. Veil only stared. Liam followed her line of sight, and realized what had the girl spooked. "Nothing to worry about, that's just Rory. See the hair? I told you it was bright. I'm sure Niall is around here somewhere as well. They help us work the farm. They're good boys, the lot of them. It doesn't look like Kellan has made it back from the field, though. Come along, lass, I'll show you what's inside." Veil, trusting his words, accepted his offered arm and followed.

The large barn doors were wide open, and the horses were the only creatures Veil could see. The one Liam had called Rory was nowhere in sight. The barn held about seven stables, far fewer than back in the barrows. Bales of hay were haphazardly stacked along the walls, and much more was stored in the loft above. Liam merrily walked Veil over to the nearest pen, where a light brown mare was tossing her mane around.

"Veil, meet Nora," Liam said. She's something, isn't she? Best mannered of the lot. She is a sneaky one, though. Will steal your lunch right out from under you, so keep a good watch."

"She's gorgeous," Veil agreed. "Really she is, Liam."

"Glad you think so. You can pet her if you like...well, any of them—except maybe that big boy there." Liam motioned his head toward a huge black horse a few pens down. Veil walked closer to see. "That's Murphy," Liam said, following Veil to the pen. "Has a bit of a temper on him. Kellan's about the only one that can do much with him."

Murphy's onyx coat reflected the light streaming in from outside. He had a serious face attached to his long, thick neck. His uncommonly large eyes were dark like his coat, and they held a tenacity within them.

"Well, well, well, Liam. What have you brought for me? It's not even my birthday, yet." The mischievous voice startled Veil, and she rushed back to Liam, clinging to his orange flannel shirt sleeve.

"Now, Rory, you'd best be behaving, lad. This lass here is called Veil." He smiled, patting one of Veil's hands. "Don't you worry, he's harmless." The boy with the bright red hair had a crooked smile that filled most of his dirt-smeared face, and he used his finger to push at something perched on his nose. "Still haven't gotten those blasted things fixed yet?" Liam asked. "They're going to fall off your nose and into a big pile of horse mess if you're not careful."

"Naw," Rory replied easily. "These are my lucky glasses. I get all the birds with these—they just can't resist. Speaking of birds." Rory turned his attention to Veil. "Your eyes sure are amazing."

"Uh-huh, sure thing, lad," Liam said, laughing. "Even Veil here can smell your bull over the manure. Pay him no mind, lass." Rory joined in with Liam's laughter, and Veil did her best to keep up with their playful banter.

"It's nice to meet you, Rory," she said.

"Oh, believe me, the pleasure is all mine," Rory replied seductively, or attempted to, before taking her hand and kissing the back of it.

"Blimey, Rory," said another voice. "Let the poor girl breathe. Sorry about him, miss, he really can't help it." The new voice came from above. Veil spun around, looking up in search of its owner. In the loft, she found another man. He wore what might have been a white shirt, but with all the hay stuck to it, it was hard to be sure. In fact, he was covered in hay. It clung to his pants and poked out of his shoes; he even had hay stuck in the curls of his dark brown hair.

"Ah, Niall, there you are, son," Liam said, smiling. "Don't you worry about the rest of the hay. I'll finish stacking it this afternoon. Come on down and meet Veil."

Niall quickly descended the ladder to the loft and made his way over to shake Veil's hand. Dark freckles dotted his light brown skin, though he didn't have nearly as many as Rory, whose pink-white face was marbled with them. Niall's umber eyes danced as he chuckled and asked, "Is this what has Kellan in such a fine mood this morning?"

"You lads know how he can be—stubborn as a mule, that one, just like his mum. But he'll come around sooner or later. Rory, Niall, Kellan, and Connor have been friends since they were in diapers, Veil."

"Aye, we have. So what has you visiting McGrath Farm, Veil? On holiday? You're too pretty to be related to Kellan and Connor," Niall teased.

"She most certainly is *not* on holiday." Kellan stood with crossed arms in the barn's doorway. His muscles were rigid underneath his cable-knit sweater and made him far more intimidating than his angry tone alone. "Da, what are you doing? Don't we have enough to worry about without adding this girl into the mix? You and Mum are bouncing around like she belongs here, no questions asked."

Liam moved closer to Veil. "That is unnecessary, lad."

"Unnecessary," Kellan repeated. "Really? Didn't you and

Mum listen to anything I said last night?"

"You need to calm down now. Your mum doesn't want to send her off, and you didn't seem too thrilled with the idea last night either. We'll discuss this later, understand?" Kellan didn't answer his father, but he did manage to shoot Veil a scathing look before turning sharply and walking out.

"Try not to mind him, lass," Liam said with a heavy sigh. "His bark is way worse than his bite. He's just got a lot on his shoulders, is all. Niall, Rory, why don't you two try to settle him, yeah?" Rory and Niall seemed to already know the drill, easily agreeing before taking off to find their angry friend.

"He's right, you know," Veil whispered. "I appreciate all you have done, really I do, but I shouldn't be here."

"My wife is bound and determined to keep you, lass. You remind her of...well, of someone. We know you've got some secrets, and we're hoping you will learn to trust us enough to reveal them. I may not know where you're from or what has you running, but I won't send you into harm. If you have someone who will care for you, we'll get you to them. Do you have anyone, Veil?"

"No," Veil admitted. "I have no one."

"Well, that's settled, then. You will stay here for the time being and let my wife fawn over you. It will keep her from smothering the rest of us." Liam smiled and winked.

Veil, grateful, smiled back. "Thank you, sir."

Liam's smile only got bigger. "I told you, lass. Call me, Liam."

14. chapter

Liam returned Veil to the cozy cottage before he disappeared to resume his work, leaving her with a promise to show her the rest of the farm later. Inside, she found Aileen washing her numerous baking dishes and dancing to the upbeat music wafting from a small metal box resting on the window sill.

"May I help?" Veil asked. Aileen hollered, sending soapy water sloshing everywhere.

"My stars, Veil, we're going to have to put a bell on you."

"Sorry...again." Veil winced.

"Don't you worry on it," Aileen insisted. "And, yes, I'd love the help, thank you. Keeping this place up is a full-time job."

After receiving a lesson in dishwashing, Veil followed Aileen into the room she referred to as 'the den' and sunk into the couch.

Aileen dropped a basket full of clothing between them, asking Veil to help sort. Veil mimicked Aileen's movements and began to fold. Veil had only seen similar clothing a handful of times as new humans were brought into the barrows. They weren't permitted to keep them for long, though. Veil picked up a soft mint-green top, her fingers finding a tear in the sleeve.

"That's Kellan's sweater," Aileen said. "I'll have to mend it. The boy is rough on clothes, I tell you. Well, so are Connor, Niall, and Rory, I'm afraid."

This was the second time Veil had heard of Connor, but she still hadn't seen him. "Connor is your son? From the blue house on the hill?"

"He is." Aileen smirked and shook her head. "I see my lovely husband has been talking your ear off. You'll have to forgive him; he doesn't have an off switch."

"I enjoy his company, actually, and yours. Does Connor not work on the farm with the rest of you?"

"Oh, he does. He's out of town at the moment. Should be expecting him back in a few days. That's his picture on the mantel, just there." Aileen pointed toward the mantel before picking up the basket and heading for the stairs. "I'll be right back—just putting these away."

Veil busied herself with the remarkable trinkets on the mantel. Pictures such as these didn't exist back in the barrows. They had stunning paintings and tapestries, but these were incredible. Maddy, perched on a tall, green hill with her arms held out wide. Rory and Niall, standing alongside the McGraths like family. She moved on to one of Aileen and Liam wrapped tightly in each other's arms, looking at one another with the same adoration she'd seen earlier, in the kitchen. Kellan and a man that looked almost exactly like him were shown in the next, rolling on the ground, grass twisted into their hair, the smiles on their faces telling a whole story.

"They're twins, Kellan and Connor," Aileen said, making her way down the stairs with the now empty basket. "Not identical of course, but like Maddy, they take after their da." She motioned to the last picture. "That is Connor with his wife and little boy. I'm sure you will meet them when they get back." Aileen and Veil returned to the couch and heard the sound of a distant door slamming. "Well, that would be Maddy. She's going to break the door off that car."

The kitchen door opened, and Maddy yelled louder than someone of her small stature should have been capable of, "Mum? Mum, I'm home!"

"We hear you, girl," Aileen answered. "We're in the den. And don't throw your bag on the table!" Aileen shook her head and laughed at the grumbles coming from the kitchen. "Go put your things away, and come help us get lunch started."

"Us?" Maddy asked, walking into the den from the kitchen. "Oh, I'm so glad you're still here! I figured with the tantrum Kellan threw last night and at breakfast, you would have left—surprised it didn't wake you, honestly." Veil had never heard someone talk so fast.

"Goodness, Maddy," Aileen said, laughing her same cheery laugh once more. "Take a breath, child. Don't mind her, Veil. I told you she takes after her da, not a quiet moment between them."

"It's quite all right," Veil replied. "It's nice to see you again, Maddy."

"So, how long are you staying? We need more girls around here. The guys drive me mental most days. Melters, the whole bunch."

"Oh, um, well…I'm afraid I don't—"

"She'll be here as long as she needs to be, Maddy," Aileen answered. "Now, up the stairs with you but hurry back—you know the boys don't like to miss a meal." Aileen smiled, wrapping her arm around Veil and gently patting her back. "Now, how about we get to cooking?"

Aileen and Maddy cooking together was an adventure. They hustled and bustled around the kitchen in a tornado of activity, running into each other in their hurry to prepare the food. They laughed at one another the entire time, and it was lovely to see a mother-daughter relationship such as theirs. Veil was thankful to be a part of it. They taught her the basics of a dish they called 'cottage pie' with rich, savory gravy poured over fresh carrots and tender meat. Peeling the potatoes proved to be a difficult task for Veil. They tried to teach her how to remove the dark skin from the white vegetable with a knife, but she would need more practice to ensure there would be any actual potato left the next time. By the end of it, she was happy to have kept all ten fingers. Kneading the bread was a true revelation to her. She even found herself calmly humming along with the rhythm she had set. It almost reminded her of strumming the strings of her harp.

"You're quite good at that, dear," Aileen praised. "Did you bake a lot of bread back home?"

"Thank you... Um, no, I wasn't taught how to prepare food such as this," Veil said, embarrassed and not wanting to reveal why she had never learned.

"Did you have a cook or a maid that tended to you, then?" Maddy asked with a dreamy look, which made Veil giggle.

"I had Dara. She took care of me for the most part. The barro—I mean, *my home*—did have help with the cooking, among other things."

"Well, must be nice," Maddy said with a slight jealous edge. "The work here never ends."

"Oh, stop your complaining. You're luckier than you know, girl."

"Yes, Mum," Maddy grumbled. Aileen ignored Maddy's pout, and turned back to Veil.

"I bet you would love baking. Would you like to learn? We bake for Shannon's bed and breakfast as I said before, but we also bake and sell things for the farmers market."

The thought of learning appealed to Veil more than anything. She didn't care what they taught her, only they would be willing. "I would like that," she answered, smiling.

"We can never have too much help in the kitchen, can we?" Maddy cut in. "All the boys are bottomless pits."

Aileen chuckled and stole a quick glance toward the old kitchen clock. "Speaking of—they should be along shortly, so let's get the table set. Maddy, will you show Veil where the dishes and silverware are?"

Maddy wiped her hands on her yellow apron before smiling brightly. "Sure. Come on, Veil."

They had just finished the table when the boys came bursting into the kitchen. Rory, Niall, and Kellan all tried to squeeze into the thin doorway at the same time. Their raucous roughhousing was quite obnoxious, but finally Aileen's complaints were heard, and the trio gave in, allowing Rory to enter first.

"Thank you, Aileen. These two have not matured *at all* over the years. Plain childish, I tell you." Rory glanced back, smirking at Kellan and Niall.

"You're the one who started the blasted race," said Niall.

"Well, who can blame me with the scrumptious smell coming from the house—and the beautiful company, of course." Rory winked at Aileen, Maddy, and Veil.

Kellan let out a long groan and playfully punched Rory's arm. "All right, stop sweet-talking my mum and sister. It's gross, mate."

"I got it—mum and sister, off limits. That still leaves the gorgeous Miss Veil," Rory replied, rubbing his hands together.

"No, it bloody doesn't!" Kellan's outburst got a laugh from everyone but Veil, who didn't mistake the red in his cheeks for embarrassment.

Rory's laughter was replaced by an impish grin. "Oh, I've struck a nerve. Just look at you, you beamer. I can't wait to tell Connor when he gets back—he's even more ruthless than me."

"You'll keep that trap you call a mouth shut, you understand me?" Kellan's good mood was gone, and Veil did her best to avoid his eyes, which were filled with a fire-like intensity.

"Easy, Kell," Rory said, his voice placating. "We're only teasing. Don't get your knickers in a twist, mate."

"Yes, Kellan," Aileen chastised. "Listen to Rory, and sit your bottom down in that chair, right now. I'm assuming you have all washed up? The girls and I have worked hard to make your lunch."

"Yes, Mum," Kellan said begrudgingly, pulling out one of the chairs. Niall and Rory took their seats as well.

"Good. Now, where is your da? He doesn't like to miss a meal either."

"No worries, love!" Liam shouted. "Your knight in shining armor is here. This kitchen smells amazing!" Liam entered with a spring in his step and scooped up his wife. He planted a loud kiss onto her cheek, and though Aileen attempted to bat him away, her giddiness was out for all to see.

Maddy, gagging dramatically, threw her hands up to shield herself from their open display of affection. "Ugh, Mum! Da! We're trying to keep our appetites over here."

"Hush, girl," Liam teased. "Can't you see I'm trying to woo your mum here?"

"And what a good job you have done, Liam," Aileen said, lightly tapping his cheek. "Now let me down so we can feed them before the poor lot waste away."

Rory rubbed his stomach. "Well, thank the Lord for that. I'm starving."

Maddy shooed Veil into the spot between Niall and Kellan before sprinting to nab the empty seat beside Rory. Liam and Aileen took their seats, leaving three chairs unoccupied, one of which held a booster seat. Liam settled the group, and they all reached out, joining hands. Veil sat, unsure of what to do, until Niall took her hand in his with a smile. Following Niall's lead, she turned her attention to Kellan and tried to grab his hand. But when she grazed it, a shock jolted them both. He yanked his hand away from hers, and though his reaction shouldn't have hurt her, it did.

"You shocked me," Kellan said, rubbing his hand. Veil apologized, hoping he knew that she meant it. She was sorry, not only for the shock but for all he had gone through after being stuck with her. Kellan's deep blue eyes lost most of their aggression. All that remained were questions that Veil was sure she would have to answer eventually. "It's okay." Kellan determinedly took hold of Veil's hand once again, both choosing to ignore the odd tingles crawling up their arms.

"Well, that was shocking, wasn't it?" Liam joked.

"Ugh, no more of you lame jokes, da," Kellan said, rolling his eyes. "We're starving here."

"Kids today don't know good comedy when they hear it," Liam muttered. "Fine then, whose turn is it to say the blessing?"

Maddy cleared her throat. "Let this food restore our strength, giving new vigor to tired limbs and new thoughts to weary minds. Let this drink rebuild our souls, giving new life to wilted spirits and new warmth to cold hearts. Once we are nourished and refreshed, let us give thanks to who gives us all. Amen. Oh! And please bring home Connor, Farrah, and Gavin soon. Also, thank you for bringing my new friend, Veil. I hope she stays for a long while. Amen!" All but Veil's eyes were shut, so she didn't miss Maddy's smile as she ended the prayer.

"Amen indeed, daughter," Liam proudly rang out. Many hands began to reach for food at once, and after serving themselves, they would pass each dish along to their neighbor. Loud but joyful conversations happened all around Veil, and her senses were oveloaded. Mealtimes had never been like this back in the barrows. The food and drinks were prepared and served mostly by humans, who were clouded to do it without complaint. Occasionally, there was mild conversation when Veil's family got along, but not much was directed at her.

"The bread is grand," Liam said, practically moaning. "Would you like some, Veil?"

"Oh...yes," she answered. "Thank you." Liam passed the overflowing bread basket to Kellan, who held it out to Veil, eyeing her. She gingerly grabbed one of the golden-brown rolls. It was still warm, and the sweet and heady scent of yeast rose in the air. "Thank you, Kellan."

"Don't mention it...Veil." Veil felt a strange warmth inside when Kellan said her name; it was the first time he hadn't referred to her as 'girl.'

"You know, Veil here is the one who made the bread, and a proper job she did too," Aileen bragged. "Maddy and I are going to teach her how to bake. Right, Maddy?"

"That's right. She'll be brilliant, I just know it."

"So you'll be staying a while longer, then?" Rory asked. "I'd love to show you around Kenmare. Lots to see there, and we could even go to Kenmare Bay—it's bloody gorgeous. What do you say, Veil? Fancy a trip?" Not knowing how to respond, Veil stammered and stalled. Thankfully, she was saved from answering.

"Language, Rory Quinn. She'll not be going anywhere with the likes of you. She might pick up some of your bad habits, and what a shame that'd be, wouldn't it?" Aileen's question was followed by a sarcastic grin.

"Oh, come on, Aileen," Rory replied defensively. "I'm a right proper gentleman, I'll have you know."

"Oh, yeah, and I'm a pink elephant," Aileen scoffed.

"All right, all right," Liam snickered, "why don't we show young Veil here the rest of the farm first, hmm? Then, maybe we can venture out farther—*if* she's comfortable."

"I'd like that, Liam," Veil answered. "Thank you."

Liam smiled. "It's no problem, lass. I'm sure I'll have time—"

"I'll show her," Kellan cut in, staring down at the table.

"Kellan... Are you sure, son?"

"Why not, Da? Looks like she's going to be here awhile. Probably best we get to know one another." Kellan's eyes said what his words had not. Veil was sure it wasn't the farm he wanted to talk about.

"Umm," Veil mumbled, "yes...yes, of course."

A shrill ringing filled the room, thankfully ending the conversation. Aileen jumped up from her seat and rushed over to a black contraption hanging on the wall. She pulled a piece from it, placing it to her ear, and left the kitchen for the den.

"Hello? Oh, Connor! Thank goodness. What did you find out?"

15. chapter

The next few weeks on McGrath Farm flew by. Veil discovered what Liam and Aileen referred to as 'farm life' was extremely busy, with a workload that never seemed to end. Veil began rising before dawn with the rest to help out in any way she could. She was mainly put to use in the kitchen with Aileen and Maddy, except when Maddy was in school. School was a place for humans to learn, and the concept intrigued Veil greatly. When asked where she had attended, Veil could only answer that her tutoring was given within her home. She wasn't questioned further, but she knew her origins troubled them. Veil had gotten quite used to Aileen's concerned looks.

Aileen had been acting peculiarly since the afternoon of the ominous call from Connor. When she had returned to the table, Veil could see the sadness in her eyes, though she didn't say what was wrong. She shared a long look with Liam in which a silent message was sent, though everyone but Veil appeared to be in the know as well. Since that first call, more had followed, and each time Aileen's mood plummeted even more. It bothered Veil to see Aileen in such distress.

Veil had taken to the gracious family as much as they had taken to her—all except Kellan. He wasn't nearly as hostile as he had been the first couple of days, but he had taken to avoiding Veil whenever possible. Mealtimes were the only times they were together, and no more than a few words were ever exchanged between them. They had not yet gotten to him showing her the rest of the farm, as they were all consumed and exhausted with the planting of the crops. Liam had told Veil they primarily grew corn, and though most of the harvest was sold to other farmers, they kept enough to feed their own cattle through the cold winter months. He also claimed their farm was tiny compared to most, but she could sense his pride for it. The crops were the main topic of discussion whenever they gathered, particularly during the morning meal. Liam enjoyed his breakfast, drowning his Irish toast in warm butter and syrup.

"Harvest season will be here before we know it, and there's still so much to do!"

Aileen chuckled, watching him inhale his plate. "Don't talk with your mouth full, dear. Do you think this crop will be better than last year?"

Liam made a point of chewing his food and swallowing before answering, "I sure hope it is, love. We can't afford another one like that."

"There were problems?" Veil asked.

"Aye, lass," Liam sighed. "Last year the soil didn't bless us, but don't worry your pretty little head." He paused long enough to send her his signature wink. "We have put a lot of love into it this year and plenty of fertilizer. It should be grand."

"Better be, with all the work going into it," Kellan said, yawning.

"Oh, a little hard work is hardly something you're new to, son. Have faith and maybe the fairies will show up to help us out."

Kellan shook his head. "We need more than fairies, Da."

"Fairies?" All eyes landed on Veil, and the ever-present blush heated her cheeks. She looked down at her plate, trying to escape their stares.

Aileen was the one to break the awkward silence. "Yes. Surely you know of fairies, Veil? This is Ireland, after all, and tales of the sae practically grow from the ground." Veil shook her head, so Aileen continued. "Fairy lore runs deep here. Even those that claim not to believe will not usually test them. Bad things have been known to happen to those that do."

Intrigued, Veil asked, "What sort of things?"

"Bad crops, strange accidents, and tales of people going missing," Liam said dramatically. "There are stories of people being taken to another world, one past the veil. They say most never return, and the few that do barely remember a thing." Veil's eyes grew wide—Liam spoke of the Sidhe. This was what Dara had meant that morning—the humans didn't remember them as they truly were and had instead reduced those beneath to nothing but tall tales.

Kellan rolled his eyes at his father and said, "A bunch of bollocks, it is. All of it."

"Language in front of your mum, Kellan," Liam snapped. "It would do you good to remember the things you were taught. Hard to believe a couple years in the big city could change a person so much."

Kellan snatched up his plate and returned it to the sink. "I'll be in the barn." Veil jumped when Kellan slammed the door behind him, and Liam sighed, shaking his head.

"Sorry about that, lass. He didn't use to be this way."

"You know there's a lot going on with him, Liam," Aileen said. "He's worried about things around here and disappointed about university. It hasn't been easy on any of us."

"I know, but he's got to shake off that chip on his shoulder, Aileen. We're all worried, and his attitude isn't making things any easier. Now, if you ladies will excuse me, there's lots to do."

Liam gently put away his plate. He gave Aileen a goodbye kiss before walking around to Maddy and Veil for a quick peck to the top of their heads. Veil had been shocked still the first time he had included her in his morning ritual. He treated her the same as his daughter, and while she was thankful, it made her miss her own father that much more.

"Have a good day at school, Maddy," Liam added. "Only another week before the summer break. Veil, we'll try to make time this week to finish that grand tour we started, yes?"

"I would like that, thank you." Veil smiled at the thought of Liam being the one to show her more of the farm instead of Kellan.

"Good, good," Liam replied. "And you, my beautiful wife— do try to behave today. Try not to think on things too hard."

"I'll give it my best go, dear," Aileen answered, gazing at him over the rim of her cup as she sipped her tea.

Liam was not perturbed by Aileen's dry sarcasm. It brought an even bigger smile to his face as he headed out the door. "See to it you do, love."

"Ah, what to do with him?" Aileen sighed, placing her cup down on the table. Veil didn't know if she would ever get used to the way Aileen and Liam were with each other. There was no doubt in her mind they would share the true mark if humans could. "Oh! Time for you to go, Maddy," Aileen said, eyeing the clock on the kitchen wall. "You don't want to be late."

Maddy rushed to the sink with her dishes before dashing to grab her book bag. "Bye, Mum! Bye, Veil! Mum, please wait for me to show her how to bake the pies, okay?" Maddy disappeared through the door without waiting for an answer. Her tiny blue car rumbled to life and soon faded away.

The telephone rang. Aileen was up and answering it in the blink of an eye. "Hello? Connor, what is it?" She slumped with what appeared to Veil to be relief, yet she still seemed disturbed by what she heard. "Okay. You're sure nothing has happened? Yes, yes. Okay. We will see you all this afternoon, then. Okay, good. Safe travels, Connor. Love you too, dear. Goodbye." She placed the telephone back into its holder. Aileen still had her back to Veil, and Veil could see her take a deep breath in.

"Is everything all right, Aileen?" she asked.

"Looks like you'll finally get to meet the rest of our lot," Aileen answered. "Connor said they'll be traveling home today."

"And this is a bad thing?"

"Oh, no, of course not. It's just...he didn't say much. But there's no use in worrying until they get here. It'll be good to have them all home."

"All is well, then?"

Aileen walked over to the kitchen window and stared out at the fields. "I pray it is, Veil. I pray it is."

Aileen soon left in search of Liam. When she returned, Veil noticed that she had been crying. They quietly resumed their routine. Tending to the laundry, dusting, and sweeping were among the chores Veil enjoyed, though Aileen said she didn't understand how anyone could enjoy doing laundry. Lunch arrived fast, but despite sandwiches made from Veil's fresh-baked bread, everyone's mood was low and the conversation slim. Their behavior at the table was strange, but it was only after lunch that the normal routine was truly broken.

The den felt small with so many piled into it, and a few extra chairs from the kitchen had to be brought in to accommodate. Veil remained silent as the others sat quietly, looking out the windows. She didn't understand why they'd not headed back out to the fields, and their unease made Veil extremely nervous. Even Rory wasn't his usual flirtatious self.

"They're here!" Niall's words initiated a stampede for the door. Veil moved to follow but stopped in the large archway between the den and kitchen, unsure of her place. She didn't have long to contemplate it before the door was opened once again.

The group flowed back inside with Aileen leading the way. A little boy clung to her, and she squeezed him tightly, kissing his fair hair over and over. "Oh, Maimeó is so glad you're home."

"Aileen, please, let the boy breathe," Liam teased. Aileen poked her tongue out at him, and he laughed at her immaturity. "Yes, go ahead and teach the lad bad habits, hmm?"

"You just hush up. You know how I've missed him," Aileen said, squeezing the young boy a little bit harder.

"What about me, Mum? No love for your favorite son, then?" Veil was finally looking at Connor, the man from the picture with Kellan, and the resemblance was uncanny. They were not quite identical, but there was no doubt they were brothers.

Kellan cackled, slapping his brother's back. "You bloody well know I'm the favorite, Connor."

"I bloody well do not," Connor said, punching Kellan's arm.

"Language. Besides, there's no point in arguing; everyone knows Gavin here is my favorite." Aileen winked at the boy she carried.

"Yes, Mum," Kellan and Connor drawled.

"That's about right," said a woman with the reddest hair Veil had ever seen. "Once the grandbabies get here, the rest of us become meaningless."

"Nonsense," Aileen replied. "I need you all to bring me many more grandbabies. See? Lots of meaning left." The room erupted with laughter, but the red-haired woman stopped when she noticed Veil.

"Oh, how rude of us, carrying on and such, and we've spared no time to introduce ourselves. I'm Farrah, this lug's doting wife." She thumbed toward Connor. Veil studied the friendly woman for a moment. Farrah was much shorter than her husband, and her fire-red hair was tightly sheared off at the base of her neck. *She looks so familiar*.

"Really, there is nothing to worry about. I'm Veil," she said at last.

"Ah, you're the one who has been causing this other giant to pout."

"Oi!" Kellan let out. "Not you too, tiny. I have plenty here that give me a hard time without you adding to it. And I do not pout."

"You should be used to it by now, Kell," Farrah teased. "Besides, this is just too good to pass up. Aileen was right—she's a pretty thing, a far better sight than that other one you tangled with." Veil knew her embarrassment was showing, even as she tried to hide behind her hair.

"Don't let my sister get to you, Veil," Rory said. "She's like a shark when she smells fresh blood. Made my life miserable growing up, she did."

"Oh, please, little brother. I was, and still am, an angel."

Rory scoffed as his sister innocently batted her eyelashes. "I beg to differ. You've only gotten worse since taking up with Connor."

"I'm the innocent one," Connor said, trying to defend himself. "Your sister was the one who always got me into trouble."

"Connor, dear, you haven't been innocent since you were a wee babe," Aileen interjected. Connor looked at his mother, incredulous.

"Thank you, Mum, really."

"Okay, enough of this." Aileen chuckled. "Veil hasn't yet met the most important person here. Gavin, can you say hello to Veil?" Aileen cooed at the little boy, who still hadn't lifted his head from her shoulder. She brought him closer, turning so that Veil could see his sweet cherub face. He appeared to have only seen three years, maybe four, and took after his father's side with his light hair and deep blue eyes. He was beautiful—and a prime example of a child the creatures from Veil's home would love to steal. Veil searched Gavin's eyes for any signs he might have been the victim of the puca's switch, but all she could see were curious human eyes looking back.

"Hello, little one," she said, smiling. The boy didn't answer, but his eyes never left hers. Innocence and curiosity swirled within them, along with something else she couldn't quite put her finger on. She sensed he had a story he had yet to tell.

"Sorry, our little man here is quite shy," Farrah explained. "He's autistic."

Gavin reached both arms out to Veil. Everyone in the room went silent as the boy spoke. "Ve...Ve. Ve-Ve." His soft voice pulled Veil in. She moved closer, reaching out to him as well. He was quick to scramble out of Aileen's arms and fling himself into Veil's, winding his skinny arms around her neck.

"Well, would you look at that," Connor uttered. "He's never done that before."

"No, he hasn't," Farrah said in awe. "Well, that settles it. Now we have to keep her around. It wouldn't be too much of a chore for you lot—would be marrying up, I'd say."

Veil's cheeks went scarlet, and Liam's grin widened. "She does have a pretty blush, doesn't she?" he said.

Aileen shook her head. "We'll be lucky if she stays one more minute with your unfiltered mouths. Veil, you'll have to excuse them. I've tried for many years to instill some manners, but alas, nothing takes."

"I think you have a kind family, Aileen, honest."

"Thank you, dear. Though I must say you do look proper with a babe on your hip."

"Look whose mouth is unfiltered now, love." Liam snickered. All but Kellan began to laugh along with their teasing. Kellan only stared at Veil as though he couldn't understand why everyone was so drawn to her.

Veil turned back to Gavin to escape Kellan's glare. She took the time to study the small boy. He had some blue-tinted discoloration under his eyes, and his breathing appeared shallow. Gavin must have felt Veil looking him over for he raised his eyes to meet hers.

"How long has he been ill?" she asked, her eyebrows drawing together. The merrymaking ceased, and once again everyone grew quiet.

Aileen's tone was cautious as she asked, "Veil, how do you know Gavin is sick?"

"Can't you see it?" Veil asked, keeping her eyes on Gavin's. "It's all here...in his eyes."

16. chapter

Veil woke the next morning with a headache from tossing and turning all night. Her mind would not shut off, and she regretted her words about Gavin. Connor and his family had left soon after Veil's mouth ran away with her, claiming they needed to unpack from their trip and rest. Veil couldn't help but think she had somehow offended them. They had all watched her with suspicious eyes, like she was someone to be wary of. She couldn't fault them for it, though. They didn't know her. And if they did, their wariness would be merited.

Veil was slow to dress, trying to avoid the day. She slipped on a light brown dress with long sleeves that clung to her wrists. The color reminded her of the deer she and Dara had encountered the day everything in Veil's life had changed. Images of Dara's face flashed through her mind. Veil sat back down on the bed and closed her eyes, letting the memories of Dara come for they were all Veil had left of her. Veil's eyes opened, brimming with tears, but she swept them away and continued getting dressed. As she laced up her boots, she heard a tap on the door.

"Come in," she called out. Aileen, still dressed in her night-clothes, peeked in.

"Oh, good, you're awake."

"Yes," Veil answered, biting her lower lip. "Did you need me for something?"

"Oh, no, no," Aileen said reassuringly, "I just wanted to speak to you about yesterday…about Gavin."

Ashamed and worried, Veil dropped her head into her hands. "I'm so sorry if I said or did anything wrong—"

"Oh, goodness, dear, it's nothing like that," Aileen cut in. She walked over to the bed and sat next to Veil. "It was just a shock to us that you knew. Connor and Farrah do not wish to discuss it, especially until they find out what is wrong and, Lord willing, a way to make him better. I'm sure they think one of us told you. Did someone tell you, Veil? Rory or Maddy, perhaps? Or, maybe you overheard one of us talking?"

Veil lifted her head and studied Aileen's face, noticing how tired she seemed. The stress over the situation with the boy had unde-niably played its part. Veil wanted to help ease some of Aileen's worries, but she couldn't lie to do it.

"No," she answered honestly.

"Are you sure?"

"Yes, I'm quite sure."

"I didn't think that was the case," Aileen said, sighing. "Can you tell me how you knew?"

With eyes glued to the floor, Veil took a deep breath while

Aileen tenderly rubbed her back. Aileen deserved some answers—they all did.

"I'm not like you," Veil answered, her voice nothing more than a breathy whisper. "I was raised differently and by very different people. I wasn't permitted to leave my room often, but my guardian, Dara, was a healer, and she would sometimes allow me to accompany her outside. She started teaching me the trade when I was young. She taught me what to look for in both nature and in people."

Aileen's face went slack from astonishment and then pinched with disgust. "Veil, were you mistreated growing up?"

Veil gazed at Aileen curiously, not fully understanding her question or her concern. "I was not accepted by many, if that is what you mean. Most of my family was not proud to have me, but I was not completely alone. I feel blessed to have had the few who cared for me."

Aileen sat in sad silence for a moment, lost in thought. She scooted closer to Veil and took hold of her hand. "You know, we're not completely different, you and me. You actually remind me of myself in so many ways. I wasn't born here—in Ireland, that is. My parents were native here, but my da took a job in the States when my mum was expecting me. I lived there until I was four years old. That's why my accent is a little odd at times." She chuckled softly before her face turned serious again. "There was an accident, you see—a car crash—and I was the only one to survive it. I was sent back here to live with my mum's sister, and let me tell you, she did not want another mouth to feed. It didn't take her long to decide she wanted me gone, the horrible woman that she was. She signed me over to the most amazing person, though, so I guess I should be thanking her.

"I was taken in by a friend of Liam's family. Her name was Lilli, and she was his mum's best mate. She took to helping out on the farm and with raising the children after Anna died. That's how I met the big lug—we grew up together." She paused long enough to shake her head and display a tiny grin. "Lilli was a blessing in so many ways. She saved me, and I miss her terribly. So you see, our stories have much in common. We all have secrets we must carry, but that doesn't mean we have to carry them alone. Not even you, dear."

Aileen had been through a tragedy, and she was stronger because of it. If Aileen could survive all that, Veil could surely make it a couple of months. The McGraths had taken Veil in and renewed her faith in kindness. No longer able to hold back her emotions, Veil plowed Aileen over with the force of her hug.

Aileen chuckled again. "*Oof!* Easy, dear. I'm not as young as you—my body has some wear on it." Veil pulled back sheepishly. She started to apologize, but Aileen cut her off and pulled her in tighter. "None of that," she whispered. "I don't think you've been hugged enough, dear. I—*we*—all want to help you, Veil. In any way you'll let us. I know you have a story of your own, but we'll wait for you to be ready to tell it. I want you to trust us and feel safe here."

"I doubt Kellan shares your opinion, Aileen," Veil replied, "and I don't blame him."

Aileen lovingly patted Veil's back before releasing her. "Kellan will come around, dear. I think it's time for you two to go on that long-awaited tour, yes? The fields are just about finished, so we will make the time for it today."

Though Veil had agreed to the tour, in truth, she didn't want to go anywhere alone with Kellan. He wanted answers, and she didn't think he would be patient like Aileen. But Veil owed him. She owed them all.

11. chapter

Kellan had been avoiding Veil like the plague, so it had surprised her when he had readily offered to take her around the farm. There was no way he would be nice about it though, no matter what Aileen said. The time had been set for Veil to meet him in the barn, and she counted down the minutes, not with anticipation but with dread. She had no idea what she would say to him. After all, what could she say?

Veil stood at the sink, filling the copper kettle for the tea Aileen had sworn would make her feel better. Aileen had assumed that Veil's sullen mood was from the way Kellan had reacted when it was announced over breakfast that Veil would be staying...*indefinitely.* Veil's prediction had been correct—he hadn't been too thrilled. Liam and Maddy, however, were over the moon with excitement.

Aileen watched Veil with a smirk. "You're overflowing there, dear."

"Oh, goodness!" Veil shouted. Water gushed from the spout and onto the floor. Veil hurried to grab the dish towel from the counter, and Aileen helped her clean up the mess she had made. "I apologize, Aileen. My mind's off a bit, I'm afraid."

"Oh, shush, dear," Aileen said. "It's only water and will wipe right up. This kitchen has seen much worse, I can tell you that." How easily Aileen forgave amazed Veil. An accident such as this would have resulted in at least a few painful barbs back home. Aileen smiled and wrapped her arm around Veil's shoulders.

Veil was filled with an emotion she wasn't the best at expressing, so instead she softly muttered, "Thank you."

Aileen and Veil broke apart when the door swung open, surprising them both.

"Oh, thank the Lord you're awake!" Farrah said, her hair matted and her face haggard. "Veil, will you take him, please? He hasn't stopped crying all night and keeps saying 'Ve-Ve.' I don't know what's the matter with him." Farrah had dark circles under her eyes, and poor Gavin had large crocodile tears leaking from his. Veil took the boy from his mother's arms. His crying stopped, but his tiny body continued to shake with the aftershocks of being upset for so long.

"Shh, little one," Veil whispered into his tiny ear. "It's all right."

"Oh, thank goodness," Farrah breathed. She let out a long relieving sigh. "Veil, you're an angel."

"My, I've never seen him this way," Aileen said. "Have you?"

"No, but I'm far too tired to question it. Poor Connor, he was barely awake when he left for the fields. Gavin has always slept so well. I'm afraid we're not used to this."

Aileen nodded sympathetically. "Go lay in the den for a bit, Farrah. We'll watch him while you sleep."

Farrah yawned. "Have I told you both how much I love you?" She walked toward the den in a sleepy daze.

Gavin lifted his head from Veil's shoulder and stared into her eyes. He observed her for quite some time before giving her a large toothy grin. Happy to see he was calmer, Veil tried to place his feet on the floor, but he drew them up, wrapping them securely around her waist.

"What's the matter, little one?" His curious eyes gazed at her again. She could see the way they searched. She could see the wonderment in them, and then she understood. He knew what she was. Cace had said that some humans were open to the Sidhe's existence, that those with willing minds could sense them—especially children. Veil couldn't help but feel relieved that he couldn't tell the others.

"I've never seen him take to someone so fast," Aileen uttered, her voice curious.

"It is strange indeed," Veil whispered.

Gavin fell asleep in Veil's arms shortly after his mother had dozed off on the couch. Aileen quietly took him to her room to rest so that Veil could have a reprieve. She soon returned and gave Veil a thankful smile.

"You've fallen right in with this family, dear, and I'm so glad for it." Veil's cheeks blazed. She tried to distract Aileen's attention away by beginning to wash the few dishes left from breakfast.

"Oh, no, none of that," Aileen said, taking the soapy plate away from Veil. "It's time for you to head to the barn. Kellan will meet you there soon."

Veil scrambled for an excuse. "Are you sure today is the best of days for this, Aileen?" she asked. "There are the crops. *Oh!* And what if Gavin wakes up crying again?"

Aileen started shaking her head before Veil had even finished speaking. "All will be well, dear. You have nothing to be concerned over. Kellan will be on his best behavior, and if he isn't, you just let me know and I'll handle him." Veil was slow to remove her apron, but she couldn't put off the inevitable any longer.

There was no one at the barn when Veil arrived. No one except the horses. They whinnied when she came closer, apparently excited to have a visitor. She approached Nora first, and the mare met her hand with enthusiasm. Veil stroked the beautiful creature from nose to ear. Soon Murphy began kicking the walls of his stall.

"What is it, Murphy? You want to be the center of attention, do you?" Veil gave Nora one last pat before heading toward the magnificent black stallion.

"Didn't my da tell you not to mess around with Murphy?" Startled, Veil dropped her hand and turned toward the person chastising her. *Kellan.*

"I'm sorry, he-he wanted me to," she stuttered.

"What nonsense are you on about? Murphy doesn't like to be touched, especially by strangers. I can barely keep him under control, and I've been working with him for years. Now, come on, let's get this over with." Kellan spoke to Veil as though she was an idiot. She was sure he could see the hurt in her eyes, but he didn't stop himself. "We'll need to take the horses. I'm not walking the entire farm to play tour guide with you. Here, you should be able to handle Nora."

When Veil didn't answer, he turned her way. "Why are you looking at me like that?"

"I don't know how to ride," she muttered, embarrassed.

"What?" Kellan snapped. He walked past her toward the saddles. "Speak up, will you?"

She kept her eyes on the ground as she tangled her fingers together, fidgeting. "I don't know how."

Kellan shook his head and yanked one of the saddles from the wall. "I don't know how you expect me to hear you when you're mumbling to the bloody floor."

Veil's anger erupted. The feeling was unfamiliar to her; she had always been taught to be passive and to follow instructions, but the way Kellan spoke to her pushed her to the edge. "I said, I don't know how!" Kellan paused, the saddle in his hand; her outburst seemed to have shocked him. She was immediately flooded with guilt. "Kellan, I know that you hate me, and you have every right to."

He stared at her for what felt like hours before he shook his head and looked away. "I don't hate you. I just don't understand what happened that night I found you. Then, my family takes you right in like you've been part of us forever. I feel like I'm losing my bleeding mind. I need to understand what's going on, Veil."

She had no idea why it bothered her so much, but she couldn't stand to see him so upset. She started to pace, questions swarming her mind. Could she trust him? Was he capable of understanding?

All it took was one more glance into his anguished eyes for her to ask, "Can we go somewhere else, a place we're less likely to be overheard?"

Kellan's eyes widened. He nodded, placing the saddle on Murphy. "I know just the place. Now, let me give you a short lesson in horse riding."

Veil had taken to riding fairly well, in her own opinion. She was, at least, able to keep up with Kellan as he showed her more of the breathtaking land the McGraths called home. The fields were much larger than Veil had thought, and the newly tilled dirt showed promise of what she imagined would be a healthy crop. Niall and Connor waved from the far end of the field. They were near an enormous machine she had been told was a tractor. *Such strange names these humans give to everything.* She smiled, returning their greeting as Kellan led her farther out. He guided her down a small hill to a stream. Once she figured out that the stream was too shallow for merrows, she was entranced by the gurgling sound the water made as it ran over the rocks. *It really is the perfect place.*

Kellan was the first to dismount, and he told her that Murphy and Nora would be fine wandering on their own. He released Murphy's reins and walked to the edge of the stream, choosing to sit in a large patch of shamrocks. Veil reluctantly let go of Nora's reins and pet her one more time in thanks. Horse riding had been exactly as she had imagined it would be—exhilarating.

"Not bad for your first time," Kellan said.

Veil was quick to turn away from his praise, hiding her face. "Thank you," she whispered. "I've always wanted to learn."

"Then why haven't you? It's clear how much you like it."

"I wasn't allowed," she explained. "My father is protective of me. There are many things he did not wish me to learn or do."

Kellan snorted. "Well, if your da is so protective, why were you on the road in the middle of the night? During a storm, no less."

"It's a complicated story."

"Uncomplicate it, then."

The eggs Veil had for breakfast sat heavy in her stomach. She rubbed small circles over her belly, trying to control her nausea.

"Hey now," Kellan said, his voice becoming more soothing, "just calm down, all right? It can't be that bad."

It was Veil's turn to snort. "It can be that bad. I don't want you or your family in danger. The less you are involved, the better." She turned to face the stream. "You probably wouldn't believe me, anyway."

"Try me."

Veil stared back, hoping in vain he would relent, but—*of course*—he didn't. She closed her eyes and let what she felt was enough be said. "I fell down a hill and landed in front of your truck that night. I was running and I tripped."

"Running? What were you running from?"

"Visitors came to my home... I'm promised to one of them."

"Promised?" he repeated, slowly. "Like in an arranged marriage?"

"My family calls it bonding, and it's forever. The man I'm meant for... My father feared for my safety."

Kellan's mouth hung open as Veil explained. He shook his head, trying to take it all in. "I didn't know arranged marriages even happened around here anymore. It's 1999 for Lord's sake."

Veil shrugged her shoulders indifferently. "It's a fairly common practice among my kind."

"Your kind? What are you talking about?"

"Kellan... I'm different," Veil murmured. She didn't know what else she could say that wouldn't reveal what she truly was. "I'm just different."

Kellan rolled his eyes dramatically. "Oh, I'm well aware of that. You aren't going to tell me, are you?"

Veil hung her head, letting her hair fall around her like a shield. She preferred to concentrate on the tiny ripples in the water than to answer. She heard his loud "humph" before he started to pull at the poor shamrocks.

"I'll take that as a no. Well, will you at least tell me who was with you that night? What did that woman do to me? I know it sounds daft, but I can feel her in my head."

The stress in his voice persuaded Veil to look up at him. "No, you have every right to feel that way. That was Dara and my cousin, Cace. Dara is the one who did that to you. You won't be able to disobey. I'm sorry."

Kellan scowled at her. "Did what? And what do you mean, disobey? I don't have to obey anyone."

His tantrum began to grate on Veil's nerves. "Yes, you do," she said firmly. "She put it in your mind that you have to keep me safe, and you won't be able to fight it."

"So you want me to believe some lady roaming around in the rain with you and some other loon—who pulled a sword on me, by the way—hypnotized me or something?" He didn't wait for an answer. "You're barking mad, girl." The idea of something beyond this world was too outrageous for Kellan's kind. Faith was a lot to ask; humans needed proof. They needed to see and touch.

"If that is how you feel, I guess you won't have any problem with me leaving the farm?"

With his arms stubbornly crossed, Kellan turned his head away. "Absolutely not. Go on, then."

"Fine," she mocked. "I'll just be off. Goodbye, Kellan." Veil rose up from the ground, but she hadn't even taken one full step before Kellan jerked her back. She fell against his solid chest. His heart pounded against her ear. She glanced up but couldn't get Kellan to meet her eyes.

His body quivered, and his skin beaded with sweat. "How can I make it stop?" he asked.

"You can't. Someone like Dara will have to free you."

Kellan finally met her gaze, she could see the hurt in his eyes. "You aren't like her?"

Veil sadly shook her head. "No, not exactly. I haven't had enough practice."

"Can you take me to someone who can do it?"

"No." Kellan's body tensed. She gently touched his arm. "It's too dangerous."

Kellan released a heavy breath. After a moment, he gently removed her hand from his arm and scooted her off of his lap. "All right," he agreed, his voice breaking. "So what do we do now? We can't stay like this forever."

"I know. Dara said I only need to survive until winter, and then all will be all right. Will you please help me?"

"I must be out of my bleeding mind," he grumbled. "All right. For now, we keep things the way they are, and we both try to figure a way out of this by winter, yes?"

Veil knew Kellan didn't fully understand, let alone believe, but at least he hadn't dismissed her entirely. "Agreed."

Kellan pushed himself up and headed in the direction of Nora and Murphy, who were grazing contently along the stream, swishing their tails to keep the bugs off. Before he reached them, he stopped and turned back to Veil. "I won't pretend to know exactly who or what you are. Honestly, I'm not sure I want to know. But I do need to know this, Veil: are you a danger to my family?"

"I'll never hurt them or you, Kellan. I promise."

"You know, not everyone keeps their promises."

"I do," she swore. "A promise is not taken lightly among my people."

Kellan searched her face. When he seemed satisfied, he said, "All right. Let's head on back. It should be about lunchtime, and I'm sure Mum will want to know I wasn't a *complete* arse to you." For the first time since they'd met, he gave her a real smile. Veil felt her knees wobble and heard Dara's voice in her head.

"*Get a hold of yourself, girl.*"

18. chapter

Kellan and Veil made it back to the house only to find it abandoned. A pot simmering on the stove was seconds from spilling over, and a large lump of dough still sat on a sprinkling of flour, untouched. Kellan rushed to move the pot and let out a curse after touching the hot metal handle. With his fingers in his mouth, he called for his family. No one answered. His pained look morphed into one of worry, and he darted out the door at a full sprint, heading in the direction of the blue house on the next hill—his brother's home. Veil hesitated for only a moment before taking off after him as fast as she could run.

Kellan didn't bother knocking, all but breaking down the lovely yellow door. Veil slowed her pace and carefully crossed the threshold. As soon as she was inside, she heard the commotion. They were all there. Rory and Niall sat at a round, white table, their heads cradled in hands still dirty from their farm work. Connor and Liam consoled Farrah and Aileen as the two women openly sobbed. In the middle was Kellan, eyes closed and fingers desperately pulling at his hair.

Connor, still hugging a distraught Farrah, explained. Apparently, Gavin had woken up gasping for air. In her exhausted state, Farrah had forgotten his medicine at home. By the time they gave him his inhaler, the skin around his lips had turned blue.

"It's all my fault," Farrah wailed. "He could have died, and it would have been all my fault."

Connor grabbed her firmly by the shoulders and gave her a little shake. "Stop that, right now. You made an honest mistake, Farrah, and he's all right. We'll both try harder."

"We all will," Aileen agreed.

Veil stood silently as they spoke, but it wasn't long before she was noticed. It was Farrah who pulled her in for a crushing hug. Veil awkwardly wrapped her arms around the weeping mother and patted her back.

"He's sick, Veil, just like you said. He's so sick, and I don't know what to do."

"What's wrong with him?" Veil asked.

"The doctors in Dublin didn't know," Farrah whimpered. "We were there for weeks. They say his lungs are failing him, but they don't know why or how to stop it. I don't know what we're going to do."

Veil looked around the room; everyone wore the same hopeless expressions. She wished Dara was there, for she would know exactly what to do. But she wasn't. It was all left to Veil. *I have to do something*.

A full moon hung high in the sky, glowing eerily through the clouds. Veil's bare feet were already caked with mud. She needed to hurry back to the house before anyone noticed she was gone, but the darkness hampered her hunt. *The little one is depending on me.*

She had never been more grateful for Dara's lessons. If she could find the necessary plants, then maybe—*just maybe*—she could help Gavin. The problem was, she didn't know the land, and that made her quest much more difficult. So far, she had only been able to find the dandelions. She still needed sage, mullein, yarrow, and corn silk. She searched for what felt like an eternity, but she had no luck locating them. She finally gave into exhaustion and morosely began the long trek back toward the house.

The house was still dark when she arrived. She cringed as the old door creaked open. Making sure to be extra quiet, she slipped in and tiptoed to the staircase. She made it without detection all the way to what the family now referred to as *her* room. She shoved the dandelion-filled basket under her bed before collapsing on top of the covers, filthy feet and all.

Veil rested her head on her arm at the kitchen table. She could barely keep her eyes pried open. She had taken to staying out much later than she was accustomed to, until the first light of the dawn sky crept through the door with her. She had only just reached her room when she heard the others' footsteps on the stairs. The lack of sleep had caught up with her.

She had also taken to searching during daylight hours, but she found it more difficult to sneak away, especially with Maddy out of school and wanting to bond with her new 'sister.' Veil enjoyed Maddy's company, but she was on a mission that her new friend wouldn't fully understand. Fortunately for Veil, she had discovered that she could distract Maddy with Rory. Veil was almost certain Maddy was sweet on him. It was always an easy escape for Veil when he came around.

Gavin's growing fascination with her also made Veil's daily outings challenging. He would cling to her when they were together, refusing to let her go. Luckily, Farrah didn't seem to think twice about allowing her to take him along on her walks. It was risky, bringing Gavin along, but it was necessary. He was becoming weaker every day.

She secretly dried the plants in her hidden place under the bed, but she still needed the mullein, yarrow, and corn silk before she could complete the remedy.

"Veil, are you feeling well, dear?"

Veil jerked her head up at the sound of Aileen's voice and knocked over her large glass of juice. The orange juice splashed all over the table and onto Niall and Kellan's plates, ruining their breakfast. In her haste to get a dish towel from the sink, Veil almost tipped over her chair too.

"Bloody hell!" she yelled. "I'm so sorry!"

"Veil, are you all right?" Liam asked, his eyes widening. "I don't think any of us have ever heard a naughty word come from your mouth, lass."

Veil looked from Liam to all the other concerned faces. She sat back in her seat and apologized once more.

"Oh, it's all right, dear," Aileen said, reaching over to pat Veil's arm. "I knew this trouble making lot would probably rub off on you sooner rather than later. But maybe you should go back to bed?" Veil declined Aileen's sweet offer with a shake of her head; she couldn't afford the time to rest. "Well, no house chores for you today, then. You need to take it easy, dear."

"You know...I've been feeling *exhausted*," said Rory. "Maybe I should keep our little Veil here company."

Niall and Kellan snorted into their juice, and Aileen was quick to retort as always. "Rory, my dear, dear boy. A large, strapping man like you doesn't need a day off, so suck it up. And manners, the two of you." She pointed her finger at Niall and Kellan.

"Yes, Mum," they said in unison.

"Why doesn't Veil come to keep me company in the barn?" Niall asked. "The horses have sure taken to her; even Murphy seems to have a soft spot for her."

Veil was surprised by Niall's invitation. She had not yet had the opportunity to get to know him well; they had all been too busy with the fields. She would have loved to spend time with him, but she needed to continue foraging. "Oh, that's all right," she insisted. "I know how busy everyone is, and I don't want to be a burden."

"Nonsense, I'd love the company. Unless you have something else you're going to be doing?" Veil could see the accusation in his fake smile, but all she could do was shake her head. "Well, it's all set," Niall replied smugly. "Nora likes a bright red apple first thing in the morning. Not patient at all, that one, so we'd best be going."

Veil rose shakily from her chair to follow him. As she slid her chair back into place under the table, she felt a soft touch to her forearm. Kellan looked at her with questions written all across his face. The best she could offer him was a subtle shrug before she reached the kitchen door and stepped out into an uncertain day.

Niall hummed a tune as he and Veil walked to the barn but didn't speak a word. Neither did Veil. It wasn't until they had fed the horses and begun to clean the muck out of the stalls that he offered up any conversation. "So, how are you taking to the place?"

"I enjoy it here," she answered. "It's been a blessing."

"Good people, the McGraths. Kind-hearted and trusting. It would be a shame if someone was to take advantage of that, you know? Would hurt them, greatly."

Veil paused, shovel still in hand, and pressed her eyes closed for a moment. "I'm not here to hurt them."

Niall also stopped shoveling. He folded his hands and rested them on the handle, casually propping his chin on top. He appeared relaxed, but something was off about his behavior. After quietly looking her over he finally spoke. "Then why are you here?" Veil began to fumble for an excuse—*any excuse*—but Niall wouldn't allow it. "Did you know that I help out with other things around here too?" he asked, his eyes never leaving hers. "Just little things, like doing the laundry from time to time. Getting everything on the line can be quite a chore for Aileen, especially the linens." Niall calmly walked over and removed the shovel from Veil's shaking hands. "I know you've been sneaking out, Veil. Where have you been going?"

"I'm exploring," she answered, but her dishonesty was clear even to her own ears. "Just trying to get a feel for the farm."

"Exploring at night, of all things. Strange, that. You know what else is strange?" Veil, in the midst of panic, shook her head hastily. "Pretty. Little. Dandelion. Flowers." He pronounced each word slowly and tilted his head to the side, looking her over.

Veil said nothing.

"Why would you be out collecting a common weed in the

middle of the night and barefoot to boot?" Niall squinted at her, demanding an answer. Veil knew when his mouth dropped open that he had finally found it. "You're one of them, aren't you? You're a sae."

Veil began to fidget as her heart began to race. "I have no idea what you're talking about, Niall."

"That's it, isn't it?" he whispered. "It all makes sense now— you arrive out of nowhere, working Kellan up so bad he can't properly function, but he can't explain why that is... And your *eyes*. I don't know why I didn't see it before. My grandmum use to tell me stories about you before she died." Niall's eyes grew wide and his face paled. He began backing out of the small stall. He squeezed his eyes shut.

"Niall, please!" Veil pleaded. "I need you to calm down. I will not hurt you."

"No!" he shouted. "I know what you can do. Grandmum told me."

"Niall, I'm not like them. Please, listen."

Niall scoffed. "Why should I? You could take and kill us all!"

Veil grabbed Niall's arm. "No! I'm trying to help. I'm trying to save Gavin—"

Niall opened his eyes at the mention of the little boy. He flung Veil's hand off him and shouted, "You leave that boy alone, you hear? You can't have him!"

Veil backed away from his hateful screaming, her hands coming up in a placating manner. "I'm not going to hurt him, Niall. I'm trying to help him get better. That's why I've been sneaking out every night. I'm trying to find the plants I need."

Niall stopped yelling long enough to search her face for lies. "Can you make him better?" he finally asked.

"I'm not an experienced healer. I can only try." Veil let herself relax when Niall's eyes lost some of their animosity. But his fear was still there.

"You won't take off with him?"

"I only want to help, if I can," she said. "This family means so much to me, and so do you."

Niall walked over to the nearest wall and let his body sag against it. "I can't believe you're one of them. Grandmum always said the sae were a lot like us. 'Some good, some bad,' she said. I thought she was just telling old tales."

Veil kept her distance, giving Niall the time he needed to come to grips with all she had told him. "We're called Sidhe, and there are some bad ones. They aren't the only creatures to be wary of, though."

"Are you one we should be wary of?" he asked, his voice quaking once again.

Veil shook her head. "I've never taken anyone." Niall didn't look like he believed her.

"What of Kellan, then?"

"Dara made him bring me here to keep me safe. She's the one who clouded him—I would never do that... I'm not even sure that I can."

Niall frowned. "Not following you there."

"We have to build up our gifts through practice," she explained, "and I haven't exactly been allowed much of that. My mother was human, so there's a possibility I'll never be able to."

"Human? How is all this possible?" Niall pulled a rag from his pocket and wiped his face.

"Listen, Niall, I understand this is a lot to hear, but you must keep it a secret. Most humans have forgotten us, but my kind has been around a long time. I don't want anyone harmed because of me."

"Who in their right blooming mind would even believe me?"

"Please, Niall? I'll only be here until the winter."

"Why winter?"

"There are people after me. They're dangerous, and I need to stay hidden just a little while longer. I will go back when it's safe."

"Just until winter?" Niall confirmed. "And you'll help Gavin?"

Veil approached Niall until she was mere inches from him. "Yes, I will."

Niall pressed his fingers to his temples. He finally drew in a deep breath and released it slowly. "Okay. I won't say a thing, but if I think for one minute that any of us are in danger, all deals are off. Understand me?" Veil nodded, thankful that he had even considered keeping her secret. "All right," Niall said. "How can I help the boy?"

19. chapter

Niall started joining Veil on her nightly outings. They eventually found the yarrow with its tiny white flowers. She would need both the petals and the leaves to make the remedy. She was careful, plucking the flowers and placing them into the basket the way Dara had taught her. Yarrow was a blessed plant, so she closed her eyes and said a silent prayer of thanks.

"We do that with yarrow too," Niall said. "Legend says it wards off evil, ironically."

Veil rolled her eyes at his barb. "How many times do I have to tell you? I'm not evil."

"Oh, I know that now," he answered, laughing. "I just find it funny that your kind would use such a plant."

"We aren't all evil, but in my experience, there aren't many who are kind either. Dara used to say that all creatures have the ability to be both cruel and kind, but they choose one far more often than the other." Veil stood up, wiping the dirt from her hands. "And I'm not aware of a plant that wards off all evil, unfortunately."

"I'm sure glad you lean toward kind." Niall bent over to pick up the basket. He handed it to her with a smile. "It's been a pleasure getting to know you." Veil returned Niall's smile with a soft one of her own. They had gotten to know each other well over the last couple of weeks, and she was thankful for his friendship.

"So, how did you come to live with the McGraths?"

Niall's jovial face turned sad, but only for a moment. "I've been best mates with Kellan, Connor, and Rory since before we all could wipe our own bottoms," he said, "and Aileen and Liam have always treated me as one of their own…" He looked down and shook his head. "Let's just say I know a thing or two about having a family that doesn't accept you." Veil said nothing. Instead, she reached out and grabbed his hand. The tension melted from his shoulders. His eyes met hers and a smile stretched across his face.

"I know the feeling all too well," Veil replied. "Most of my family shunned me. I wasn't like them, so they kept me hidden away." Opening herself up without the dread of revealing too much was like a healing balm to Veil's spirit. She put her hand on Niall's chest, over his heart. "Dara always used to say that a person's worth does not come from the approval of others, but from within themselves."

Niall covered Veil's hand with his own. "Thank you," he whispered. He cleared his throat. "You know, your Dara sounds a lot like my grandmum. She took care of me after I left my parents. I was only sixteen when she passed, but the McGraths took me in, no questions asked. I tried to move out when I turned eighteen, but Aileen was having none of it." He chuckled as he described a disheveled

Aileen throwing one of her motherly fits. "So here I am, twenty-one and living in the apartment she demanded be built for me—that way I'm not too far from home. Plus, it's attached to the barn so I can wear my pajamas during calving season." Niall winked at Veil and together they shared a laugh.

"Thank you, Niall," Veil said. "For trusting me... For giving me a chance."

"Don't get all mushy on me now," he teased. "We should head back, it's almost five."

"Yes, you're right," Veil agreed. "This is just taking so long— too long. I still need the mullein and corn silk to complete the tea. I've got the sage ready to be burned, but the tea is what he really needs."

Niall offered Veil his hand again as he started back in the barn's direction. "You'll have all the fresh corn silk you need come harvest time," he said, "but I think we'll have to leave the farm to gather the other one."

The thought of leaving the safety of the farm terrified Veil. "What if I'm seen by another Sidhe? My cousin said our kind walk freely around."

"Think what will happen to the boy if you don't."

Veil's breathing picked up, the dreadful possibilities entering her mind. "I know," she mumbled.

"Sometimes, you just have to take the risks," he said, gently squeezing her hand. "You know I will stay by your side."

Veil squeezed back, his assurance bringing her some relief. "Thank you. When do we leave?"

"How about today? I'll offer to pick up the supplies Aileen needs for the upcoming farmers market, and you can say you wish to see more of our quaint little community—finally."

Veil laughed. Niall had called her a hermit more than once

since they had tethered their friendship. "All right, but first we have to get back. Breakfast can't come soon enough—I'm famished."

"You've been spending way too much time with Rory, you poor soul." Niall snorted.

"Necessary evil, I'm afraid." Veil giggled. "It's the only way for me to shake off Maddy."

The two friends continued to laugh until the barn came into sight. The loft had become one of Veil's favorite places and now also served for drying the plants. She could see so much of the charming farmland from the large loft doors, and the smell of hay reminded her of the stables from back home.

They carried on with their banter, Niall entering the barn first, when suddenly he stopped and threw his arm out in front of Veil. "Oh, it's only you, Kell," he said, his hand coming to his chest. "You just about gave me a heart attack."

Kellan's clenched jaw stood out in the lamplight. "Nice night, isn't it? Decided to take a little stroll, did you?" Niall and Veil both flinched at Kellan's tone.

Niall raised his hands. "Kell, what are you on about, mate?"

"Oh, just pointing out how chummy the two of you have gotten over the last few weeks," Kellan answered. "I bet if you knew the truth, you wouldn't be skipping through the woods at night with her. *And you*—" He turned to glare at Veil. "If you think I'm going to let you do to him what you did to me..." His hateful remarks hit Veil square in the chest, and she rubbed at the pain.

Niall placed himself in front of Kellan, shoving him back and blocking his view of Veil. "That's quite enough, Kell. It's not like that and you know it. She's done nothing wrong. She's trying to help, you dumb lug."

"Help with what, Niall? She's been nothing but a nuisance

since she arrived. Like I said, you wouldn't be defending her if you knew—"

"I know plenty," Niall cut in, taking another step toward Kellan. "I also know that you're being a right arse."

Kellan looked over Niall's shoulder until his eyes found Veil's once again. "You told him? What happened to all the hush-hush talk, hmm? It doesn't apply to him, or am I the only one you refuse to tell?"

Veil could feel the pain in his voice. She realized he was more hurt over the possibility of her confiding in Niall than he was angry. "Kellan, he figured it out. And I only wanted to keep you safe."

"I don't need you to take care of me," he snapped back. "I can take care of myself perfectly fine. Now, what the bloody hell is going on?"

"You're way out of line," Niall said. "I did figure some of it out, unbelievable as it is, but it's no wonder she keeps it to herself. She'll be the one to tell her secrets, if and when she wants to. She is trying to help our family, mate; she's trying to cure Gavin. She needed some help finding her way around, so that's where I came in."

"Cure Gavin?" Kellan gasped. "You can do that?" Kellan's mood changed so abruptly it was difficult for Veil to keep up.

"Maybe," she replied timidly. "I've only been taught a little healing, but I think I can make what he needs."

"How? What do you need?" Kellan's eyes followed as Veil gestured to the basket she held in her hands.

"I still need mullein and corn silk to complete the tea."

Niall stepped back and stood beside Veil. "I'm taking her out today to look for the mullein. The fresh corn silk though…"

"Corn silk," Kellan repeated. "But there's a market just there in Kenmare."

Veil bit her bottom lip. "No, Dara said it has to be the freshest we can get—straight from the soil."

"But the harvest won't be ready until October, September at the earliest." Kellan's shoulders slumped.

Niall walked over to him, laying his hand on Kellan's shoulder. "We know. We'll figure this out, mate."

Kellan dropped his head as Niall squeezed his shoulder and whispered in his ear. He listened to what Niall had to say before he looked up, staring at Veil. "I'm sorry," he said. "I feel like I'm losing my bleeding mind. Thank you for trying to help... And it's really none of my business if you prefer talking to Niall over me."

Niall burst out laughing until tears streamed down his face. "Really, Kell? Is that what you're worried over? You know me; she's definitely not my type." He glanced at Veil, smiling widely. "No offense, Veil."

"Worries, what? I-I don't have any," Kellan stammered. "I'm not concerned a bit!"

Niall, still laughing, wiped away his tears. "Sure, mate. Whatever you say."

Kellan huffed and swatted Niall's hand away before stomping off toward the door. It was obvious that he desperately wanted to flee the conversation. Before leaving, he turned to say, "I'll take her today... if she wants?"

"I would like that, Kellan," she answered, surprising herself.

"Yeah, well, I only want to help my nephew, so..." Kellan's flustered words faded as he stepped through the barn door.

Niall chuckled until Kellan was out of sight. "Whew! That boy has it bad."

"Has what?"

Niall didn't answer, but his cackling made it clear that she had missed something.

20. chapter

Veil stared out the passenger window as Kellan's truck rumbled past familiar hills. The memory of the night they had met still haunted her, threatening to spill tears down her cheeks. Veil wiped her eyes. Dara would be disappointed by her inability to keep her emotions in check. But the more time she spent with the McGraths, the safer she felt letting everything out.

"What's wrong?" Kellan asked.

Veil pulled her eyes from the window and focused on her hands, which lay crossed on her lap. "Are we close?"

"It's just a little ways more. Kenmare is just up the road—"

"No," Veil interrupted. "Close to where you found me?"

"Oh...*no*. That was near Killarney, in the other direction."

Veil remembered when Aileen had questioned her about

Killarney, a conversation that felt like so long ago. "What is Killarney?"

"Killarney is a bigger town just north of us," he explained. "It's only about half an hour's drive."

Veil turned to Kellan. "Why were you there that night?"

"Pretty nosy today, aren't you?" Embarrassed, Veil turned back to the window and mumbled a small apology. Seconds later he released a loud sigh. "I went to meet up with my roommate, Shane, from uni. He did me a favor, meeting me in Killarney so I could get the rest of my things without having to drive all the way to Cork."

"Uni?"

"Yes, uni. You know, university? Well, I guess you wouldn't know, now would you? It's a place to study."

Whether Kellan meant to or not, the way he spoke to Veil made her feel small. His jabbing remarks only highlighted how little of this world she knew. Still, she asked, "Like the school Maddy goes to?"

"Kind of. It's way bigger. And the town it's in, Cork, has so much more to do compared to here." There was bitterness in Kellan's tone.

"You want to be there?"

"It doesn't matter what I want. My family needed me when Gavin started getting sick, and like a proper son, I came back."

"If we can make him better, will you leave again?"

Kellan cut his eyes from the road over to Veil. "Not like I can go anywhere with this bleeding curse on me." His wounding remarks sent a nagging pain to her chest. Out of the corner of her eye she saw him rubbing at his own chest. "*If she feels pain, so should you.*" That's what Dara had said.

"Hey, listen," he said. "I didn't mean to unload on you like that. I know you're new to all this and have issues of your own, and I shouldn't be a git about it. I'm sorry." He looked over at Veil long enough for her to give him an encouraging smile. "To answer your question, I'll probably go back. I only have a year left. Mum and Da want me to stay—they never wanted me to leave in the first place, actually. All I've ever done is farm, and I just... They just don't get it. I love the farm, but I want to make my own decisions about what to do with the rest of my life."

Veil reached over and placed her hand just above his knee. "That I do understand," she replied.

Kellan's cheeks reddened, and he glanced down at her hand. "Okay, then," he said, sucking in a breath. "What does this plant we're searching for look like?"

Veil brought her hand back to her lap, clasping it tightly with her other one. She couldn't blame him for his reaction. She had been nothing but a burden since he had found her. "Oh, umm, mullein is a strange plant with yellow cup-like flowers," she finally answered. "Dara sometimes called them a 'velvet plant' because the leaves have a fuzzy feel to them."

"I think I know what you're talking about. I've seen those along the road before. I thought they were only weeds."

"Dara always went to collect them," Veil said, smiling. "She said they were farther out than I had any business going. She taught me how to prepare them, though."

Kellan was silent for quite some time. Veil thought he was concentrating on looking for the mullein and was surprised when he asked, "Veil, what was life like for you? You know, before I almost killed you with this motorized rust bucket."

Veil let out a facetious little chuckle. "Nothing like a day with you and your family. There were few I could trust, and the rest didn't at all care for my existence. I was kept hidden like a horrible secret for a good portion of my life. Father and Dara said it was for my protection.

I appreciate them for keeping me guarded for as long as they did."

"Safe?" Kellan asked, his face tightening. "It sounds like you were kept prisoner."

"In a way, I guess," Veil replied, thinking it over. "But safety behind locked doors was preferable to facing those allowed to freely roam. Remember, we are from different worlds, Kellan."

Kellan released a heavy sigh. "Always holding back... Will you ever trust me enough to tell me?"

"It's not about trust. You've kept me protected; now it's my turn to keep you and your family safe. If you aren't a liability, no one should bother with any of you when I return home."

Kellan gripped the steering wheel and clenched his jaw. "You can't actually want to return? That's no way for anyone to live."

"Come winter, I'll have no other choice. Lives depend on it."

Kellan nodded slowly. "Different worlds or not, we all know about sacrifice, don't we?"

"That we do," Veil agreed. "But I have seen joy, as well. You're incredibly lucky to have the loving family you do."

Kellan briefly closed his eyes before he attempted to speak again. "Veil—"

Something bright yellow caught Veil's attention. Her face lit up and she pointed excitedly, interrupting whatever Kellan was about to say. There, just off the side of the roadway, was the mullein.

"Look!" she yelled. "We found it, Kellan!"

Kellan laughed as she bounced off the seat, and just like that, their heavy conversation was forgotten.

The basket sat full between Kellan and Veil as they carried on with their journey. It hadn't been hard for them to get out of the house; Aileen had been positively giddy when Kellan offered to go into town for supplies and bring Veil along.

"Oh, thank you, dear," Aileen said, smiling. "We're expecting a huge turnout at the market, so I really need the flour we ordered. Please don't forget the vanilla. And thank you for taking Veil. It's about time she got to see what our small slice of the country has to offer." She turned to look at Veil. "It's positively gorgeous, dear. You're going to love it."

After stopping to collect the mullein, they were quick to get back on the road. Eventually, the rolling hills were replaced by brightly painted buildings that all appeared to be connected to each other. Kellan announced that they'd reached Kenmare, and Veil marveled at the beautiful town. Some buildings were tall and lean while others were short and wide. She smiled at the brilliant blues and the rich yellows. Cars and trucks were parked on the side of the narrow road, and scrambling along the sidewalk—*so many people.*

Veil smushed her face flat against her window, trying to see it all. She glanced at him over her shoulder and yelled, "It's incredible!"

"Aye," Kellan said, shrugging. "I guess it's okay for a small town. Doesn't get as many tourists as Killarney, so there's not as much to do or anything."

"Tourists?"

"Yeah, tourists. They're the people who aren't from here and come to visit… See the sites and such."

She wondered about his answer before asking, "So, I'm a tourist?"

He laughed heartily at her, a sound Veil decided that she liked.

"Veil, you are a great many things, but a tourist is not one of them." He wheezed.

Veil didn't understand what he meant, but she was too focused on all the lively people rushing in and out of the many buildings to question him further.

"What are all these places?"

"Mainly just some places to eat and a few hotels. Farrah and Rory's mum, Shannon, owns one of the bed and breakfasts just up the way. There are a couple of bakeries... Oh, and of course, a pub or two."

"There's so many!"

"Not as many places to see as Killarney or Dublin...or Cork, but it's all right."

Veil shook her head. "Not the places. Humans... *So many humans.*" She ignored Kellan's strange look, searching past him to watch the people milling about the sidewalks in front of the stores.

"Come on, Veil, let's find a place to park and try to take on Mum's list." Kellan pulled into an open spot. He opened her door and offered his hand as she stepped out. "This is it."

He gently placed one of his hands on the small of her back. The crowd was thick, overwhelmingly so. Some walked fast and carried bags filled with things Veil could only imagine. Others held hands and strolled along without a care. But the families amused her the most. She saw mothers and fathers struggling with their broods, little ones who pulled their parents along. She watched the humans with curious eyes, and she noticed Kellan watching her in much the same way.

A tiny store, the color of ash and trimmed with white, stole Veil's attention. It had enormous windows. Veil came to a sudden stop and dashed over to watch the sun catching on the stones that were so brilliantly laid out on display. Entranced, Veil gazed at all the shining pieces.

Kellan reached her side and chuckled. "A girl who likes jewelry, imagine that. Maybe you're not so different after all." He jabbed her side with his elbow. "Well, what's your fancy? Are you a diamond and gold gal...or maybe emeralds and rubies?"

"What are those?" Veil asked.

"What are what?" She pointed back to the display which held stones far different than the rest, their colors hazy and their edges jagged. "Oh, those? They aren't ready yet—they're raw. They're there for people to pick out which one they like, and the jeweler will cut it for them. It'll look like those when it's finished." He motioned toward the shimmering glass-like stones on the opposite side.

Veil frowned. "Why would they want to change something that is already so beautiful?"

Kellan gave her another odd look. "Umm, because most people like them that way, I guess. What, you prefer them straight out of the ground?"

"I think they're beautiful as they are. They may not be perfect, but they are real." Veil bit her lip. "Is that wrong?" Kellan stared back at Veil with a strange, soft look. She felt the slightest touch of his fingers skimming against her own. The familiar tingling began to crawl up her arm.

"No, it's not wrong," he murmured.

"Special occasion, Kellan?" A gorgeous woman with hair the color of beech bark stood a couple feet away. She was flanked by two more that were just as pretty. When Kellan saw her, he jerked his hand away from Veil's, rubbing the back of his neck with it instead.

"Bridget," he said. "Hi." His greeting was low and sounded lukewarm at best.

Bridget stood with one hand perched high on her hip. She raised one perfectly shaped eyebrow and looked Veil up and down.

"Hope we aren't interrupting anything. Who is this?"

"Veil's, uh... She's just a family friend," Kellan floundered. "What are you doing back here?" If Kellan's rude tone bothered Bridget, she didn't let on. She flicked her long hair over her shoulder dramatically.

"It's summer, Kellan. We're all on break, you know? Well, you would if you hadn't left. You really should come back. We had a lot of fun, didn't we?" Bridget reminded Veil so much of Nessa, especially when she attempted to glide her hands up Kellan's chest. Veil was surprised when Kellan pushed them away and took a giant step back.

Bridget's mouth hung open after Kellan's rejection, and it didn't take long for her to turn her wrath on Veil. "So this is what you're into these days, huh? Nice clothes, sweetie. I haven't seen anything that homely since I visited my gran." She laughed while pinching the old lace trim at the end of Veil's long blue sleeve and smirked as Veil gently pulled her arm away and wrapped it around her middle, trying to disappear.

Bridget's gloating was short-lived. Kellan pushed his way between them, blocking Veil from the other girl's hateful eyes. "Classy, Bridget. There's no need for that. Don't you have better things to be getting to? Take your crew and move along."

Bridget let out a loud "*humph*" before saying, "Yeah, you're right, I do have better things to do. Have fun with whatever that is behind you. It's about right you'd find a plain girl to match that simple life you're stuck with." Still hidden behind Kellan, Veil peered around to watch Bridget and the two other women leave, stomping their way down the concrete sidewalk, their screeching voices annoying the crowd.

"Sorry about her," Kellan said, turning to face Veil. "She's never been very nice, I'm afraid. Though it did take me a while to realize just how horrible she truly is.”

“I don’t think she cares for me much,” Veil replied, her eyes still following Bridget. “Is she your intended?”

“My intended?” Kellan nearly choked on the words. “As in, am I supposed to be marrying her and all that?” With Veil’s nod, Kellan’s eyes grew even larger. He shook his head and chuckled. “Goodness, Veil, the way you speak. We dated—briefly. Too much drama from that one, and apparently I, alone, wasn’t enough for her. So, no, I definitely have no intentions with Bridget. Thank the heavens for that.” He shoved his hands into his pants pockets. “Look, let’s get this shopping over with. I wanna take you to see something.” He started toward the supermarket without another word and Veil followed, her smile growing.

They stood at the edge of the largest body of water Veil had ever seen. It appeared to go on forever. Reflections of the sturdy mountains, vivid green hills, and fluffy white clouds danced across the surface. The beach was mainly rock, but her bare toes wiggled in what cool sand there was. Kellan smiled as she rolled up the ends of her pants to dig her toes in deeper.

“This is Kenmare Bay,” he said, gesturing toward the water. “Aren’t your feet cold?”

Veil waved off his concern with a smile. “I’ve never seen any place like this before. There’s so much water, and the stones along the sand are so smooth.” Veil’s feet were cold, but she loved being able to *feel*. Dara had always called it ‘earthing.’ It allowed the Sidhe to make a better connection with nature. *Well, most Sidhe anyway.*

Laughter and the sounds of play reached Veil's ears. She followed the sound until her eyes landed on a group of children. Some ran along the water's edge while others had stopped to collect rocks.

"Do they not worry about being so close to the water?"

"They're just having a merry time, and it looks like their parents are right there," Kellan reassured. "Nothing to worry over."

Veil followed his line of sight, and sure enough, a group of adults were not too far off. Their faces held tenderness, watching the young ones, and they lounged happily, seemingly without a care in the world. But Veil knew exactly how fast that happiness and peace could be taken away. She turned back to Kellan and asked, "Are you not afraid of what's in there?"

"Like what? The current would probably be the most worrisome, I'd think."

Veil gasped, her overactive imagination running away with her. She clenched her eyes closed against the horrifying images. "There are far worse things within the depths. You won't go in there, right?"

Kellan nodded very slowly. Her anxiety soothed. She was finally able to release the breath she'd been holding. "Someday, I'm going to get you to be a little more elaborate," he mumbled. Veil gave him a crooked grin and shrugged. Kellan chuckled and shook his head. "All right, well, pick up those shoes. It's time to be getting home. Mum will be needing to get a head start on the baking for the market this weekend, and we still need to figure out what to do about the corn silk, yes?"

"Yes, the corn silk," she agreed. "Are you sure there isn't a ready crop somewhere?"

"Naw, not until October, September at the earliest."

Disappointed, Veil knew there was only one thing left to try.

"Kellan, will you take me out to the fields tonight?"

"Why? I told you there won't be any ready for months."

"I know," she said, her apprehensive eyes on the rocks and sand, "but there's something I want to try."

21. chapter

Kellan and Veil arrived home and unloaded the supplies for an extremely happy Aileen. Veil then politely excused herself to the comfort of her room. She laid on the cushy bed, staring up at the ceiling. So much depended on her, and her lacking abilities weighed her down. She remembered the things Dara had been capable of and wished she could do even a portion of that. Dara had said the connection would come when the time was right. Veil closed her eyes and prayed that time was now. She was jostled awake by two large hands.

"Hey, it's time."

Veil tried to focus on Kellan's face, hovering above her own, but the room had turned dark with only the moonlight drifting in from the window. She must have been asleep for hours.

"Sorry, I didn't mean to fall asleep."

"It's okay. You missed supper. Mum and Da were pretty worried, but I told them the trip to town probably wore you out."

Veil picked at the yarn of her blanket. "I didn't mean to make them worry..."

"None of that now. Niall told me how much sleep you've been missing. I'm surprised it took you this long to crash, honestly. He's going to meet us at the barn. Are you ready to do whatever it is you're planning?"

Veil gnawed on her lower lip and thought again of what would need to happen for this to work. She had no idea whether she could do it or not. Still, she had to try. More determined than ever, she got out of bed. "Let's go."

They met up with Niall, the three of them jogging to the fields where neatly planted rows of corn poked through the soil. The night was dark, but by the light of the torch Niall shone across the ground, they could see the tiny sprouts.

"See? They won't be ready for quite some time," Kellan said. "Are you sure it has to be straight from the dirt?"

"Quite sure, yes," Veil answered, slipping off her shoes. "Dara said the healing qualities of nature are always greater when you can still smell the earth on the plants. I have to harvest them directly from the ground or we'll risk a weak batch of tea. Gavin looked awful this morning at breakfast."

"Okay, want to tell me how you plan to get fresh corn silk from those few leaves, then?"

"Just give her a moment, Kell," said Niall. Kellan shut his mouth and stood watching with his customary pout. Veil nodded her appreciation to Niall and made her way out onto the cold, tilled dirt, careful not to step on the new growth. She took her time, trying to remember all Dara had taught her about tapping into the connection.

Veil's eyes turned up toward the moon, examining its half full form. The night sky was filled with twinkling stars. She watched in wonder as one dashed across the sky, and then another, and another. She listened to the chorus of frogs singing in the distance. She closed her eyes and took a deep breath. The smell of rain hung in the air; a storm was not far off. She dropped to her knees to study the corn. The green shoots twisted up from the ground and held only three delicate green leaves each. Kellan and Niall stood behind her. There would be no logical way for her to explain the connection to either of them if this worked. There would be no going back.

"Don't think on it, Veil. Just do it," Niall encouraged.

"Do what?" Kellan asked. "What's happening?"

"Shh, Kellan," Niall answered. "You can do this, Veil. Think of Gavin." Veil turned her focus back to the corn and caressed the smooth surface of the leaves before allowing her fingers to graze the dirt just beneath. She closed her eyes again, and with her next breath she dug her hands into the soil and *reached*.

Nothing. Like all the times before, she felt nothing.

She tried again. She could practically hear Dara's voice telling her to focus *more* and to reach *deeper*. She tried once more, plunging her hands in up to her wrists, all of her muscles tensing. She pulled one hand back and smacked the dirt with her fist. She dropped her head, her exhausted body shaking with racking sobs. She had failed Gavin. She had failed them all.

Veil didn't notice Kellan making his way over to her. He

kneeled beside her and delicately brushed the hair away from her face. Veil could feel him examining her, but she was too ashamed to meet his eyes. He tenderly cradled her face with both of his hands, gently encouraging her head up. His dark blue eyes were too much. She let her tears fall.

"Hey, enough of that," he said, delicately wiping them away with the pads of his thumbs.

"I'm so sorry. I can't do it—I can't…"

"Veil, I don't know a whole lot when it comes to you, but I think from all I've seen and felt, there isn't much you can't do." Veil searched for any signs of deceit in his words and found none. Her life had been filled with the malicious words of those who took delight in tearing her down. Their voices now fought to be heard, their destructive calls mocking her attempt. Where once she would have folded under the weight of their spitefulness, this time she tried pushing back. An unfamiliar sense of self-assurance spread throughout her core.

Veil covered his hand with one of her own and that's when she felt it—*a nudge*. Something moved through her body, small at first but growing, trying to push its way into her mind. *The connection.* Her mouth dropped open and her eyes went wide, staring down at the hand still buried in the soil. As the feeling grew, so did the plant…and the next one, and the next. Kellan gasped, and the two watched as Niall disappeared behind the thick green stalks. The firm shape of the corn expanded within its husks, and Veil removed her hand from the soil.

Kellan's eyes were round as saucers. He shakily removed his hands from her cheeks and placed them heavily on her shoulders, leaning on her to keep himself upright. When his trembling stopped, they both stood up, and she watched him warily, unsure of what was to come. Finally regaining his bearings, Kellan reached out, plucking an ear of corn from its stalk. He peeled away the husk to reveal the gold within.

"What are you?" he asked, his amazement tinged with a hint of fear. Veil clutched at his hand, her eyes pleading for him not to be frightened of her.

"Oh, bloody hell!" Niall yelled, barreling toward them. "Are you seeing this, mate? It's amazing. She's bloody brilliant!"

Kellan and Veil stayed locked onto one another, and time seemed to slow. Until lightning flashed across the sky, and the clouds finally released the rain, drenching them all. And yet, his eyes never left hers.

"Sorry to interrupt, but how do we explain this?" Niall's question broke whatever magic had passed between Veil and Kellan. She dropped his hand, her body shaking with alarm. Kellan stepped forward, grasping both of Veil's shoulders to calm her.

"Hey, deep breaths, okay? It'll be fine, Veil."

"How?" she asked. "What have I done? There's no way around this—"

"You gave Gavin a chance, is what you've done. Please, no regrets, okay? I swear to you that all will be fine."

Veil's nerves were still frayed the next morning as she helped with the morning meal. Maddy had tried to teach her how to flip pancakes. Maddy's carefree laugh carried through the house as Veil's many failed attempts piled up in the trash, and the batter splattered on the floor.

"No worries, Veil," Maddy teased. "It's a practiced talent."

"So I see," Veil said, her voice thick with sarcasm. Maddy covered her mouth to hide her wide smile while Veil cleaned up the mess.

Liam soon joined in with Maddy's taunts. "Now, don't tease her, lass. Veil's got many talents in the kitchen. Perhaps just not when it comes to making pancakes." Veil poked her tongue out at the both of them but eventually she caved, and their laughter echoed off the kitchen walls.

Aileen pretended not to be entertained by all the chaos and shook her head with an amused smile. "All right, you three, enough of that. Your shenanigans could wake the dead, I tell you. Now girls, we have lots to do today. We'll get the boys fed and out of the kitchen so we can prepare. Saturday will be here before we know it."

Liam rubbed his belly as Aileen listed all the baking that was to be made. "I can't wait for lunch."

"I'm afraid it'll be sandwiches out in the barn for you all come lunchtime," Aileen said. "Can't risk the goods, dear."

"Oh, come on, love," he begged, batting his eyes. "Not even a small piece of apple cake?"

"Well, I guess we could make an extra one...if you'll finally get to cleaning that attic." Maddy and Veil giggled at how fast Liam got his way once Aileen got hers. Aileen stuck her tongue out at them. *Shenanigans indeed*. "All right, girls," she said, using a towel to wipe the counter. "Go ahead and wake up Kellan. It's not like that boy to sleep in. All the others should be here short—" Aileen was interrupted as the door was again thrown open, thumping loudly against the wall. Veil couldn't understand how the door stayed on its hinges with the abuse it endured.

Connor bolted in and doubled over, trying to catch his breath. "Da! Da, you got..." He wheezed. "You gotta come look!"

Aileen clutched the towel, her hands twisting the material. "Oh my Lord, is Gavin okay?"

"It's the crops, Mum, the crops!" Aileen slumped down in a chair as her knees gave out, and her hand came up to her chest. Liam jumped up from his seat and took off with Connor in the direction of the fields at a fierce pace. Maddy stood in shock, and a partially dressed Kellan tripped all the way down the stairs in his rush to investigate. He slid into the kitchen with mussed up hair, still pulling up his pants.

"What the bloody hell is going on?!"

"Connor came in—almost broke down the door," Maddy explained. "Said something about the crops. He and Da just took off."

"Oh, heavens, I hope everything is all right," Aileen sobbed. "We can't have another bad year—we just can't!"

Kellan embraced his mother, comforting her, while sharing a knowing look with Veil. "Listen, Mum. I don't think we have anything to worry about."

"Aileen! Aileen! You're not gonna believe it, love." Liam threw open the door, and with a few quick steps he crossed the kitchen to pull his wife into his arms, swinging her around the room. "Aileen, you're not going to believe it! The crops—it's a bleeding miracle!"

"What in the world are you on about?"

Liam laughed and squeezed her tighter. "The crops are ready. I don't know how, but they're ready—taller than me and the finest corn you ever did see."

"How can that be?" Maddy asked. "I was out there only yesterday with Rory, and they were barely out of the ground."

Liam released Aileen and laid a hand on Maddy's shoulder. Liam's joy was contagious as usual, and soon all but Veil's worried face matched his. "I don't know, lass. Like I said, a miracle or a blessing—or Irish luck even. I just don't know..."

Kellan smiled. "Maybe it was all of them."

Liam turned to Kellan with pride. "Aye, lad, maybe it was. Come, all of you. You really must see it." Liam all but dragged Aileen out the door, and a bouncing Maddy followed close behind. Kellan lagged behind with Veil, giving her that same strange look she didn't understand. She tried to hold his gaze, but it was a difficult task with so much of his skin showing. Her eyes explored his naked chest, following the dusting of fair hair until it disappeared beneath the waistband of his low-slung flannel pants. He cleared his throat. Veils' eyes snapped back up to his. At first she saw amusement within them and then a dawning realization.

"You're one of them, aren't you?" he said. "It all adds up now—my mind, your eyes, and last night... You're a sae, just like in the stories."

Kellan's tone was stern and intimidating, but this time Veil didn't back down. "Sidhe," she corrected. "We are called Sidhe, and we're not just stories."

His reaction to her admission was not what Veil had expected. "You can fix me," he insisted. "After what you did last night..."

Veil shook her head and firmly answered, "No."

"No?" he asked incredulously. "What do you mean, no? I saw what you can do, so I know you can." The desperation in Kellan's voice hurt Veil. But still, she shook her head. She would never purposely enter his mind and manipulate him. She couldn't risk hurting him further.

"I promise I will find someone else—"

"Someone else? Who? And when?" His voice rose as he spoke, reaching a hysterical pitch. "How long do I have to stay like this? You're in my mind all the time—it's driving me mad! I thought there might be another reason, but it's you, you're controlling me."

Veil dropped her eyes from his, quietly denying his accusations. His mental bondage was not her doing, but it was her fault. Still, she couldn't risk it. "I'm so sorry, but I can't, Kellan."

"Can't...or won't?"

22. chapter

The divine scent of vanilla and the comforting aroma of toasty spices filled the kitchen.

"You want to make sure you sift the flour well before you blend all the dry ingredients together," Aileen instructed.

"Like this?" Veil asked, shaking the flour through the sieve.

Aileen smiled proudly and patted Veil's back. "Exactly like that, good. Maddy, have you got all those apples sliced, dear?"

"Yes, Mum," Maddy sang.

"Brilliant," Aileen said, beaming. "Maybe putting this cake in the windowsill will draw the boys in. Apple cake is Kellan's absolute favorite! Do you think if we bribe him with the first piece he'll help us load all this up?"

"Maybe," Veil muttered. The mention of Kellan brought on

the throbbing pain in Veil's chest. He had resumed avoiding her after she denied him, and she missed him deeply, not that she blamed him for his anger. It would be the first time in three days that he'd be forced to endure her company for more than a few moments.

"Aren't you excited, Veil?" Maddy asked, slicing the last apple. "Your very first market! It's a lot of work, obviously, but so much fun. And you'll get to meet so many of my friends and probably most of our neighbors. You'll love it, you'll see!"

"I'm sure it will be lovely, Maddy." Veil tried to keep her emotions over Kellan hidden, but she could see Aileen eyeing her with concern.

"Veil, are you all right, dear?"

"Yes, of course." Veil tried to answer convincingly, but her effort was wasted. Aileen frowned at her, and Veil hid behind her curtain of thick hair like a coward.

"Veil?"

"Everything is fine," Veil assured her. "I'm probably tired is all." That was partly true. Veil was still keeping late hours in the loft preparing the tea, with only Niall along for company. Niall hadn't been surprised when only Veil had shown up. The pity written all over his face told her that Kellan had spoken with him.

"Try to be patient with him, Veil," he said. "I've known Kell a long time and he's more stubborn than a bull, that one is. He'll come back around, you'll see." They didn't pursue the subject any further, instead putting all their effort into the task at hand. There were more important things to worry over than a spat, and their diligence paid off. She only needed one more night, and Gavin's tea would be ready.

"You do look a little dark around the eyes, dear," Aileen remarked. "Are you sure you're up for all this? The market can be overwhelming, even to those of us who have been many times. Maybe you should stay back and rest."

"I really am fine, Aileen. I'm truly looking forward to it."

Aileen searched Veil's face. Finally, she nodded. "All right, then. Well, let's round up those boys and get going, shall we? Oh, and you might want to grab a jumper. It's supposed to be a windy one." Veil followed Aileen's advice and headed up to her room to fetch the light pink cardigan Maddy had loaned her. As she made her way back down the stairs, pulling on the cardigan as she went, she heard Aileen raise her voice. "Kellan, I know you've done something to upset her," Aileen accused. "She's been walking around like the dead for three straight days. Now, what is going on? I thought you two were getting along so well."

"Mum, I love you, but it's none of your business," Kellan answered matter-of-factly.

"The bloody hell it's not," Aileen snapped. "That girl has been through hell and back. I'm fairly certain she was brought up by heathens or...or a cult that kept her secluded from the world. And she's a good girl, Kellan. She's a good fit for this family, and she would be good for you."

"Good for me?" Kellan asked, his voice now rising too. "She's no more than a child, Mum. She might be close to nineteen, but she's more naïve than Maddy. I don't know what you were hoping for, but me staying here on this farm and shacking up with someone we barely know is not it. And trust me, Mum, we do not know her."

Veil's head fell back to rest against the wall as she heard the kitchen door slam.

"He didn't mean it," Maddy said.

Veil turned with a start. "You scared me, Maddy."

Maddy placed her hand on Veil's shoulder. "He didn't, Veil."

"It doesn't matter," Veil whispered. She turned away and

continued down the stairs.

They found Aileen sitting at the kitchen table, her head in her hands. She didn't seem to notice she was no longer alone. When she finally raised her head, her hands flew up to her chest.

"Bells for the both of you." She yelped. "Are you sure you're okay, Veil?"

"No, she's not," Maddy answered, crossing her arms with a huff. "I swear my brother is the biggest a—"

Veil was quick to cut Maddy off. "I'm right as rain, Aileen." Maddy didn't act thrilled with Veil's interruption but kept her mouth shut. Aileen eyed them both, but when neither Maddy nor Veil broke, she let it go.

The ride to Kenmare Square was a short but tense one. Maddy and Veil had been crammed into Kellan's old truck, and the awkward silence was suffocating. Thankfully, they didn't have to suffer long.

The square was impressive, with rows of tents as vibrant as the buildings in Kenmare. Each held tables filled with wares, packaged and ready to sell. Veil smiled at all the people, scurrying in their hurry to set up before the day started.

"Pretty grand, right?" Maddy asked, her joyful manner returning.

"It's quite a sight," Veil agreed. "Do you do this often?"

"Oh, yes. We used to come every week to work our booth, but when Gavin got so sick, we had to cut back."

"Will you two hurry up? The least you can do is help unload."

Kellan didn't wait for a reply; he walked past Maddy and Veil carrying a large case of jelly.

Maddy rolled her eyes at his back before grabbing two baskets filled with the loaves of bread Veil had made. "Here, we'd best get to it," she said, passing Veil one of the baskets. "Won't be long till it starts." Maddy guided her through the crowd and stopped at a booth near the end of the row. Aileen and Liam were already there, organizing the goods.

Liam rushed to take the baskets from the girls. "Veil, these smell so good," he said. "I bet they go first. You two about ready? It's opening time."

Veil soon learned that she was most certainly not ready. Aileen had warned her that the market could be overwhelming, and she discovered that this had not been an exaggeration. Once opened, people swarmed the walkways and began filling their totes with fruits, vegetables, and just about anything baked. Children were especially drawn to the McGrath booth or, more accurately, drawn to Veil. The booth stayed so busy that Veil didn't have time to worry about Kellan. He stayed clear across the booth and helped those who wanted one of Aileen's delicious pies, while Veil stayed with Maddy, helping with the fresh bread and chicken eggs. Around noon, the crowd dwindled to a much more manageable size. It was a good thing too, for they were out of practically everything.

Maddy had already started to clear away the empty crates when she asked, "Pretty good turnout, yeah?"

Veil swiped the hair away from her face, exhausted. "Is it always this way?"

Maddy shrugged. "Mostly."

"Aye, lass, it was a good day," Liam agreed. "It's about time to clean up and head out. Kellan, will you stop pouting long enough to bring the empties back?" Kellan didn't answer his father but did start stacking the crates. He piled them high, and when he could hold no more, headed back to his truck. Liam shook his head. "Don't know what to do with that boy," he said with a sigh. "Maddy, please help your brother. And Veil, would you mind helping Aileen with the last bit of jams?"

"Of course," Veil agreed. She found Aileen at the front table speaking to a man who looked to be about her own age. "So glad to see you out today. Here, I held a couple of jars back."

"Strawberry—thank you, Aileen," the man said. "I tell you, you're the sweetest thing, but don't tell my wife I said that."

Aileen laughed as she placed the jars into a sack for him. "So, where is that lovely wife of yours?" she asked.

"You know, I should keep a better eye on that lass—always wandering off, I tell you," the man joked. "But I love her to bits." As Veil got closer, she could see that the man had a monstrous set of scars that started near his hairline. They trailed down the left side of his face and across one milky eye, disappearing under the collar of his brown checkered shirt.

"Ah, there you are, dear," Aileen said, waving Veil over. "Veil, I'd like you to meet a friend of mine. This is—"

The man, now ghostly pale, stood slack-jawed. "Maeve?" he whispered.

Veil's heart pounded.

"I can't believe it," the man said, his voice wavering. "It's you!" Veil turned to Aileen for help, but she was just as astonished as Veil. "Oh, my heavens, Maeve! I can't... I just can't!" The man babbled incoherently as he rushed around the table. He collided with Veil, knocking them both to the ground. Veil tried to scramble away, but he was stronger, pushing forward and grabbing onto her.

Veil couldn't see all the people the commotion had drawn in, but she did hear their shouts. Aileen and Liam's voice were in among the mix, but it was Kellan that pulled her to safety and tucked her securely into his chest. She held onto him for dear life.

"Jack? Jack!" A dark-haired woman pushed her way through the throng of people. When she finally reached the man, he was sobbing. Jack didn't remove his teary eyes from Veil, not even when the woman tugged at his arm.

"Evelyn, look!" Jack said. "It's Maeve! She's come home, Evelyn."

"Maeve? Jack, you know that can't be...." Evelyn's words drifted away when she saw Veil. She studied her with awe. "Jack, look. She's not her, love—look at her eyes." Jack did as he was told, focusing his one brown eye on Veil's blue.

"But look at her, Evelyn."

"I know, love," Evelyn said. "Come, let's get you home." Evelyn stood up, pulling Jack up with her, and began escorting him away. Jack looked over his shoulder at Veil. His woeful features burned themselves into her mind.

"I'm sorry," Veil whispered. She could hear Kellan's heart pounding against her ear.

It wasn't Jack, but Evelyn, who turned to reply. "No worries, dear. We're the ones who are sorry. You do look just like her...all except the eyes." Those final words left her lips, and she pulled Jack along, disappearing into the crowd.

23. chapter

Back at the farm, the family sat quietly around the kitchen table. Aileen and Liam had each attempted to speak several times, but they, too, seemed shocked to silence by the incident. Veil kept her eyes glued to the wooden tabletop, a cup of hot tea in her hands. She hoped that by avoiding eye contact, she would be saved from the talk that was sure to come. She didn't think she could handle any more questions she couldn't answer. Liam appeared to be gathering his courage to say something, but the phone began to ring. He sighed deeply before rising to answer it. He wasn't gone long.

"That was Evelyn," he said. "She wanted to apologize again. She said Jack hasn't had a fit like that in years and was just beside himself for scaring Veil." He reclaimed his spot at the table and rubbed his face with his hand. "Maddy, Kellan, would you mind excusing us?

I think we need to speak to Veil privately for a moment." Liam's tone alarmed Veil. She was scared of losing them like she had lost everything else, and that fear overtook her. She struggled to breathe. Panicked, she swiftly stood up from the table. A wave of dizziness hit her full force, and she fought to remain conscious, grabbing hold of her chair. The same hands that had pulled her to safety at the farmers market held her up.

Still gasping, she begged, "Please, please, don't. Don't leave me too!"

Kellan whispered soothingly into her ear, "Shh... You listen to me. I'm not going anywhere. Now, take deep breaths, Veil. Breathe with me." In and out, she tried to match his breaths until eventually her vision returned to normal. He tilted her chin up to see her face. Without taking his eyes off hers, he said, "I'm not leaving her, Da."

Maddy crossed her arms in a stubborn display. "Neither am I. She's family now, Da."

"Oh, Maddy, of course she is," Liam replied. He turned to Veil. "Aileen and I have thought of you as a McGrath for quite some time now. We want you here. Don't ever doubt it, lass." Unused to hearing such things, Veil searched Liam's eyes for signs of deception or regret and found none. He held out his arms to her. Veil threw herself into them. Liam gently laid his chin on top of her head and squeezed her. "Shh, all will be fine, lass, you'll see. You've got us, whether you want us or not."

"Thank you," Veil murmured.

Liam cleared his throat, his voice thick with emotion. "Ah, now, none of that. But I do think it would be best if we talked, lass."

Veil nodded, and the soft material of Liam's teal plaid shirt rubbed against her cheek. She released him, turning to look at the others. It dawned on her that she could trust them completely; they wouldn't turn their backs or abandon her. The feeling of security was immeasurable to Veil. Kellan took her hand, and they sat back down at the table. With everyone settled, Veil waited with bated breath for Liam to speak.

Veil sat on the edge of the loft's large opening, letting her legs dangle off the side while she stared out into the darkness. The sky was overcast, blocking out the light from the stars. Physically and emotionally drained, she leaned back onto her hands, and the hay that covered the loft floor crunched beneath her palms. The sound of bubbling water soon reached her ears. Beside her, a pot sat on a borrowed crate, where a small flame from the camp burner Niall had brought her cooked away.

"I thought I'd find you here," Kellan said, reaching the top of the loft's ladder. Veil was not surprised to see him. It had only been a matter of time before someone would come looking for her. "You know Mum and Maddy are worried to death about you. Da said you just needed a walk to clear your head." Guilt bubbled up within her. They had talked and she had listened, never admitting or denying a thing. She hadn't considered anyone's feelings when she'd abruptly left the house after they were finished. When Veil failed to acknowledge him, Kellan sat next to her and threw his long legs over the edge too. "Are you okay?" he asked. Veil wasn't sure how she felt. Nevertheless, she nodded. "Come on, Veil. This whole thing is...it's just unbelievable," he said, shaking his head. "I mean, everyone around here knows the story about Jack. Da would always use it as a lesson, to teach us to respect the land and our culture. I never *ever* thought it could be real." Kellan was having a difficult time coming to terms with it all and Veil understood.

"I didn't know," she said, staring into the dark sky. "My father only told me about my mother the same night you found me. It was the first time he'd even told me so much as her name. He barely mentioned her brother, only said she had gotten lost in the woods searching for him."

"Why would your da not tell you about your mum till now?"

Veil finally looked at Kellan. She could see the concern in his eyes. "I used to believe he blamed me for her death, but Dara said it was my mother's memory; it simply brought him too much pain. They were never meant to be together, but they developed feelings for one another. Father told me she changed him...for the better, he said."

"Perhaps, you should talk to him—Jack, I mean."

"And say what? Hello, I'm the only child of your long-lost sister, who is dead due to my existence. Oh! And so sorry for all the terrible things that happened to you because of my father." Veil ran her hands down her face before using them to cover her eyes. "His poor face, Kellan. How could anyone forgive that?"

Kellan slid over until his leg touched hers. "You aren't to blame, Veil, for any of it." He reached out and grabbed her hand before continuing. "I know you have no reason to believe me when I tell you how sorry I am. I've just been so bloody angry with everything, and I've made a habit of taking it all out on you. I'll do better by you. I swear it." Kellan's words sounded sincere. Despite what he had said in the kitchen to Aileen, she couldn't seem to ward off the warmth that always settled in her chest when he was near.

She cleared her throat and waved off Kellan's kind words. "I never blamed you for being displeased with me—look at what you've been through. You have every right to be angry. I promise I'll find someone who can help you... Someone who can free you." Kellan's hand was locked with hers, his thumb gently gliding across her skin. A light summer rain began to fall, and the musky smell of the tea filled her nose. She checked the rumbling pot to find that the water had turned a rich honey color. "Look!" she said, her eyes bright once more. "The tea, it's ready!"

Kellan almost fell off the edge of the loft in his hurry. He pinched his nose as he leaned over the pot. "Blimey, that smells terrible. Are you sure it's ready?" Veil nodded with the biggest smile she had ever worn. Kellan lifted her off the ground, hugging her tightly. She didn't have the time to process what was happening before he began swinging her around. "Thank you... Thank you... Thank you, Veil," he mumbled into her hair. Kellan's excitement was catching, and Veil laughed with him as he spun her in the air. Finally, he placed her feet back onto the loft floor. "Come on, then. Let's go save him!"

Veil turned toward the pot, her hand grazing the handle before a thought pushed its way into her mind. "Umm, Kellan...what about Connor and Farrah?"

24. chapter

The first time Veil had entered the blue house on the hill was the day Kellan had taken her to his perfect place. It was the same day Gavin had had one of his worst spells. Veil had not been able to truly appreciate just how pretty their modest home was. The cream walls contrasted beautifully against the dark wooden floors. Most of the furniture was white and wonderfully simple in design. But Veil's favorite feature was the staircase.

"Kellan carved that, himself," said Farrah.

"Kellan did this?" Veil reached out to touch the railing.

"He is quite talented, though good luck getting him to admit to it." The craftsmanship was proof of what had to have been be many hours of hard work. Veil ran her hand along the detailed designs. Several circular symbols were deeply etched into the brilliant brown wood. They were all a little different, but each had four distinct corners.

"What are these?" she asked.

"They're Celtic Knots," Farrah answered. "They're meant for protection. Old tales say they'll ward off evil and bad luck."

Veil took her eyes off the railing and glanced at Farrah. "Do they work?"

Farrah traced the carvings herself, releasing a cleansing sigh. "Veil, anything will work if you believe in it enough." Veil didn't think she was referring to the stairs. Dara had told her that most humans were fickle when it came to faith, but in Veil's time with the McGraths, she had learned their will was strong and their kindness unlimited. Together, the family could accomplish anything.

"Farrah, Veil?" Kellan called out. "Will you come here?" The two women entered the kitchen, where Veil was met with a steely-faced Connor.

"My brother here is trying to convince me to let you use some herbal hocus pocus on my son."

"Connor, come on," Kellan said, trying to calm his brother. "Just listen to her. She's trying to help."

The air in the small room began to feel thick to Veil as Connor's hostility built. "Bleeding hell, the doctors can't even figure out what is wrong with him," he snapped. "Actual educated doctors, Kellan. Do you really expect me to believe she can do what they can't? That the miracle we need for our son is a tea some bird you found on the side of the road made from a bunch of weeds?"

"Connor, what in the world are you talking about?" Farrah asked, her brow furrowed.

"Exactly what I said, Farrah. Kellan claims *she* can make Gavin better with nothing but some bloody plants." He turned his face to

Kellan and Veil. "Well, you're both loony if you think I'm letting either of you near my son with that mess."

Farrah gasped and grabbed Veil's arm. "Is it true, Veil? Can you help my baby?"

Connor's eyes widened. "Farrah, you can't possibly be buying into this load of bollocks?"

"Hush, Connor," Farrah hissed before repeating her question to Veil. "Can you help him?" Farrah's grip was tight on her arm and Connor's angry glare bore down on her.

All Veil could do was shake her head. "Nothing is certain, he's very ill—"

Connor's scoff was loud enough to interrupt her. "See, Farrah? She can't help us."

Farrah released Veil's arm and crossed the room, kneeling at her husband's side. "Connor, our son—Gavin is dying. If there is even the smallest chance she can save him, shouldn't we allow her to try?"

Connor stared into Farrah's desperate eyes before taking her hands in his. He rested his forehead against hers. A moment later, he asked, "Do you think you can do it, Veil? Do you think you'll be able to give him a chance?"

Veil couldn't look away from Connor and Farrah. There was hurt on their faces and pain in their eyes, but she could also see their hope. If they were able to keep their faith alive, so could she. "Yes, Connor," she said, her head held high. "I believe I can."

Connor kept his eyes on Farrah. "All right," he said. "I sure hope you know what you're doing."

July came and went. Winter drew nearer with each passing day, and while the fear of what was to come lurked within the corners of Veil's mind, she tried to keep it locked up tight. She still had some time, and there were more important things to worry over. This was the day they would find out if the tea had worked.

Gavin had not cared for the tea. The smell alone was hard on the senses, and the taste... For days he had silently refused to swallow a single drop. His parents had all but given up. On the fifth day, Veil had finally had enough. Enough of watching the precious boy wither away. Enough of watching the family she cherished sinking deeper into despair.

"Mind if I take him for a walk?" Connor and Farrah raised their heads from the table, where they'd collapsed when Gavin had refused the tea, yet again. "Please?" Veil asked again. "I won't take him far." They gave Veil the smallest of nods, and she pulled the small boy from his chair. Kellan, looking just as miserable as the others, stood to accompany them, but Veil shook her head. "I wish to take him alone." She perched Gavin securely on her hip and held his cup as they walked out into the bright sunlight, heading toward the barn.

Nora seemed glad to see them. "She's a gorgeous one, isn't she?" She petted the mare's velvet muzzle while Gavin rested his head on Veil's shoulder. "You know, you and Nora here have a lot in common, little one. She's strong willed too, though you might not know it simply by looking at her. She doesn't let her small size keep her from doing big things, Gavin." Gavin's hand reached out to lay atop Nora's nose. The horse nuzzled him the same way she'd nuzzled Veil, and Gavin's tiny cheeks pulled up into a smile. Nora playfully whinnied, which made Gavin raise his head to look up at Veil. "She's devoted and determined. She's a fighter. We need you to be a fighter too, little one."

Relief washed over Veil when Gavin silently took his small cup and lifted it to his mouth, gulping down the liquid inside. He then resumed tickling the contented horse's nose. Veil had never been happier. They returned to the house with an empty cup, which brought comfort to his parents. Veil showed Farrah how to burn the sage in Gavin's room, letting him breathe it in while he dreamed. They had a real shot in saving the little one's life.

It was several weeks after Veil had taken Gavin to the barn that the family gathered in the den to await Connor, Farrah, and Gavin's return from his doctor's appointment in Dublin.

Aileen paced from one end of the den to the other. "Good Lord, what time is it? They should have been back ages ago! What if something happened?"

Aileen's voice wavered and Liam pulled her into his lap. "Calm yourself, love. Dublin is a good drive from here—you know this."

"But it's been so long, and they should have called by now. They should have called and told us something."

Liam sighed, gently tucking her head under his chin. "They might not be able to just yet. We just need to have faith."

Aileen sniffled, and Liam handed her a tissue. "I know. I need him to be all right, Liam."

"And he will be, love," he said, rubbing Aileen's back. "Think about how well he's been looking. He's been eating a little more and hasn't had an attack in over a week." What Liam said was true. Gavin had been looking better and had enough energy that he wanted to play. His eyes had even had more life in them, but Veil didn't want to get her hopes up either.

Maddy jumped up from her seat, almost knocking Rory over and yelled, "Look! They're coming up the drive now." She rushed through the kitchen, leading the way outside. The family was not far behind.

Connor was the first one out of the car. He bypassed all the others and stopped directly in front of Veil, his expression unreadable. Veil felt the weight of her most tragic failure crush her. *The tea didn't work.* Connor grabbed hold of her, lifting her until her feet left the ground. He buried his face into her hair, crying. Stunned, Veil turned to the others with wide eyes. More tears fell, but they were *happy* tears.

A weeping Farrah held her little boy, whose smile was bright and healthy. "Thank you," she said. "Thank you so much, Veil."

The sun warmed Veil's face, and the grass felt nice against her back. She gazed up into what Liam had called a bluebird sky. Fluffy, white clouds danced on the wind. The peaceful moment didn't last long, however; it was broken by a high-pitched squeal. Veil bolted up.

Farrah, who was stretched out by Veil's side, started to laugh. "Easy... They're only playing around a bit. Look how happy they are." Connor chuckled as he tossed Gavin into the air. Veil took a moment to watch them. In the barrows, parents didn't play with their children like this. They never really played with them at all. Veil had never seen anyone look at someone the way Connor gazed at his son. Gavin wore his toothy smile so wide, his dimples were on full display. No one never would have guessed he had been so ill only a few short weeks ago. According to Connor and Farrah, the doctor had been astounded by the new test results, and they'd had no other option but to tell the rest of the family what they had been up to. Everyone had thanked Veil more times than she could count. Farrah sat up and gently bumped her shoulder against Veil's. "Thank you for this."

Veil gave her a small smile, her cheeks pink. "Farrah, you've already thanked me numerous times. I'm just glad he's recovering so well."

"Honey, I will thank you every day for the rest of my life for this, so get used to it," Farrah chuckled.

"What are you two hens cackling about over here?" Kellan asked, walking their way.

"Even if we were cackling, which we most certainly were not, it would be none of your business," Farrah answered.

Kellan snorted. "Whatever you say, tiny. Now, move over, I'm beat."

"Ugh, Kell. Get your sweaty body away from me!" Farrah yelled as he pushed his way between them. Her look of disgust sent Veil into a giggling fit.

"Kellan, quit torturing my wife," Connor called out.

"I did nothing of the sort," Kellan replied. "Plus, she likes it, deep down."

Farrah gagged, pinching her nose. "I most certainly do not. As grateful as I am for the blessing of two crops in one season, I don't know if my delicate nose can handle the stink on you lot from working it." As Kellan and Farrah continued their banter, Veil looked out over the field to see Liam, Rory, and Niall walking along the mounds, heading back their way. Veil swore she could see the pride on their faces even at a distance. The crop that had been brought on by Veil's touch was long gone, and Liam had been ecstatic with the idea of a second one. They had replanted as soon as the ground was prepped, and the field was already filled with rows of short green stalks. Farrah playfully shoved Kellan into Veil, giving them both a wink before leaving to join

Gavin and Connor.

Kellan leaned back on his hands and sighed. "Grand, isn't it?"

"Yes," Veil agreed. "Niall said this one should be ready right on time."

"I wasn't really talking about the crop, but aye, that is quite the sight as well. I was talking about *that*." Veil followed the direction Kellan gestured and saw the beauty he was referring to. Liam, Rory, and Niall had finally made it and joined in the fun with Gavin and his parents. The little one was in the middle, literally the center of attention, right where he belonged. He appeared to be loving it.

"Yes," Veil sighed. "That's one of the most beautiful things I think I've ever seen."

Kellan's eyes were locked on the ground, his fingers pulling at the grass. "You ever think about that?"

"Think about what?"

His eyes never left the grass he tore into tiny pieces. He cleared his throat, and said, "You know...kids. Having a family of your own."

Veil shrugged, watching the merry scene playing out before her. "I don't know," she answered honestly.

"What if you found a safe place, a place you'd always belong? What then?" His eyes shone with possibilities, and Veil let herself fall into them.

"Like a true mark?" she whispered.

"A true mark?"

"All right!" Liam said, his arrival cutting off their conversation. "The fields are looking mighty fine, and I think we could all use a day off. The Puck Festival starts tomorrow and we're going!"

Veil's mind was filled with a million questions. Instead of asking the ones she truly wanted to, she settled for a question that felt safe to her heart. "Kellan...what's a puck?"

25. chapter

Killorglin. The small town would be the farthest Veil had ever traveled from the farm—or from the barrows for that matter. Kellan had explained that the Puck Festival was the oldest fair in Ireland, filled with markets and music. He also tried to explain something about a goat, then chuckled at Veil's confusion and said she would see when they arrived.

"Aren't you so excited, Veil?" Maddy asked eagerly. "We're almost there!" Maddy hadn't been still since they began the long drive to Killorglin. Veil wondered where she found the energy.

"I am," Veil answered, smiling. "And I see you are as well."

Maddy bounced in her seat, clapping loudly. "Oh, the Puck Festival is one of my all-time favorites!"

"Maddy, you say that about all of the festivals," Kellan said, shaking his head and laughing.

Maddy began to laugh as well. "Oh, you shut it, Kellan. You know you're just as excited as me." Though Kellan didn't admit it, Veil knew Maddy was right; he hadn't stopped smiling the entire trip. He'd been in high spirits since Gavin's trip to the doctor, and they hadn't had a single argument since he had apologized to Veil in the loft. Maddy had told Veil in secret that she was thrilled to have her brother back to his old self. "Look, Veil," Maddy said, pointing toward a town. "We've made it! Oh, I just can't wait to show you everything."

"Let's find a place to park this old thing first, little sister. Are the others still behind us?" In her hurry to look out the back window, Maddy's braid swung wildly around, forcing Veil to press into Kellan's side while dodging it. Veil apologized and began to scoot away, but Kellan draped his arm across her shoulder, pulling her in instead. "It's all right," he whispered, his breath warm in her ear. "You're right where you belong." Kellan kept his eyes on the road, making it impossible for Veil to read his face. His behavior lately had been so different than when he first brought her to the farm, and while she enjoyed seeing him so happy, his actions confused her.

Maddy snickered. "Well, in case you two are still wondering, everyone is right behind us."

They crossed a charming stone bridge stretched over a winding river. On one side was a sculpture of a crown-wearing goat posing proudly on a rock.

"Is that the puck?" Veil asked.

Kellan nodded, tugging her closer. "Aye, it's a statue of King Puck. You'll see the live one soon, just wait and see."

Killorglin reminded Veil a lot of Kenmare, especially in the way the brightly painted buildings lined the street, each connected to the other. She didn't see a way for anyone to actually get into them though, with all the people swarming the street.

"Are there always this many people here?"

"Not usually," Kellan answered. "They're here for the festival. Stay close to me, all right?" Veil squeezed the hand Kellan offered, and along with the rest of the family, they made their way into the crowd.

Although overwhelmed, Veil couldn't help but be amazed by everything. Multicolored tents sold food, jewelry, clothing, and all manner of trinkets. Young girls, adorned in long-sleeved knee-length dresses, jumped and tapped their toes to the rosy music played by a band of fiddles, flutes, and drums. Lines of flags were draped from one building to another, waving in the wind. When they reached a tall white tower in the center of the street, she finally learned about the goat. The creature had been placed in a small cage to keep it secure and wore a regal crown atop its horns. Next to the goat was a pretty little girl. She wore a flowing white dress, secured around her middle with a sparkling green-and-silver belt. She also had a crown of her own.

Kellan pointed toward the goat. "See, that's King Puck," he said. "The locals go and catch him out in the wild, and he's treated like bleeding royalty for three days. The little lass is this year's Queen of Puck, and she's the one who gets to crown him."

"Kellan, what happens to him afterward?" Veil asked, biting her lower lip.

"Don't fret," Kellan answered, squeezing her hand. "On the last day, he is returned to his home. It's called Scattering Day. Now, come on, there's so much more to see!"

The family browsed several tents, Aileen loading her arms and Liam's with bags, most of them containing items Gavin had taken a liking to. Connor had fallen behind and returned with delicate baby's breath crowns. He placed a crown on each of the women's heads.

The sea of people made it a struggle for the family to stay

together, and they lost Rory somewhere in the mix. Veil popped up on her tiptoes looking for his notorious red hair, but she had little luck with all the people dressed in what Kellan had called costumes.

"No worries," Niall said. "I'm sure he's just found the brewery or a lass to aggravate."

"Are you sure?" Veil asked, her eyes darting between Niall and the crowd. "There are so many people here. How will he find us?"

Niall let out a hearty laugh. "Trust me, Veil. The boy is like a hound. He doesn't stray too far and always finds his way home. Now, let's dance!" He pulled Veil into a small clearing in the middle of the street. Many others were already there, dancing and spinning around, and most were in fanciful garb. The dance was a lot like the ones Veil had learned growing up, and she was able to seamlessly fall in.

"Where'd you learn to dance?" Niall asked, raising his eyebrows. "You're quite good."

"There are celebrations where I'm from, too. Music and dance were among the skills I was encouraged to learn, and Dara was an excellent teacher."

Niall took her hand in his, twirling her around. "Indeed she was. You said you were taught music as well? Like an instrument?

Veil's movement momentarily stalled. "Yes, a harp."

"A harp, you say?" Niall didn't seem to notice Veil's wariness, and he didn't wait for her reply. He stopped their dance and tugged her hand toward the stage where the band played. His eyes told her that he was up to no good. "You wait right here," he said. He winked and left her. He didn't go far, though.

Niall approached a burly man with a silvering beard standing near the large burgundy curtain that hung behind the band. Niall's hands waved around as he spoke, and soon the man turned toward Veil and grinned. He then disappeared behind the curtain. Niall jogged back to Veil, his face glowing with excitement. He pulled her to the stage, where the band had just finished their last song. The burly man brought out a harp, and Veil understood what Niall had done.

She jerked away. "No. I can't, Niall."

Niall reached out and laid his hand on her shoulder. "And why not?" he asked, his voice kind. "You know how, you said."

Veil glanced from the crowd to the familiar instrument and back to Niall again. "I do, but I—"

"Then I want to hear you," he insisted. "And I'm sure I'm not the only one." Niall hauled Veil onto the wooden stage and headed directly for the harp. He gave her a firm hug before skipping away to rejoin the McGraths. Veil's hands grew sweaty, and she nervously rubbed them together.

"You got this, Veil!" shouted Maddy. Still unsure, Veil glanced at each family member, stopping when her eyes landed on Kellan. He nodded in encouragement. It was nearly impossible for her to look away from his face.

The burly man appeared at Veil's side, still grinning. He took hold of her hand, escorting her to a small wooden stool. "Here you go, lass. Wouldn't make them wait too long, this bunch can get a little batty, if you know what I mean." He presented Veil with a dramatic bow and stepped off the stage.

Veil sat in the center of her audience, the band at her back. They all stared at her. She hesitated, and the people did indeed begin to act out like the man had warned. They started to clap and yell, demanding to be entertained. Veil reached up and placed her hands into the correct position, and the noise from the crowd seemed to magically disappear. The harp felt sturdy *and safe*, just like her own. She let herself go, singing along as she rhythmically plucked the harp strings. The song she played had been one of Dara's favorite pieces, a slow song about a girl longing for her lost love.

Veil strummed the last note and turned back to the audience to see that a row of wide-eyed children now lined the front of the stage. Everyone stood silent. All except Kellan, who made himself known seconds later, pulling Veil up from her seat. He was fixated on her with an expression she had never seen from anyone. She blushed and lowered her head, trying to escape the intensity of it. He gently cradled her face, bringing her eyes back to his. Veil's feelings for Kellan were there and growing, but she would need time to banish the dark thoughts she had about herself and come to terms with his obvious affections. Veil's isolated upbringing had left her with little understanding of intimacy, which Kellan was embarrassingly aware of. He had called her naïve—*no more than a child.*

Kellan must have picked up on her worries, for he began to stroke her cheeks as he held them between his strong hands. He searched her eyes—for what, she didn't know. He placed a soft kiss, like the brush of a feather, upon her forehead. He pulled back, grinning and satisfied. It was enough for Veil to believe his affections might be real. She gazed at him, her grin matching his. It felt like the first time she'd ever truly seen him. The uproarious cheering from the onlookers broke the spell, and Rory, who had found his way back, hollered louder than all the rest. Veil buried her face into Kellan's mustard yellow sweater. Her cheeks had never been redder.

"Pay Rory no mind," he said. "He won't be laughing in the morning when that hangover hits." Kellan's chuckle turned to full out laughter when he saw the baffled look on Veil's face. "Oh, Veil. Don't ever change, you hear?" His words faded away as he rested his forehead against her own, the spectators cheering even louder. The feeling of warmth that only Kellan seemed to bring filled Veil's chest. She allowed it to engulf her, taking over her senses. If she hadn't, she might have noticed the eyes watching them—*watching her.*

Veil saw the hooded man out of the corner of her eye. It was unnatural, the way he stood so still among the busy bystanders. His hood was pulled securely up, casting a shadow over most of his face, but Veil caught a glimpse of his eyes.

26. chapter

Days passed, filled with worry and stress. After Veil had spotted the hooded man with eyes so much like her own, she had dragged Kellan off the stage and attempted to disappear into the crowd. The man never approached, but Veil sensed his gaze penetrating the back of her head as she fled. Thankfully, the family had chosen to leave the festival right after Veil's performance; she rushed them all back to the safety of their vehicles, her head on a swivel. She thought she would feel relief once they put some distance between themselves and the man, but nightmares of the hooded man plagued her sleep and seeped into her waking hours on the farm, where she swore she would catch a glimpse of his shadowed form around every corner. Eventually, the days began to pass with fewer dreams and even fewer sightings. In the end she chalked it all up to paranoia.

Veil's ease continued as the crops thrived, and the farm was busier than ever with several of the cows pregnant and due at any time. Maddy said she hoped the calves would make an appearance before she had to start back at school. Gavin had been doing so well that Aileen was able to start baking again for the weekly market. She was rarely seen without a layer of flour covering her head to toe.

Then there was Kellan, who had barely left Veil's side since the festival. Even when there were chores that needed tending to, he always suggested a reason for Veil to tag along or an excuse to hang around the house when she helped Aileen. He acted as if he craved her touch, whether it was a simple hug or shyly holding Veil's hand. Kellan was happy, and she liked seeing him that way.

Kellan and Veil had snuck off one day after dinner and ventured out to his perfect place. They lay down together, her head on his shoulder, and talked. He learned that her favorite color was green and she found out that his was blue. He asked questions she thought were strange, like what her favorite flower was.

"How can one choose a favorite flower?"

Kellan shrugged. "I don't know... There's gotta be one you like more than the rest."

So Veil had described to him a bloom which only grew in her realm. The flower, known as the 'wind flower' to Veil's kind, had always been Dara's favorite. It grew everywhere in the In Between, but only in the winter, near Veil's birthday. The flower was uniquely beautiful, with white petals that faded to a deep blue before its stamens turned the deepest black.

Veil was brought back to the present by Aileen's voice. "Finally got that boy to leave you be, did you? You know, I don't think I've ever seen my son this way."

Veil grinned at the memory of Liam dragging Kellan out to

the field after lunch. "It was Liam who came to claim him."

Aileen submerged her hands in the soapy water and scrubbed away at a stubborn bit of batter clinging to a bowl. She handed the clean dish to Veil to rinse and dry when she was finished.

"I'm serious, you know. Kellan hasn't been this happy in a long while. He seemed content when he was attending uni—when we even got to see him, that is. But even then it felt like he was searching for something. I think he's found it now." Soapy hands and all, she pulled Veil in for a hug. Veil couldn't believe that Kellan's mirth was all due to her. Not knowing what to say, she just held on tightly to Aileen.

Maddy barreled through the poor kitchen door, flushed and sweaty from running. "Mum! Veil! One of the cows is in labor. Come on, you gotta see this!" Once she had delivered her message, she turned on her heel and sprinted back the way she came.

Aileen shook her head as her animated daughter rushed out. "I don't know how my door handles all the mistreatment it gets from this family. You go on, Veil. I'll finish up here."

In truth, Veil was as excited as Maddy, though she kept hers better managed. She had never witnessed any creature bring forth new life; it would be one of the biggest blessings she could ever imagine receiving. Veil thanked Aileen before pulling the apron over her head, hanging it on the rack, and rushing after Maddy. She found Maddy inside the barn, along with Kellan and Rory.

Kellan's face lit up when he saw her. "Ah, Mum released you, did she?"

"You know I enjoy her company," she answered, smiling.

"But not more than mine, right?" Veil shook her head and Kellan laughed at her pinkened face. "Good. Now, come and see Elsa here before Maddy bursts." Veil approached the wooden railing, carefully peeking over at the mother-to-be. Elsa was a girthy white cow with a few black spots and eyelashes so long they curled. Rory and Kellan had prepared one of the empty stalls with a fresh layer of hay along the floor. Elsa lay in the middle of it and appeared quite comfortable. Kellan came to stand behind Veil, enclosing her within his arms and resting his chin on her shoulder.

"Is it happening now?" Veil whispered, trying not to alarm Elsa.

"Oh, I think she's got a ways to go yet," Kellan answered. "These things take time. Could be tonight or in the morning even. We may have to sleep here to keep an eye on her—let Niall have a night off."

Veil's body vibrated with excitement at the thought. "Can I stay as well?"

"Sure, why not," Kellan chuckled.

"All right!" Maddy yelled, pumping her fist into the air. "Slumber party in the loft tonight."

The sky was completely dark, but the flickering lanterns threw off a soft glow. Rory and Maddy had given into sleep long ago, although Veil had no idea how Maddy slept over the sound of Rory's snoring. Kellan returned from below and glanced toward Maddy, shaking his head.

"That girl can sleep through anything, I tell ya."

Veil covered her mouth to muffle her laugh. "It is quite the talent," she said. "How is Elsa?"

"Not much longer now, probably a couple more hours. We'd

best rest while we can."

Veil scooted over on the blanket, the hay crunching beneath it. Kellan lay down and turned onto his side, facing her. He stared at her silently, but she could sense that he had something on his mind.

"All is well?" she asked. He started to speak only to abruptly stop again. "Kellan, what is it?"

Kellan cleared his throat and tried again. "I... It's just," he stuttered. He lowered his eyes, finally getting out what was bothering him. "It's almost fall, Veil."

"It is," she agreed. "Does the season bother you?"

Kellan lifted his eyes back to hers. "No, but the season that follows does."

Veil sighed. "Don't worry," she said, trying to comfort him. "I gave you my word. Come winter I will find a way to help you."

"No, Veil... I don't want you to leave."

Kellan's intense gaze bore into her, and Veil found she had to look away. "I have to," she whispered.

"You don't," he insisted. "You can stay here with me."

"What about my family? Kellan, I don't wish to leave, but they're hunting me." Veil's voice dripped with desperation. She became more upset with each word that left her mouth. "Every moment I'm here, I put you and your family in danger. I cannot bear the thought of something terrible happening to any of you because of me."

Kellan pulled Veil closer to him until there was not an inch of space between them and whispered into her hair. "Shh. We'll figure this out, I swear it. I can't lose you... Not now." Kellan caressed her face, her wild hair curling around his fingertips. He leaned in, his rough lips brushing lightly against her flushed skin, following the trail of freckles along her cheekbone. Her breathing faltered and her trembling hands rose to rest on his chest, his heart pounding against her palms. When his lips grazed hers, the connection they shared—that spark—ignited, sending white-hot heat through every nerve.

Rory let out a deep, rumbling snore.

Kellan grumbled under his breath, pulling away. But in his eyes, passion still swirled. Veil could see everything she had ever longed for within them, and the intensity of it all was enough to take her breath away.

21. chapter

Veil's eyes blinked open. She was met with Kellan's eager face.

"Good morning," he said. "Are you ready to meet the newest addition to McGrath farm?"

"The calf—it's here?"

A smile spread across Kellan's face as he helped Veil to her feet. He held her hands in his, rubbing his thumbs across her skin. "She's healthy as can be. Come and see."

They climbed down to where a sleepy-eyed Rory was tending to the new mother and baby. She hurried to the pen, peeking over to see the suckling calf. Kellan followed and stood beside Veil, draping his sturdy arms across the wooden railing.

"Isn't she gor...ge...ous?" Rory yawned.

"She is," Veil agreed. "What's her name?"

"Well, Rory and I thought you might like to name her." Veil gasped and turned, nearly bowling Kellan over with a hug.

"I must wake Maddy! She can help!" Veil scurried back up the ladder to the loft with the boys' laughter following her. Before she could wake Maddy, movement at the edge of her vision caught her attention. Curious as always, she looked closer.

A black-winged butterfly.

Dara's warning rang in Veil's ears. The creature fluttered in the early morning light while Veil stood still, barely breathing. She followed it as it flew out, to see what direction the infernal thing would take. It headed straight for the blue house on the hill. Veil practically fell down the loft's ladder. She sprinted toward Connor and Farrah's home, ignoring the concerned shouts from the barn. She was almost to their front door when the butterfly stopped and hovered right outside a cracked bedroom window. *Gavin.* Veil threw open the door to see a wide-eyed Connor sitting at the kitchen table, drinking what looked to be a cup of tea.

"Veil?" he stammered. "What's wrong?" She disregarded Connor and ran up the radiant staircase, sliding to a stop in front of Gavin's closed bedroom door. She turned the doorknob with caution and entered. Gavin stood, wide awake, next to his small bed. Relief filled her.

"Good morning, little one. Did you sleep..." Veil's words drifted away when he looked back at her. Her knees buckled and she fell to the floor. Gavin's eyes were still the same pretty shade of blue, but their innocent light was gone. Veil heard shouting as Kellan, Rory, and Connor all rushed into the room. The creature sent Veil a sinister grin.

"What on earth is wrong, Veil?" Kellan asked, dropping to his knees beside her. Tears welled up in her eyes, falling and flowing down her face. "Veil, please talk to me." The worry was thick in Kellan's voice, but there was no solace she could provide. What she feared the most had come to pass; they had found her. And they had taken Gavin. There was only one way to fix it.

Veil squeezed her eyes closed. "You have to take me back."

Aileen's kitchen, which was once a place where Veil could find peace, now held a much different feeling. The room was filled with the chaos of everyone trying to speak over one another, and the look-alike fed on the negative energy. These creatures thrived on destruction, and the evil glint in this one's dead eyes showed exactly how much it enjoyed watching the family tear itself apart. The mayhem was more than Veil could take.

"Enough!" The room went from deafening to pin-drop quiet.

Liam tried to speak. "Veil...lass, we're trying to understand, but—"

"This might be easier if everyone sat," Veil suggested. No one moved except Aileen. She approached Veil, searching her eyes. Veil knew she was looking for some kind of logical explanation. Unfortunately, Veil wasn't able to give her one. "It's time, Aileen. It's time for you to hear my story."

Aileen squeezed Veil's hand. "Then we will listen, dear."

Veil took her time gazing around the room. She studied the troubled faces of those who had taken her in. Liam sat beside Aileen, tenderly stroking her hand and trying to ease her tension. Maddy, with eyes that betrayed how worried she was, sat close to Rory, who had her tucked protectively under his arm. Niall and Kellan both refused to sit and paced the worn kitchen floor. Veil's eyes then landed on *it*. The little monster hung to its 'mother' while Connor lovingly patted its back, not knowing the truth of what Farrah held in her arms. But soon they would all know. Veil said a quiet prayer, asking that they would accept what she had to say. And that they would be able to find a way to forgive her.

"I was not raised like you," she began. "Or even like the others from my home. I spent most of my life behind locked doors, unable to leave without permission and never without someone to accompany me—"

"What do you mean, '*the others*?'" Connor asked. His was the first of what Veil thought would be many questions.

"There are many of us who live within the woods, deep under the ground and within the barrows," Veil explained. "We're called the Sidhe."

"*Sidhe?*" Connor repeated.

"Yes, Sidhe. Though I have heard you call us by many names—sae, fairies..."

Connor started to laugh. "Flipping fairies? You're pulling one on us."

"Connor, you will hush and let her finish," Aileen ordered.

Veil gave her a small nod of appreciation before continuing. "I know this will be hard for you to hear, much less accept, but know what I say to you is true. My kind exist and have been around since the beginning of creation. Just as humans do, Sidhe have the ability to either choose a life of light or a life of darkness."

Rory's jaw dropped. "Humans? Light and darkness? Bloody hell, you're not joking, are you?"

Connor rolled his eyes. "Rory, don't tell me you're actually believing this, are you?"

Rory continued to stare at Veil while he answered Connor. "Think about it, mate. She comes out of nowhere, and Kellan can't make heads or tails of it. And Gavin, who doesn't take to anyone, looks at her like she's hung the bleeding moon. Not to mention she's able to mix up some miracle cure for him. And look! Remember all the stories we were told growing up? Really look at her eyes, Connor."

For the first time since Veil's story began, Niall spoke. "What she says is true. Kellan and I have seen her do impossible things— Gavin's medicine and the crop."

"The crop?" Liam asked, bewildered. "You're the one responsible for that?"

"Yes," Veil admitted.

Connor scoffed. "Okay, let's pretend for a minute that this is actually possible. Why exactly are you here, then?" Veil could hardly blame him for his disbelief. Humans preferred a life of logic, to live in what they knew as their 'reality'.

"On the night Kellan found me, I had been told for the first time about certain circumstances of my birth, circumstances which are rare and deemed valuable among some. My father spoke of a moon that only shines during the Winter Solstice and will shine again in the winter of my nineteenth year—*this year*. The same moon that shone upon my human mother as she gave her life to grant me mine."

"Maeve," Aileen whispered. "Your mother was Maeve."

Veil looked to the floor. "She was."

"How? How can any of this be possible?"

"Father said she was lost in the woods, searching for her brother, when she accidentally wandered through our borders. He found her...and he took her."

"Your father *stole* your mother?"

Veil slowly nodded her head in agreement, her eyes focused on her feet. Doubts about everything her father had said and done had been festering in her mind since her run-in with Jack at the farmer's market. Whatever her father's reasoning was, what he had done was wrong. She tamped down her anger and disappointment enough to continue.

"Not exactly stolen. At least, not in the way you're thinking, though the result is the same. Sidhe possess certain...abilities. What we call the connection allows us to tap into all things in nature, even the human mind. That's how my mother was taken; she was clouded by my father. He said she was the most amazing person he had ever met and they fell in love. He claims she chose to stay. I was the result."

"That's why they never found Maeve's body. Everyone thought she had been taken or killed by a madman, the same they said attacked Jack. He tried to tell them—" Aileen's voice broke and Liam placed his hand on her shoulder to comfort her. "He told the truth, and no one believed him. Everyone thought his mind was gone from the shock."

"Well, while that story is tragic, it still doesn't answer why you're here," Connor spat.

Veil tried to ignore his anger, remembering that this had to be difficult to accept. "The circumstances I spoke of—that's why I'm here," she said. "My father, while placed in a desperate situation, signed an agreement. One of his heirs was promised to the clan our people were at war with. Father thought that if he produced another heir, I would be protected, but all did not work out as planned. My half-sister was bound on May Eve, making me the only eligible heir left to fulfill the agreement. When Father tried to keep them from taking me, he was punished severely, and I was forced to escape. That's how we came across Kellan, and that's when my guardian clouded him.

She made him bring me here and compelled him to protect me. I was told only that I must survive until winter while they try to renegotiate the terms."

Everyone turned from Veil to Kellan, who now leaned against the kitchen wall. Aileen rose from her chair and slowly approached him. "Son, is this true?" she asked. Kellan's head barely moved, but his answer was there all the same. Aileen turned her hard eyes on Veil with the look of betrayal Veil had always feared would come. "Take it off him," she said, jabbing her finger in Veil's face. "Take it off now."

"No, Mum," Kellan said. "I don't—"

"No," Veil interrupted, her voice strong.

Aileen took a threatening step toward her. "What do you mean, no? We let you into our home, into our family, into our hearts, and you still won't let him go?"

"I will not risk hurting him, Aileen. The crops were the first time I have ever successfully connected, and I care too much for him to risk it. I'll get someone to help him when I return."

"When you return?" Aileen scoffed. "It's only the middle of August, Veil. Winter is still months away. And if you think for one minute I'm allowing you to—"

"No. Not months from now, and not in the winter. Today. I'm returning today."

With a few long strides, Kellan had crossed the room and pulled Veil from her seat. "No, you will not, you hear? You're not leaving me, Veil!"

"Staying is no longer an option, Kellan. There was a man wearing a hood at the Puck Festival... *A Sidhe man*—"

"I can take you somewhere else. I can hide you better, I promise."

Veil's gaze traveled over Kellan's shoulder to the ominous eyes of the changeling once again.

"They have Gavin."

They all stared at the thing in Farrah's arms.

"Veil, he's right there," Kellan said.

"No, that's not him, Kellan. There are other creatures beyond the border. They long to be here, in this realm, and they serve the Sidhe for the chance to take the place of children the puca take. They have Gavin, and I can prove it." Veil didn't wait for anyone to react. She grabbed a skillet from the stovetop—*iron*. As Veil approached Gavin, Farrah jumped from her seat and scurried away with the creature until her back hit the wall.

Connor quickly blocked Veil's path. "You'll not go near my son," he said.

"That is not your son."

Kellan stepped up to Veil's side. "Let her do it, Connor."

"Kellan, you've lost your bleeding mind if you think I'll let her hurt him."

Kellan raised his hands, attempting to placate his brother. "Connor, think. When has she ever tried to hurt Gavin? She saved him, remember?"

"If you think I'm going to hurt him, you do it. All you need is a touch of cold iron."

Veil could tell Connor was wary as he looked first at her, then down at the skillet in her hand. He closed his eyes and said, "Farrah, bring him here."

"But, Connor..." Farrah stuttered, her eyes wide.

"Farrah, all will be fine," he assured her, though he didn't seem very sure, himself. "Just bring him."

The 'boy,' who had been peacefully settled within Farrah's arms, began squalling and wrestling to be free. The rest of the family stared in disbelief at its sudden change in behavior. Connor studied it with narrowed eyes, the thing continuing to struggle against Farrah. Connor glanced down at the iron pan in his hand. He touched the creature's arm. The thing let out a scream and began to thrash, red blisters and boils appearing where the skillet had touched its skin. It savagely clawed at Farrah's arms, and she dropped it to the floor. It rolled onto all fours, spitting and hissing, and morphed back into its true form with large pointed ears and a thin-skinned skeletal face. Its sandy blond hair began to fall out, and its eyes changed from blue and white to an endless black. The changeling's head darted left then right, searching for an escape. If there was any further question that this creature was not Gavin, the way that it leaped up from the floor and disappeared with a crash through the window removed all doubt.

28. chapter

Veil rode with Kellan, who had barely said a word since they had departed. His silence tore Veil apart.

"I will get him back, Kellan. I promise you, I will."

"And what of you?" Kellan asked. "Will I get you back?"

"Kellan," Veil pleaded. "Aileen is right. What Dara did... It was wrong. When we arrive, one of the others will free you of me."

"You think I want that? That I want to risk losing what I feel for you?"

The hurt in Kellan's voice set off the pain in Veil's chest. "Kellan, please," she begged.

"Please what?" he shouted, hitting the steering wheel with his fist. "You just expect me to let you go? I can't!"

Veil held back tears, feeling utterly useless. She let the silence take over once again. Kellan finally pulled over onto some grass off the roadway. The rest of the family parked behind him and followed Veil up the same hill she had tumbled down all those nights ago. When they reached the tree line, Veil stopped to gather her courage. Once she entered the woods, there would be no going back.

At first, their forested surroundings all appeared the same. It took Veil some time to find the way, but as they neared the In Between, she felt it. *The pull toward home.* She let it draw her in until she could see the border a short distance ahead. They were not the only ones approaching it. On the other side, Bidalia and Lorcan led an entourage of armed Sidhe through a meadow, trampling the grass and halting just shy of the shimmering curtain. A howl sent shivers up Veil's spine—*the wolves.* The beasts that had taken Dara's life were even more terrifying in the light with their haunting black eyes and long blood-stained fangs.

"What is it?" Kellan asked, stopping short to avoid a collision. "Why'd you stop?"

Confused, Veil turned her head to look at him. "You can't see them?"

He scanned the clearing in the direction she gestured then shrugged. "No, I don't see anyone." Dara had told her that most humans would not be able to see into their realm. It wasn't until her grandmother and the others stepped through the gauzy boundary that they were revealed.

"So, she has finally decided to come home, has she?" Bidalia's question dripped with contempt.

"Now, Bidalia, don't be so bitter," Lorcan said, taking another step toward Veil. "I'm sure the girl realized to whom she belonged, and her return had absolutely nothing to do with this."

He waved his hand, and Moira suddenly appeared behind

him. She sauntered their way, carrying Gavin. Upon seeing her only child in a stranger's arms, Farrah took off toward him. The wolves began to snarl, their hackles raised. Connor immediately picked up on the danger and tackled Farrah to the ground while Veil ran between them and the growling beasts.

"Stop!" Veil yelled, throwing up her hands. "Stop this!"

Lorcan tossed his head back and laughed. "Oh, how sweet," he cooed. "She's protecting her humans. You should let her come. I'm sure my pets would love a little snack."

"Please!" Farrah begged. "I only want my baby."

"Well, it looks as though we have ourselves a little problem then, don't we?" Lorcan taunted. "I have something you want, and you have something I want. Oh, whatever should we do?" Veil's body sagged in surrender. She turned back to Kellan, whose eyes flashed with fire.

"No, you can't have her!" he yelled. He tried to push himself between Lorcan and Veil. But the wolves wouldn't allow it. One wolf broke away from the others and pinned Kellan to the ground, its bared teeth dripping drool onto Kellan's face as its chest vibrated with monstrous growls.

"Oh, look what we have here, son," Lorcan said, looking Kellan over.

"Looks to me like he's challenging us, Father," said Colden, his voice deadly calm. "Is that it, human? You wish to challenge me for her?"

"No!" Veil shouted. Her heart raced, and her mind struggled to stay focused on this game they played. All eyes were fixed on her. She had their attention, now she had to choose her words carefully. "No, he doesn't. You can have *me*—me for the boy."

"Just like that?" Lorcan asked. "Without a fight? What a pity."

"Just like that," Veil repeated. "But I want a vow."

"A vow?" Lorcan scoffed. "You know we could simply take you and eradicate the vermin you brought with you." That was exactly what they would do if she didn't sweeten the deal.

"In return, I will vow never to escape... Ever."

Lorcan's predatory grin made her stomach turn. "You do present a tempting offer," he replied, rubbing his chin. "Yes, *very* tempting. All right, name your terms, my dear."

"First, tell me where my father is."

"Ah, yes," Lorcan said. "Cace, would you like the honor of telling her?"

Cace stepped forward. He stared angrily at Lorcan before his tormented eyes met Veil's. "I'm so sorry, cousin. I couldn't get to him."

Veil's fragile heart plummeted. Despite the hurt he had caused her, he was still her father, and he was slowly dying within the Saeculum. "I want him released now."

"Well, Colden, looks like you got yourself a feisty one."

Colden's eyes glittered with amusement. "Oh, I do like it when they play hard to get."

"Indeed, " Lorcan agreed. "I can hardly wait to taste her."

Behind Lorcan and Bidalia, Nessa gasped. She turned to Moira. "Mother, what is he talking about?"

"Nothing for you to concern yourself over. Now, hush."

"But, Mother—"

"I said quiet yourself!"

Nessa, not used to being scolded, turned and tucked her face into Haven's chest. He cradled her head, sending Moira a scathing look.

"All right, enough!" Lorcan shouted. "I'm becoming impatient, so let's finish this. Free Darragh and return the boy. Anything else?"

Veil lifted her chin and looked at her captors defiantly. "Yes, Lorcan. You will return these humans safely to their homes, never to be bothered by our kind again."

He balked at her request. "Do they mean so much to you? They're only humans."

"They mean everything to me," she answered fiercely.

"Very well, my dear," Lorcan replied, holding his hand out invitingly. "Come to me." Veil met Lorcan halfway, and the wolf moved away from Kellan to rejoin the pack. She could hear Kellan's panic-filled shouts as Liam, Connor, Niall, and Rory all held him back. His struggling only worsened when Lorcan wrapped his arm around Veil's, elbow to the wrist. Lorcan's connection touched her mind, and a burning pain pulsed within her arm. His eyes were victorious as the vow left his lips. "Take my arm and keep your promise, for lies will only lead to your demise. Consider the words, for once they are set, your vow to me will ensure they are met."

It was Veil's turn, and though it ripped her apart, she took the vow. Her arm blazed with each word she spoke. "Take my arm and keep your promise, for lies will only lead to your demise. Consider the words, for once they are set, your vow to me will ensure they are met."

The pain boiled until it erupted, and a golden fire engulfed their arms, momentarily searing them together before dissolving into their skin. As soon as the fire vanished, Veil jerked her arm from Lorcan's, trying to rub the pain away.

"Excellent," Lorcan purred. "Shall we, my dear?"

"Give me the boy and release my father," Veil said, her eyes misting over. "And allow me to say goodbye...please?"

"That wasn't part of the deal," Lorcan taunted, "but I suppose I can be merciful every now and then." Lorcan turned to Cace. "It looks like you're finally going to get your way. Go and release Darragh." Cace immediately sprinted for the tree hollow.

"Moira, please bring our little guest, will you?" Moira smirked as she handed Gavin over to Veil, who crushed him to her chest, swaying back and forth. "Best not take too long, my dear," Lorcan warned. "I told you my patience is wearing thin." Veil obeyed and walked Gavin back to his family. She handed him off to a grateful Farrah and smiled sadly at Aileen and Maddy. Their mournful eyes followed her as she made her way to where the men still restrained Kellan. Most of his fight appeared to have left him with the completion of the vow.

"Release him, please."

They did as Veil asked and Kellan immediately pulled her into his arms. He poured everything he had into their embrace. "Why, Veil? Why did you do that?"

Veil squeezed him back, her cheek laid over his heart. "To save you—the way you saved me." She leaned back and looked him in the face. "And now, you have to let me go."

Kellan shook his head, his eyes brimming with tears that threatened to fall at any moment. He gave her a single grief-stricken kiss and whispered against her lips, "I can't. You know I can't."

She already regretted what she was about to do. "I know, but all will be fine. Look at me." The connection came as naturally as it had in the cornfield. Kellan's body went rigid as their eyes met, and she could see the betrayal he felt. A stabbing pain tore through her chest. She didn't want to be the one to do this, but there was no one else she could trust. "Don't worry, Kellan," she said, her voice soothing and hypnotic. "Everything will be all right, you'll see. You and your family will return home, and you will no longer feel the burden of me in your lives. Live the life you choose, Kellan. *I free you.*"

His tears finally fell.

The connection was brutal as it broke apart. They let out a scream as the stabbing pain turned into crippling torture, its vice-like grip squeezing their hearts more and more with each beat. Their bodies lit up with a blinding flash crackling with energy, and they collapsed to their knees. Kellan's family jerked him away as cold hands latched onto Veil, dragging her through the border. Colden's brilliant green eyes filled her vision. The last thing she heard before the fog filled her mind was, "You are mine."

Then everything faded away...

Part Two

Kellan

chapter 29.

Kellan slammed the door to his old truck and stomped his way to the barn. He found only Murphy there. Kellan sighed in frustration, kicking at the dirt with his shabby brown boots. Murphy let out a loud snort, apparently not impressed with his tantrum. Kellan met the stubborn beast's large, dark eyes and thought of Veil, who'd had a way of taming them both. Overwhelmed by grief and suffocating despair, Kellan doubled over, retching, his body trembling as he sobbed. His breakdown sent Murphy into a frenzy and he began to snort, kicking the sides of his stable. Murphy then escalated to bucking in the small pen. Kellan straightened up and wiped his mouth with his shirt sleeve. He rushed to Murphy and reached out a hand, attempting to calm him. Murphy huffed with agitation but eventually allowed Kellan to touch him.

Kellan closed his eyes, focusing on his own breathing. "I miss her, Murph," he whispered. "I miss her so much."

It felt like all he had done was cry since that day. He had awoken on the side of the road with his family, groggy and confused. None of them remembered how they had gotten out of the woods, but they all remembered what they had lost. They had encountered the impossible in the forest, and though Kellan had searched the place where Veil had been taken from them for months, he was no closer to finding her. Veil was gone.

Kellan was startled by a gentle pat on his back. He turned to see his father's concerned face. "Anything today, son?" Liam asked. Unable to speak, Kellan shook his head.

They had all helped in the beginning, searching for the girl who had magically appeared in their lives. They tore through those woods, combing every inch. They had searched relentlessly until the farm started to fall apart. The newborn calves, the second crop, and the markets all played a part in their surrender. The family had resumed life as best they could, taking up Kellan's chores so that he could continue searching, but Kellan couldn't cover much ground alone.

Finally finding his voice, Kellan asked, "How are the girls and Gavin?"

Liam had to clear his throat before he could answer. "Not good... They're not good at all, son."

Maddy and Farrah had both taken the loss of their claimed sister hard. Maddy had been so traumatized over the events from the woods that Aileen and Liam had pulled her from school, choosing to complete her final year at home. Farrah felt as if she owed Veil everything. Not only had Veil brought the family closer, but she had saved Gavin—*twice*. And though Gavin's physical health was still good, his emotional wellbeing had declined, his eyes losing a little more light every day that Veil was gone. Then there was Aileen, who blamed herself for casting Veil aside so harshly.

"We're worried about you too, son," Liam continued. "It's been months with no sign of the lass...and your nightmares. You can't go on like this, Kellan; you're fading away before our very eyes. I spoke to your mum, and we both think you should consider going back to uni—"

"I'm not leaving," Kellan interrupted. "How can you even suggest it? I need her Da..." Liam, who had never seen his son break down, pulled Kellan in, hugging him hard.

"I know, son... I know. We all miss her. We just thought some distance might do you some good. We can't lose you too, Kellan." Liam tightened his arms around Kellan, and Kellan let his father comfort him. He understood his family's concern. Especially with the dreams that came to him every night, though he wasn't sure they were only dreams. *Lord, please let them be dreams.*

The roar of thunder broke Kellan and Liam apart. The wind caught the barn doors and they flew open, hitting the barn walls with a loud bang. Where the sky had been bright only moments ago, it was now a haunting gray. The wind caused havoc as it whipped across the farm, bending the grass and churning it like turbulent water. The old barn doors rattled and shook as they struggled against it.

Liam approached the doorway, his eyes widening. "What in the bleeding hell is this?"

Kellan joined his father and stuck his head out, pulling it back in just as large raindrops started to fall, pelting the ground. "I have no idea," he answered.

"Kellan! Liam!" Niall yelled. Kellan and Liam followed the sound of his shouting to see Niall sprinting up the next hill toward them. He finally reached them and doubled over, trying to pull air into his desperate lungs. Water dripped from the ends of his curls and landed on the dirt floor of the barn. His shirt sleeve clung to his arm as he reached up to wipe his face. Kellan had never seen Niall in such a state. When he recovered, he said, "Kell, you need to get to the field—they're here."

"Who is here, Niall?" Kellan asked.

"*They*, Kellan—the people from the woods." With that, he pulled them out of the barn and into the rain.

30. chapter

Kellan's lungs burned. Surprisingly, Liam and Niall kept pace with him as the three of them slipped and slid on the wet grass, reaching their destination covered in grime. The only sound was the rain and their labored breathing.

"Where are they?" Kellan asked.

"They were right here," Niall said, his head swinging from left to right, searching. "I tell you, I nearly pissed myself when they appeared."

Kellan slowly walked toward the first row of corn. The stalks were tall and thick, making it nearly impossible to see into the field.

"Hello?" Kellan called out. "Are you out there?"

"We are," came a familiar voice. The cornstalks began to shake. Kellan jumped back and lost his footing. Luckily, Liam and Niall were there to catch him. A man with a sword hanging from his hip stepped out. "You recognize me, human?" he asked, smirking.

Kellan brushed away Liam and Niall's hands, and crossed his arms. "You know I do," he said. "Where is she?"

"Not in this realm, I'm afraid." A look of regret swept across the man's face before he squared his shoulders. "It is safe to come out. They'll not try to harm us—if they're smart." Two more walked out with a third between them, his arms draped over their shoulders.

"Who are you?" Kellan asked.

The injured man answered, "No need to be frightened, I'm Darragh. This is Haven and Nessa." The woman, Nessa, resembled a porcelain figure more than a living being, too perfect to be real. Darragh nodded toward the man who had been the first to walk out of the field. "I believe you have already had the pleasure of meeting Cace."

Kellan nodded and dropped his arms to his side, freeing them for a possible fight. He had not forgotten when the man had shoved a blade in his face. "Aye, I guess you could say that," he said. "Bloody fool tried to kill me."

Cace gave Kellan a flirty wink. "I'd say I'm sorry about that, but I'm not. I wouldn't want to start our relationship off with a lie— wouldn't be proper, would it?"

Liam stepped between the two, placing one sturdy hand on Kellan's chest and holding the other out toward Cace. "I'd say that's enough of that," Liam said. "Now, why are you all here?"

Darragh dropped his arms from Haven and Nessa's shoulders to stand on his own. "We're here because you have all been parading around our woods for weeks now. We're not bothering you if we're all searching for the same thing, are we?"

Kellan took a step around his father. "Where is she?"

Darragh hung his head in shame, a feeling Kellan understood

all too well. "As Cace said, she's not in this realm."

Kellan threw out his arms as his frustration bubbled to the surface. "Then which bloody realm is she in? Yours?"

"She is—"

"Why haven't you saved her yet?" Kellan demanded. "Don't you know what's happening to her? The things I've seen!" Kellan shut his eyes and shook his head, hoping to chase away the horrifying images filling his mind. Kellan opened his eyes to see Darragh and the others exchanging the strangest of looks.

"You see her?" Darragh whispered. "That's not possible." He turned to Nessa and Haven. "You said that Veil released him from Dara's hold."

"She did," Haven assured. "We both saw her do it before they dragged her off, but the reaction—I've never seen anything like it. The power from it blew them apart."

Darragh limped toward Kellan, closing the remaining distance between them. It was a foolish act to maintain eye contact with any of them, but Kellan stood his ground as Darragh appraised him.

"It's just not possible," Darragh mumbled. "Unless... But how can that be? Those with the mix can't bear a true mark."

"True mark?" Kellan asked, his eyes lighting up. "Veil said that before. What does it mean?"

"It means you're fated. It will even tie your lives to one another if you are ever connected. If you are Veil's true mark and Dara linked the two of you, she could have unintentionally started the binding." Darragh appeared perplexed, his brow pulling down. "But only pure-blooded Sidhe can withstand it. In all our histories, there has never been a telling of a halfling, or a human of all things, wearing it. There must be some other explanation. Veil lacked in her abilities. That must be it. She failed to fully release you from Dara's tether."

Kellan didn't like the way Darragh spoke of Veil. To Darragh, she was lacking, but to Kellan, she was everything. "You must not know her very well, then," he countered. "She's so much stronger than you give her credit for."

"Oh, I think I know her quite well," Darragh argued. "After all, she's my daughter."

Kellan's body trembled with outrage, and he advanced on Darragh until their chests were touching. "Your daughter? If she's your daughter, you should already know how wonderful she is. And why haven't you done anything to help her? She's been gone for weeks, and you've done nothing."

Regret flashed across Darragh's face before it was masked by fury. "Human, you know nothing of our world. Don't you think I wanted to go after her? She's my blood!"

Kellan stood toe to toe with Darragh, the man who claimed to care so much about a daughter whose life he had signed away. Anger was what Kellan wanted to feel, but as he looked Darragh over, pity was all he could muster.

"I may not know much about the world you're from, but I do know my feelings for Veil are real. She broke the link that woman put on me—I felt it. I love Veil, perfect true mark or not, and I won't stand here and allow you to demean it."

Darragh took a step back and held Kellan's hard gaze until his own finally softened. "You really believe that, don't you?"

"I know it," Kellan answered, chest out. "With everything inside of me, I love her."

"Are you willing to die for her?" Darragh asked, his voice more serious now. "Because that's likely what awaits us if we attempt to bring her back."

"I'll face the fires of Hell if I have to."

"I'm afraid Hell's fire is not what we have to worry about," Cace chimed in. "Hell is a lot warmer than where we're going."

"Anywhere. I'll go anywhere for her."

"All right, gather your people," Darragh said as the rain finally let up. "We'll begin when we return."

"Begin what?" Niall asked, sounding as though he wasn't sure he really wanted to know.

"Training, of course. We only have a short time until the Cold Moon, and with it, Veil will be lost forever. Human minds do not fare well in our realm, and despite what you may believe, we are not the worst things to inhabit it. You will need to learn how to protect yourselves if you are to have any hope of survival." He turned, and with the assistance of the other three, headed back into the corn.

"Wait!" Kellan yelled. "How will we know when you're coming back?"

Darragh turned his head and gave Kellan a smile that chilled him to the bone. "Just wait for the storm."

31. chapter

Kellan and Liam sat in Kellan's truck. They had pulled up to the house nearly ten minutes earlier, neither getting out. A woman walked out the front door and leaned heavily against a wooden post. She didn't appear too thrilled to see them.

"Evelyn's on the porch, Da."

"I guess we'd best get this over with," Liam said with a sigh. Both men opened their doors.

Evelyn was already laying into them as they stepped out of the truck. "I don't know what this is all about, Liam, but Jack is still reeling from the incident at the farmers market. You know how fragile he is."

"Evelyn, I promise you we're not here to add to his suffering, but this is life or death. It's about the girl."

Evelyn uncrossed her arms with wary eyes, gesturing Liam

and Kellan inside. The little green house was cozy, a warm fire in the hearth fighting off the chill of autumn. Jack sat on a brown leather couch, quietly staring into the flames. Liam and Kellan sat across from him, and Evelyn sat down beside him and whispered in his ear. When she grasped his hand in hers, he looked up and gave them a small nod.

"Evelyn says you need to speak to me."

"Aye, Jack," Liam answered. "It's about Veil, the girl you met at the market."

Jack closed his eyes, his face etched with regret. "I didn't mean to scare her... She just looks so much like Maeve."

Liam reached out to squeeze Jack's knee. "I know you didn't, Jack," he said, sitting back once more. "We're not here about that, but I do need to talk to you about Veil...and Maeve." Liam turned to Kellan a final time, silently asking if Kellan was sure this was what he wanted to do. Kellan nodded. Liam cleared his throat before he began. "Jack, mate, there really is no easy way to say any of this, but here it goes. A few months ago, Kellan was driving home from Killarney when he came across a girl, Veil, in the road. But she wasn't alone." Jack and Evelyn stared at Kellan, their foreheads wrinkled with confusion.

Kellan took up where his father had left off. "She appeared out of nowhere in the middle of a storm. There was another woman, Veil's guardian, and she did something to me. She forced her way into my mind and made me take Veil under my protection."

"Could you hear it?" Jack asked, his eyes wild. "The music, the voices? Could you hear them?"

"I could. But Dara's voice was the strongest. She linked me to Veil, and I had no choice but to bring Veil home with me."

Evelyn slowly brought her hand to her mouth. She took a moment to compose herself before asking, "What does this have to do with Maeve?"

Kellan looked at her sadly before turning back to Jack. "Veil is Maeve's daughter."

"I knew it," Jack whispered. "I *knew* it! See Evelyn, she's alive!" He leaped up from the couch. "Where is she, Liam? Where is my sister?"

Liam gently placed his hand on Jack's shoulder. "Mate, I think you really should sit back down."

Evelyn rose from her seat and grabbed Jack's hand again. She kept her eyes on his and said, "Go on, Liam, let's hear it."

Liam let out a heavy sigh, glancing to Kellan to finish the grisly tale. Kellan kept his eyes glued to his lap. "Veil said her mum died during childbirth—her birth." Jack's eyes stayed locked on Evelyn's, neither of them reacting to the devastating news.

"Jack, I know this is a shock, mate, but there's more," Liam said, his voice wary.

Jack shook his head and blinked, letting the tears fall. "What more could there be?"

"Your niece, Jack," Liam answered. "They have Veil."

"Who has her?" Evelyn asked.

"We call them saes and fairies, but Veil said they are known as the Sidhe," Kellan explained. "All the stories we grew up hearing are true."

Jack desperately searched Evelyn's eyes, and something appeared to pass between them. Without taking her eyes off Jack, Evelyn said, "How can we help?"

32. chapter

Veil thrashed her arms as far as the chains would allow. Her blood-soaked arm shook from the effort it took to keep it from him. Colden laughed hysterically, dodging her swings. The chains clanked as he pushed her arm flat against the stone wall, displaying her wounds as one would a work of art. Colden's pupils expanded, spreading like bleeding ink. He placed his hand over a patch of ice that clung to the rocks. The icy shards began to quiver and expanded to surround Veil's arm in a spiked cage, locking it in place.

"Now, let's see how sweet you are," Colden purred. He leaned in and glided his nose across her wrist, smearing the blood and hovering over her pulsing veins. Veil struggled against the ice, her chest heaving as her fear threatened to choke her. As his tongue raked over the mangled meat of her palm, the stinging sensation sliced through her exposed nerves like razor blades. A horrifying scream left her mouth, the last she could summon before she succumbed to the darkness.

Veil sensed a presence next to her, but she did not dare open her eyes. She lay on what she guessed was a bed, though she didn't know how she had gotten there. The last thing she remembered was the image of Colden's dark eyes, filled with ecstasy, and her blood dripping from his teeth.

She felt a cold hand grasp her own and a sharp stinging pain. She tried to pull free as something rubbed across her sensitive wounds, but the stranger's grip held tight. She opened her eyes to find a man sitting beside her, still cradling her hand. He was tall, his long and lanky body underfed. Most of his dusky skin was covered by dark, tattered dressings, and his long black hair was beautiful, even in its neglected state. He tended to her injuries, saying nothing, his body moving systematically.

"Who are you?" Veil asked. But the man didn't acknowledge her or pause in his movements. Tired of being ignored, Veil pushed his hand away. "I said, *who are you?*" Tremors shook the man's hand and spread to the rest of his body. Beads of sweat formed on his brow as he fought to reclaim her hand. He struggled, the muscles in his neck contracting and straining. Understanding took hold of her: he fought because he was clouded. "Look at me," she instructed. "Keep your eyes on mine." The man's entire body quaked as he fought harder against her, but the connection came easily. Ever since that terrible day in the woods, it bubbled right beneath her skin. Veil's eyes remained focused on his pupils, and she asked, "What is your name?"

The man grunted, and blood began to pour from his nose. "Daniel."

Veil took the cloth from his hand and gently held it to his nose to stop the bleeding. "Daniel, I won't harm you," she reassured. "Just keep your eyes on mine and listen. You are no longer bound. Your mind is your own once more, do you understand?" She waited, all the while patiently trying to pull him back. The moment he finally broke loose of his clouding, the light of life returned to him. His large brown eyes bulged out of his gaunt face, holding confusion and fear within them. *He must have been under for so long.* "I won't hurt you, Daniel," Veil whispered. "Come back to me now." Daniel looked around the dark room like a frightened animal seeking an escape. "It's all right. It will all be all right now."

"Who are you?" Daniel asked gruffly.

"I'm Veil. How long have you been here?"

"I-I'm not sure." Though his face was haggard from the abuse, he appeared to be only a few years older than she was.

"Were you taken as a child?" she asked. He chose to nod rather than speaking. "Do you remember your family?"

Daniel's brow pulled down in concentration as he searched his memory. "I remember a woman with braided hair holding me on her lap," he said. "I think she may have been my mother."

A smile tugged at Veil's lips, the first in months. Daniel's words were filled with light, and she was pleasantly surprised that he had kept such tenderness. The sinister acts perpetrated within these wicked walls were enough to corrupt the purest of hearts, and Daniel had been confined in this grim place for a long time.

"You're not like them... The others, I mean," Daniel said.

Veil shook her head. "No. I'll never be like them."

"But you have their eyes…"

Veil shook her head again and gently took hold of his hand. "I do share their blood, but I am half human. I've been called a dirty halfling my whole life."

"Were you taken too?"

Veil turned her face away from Daniel to hide her tears. "In a way, yes, but not the same as you." Veil told Daniel her story. She told him of the agreement that had led her to flee her home. Of the loving family that had sincerely accepted her. Of those who had sacrificed everything to protect her. And of Kellan. "I dream of him often," she said, her voice heavy with sorrow. "In my dreams he searches for me endlessly. He calls out my name, but silence is all that answers him."

Daniel stayed quiet for some time. Then he squeezed her hand and said, "I know this place, Veil. I know their routines, and I know their weaknesses. We can get out together. We can escape this dreadful place." Veil pitied Daniel for his naïveté. Neither of them could leave. She was tied to the vow, and Daniel had surely eaten the enchanted food. They were both trapped.

Veil didn't get the chance to explain to Daniel why they couldn't escape, for at that moment the door to her room creaked open. Veil panicked and grabbed Daniel's face, whispering, "You have to pretend. They won't hesitate to put you back under if they know." Daniel nodded, taking up the cloth and bandages he had brought with him. He kept his eyes down and resumed wrapping Veil's hand.

In walked a woman carrying a silver tray. Her stern blue eyes were set above strong cheekbones, and her face was framed by the darkest hair Veil had ever seen on a Sidhe.

"You still haven't finished, human?" She sneered. "We may have to remind you of your place."

"Yes, madam," Daniel answered, trying to keep his voice monotone. The woman studied the back of Daniel's head while he finished securing the wrap around Veil's hand.

"Is there something you needed?" Veil asked, using her cattiest tone in hopes of distracting the woman away from Daniel.

"Colden said you had some fire in you." She chuckled. "I like fire." Veil squirmed under the woman's lustful stare which made the woman laugh harder. "No worries, sweet," she said. "Lorcan has forbidden anyone from touching you until after your bonding, and Colden has never been good at sharing." The woman tilted her head and looked Veil up and down before continuing. "I am his favorite pastime though, so he may share with me if I ask him nicely."

Veil jutted out her chin. "I'm not afraid of you."

"Then you are a fool, sweet. No matter. You've been summoned, and apparently that means I must be the one to feed and fetch you. Like I have nothing better to do than play chaperone to a dirty human lover."

Daniel's eyes widened. Veil watched in horror as he moved to speak. She hurried to cover his words with her own. "Well, I guess we shouldn't keep anyone waiting. Thank you, kind sir, for tending to me."

The woman snorted in disgust. "Disgraceful." She placed the tray on the end of the bed. "Hurry up and eat so that we can get this over with." The food on the tray shone like glass but was the color of a moonless night.

"I'm afraid I've lost my appetite."

The woman shrugged, examining her pristinely manicured nails rather than looking at Veil. "Makes no difference to me. Give it to the human you seem to care for so much."

"I'd rather I not be the one to poison him."

"You know I didn't believe it, but it's true; you really know nothing. We're not like your pathetic clan. We don't have to alter the food to ensure our humans stay. Have you looked outside? They wouldn't survive out there, and even if they did, we like it when they run."

Veil's eyes widened. They didn't curse their food. The woman turned sharply and walked out. Veil was obviously expected to follow, but as she tried to leave, Daniel gripped her hand. His eyes begged her not to go.

She gave him a reassuring smile and whispered, "All will be fine, Daniel. Stay here and stay safe." She pulled her hand free and walked out the door.

Veil tried to keep up, but her feet were still bare and tender from the torture they'd already endured.

"Can't you hurry up?" the woman snapped.

"We don't all have the luxury of fur boots," Veil muttered. The woman cackled and raised her long, deep blue skirt indecently high.

"What, these old things?" She blew Veil a kiss before letting the material fall from her hands and over her blanched skin once more.

Veil rolled her eyes at the woman's audacious behavior. "Do you all act like this?"

"Afraid so," the woman sang. "But I take pride in ranking at the top."

"Will you at least tell me your name?"

"Exactly what good would it do, hmm? It's not like we're

going to be friends... Well, we might get a little friendly—if Colden allows it, that is." The way she looked at Veil made Veil's stomach turn.

"I'll never belong to him."

The woman laughed so hard, she could barely stand. The fit threw her into the wall which she clung to keep from falling over. Veil stopped and watched her with wary eyes. She was clearly insane. Suddenly, she pushed off the wall, launching herself at Veil like a predator attacking its prey. She stopped mere inches from Veil's face. Her breath reeked of old blood. The woman's bright eyes danced as she grabbed the back of Veil's head.

"Now, you listen to me, sweet. You have belonged to Colden—to our entire clan—from the moment you took your first breath. We all know your history and the glory you will bring us. So you might as well come to terms with your fate." The woman pulled Veil's face even closer. "And my name is Morrigan." Morrigan turned and skipped down the hall, humming an eerie tune. She stopped at a large archway and waited for Veil with an all-knowing smirk. As soon as Veil was close enough, Morrigan shoved her through the archway.

Horror-struck faces encased in icy tombs stared at Veil. There were hundreds of them lining the walls, each frozen in a unique pose. Some kneeled with hands raised in defense, others stood with mouths open wide in silent screams. What they did share was the same look of terror. *This is their Saeculum.*

"What's the matter, human lover?" Morrigan taunted. "I thought you would appreciate our collection. After all, it's quite a sight, don't you agree? I'm surprised your beloved cousin didn't tell you, but I guess he was a little preoccupied with warmer bodies."

"You're cruel," Veil hissed. "You're all cruel."

"Oh, I've upset the sacred one," Morrigan said, feigning a frown. "Whatever will I do?" She rolled her eyes before pulling Veil to her feet with enough force to bruise Veil's arm. "Right through here, sweet. Fate awaits."

Veil fought to bring her courage to the surface. She was so much more than the passive girl who had escaped the barrows all those months ago. She was strong. Dara wouldn't have wanted her to show these monsters one ounce of fear. She squared her shoulders and marched past Morrigan, into the polar crypt.

When they reached the throne room Veil's resolve momentarily faltered. In the center of the room lay three of the massive beasts that had taken Dara's life. The wolves casually stretched, not at all intimidated by her presence. Veil glanced around the room. Guards loomed over her, all in dark blue cloaks, their helmets polished to a mirror finish. Her eyes met Lorcan's. He sat on his lavish silver throne with Colden at his side, lounging on a throne equally as grand.

"Ah, there she is," Lorcan said, his eyes sparkling. "I'm afraid I've been preoccupied with planning the Cold Moon ceremony. I have quite missed your beautiful face, my dear." Veil stubbornly ignored him. "Come now, surely you have missed me as well?"

Veil crossed her arms. "Can't say I have."

Lorcan snorted at her insolence. "My son told me that you haven't been adjusting to your new home very well."

"This is not my home," she spat.

Lorcan chuckled as he rose from his throne. He casually descended the stairs, stopping a few feet in front of her. "You know, not even the bravest Sidhe would dare speak to me in such a way. Most look up to me from their knees."

Veil stood tall, unfazed by his threat. "I'm not most Sidhe."

"No, you most certainly are not, but you will learn your place. One way or another."

Veil bowed, her eyes locked on Lorcan's. "Do what you will.

You can't possibly hurt me any more than you already have." The entire room erupted in laughter.

"I do love a challenge, my dear." He turned to Colden, his expression darkening. "But there are certain things that must wait until the return of the Cold Moon. The histories say the covetable are precious entities, and we must not forcibly take from them what does not belong to us, blood or otherwise, until they become ours through the binding. We must honor our histories, don't you agree?" Colden didn't appear too happy about his father berating him in front of the others; he sat back on his throne with a pinched face and crossed arms. Lorcan shook his head at Colden's childish behavior. "We're quite lucky Colden was not the one to break her skin. But I suppose boys will be boys." Lorcan turned back to Veil, his smile returning. "Now, where were we?" he asked. "Oh, yes. Restrain her." Four guards surrounded Veil. She lashed out, fighting with all she had, but was overpowered and forced to her knees. Lorcan licked his lips, holding out his hand. "Bring me the brand."

"No! Veil, no!"

Kellan fell out of his bed, his knees smacking hard against the scuffed wooden floor. He continued to tremble long after the nightmare was over and fought to draw in a shaky breath. As with all of his dreams about Veil, it was like he had been watching a scary movie. Only this wasn't a movie; their minds were connected. He could see everything she was seeing, hear her thoughts... He could feel her pain.

Kellan's door was suddenly thrown open. Seconds later, Liam

was there, hovering over him. Kellan heard a gasp and turned to see Aileen standing in the doorway, cradling Maddy in her arms. They all had tears in their eyes. Kellan's sweat-covered body seized again and he whimpered from where he kneeled on the floor.

Liam sank to his knees by Kellan's side. "Are you all right, son?" he asked.

"No," Kellan whispered. "And neither is she."

33. chapter

Kellan sat in the den, grinding his teeth and numbly watching the flames blaze within the confines of the stone hearth. It had been two weeks since the meeting with Darragh and the others, and they had yet to return. The waiting ate at him. He tried to distract his thoughts by returning to work on the farm. The second crop was ready, and they had spent an entire week harvesting. Seeing the vacant field where there had once been precious growth was just another reminder that Veil was gone. Kellan slipped deeper into depression. Nighttime was the worst.

"Are your dreams always so bad?" Evelyn asked. Kellan nodded, not bothering to look at her. Liam had offered to have her and Jack stay with them on the farm, and they had agreed. They wanted to be there when Darragh and the others returned. Although Kellan knew it was for the best, he couldn't help feeling bitter when Aileen had fixed up Connor's old room for them—*Veil's room.*

Kellan closed his eyes, the images invading again. He had seen Veil, appearing worse than she had the time before. She had lost weight, just as Kellan had, and her eyes, which had once been so alive, were dim and empty. He had shared her panic as she was overwhelmed and held down by hulking figures in dark cloaks. He had screamed with her when the black iron brand was pushed into her delicate skin. He had even smelled her searing flesh. It was a scent he would never forget.

"Mine were like that," Jack whispered. "Like I was still there living it." Kellan glanced over, hearing the anguish in Jack's voice. Evelyn, who was sitting as close to Jack as she possibly could, wrapped her arm around him.

"Do they ever get better?" Kellan asked.

"The nightmares got less intense over time, but they never left me completely. I think once you've been touched by their magic, it sticks. It's like an old wound—even though you're no longer bleeding, the scar will always be there to remind you."

Kellan closed his eyes. He would never be able to move on. Veil had opened his foolish eyes to what was right in front of him. The life he had wanted so badly to escape was beautiful and blessed. He had a family that loved and accepted him, a luxury she had never had. He wanted to spend the rest of his days making up for that. He had to get her back.

Rory cleared his throat. "It looks overcast today."

"Same as yesterday, and the day before that," Niall pointed out.

"Aye, you're right, mate." Rory hung his head. Maddy sat by his side, as she usually did, and patted his back, but he appeared oblivious to her. Kellan wished Rory would pull his head out of his rear. Even though he gave Rory a hard time, he wanted his sister to be happy and didn't have a problem with the idea of the two of them together. His little sister wasn't so little anymore. Maddy had turned eighteen the month after Veil was taken, though she had refused to celebrate until Veil was home, safe and sound.

A light rain splattered against the old windows. Everyone knew better than to get their hopes up, but they were all waiting for the storm that would signal Darragh and Cace's return. The storm they had first arrived in had been more intense than any Kellan had ever seen. The air had crackled as the skies lit up. Kellan had thought he'd heard whispering voices riding the wind as it blew. Kellan waited with bated breath as the rain picked up. Suddenly, vivid blue lightning flashed across the sky. It was followed by booming thunder that was so loud, Kellan could feel the vibrations from it under his feet. Everyone gasped.

Aileen was the first one up. She sprinted to the kitchen door and practically threw it off its hinges. Kellan and the others were right on her heels. The heavy downpour made it almost impossible to see so they stood silent, listening. They had all but given up when, finally, the strange wind started to blow.

"To the fields!" Niall yelled. Everyone leaped from the shelter of the house and sprinted across the farm.

When they reached the edge of the cornfields, Aileen asked, "Where are they?"

With the corn gone, Kellan could see all the way across the field, but no one was there. He turned his face toward the sky and prayed the rain would cover his tears. "I don't know, Mum," he said. "They said they would come... They said to wait for the storm."

Gavin, who hadn't said a single word since his rescue from the woods, began to shout, "Ve-Ve!"

Farrah met Kellan's wide eyes. "Where, Gavin?" she asked. "Where is Ve-Ve?" The boy struggled to look over his mother's shoulder, fighting so hard she nearly dropped him.

Kellan followed his nephew's line of sight. "The barn."

The barn doors were securely closed. They could hear nothing from inside, not even the horses. Kellan and Niall were the first to step forward and together, they pulled on the wooden handles. With a little effort, the doors swung wide open. At first, silence was all that met them, and then they heard voices.

"Tell me, does all your kind prefer to stay filthy?" Nessa asked, disgusted.

"Come now, Nessa, manners," Cace laughed.

"At least we have the sense to get out of the rain."

"Stop, the both of you." Darragh sighed. He turned toward the door. "Though she is right; you should come in out of the rain." Kellan cautiously stepped into the barn and regarded their strange guests. He counted five this time. They had brought another woman with them who was tending to Murphy's mane.

"You might want to be a wee bit careful with him," said Kellan.

"Save your breath, human," Cace stated. "I can assure you Calla knows how to handle herself around horses."

Calla rolled her eyes. "Don't mind him. He's just jealous I'm not handling him instead. You have beautiful creatures here. Maybe a little small, but beautiful nonetheless."

"Thank you...I think." Kellan turned to Darragh. "What took you so long?"

"We've been preparing. I don't think you understand what awaits—" Jack's angry fist connected with Darragh's jaw and Darragh, still weak from his sentence in the Saeculum, fell to the floor.

Jack stood over Darragh and glared. "Oh, but I do."

34. chapter

"Relax your shoulders," Calla instructed. "There you go. Slowly breathe in and out—now release."

"Look, Calla—bullseye!" Maddy cheered. "I did it!"

"Brilliant job, Maddy," Kellan said, a proud smile on his thinning face.

Calla laughed, and together they walked down to where the target was mounted on a bale of hay. The arrow had hit dead center, and Calla patted Maddy's back. "Well done, Maddy."

While Maddy soaked up the praise, Kellan thought about how far they had all come with their training. Calla and the others had spent weeks trying to prepare everyone for the dangers they would encounter. The training consisted of exercises such as hand-to-hand combat, sword fighting, and archery. Of all their lessons, the mental skills were the most important. They needed to learn to protect their minds from clouding.

They were only days away from the Cold Moon. When Kellan had questioned Darragh's decision to delay Veil's rescue, his only reply had been that Veil wouldn't be harmed until she was bound under the Cold Moon—but Kellan knew better.

"Do you think we're ready yet, Calla?" Kellan asked.

Calla thought long and hard before she answered. "Our world was never meant for humans. They are kept only for our needs and under our watch. They cannot survive on their own."

"But you and Veil lived there."

"That is true," Calla said. "But you must know that while creatures like Veil and I exist, we are not human." Kellan repeated Calla's words over and over within his mind, each repetition bringing more doubt that they would be able to rescue Veil. Calla laid a hand on his arm. "We will get her back. The journey will be dangerous, make no mistake, but I know we will get her back. Have faith, and try to keep your strength up."

"She's right, Kell," Maddy agreed. Seeing the worry in her eyes, which were usually bright and carefree, gutted him. Kellan knew it was obvious how much his health had deteriorated. His skin was drab and his eyes were spiritless, like that of a corpse. He only ate when his parents forced him to, and he only slept when the fatigue was so great that he basically collapsed. He turned away to escape her sadness.

Down the hill, Rory was sparring with Cace and appeared to be losing. Kellan put on the best smile he could muster and winked at Maddy. "Looks like Rory may need you to protect him. He's getting his arse handed to him."

Maddy's face turned scarlet. She turned around just in time to see Rory fall to the ground after Cace connected a blow to his stomach.

She smiled when Cace offered his hand to help Rory up, then she lowered her head. "Do you two believe in true love and soulmates?"

Kellan was about to answer but Calla beat him to it. "Of course. I've seen it. Do you not?"

"I want to," Maddy said, her smile gone. "But I'm not sure it will happen for me."

Kellan didn't know what to say. Everyone knew she had eyes for Rory, but he treated Maddy like a child. He acted as if he had no clue of her feelings for him, even though she did a terrible job of hiding them. Kellan shook his head. He turned to Calla, hoping she may have the right words to cheer Maddy up, but she was watching Rory and did not look impressed.

"Are you sure the red-haired one is *the* one?"

Maddy's face flew up, her eyes wide. Kellan let out a chuckle, but his amusement faded when he saw that there was fear within them. He walked over to her, delicately placing both of his hands on her shoulders. "It's all right, Maddy," he reassured. "Everyone knows... Everyone but Rory. If he ever comes to his senses, he'll have no problems from the rest of us."

Maddy wrapped Kellan in a bone-crushing hug. She turned to Calla and said, "Rory may not be everyone's cup of tea, but yes, I believe he is the one for me."

Calla glanced back toward Rory and Cace, but her eyes were focused solely on Cace. "It's always the ones out of reach who capture our hearts, isn't it?" She turned back and took Maddy's hand. "If he is the one, don't give up on him."

Kellan grabbed Maddy's other hand. "Come on, ladies, let's go see if Rory survived."

The sun was soon gone, and they all sat around the fire Connor had built. Kellan and Niall sat with Cace, listening to his lecture on the importance of balance when it came to swordplay. Calla sat on Cace's other side, wearing a bright smile, Maddy whispering in her ear. Across the fire, Nessa was nestled close to Haven.

Aileen joined them, carrying a tray of tea. "Would you like some tea, Darragh?"

Darragh politely accepted the chipped teacup and brought it up to his mouth, looking across the fire as he sipped. Darragh set his cup down again and said to Jack, "It appears you have something to say." Everyone around the fire stopped to listen.

"You took my sister. Made her give you a child. She was barely eighteen, and you stole her life. You stole my life."

Darragh stared at Jack over the fire, the flames dancing his eyes. "I admit that in the beginning I took what was not mine, but Maeve was not a slave to the clouding when we found love—she chose to stay. She was thrilled when she found out she was pregnant, as was I. As for your life, what happened to you was not my doing. I am the one who dragged you out so you would be found."

"And why would you do that?"

"Because even with her mind deeply under my influence, all Maeve would do was whimper for her brother. You should be grateful."

"Grateful?" Jack stood, almost knocking Evelyn from her seat. "Look at me! They all thought I was crazy! And when I stood by my story, my mum and da threatened to put me away. To this day they barely speak to me—they blame me. Evelyn is the only one who listened, even though I bloody well knew she didn't believe me. It wasn't only Maeve and me that paid the price but Evelyn as well. She sacrificed everything to stay with me."

"Kellan!" Niall yelled.

Kellan grabbed at his chest as he fell from the hay bale he was using for a seat. They all crowded over him as a frothy foam erupted from his mouth. His muscles spasmed so intensely that his body jerked off the ground.

Then Kellan's nightmare began.

Daniel untied Veil's elaborate dress and helped peel it from her body. He dipped the cloth into the cold water and dabbed at Veil's seeping wound. Though many days had passed, Veil's wound had not begun to heal. Veil remembered the day vividly. Colden had dragged her back to her room and demanded with amusement that Daniel care for her. And care for her is exactly what Daniel had done every day since.

"It'll never go away, will it?" Veil asked, her voice strangely calm.

"No," Daniel answered. "The brands are made from the iron they use to torture the puca. Their blood is practically poison. Once they push the cold iron into your skin, it will never heal."

"Cold? But it was so hot."

"It's so cold that it feels hot," Daniel explained. "It burns just the same. I'm afraid I don't know what it means, though."

Veil peeked over her shoulder and studied what she could see of the brand. There was a circle with two points: one at the top and one at the bottom. The points were pierced with what resembled a single large spear running down the center of the circle. Veil slid her arm through the robe Daniel had laid out for her, trying to avoid rubbing it against the sensitive brand.

"It doesn't matter, does it? Lorcan let Colden mark me as his own, and that is what I'll always be."

Daniel walked around to face Veil, folding her hands within his own. "Don't talk like that. We're going to get out of here, exactly like we talked about, but you have to eat and sleep or else you won't make it past the doors."

Veil knew she wouldn't make it past the doors anyway. She had taken a vow and couldn't escape. *But Daniel can.* She would find a way to get him out of the icy wastelands of Cold Valley, but he would have to travel alone. As soon as she set foot outside the rocky fortress, her life would finally come to an end. But Daniel would be free and, in a way, so would she.

"You're right, I'm sorry," Veil said.

"I promise we can do this," Daniel insisted. "It won't be easy, but together I believe we can."

"Yes, but we must be careful. I can't let anything happen to you, Daniel."

Daniel, who seemed to be finding more and more of himself, smiled. It was a mesmerizing sight.

"You really are nothing like them, are you?" he asked.

Veil returned his smile and shook her head. "No, I'm not."

Daniel sat down next to Veil on the bed. "To get out, we will need to wait until they hold a ceremony. They'll all be gathered in one spot, consumed with bloodlust. I think that's our best chance."

Veil studied the room that doubled as her torture chamber and closed her eyes, the horrid memories filling her mind. "They practice that here. They've made me watch."

Daniel nodded, staring down at the bed. He slid his sleeve up, revealing deep scars slashed across his arm. "I've been in those chains and on this bed, but when they hold a celebration, they gather in the Red Room. I'm sure you can guess as to why it's named that."

Veil stared at Daniel's arm until she couldn't stand it any longer. She reached out and skimmed a single fingertip along one of the deepest scars. Most of Daniel's scars were old and faded, but the one she followed was an angry pink. *Fresh.* The thought of being made to watch Daniel suffer in such a way made Veil tremble.

"We're getting you out of here, I promise you. When is the next time they'll all be gathered in the Red Room?"

"I have heard the others speak of a big celebration—the biggest their clan has ever seen. I'm not sure when it is yet, but there are whispers of many visitors set to arrive any day now."

The biggest their clan has ever seen. It had to be the binding ceremony; the Cold Moon was days away. "We can't wait until then. That celebration involves me, and I don't see them allowing me much alone time. We have to get you out before that happens."

"Do you have any suggestions?" he asked.

"We should go tonight. I've made it to the doors before."

Daniel shook his head. "I don't think that is the best plan. We may make it to the doors before someone notices us gone, but we need time to get far enough away that the wolves will have trouble tracking us."

"How can we give ourselves more time?" Veil asked.

Daniel thought for a moment. "Have they taken you to the well yet?"

271

"Do I even want to know what that is?"

"I doubt you do," he answered, shuddering. "The well is what they call one of the watery caverns they have here. It has a deep pool—runoff from somewhere outside. Their magic keeps it warm. They use it for bathing, among other things."

"What other things?"

"They congregate there most nights with humans that have outlived their usefulness. They call it playing with their food. The water is blood red."

"And you want us to go there?" Veil shrieked.

Daniel's finger flew up to his mouth to shush her. "No, I don't," he said. "But if we can't wait until a Red Room gathering, I think the well is our only option. When they are drunk with bloodlust, slipping away should be more feasible."

"And if we can't slip away, what then?"

"I know the risk is great, but it's our best chance."

Veil couldn't believe she was even considering it, but it did seem like their only option. "All right, we'll go to the well tonight."

Although Veil was guarded at all times, obtaining permission to go to the well was not difficult. She'd simply told the guards posted outside her chamber that she was in desperate need of a bath. She cringed when they offered to take her to the well themselves, their faces filled with lust.

"That won't be necessary," she insisted. "I have my human, and I do not wish to share. I'm sure you understand."

"Looks like the girl is finally beginning to understand how we do things here," the larger of the two said. "But unfortunately, my lady, your privileges do not extend to roaming freely about—I'm sure you understand. If you'd like to take your treat and go, we'll be more than happy to show you the way."

Veil tried to ignore her nausea and dropped into a curtsy. She made it all the way to the next hall before she could no longer ignore her stomach. She gagged on her rising stomach acid, her eyes watering. Daniel pulled her hair away from her face with one hand and rubbed her back with the other. His actions garnered inquisitive looks from their two escorts.

"All is well, masters," Daniel said, still playing the role of clouded servant. "Allow me a moment to tend to my mistress." Daniel kept his eyes on Veil, whispering in her ear. "If everything goes in our favor, we'll be free of this nightmare come nightfall."

"I'm sorry," Veil said. "I can't believe you've endured this for so long."

"I won't say I was lucky to be clouded, but there truly can be bliss in ignorance."

Veil shook her head and gave him a sad smile. "I've been taken into the fog as well, and I would rather face the torture than have my free will stripped from me. You deserve so much better."

"We both do," he agreed. "Now let's go free ourselves."

Veil set her mind to the task and allowed Daniel to lead her deeper into their frozen prison.

The entrance to the well was an ominous black tunnel which appeared to stretch on for miles. Veil could see her breath and feel the harsh jagged rocks beneath her feet. She could hear nothing—not the guards, not their footsteps, not even the water Daniel claimed was there.

Hoping the answer would be 'no,' Veil asked, "Daniel, have you ever been to the well?"

"I have...once," he admitted. "I lived through it, but the things I endured made me wish for the shackled wall. Prepare yourself. Our goal is to get in and slip out without drawing too much attention. I'm not sure how easy that will be, considering they seem to have a taste for you..." He glanced at Veil and cringed. "Sorry, bad choice of words."

The ghost of a smile haunted Veil's lips. "It's all right," she said. "I hope those beastly guards are easily distracted."

"Me too," he agreed, linking his arm with hers. "Shall we?" Veil clung to his arm as they took their first steps into the blackness together. They traveled for a lengthy time before lights appeared. Clusters of bronze lanterns were woven into the rock wall and glimmered like they were dancing to an unknown beat. She could hear the water long before she could see it. Daniel stalled where the tunnel opened to reveal the cavern. In the middle lay the pool. The water's current picked up where it flowed through a large hole in the back wall. At least a dozen naked Sidhe waded in the crimson water, and each had at least one clouded human within arm's reach. The humans were unnaturally still.

"Well, what are you waiting on, my lady?" The guard gave her a little shove forward. His question brought unwanted attention Veil's way, and to her utter astonishment, a familiar voice rang out.

"Well, what a pleasant surprise. Has the sacred one decided to join us mere peasants?" Morrigan asked, wading toward where Veil and Daniel stood. Like the others, she was entirely nude. Her dark hair dripped red down her alabaster body. "See anything you like, human lover? I must warn you, I'm much more durable than what you usually go for." Her body shook with laughter.

"Trust me," Veil answered. "I'm nowhere near attracted to you. And it has nothing to do with your breed." Though meant as an insult, Veil's words only made Morrigan laugh harder.

"You are so bold today," she said. "Much more than the last time I saw you. How is your shoulder, by the way?"

Veil flinched at the mention of the brand. "That's none of your concern."

"Whose concern is it?" Morrigan asked, winking. "Colden's, perhaps? Maybe we should ask him?" She lowered her hands until her palms grazed the water's surface. Her face froze in pure concentration until the water began to bubble and rise. With a small wave of her hand, it parted. Colden, who had been submerged, stood with his lean, muscular back to them. His white hair was stained red, and in his arms, he held a woman no older than Veil. The woman choked and coughed, trying to expel the water from within her lungs.

"Morrigan, you'd better have a good reason for disturbing me."

Morrigan rolled her eyes. She lifted her hands and let the water fall back into place. "Oh calm yourself, Colden. I have something you're going to like even better."

Colden stood and threw his head back, laughing as he turned around. "I seriously doubt—" He released the woman from his arms with a splash and shoved her away. Her body floated until it bumped into another Sidhe, who snatched her up with a grin.

Veil had seen a lot of skin back in the barrows but had never seen a man so completely exposed. Kellan had once rushed into the kitchen without a shirt on in low-hanging pants, but that was as close as she had come. And Colden was nothing like Kellan. Where Kellan was warm and stout with skin that freckled from the sun, Colden was icy and slender with skin the same shade as the snow that gripped the fortress' barbarous windows.

Colden approached, flexing his muscles. "I stand corrected," he said. Veil squirmed under Colden's scrutiny. She and Daniel had known their plan was high risk, but with both Colden and Morrigan here, she had no idea how they were going to get out of this unscathed. *So much for going unnoticed.*

"Maybe you should ask her why she's here, hmm? I don't think the human lover suddenly had a change of heart when it comes to our ways."

Colden snatched Morrigan's arms into a tight grip. "Do not insult my bride-to-be," he ordered. "She will be your queen one day."

Morrigan turned her eyes to Veil. They were full of fury. Veil held her stare and said, "It won't be by choice, I promise you that."

Colden stepped out of the water, dropping Morrigan's arm. Veil backed away until her shoulder blades scraped up against the rough rock behind her. Daniel began to move to her side, but Veil sent him a stern look.

Colden clamped his hands around Veil's upper arms, the red staining her sleeves. "I know what you think of my people, but you haven't seen anything yet," he threatened. "Morrigan isn't the only one who needs to watch her tongue."

Veil wanted to spit in his eyes, but she could see Daniel's terrified face over Colden's shoulder. There was no way to escape together, but she could get him out. She put on a mask of sincerity and answered, "My apologies, my lord—I meant no offense. I only came for a bath, nothing more."

Colden appeared to enjoy Veil's submissiveness as much as he claimed to like her fire. She shuddered, watching his body vibrate. "Then a bath you shall have, my lady," he said, bowing his head. "Why don't you undress and bring in your toy?"

"It looks like you have plenty here," she answered. "I no longer need him." She casually waved her hand toward Daniel. Daniel stubbornly stood still. He was coming perilously close to revealing that he was no longer clouded.

"I said leave!" she shouted.

"You heard your mistress, human," Colden said, still staring at Veil. "Go."

"As you wish," Daniel said finally. As he took his first steps away from Veil, her heart ached.

"Kellan, answer me, son!" Liam yelled.

Kellan slowly blinked his eyes open. He brought up his hands to cover his face, trying to hide from all he had seen. He had never had a vision of Veil while he was awake, and none of his dreams, as bad as they were, had ever been anything like what had just flashed through his mind. All he had seen was red. Red-stained bodies floating in a red pool, and red tinted lips that dripped red from their butchers' lips. The metallic tang still lingered on Kellan's tongue.

Veil had been there, in the middle of it all, covering what skin she could with her arms. The others taunted her and pulled at her hair. A lifeless body floated by, its fingers grazing her ribcage as it passed, and she lost all sense. Laughter rang out, and a strong pair of hands grabbed her by the waist. Her fear was so thick that Kellan could smell it. Her head was yanked back, and she was forced to look into a set of green eyes. The last thing Kellan had heard before all the red turned to black was a malicious voice demanding, "Look at me."

Kellan didn't know he'd spoken his nightmare aloud until Cace whispered, "The well."

"What's the well?" Niall asked.

"Not a place any human, or someone with the mix like Veil, ever wants to be," he answered.

Darragh stood and began to pace. Then he stopped and stared up at the moon, which was nearly full. "It's time," he said, closing his eyes. "We leave at dawn."

35. chapter

Darragh and Cace led the way through the woods. The air smelled of the rain that had fallen earlier, which still clung to the leaves of the trees. Kellan had come the same way many times in his prior searches. He must have walked right past the border.

"What's the matter?" Cace asked.

"Nothing," Kellan answered. "Just bloody well pissed at myself for not finding you when you were right here the whole time."

"Don't be too hard on yourself. The border is well hidden, and not many of your kind can see it. Of course, that little boy can. You should have brought him along with you."

Kellan rolled his eyes. He would never admit that the thought of bringing Gavin had crossed his mind, not that Farrah would have allowed it. She and Connor had been the only ones to stay behind.

They wanted to keep Gavin safe. The group had said their tearful farewells, and Connor and Farrah had made them promise to return safely.

"I still think it's a mistake to have Nessa with us," Cace stated. He spoke loud enough for all to hear, including Nessa.

Nessa marched right up to him and stood with both hands placed angrily on her hips. Cace towered over her but she threw her nose in the air. "Are you seriously still going on about this? I told you I wanted to help."

"And I ask again, why should we trust you? You have done nothing but help in making Veil's life hell."

For the first time, Kellan witnessed Nessa break down. Her tears fell like rivers down her too-perfect face and she apologized, an act which obviously confused Cace. He backed away, bewildered.

"It was the way Mother taught me to be," Nessa explained. "I knew Veil would be sent away if I entered into the binding with Haven, but I swear, I had no idea of what awaited her in the Cold Valley."

Darragh came to a sudden stop. "Would you two be quiet?" he snapped. "We're here. Remember, once you go through the border you must concentrate on keeping your wits about you. Don't eat, drink, or touch anything."

"You will be overwhelmed once you've crossed the border," Cace added, his focus back on the task at hand. "The colors, sounds— even the air will push at your sanity. If you can't make it through the In Between, you will likely not survive inside the barrows. And you definitely will not survive the Cold Valley. You must fight it."

Liam stepped up to stand beside Kellan. "What border?"

"It stands only feet in front of you," Darragh said. "It's what Veil was named after. It's too bad you can't see it—it is quite beautiful."

Darragh and Cace stepped forward, disappearing into thin

air. Nessa and Haven followed and then Calla. She took one last look behind her before stepping through and said, "Be brave. We've trained you well. Now is the time to use it."

Kellan was next, leading the way for the others as they all stepped through. It took them only seconds to cross over, and the effects were instant. They all rubbed at their skin as an odd sensation covered them from head to toe. It reminded Kellan of crawling insects. The voices did indeed come, and Jack was understandably the first to panic. He pulled at his hair, screaming.

Darragh tackled him to the ground, forcing him flat on his back. He straddled him and placed a hand over Jack's mouth. "You mustn't scream, Jack. Ignore the voices—you must block them out."

"The be-beasts," Jack said, his words muffled through Darragh's hand. "The beasts with the yellow eyes."

Darragh lowered his face until his nose almost touched Jack's. "They will not come for you this time—unless you scream. You have to find your courage, Jack...like Maeve found hers." Jack's eyes focused on Darragh's when he heard Maeve's name. He regained control of himself, and Darragh lifted his hand away from Jack's mouth. Jack removed his shaking hands from his head and nodded that he was ready.

Kellan didn't know what to expect when he followed Cace into the hollowed oak tree, and nothing could have prepared him. The tunnel was dark, but Kellan could see by the soft blue-green light emitting from the glowing worms that hung from the ceiling. He ran his hand along the wall, letting his fingers tangle with the ivy and press into the damp moss. He had assumed the place would smell stale, or of wet dirt, but this was not the case.

The scent of lavender was so heavy it overpowered his senses. It also calmed him, lulling him into a groggy state. He struggled to keep his mind tightly locked. The fog in his head began to thicken, but he pushed back with all his might, the way he'd been trained. He walked a fine line between coherence and derangement, but resisted succumbing completely. If it weren't for the training they'd received, none of them would have stood a chance.

Darragh and Cace were out in front, with hands that seemed to itch for the swords that hung from their hips. They traveled without incident until the sound of voices reached them. This time, the voices were not in their heads.

Darragh's hand flew up, signaling them to stop. "Each of you grab one of them. Hurry!"

Cace was the first to move, placing himself between Kellan and Niall. He grabbed their arms, and whispered, "I hope your acting skills are better than your sparring. Keep your mouths shut, your eyes low, and your faces devoid of emotion."

Neither Kellan or Niall had time to process what Cace had said before they were pulled forward. Kellan glanced over his shoulder to see that the rest of his family also had escorts. When they reached another tunnel and the owners of the voices revealed themselves, he finally understood.

Kellan had no difficulty telling which were human and which were not. The humans moved slowly and their faces were wiped of anything resembling free will. A man with solid white eyes walked by. Kellan shuddered and looked to Cace, silently asking for an explanation.

Cace shook his head. "That's the power of the ebony harp—the horned beast has him now." Kellan was horrified as a group of children merrily ran by. "Human children don't think as adults do," Cace whispered. "They see us, and they have no fear. There is no need to keep them heavily clouded because the allure of the In Between is enough."

Kellan didn't react to Cace's words, allowing himself to be dragged along as he thought about the absolute agony the children's parents must have endured. None of the others who filled the hall paid Kellan's group any mind, and the farther they traveled, the less they came across anyone, until there was no one in the hallway but them. Their escorts released them into the most enchanting room Kellan had ever seen.

"Brilliant," Maddy said, her voice full of awe.

"It is a sight," Calla agreed. "This is what we call the Great Hall. Mind yourselves, though. As beautiful as it seems, this place holds more evil than you can imagine."

Kellan and his family followed the others forward, taking in everything from the massive slab tables to the magical glass ceiling.

"I thought we were underground," Kellan mumbled.

"We are, but we can influence nature to do what we want," Darragh explained, gesturing to the ceiling. "That includes opening the earth above us if we wish."

Kellan shook his head, his mind running wild. "That's impossible."

"Maybe in your realm it is," Cace said. "But here, many things are possible." Cace entertained them with stories of how wondrous the In Between was. No one noticed that Rory had foolishly fallen behind.

Rory walked toward the raised pool that held dark water, transfixed. He ran his hand along the lip before dipping his fingers into the inky liquid. A ripple swelled a short way out, followed by a flickering shimmer beneath the surface. Rory leaned in closer.

"The merrows!" Cace yelled. "Rory, get away from there." They all watched in terror as a merrow breached the water's surface and wrapped her long black nails around Rory's neck, pulling him into the water with her.

"Rory!" Maddy screamed, bolting to the pool and diving in after him. Kellan was right behind her. He opened his eyes into the dark abyss, seeing nothing. He swung his outstretched arms ferociously, praying he would find Maddy or Rory. Instead, slimy hair slipped through his fingers and a clawed hand clasped his ankle.

The merrow pulled Kellan deeper. He saw Maddy trying to fight one of the three merrows that held Rory. Kellan's eyes widened as the scaly monsters opened their mouths, filled with pointed teeth, and clamped down on various parts of Rory's body. Kellan struggled to stay conscious and tried to swim toward Maddy and Rory, kicking to escape the painful grip on his ankle. A splash came from above, and seconds later the merrows hissed in displeasure when they saw Cace, a Sidhe, in their territory. They released their meal as they fled.

Maddy reached out and latched onto Rory's limp body. Cace and Kellan snatched them both up and began to swim toward what Kellan hoped was the surface. When they reached the edge of the pool, Calla and Niall helped Cace and Kellan over while Haven and Darragh pulled Maddy and Rory to safety. Kellan choked, his lungs burning.

"Rory's not breathing!" Maddy screamed. Aileen shoved her aside and put herself as close to Rory as she could get and, placing her hands on Rory's chest, began to pump. Minutes dragged on with no response from Rory, and Aileen's composure began to falter. Tears fell from her eyes and dropped onto Rory's face.

Just as Kellan thought all hope was lost, Rory's eyes flew open and he rolled to his side, trying to rid his lungs of water. Overcome with relief, both Aileen and Maddy flung their arms around him and held on tight.

"Decided to come home, have you?"

Darragh put himself in front of everyone and placed his hand over the hilt of his sword, facing the Sidhe man that had snuck up on them. "Faelan. We're going to get her back."

"I can't allow that," Faelan argued. "You have no idea what has transpired in your absence."

"What are you talking about?"

"Mother," Faelan answered. "She's dead, brother."

Darragh's hand fell from his sword. "What happened?"

"Moira happened." Faelan growled. "Your bride did this as soon as you left. She gave Mother a chalice filled with poison then escaped before we could imprison her. She's back in the Cold Valley under Lorcan's protection. They planned this treachery, Darragh. They planted an assassin and waited years to do this. The war never ended."

"Faelan, we will make them pay, but first we must rescue Veil."

Faelan shook his head. "I can't let you go. You'll bring death to us all, Darragh. When the Cold Moon comes and Veil is made theirs fully, they will have control. The other clans will bow to them, and Lorcan will command an entire army. We won't stand a chance—we must fall in line if we wish to survive."

Cace took a step toward Faelan. "What if there was another way?"

"There is no other way, son," Faelan insisted.

"Oh, but there is," Cace said. "In fact, it may be the only way. We must rescue Veil and rid this world of Lorcan and his kin. Once they're dead, his people will come to heel. Think about it, Father—you could rule the Cold Valley. His wolves will be yours."

Faelan's eyes sparkled at the mention of the wolves. "Do you really think you can accomplish this?"

Cace smirked as though he knew he had already won. "I know we can, Father. If you allow us access to the stables and permit safe passage to their land, we will not fail you."

Faelan rubbed his chin thoughtfully. "Very well."

36. chapter

Kellan and Liam stood wide-eyed, taking in the giant animals. Now Kellan understood what Calla had meant when she had called Murphy small. The horses that stood before him were not like any Kellan and his family had on their farm.

"How?" he asked.

Calla laughed, answering as though it were obvious, "What do you mean 'how?' They are as they are meant to be."

Cace and Haven began clearing the hay and uncovered several well-hidden packs which were filled with warm clothing, weapons, and supplies—an enormous load. It was lucky the horses were so large.

Calla led Kellan to a solid gray stallion and stroked its muzzle. "This is Glas." She took Kellan's hand and placed it on the horse's nose. "He'll take care of you if you take care of him."

"I think it would be wise if Aileen, Maddy, and Evelyn each rode with another," Cace suggested. "Their smaller statures may put them at a disadvantage when it comes to controlling the beasts."

Rory, who was mostly recovered from his near drowning, spoke before any of the others could get a word out. "Maddy can ride with me," he offered.

Liam eyed Rory before walking over to him. "She is my daughter, Rory. Can I trust you with her?" Liam loved Rory like he loved his own children, but Kellan couldn't blame his father for his concern.

Rory stood tall and met Liam's firm gaze with his own and answered, "I'll let nothing happen to her, Liam. She is safe with me."

Satisfied, Liam nodded. "All right then," he said. "Maddy with you, Evelyn with Jack, and Aileen with me."

"Now that we've settled that," Darragh said, emptying the contents of one pack, "we must clothe ourselves with everything we can stand to have on because even that will never be enough for where we are going." They layered on long sleeved tops and pants until it was impossible to squeeze into any more. Once finished, their mundane human clothing was well hidden under otherworldly tunics and what Calla called 'practical gowns.'

"Practical?" asked a wide-eyed Aileen. The slit in the olive green dress she wore opened past mid-thigh. "I'm glad I wore trousers today."

"You'll understand when you see what Sidhe women usually wear," Calla quipped. "Here, these should help."

Aileen gratefully accepted a hooded cloak. Maddy spun merrily around, her orange cape flaring out wide around her, the gold threading catching the light.

"If you all are quite finished," Faelan admonished. "There is still the small matter of getting you into the Cold Valley."

Though the tunnel Faelan led them down was larger than the one they had used to enter the barrows, the horses' heads still scraped the ceiling. The passage started to descend toward the center of the Earth. Kellan wondered how far they would have to go before they reached the end. He didn't have to wonder for long.

Their warm breath turned to fog as it left their mouths. The temperature was falling drastically. They continued until Faelan stopped short of a closed door, which blocked their path. The deep burgundy door was circular, with carvings that were similar in design to Kellan's banister. The door had no handles, and the ice around its edges locked it in place.

"What now?" Niall asked.

"Patience, human." Faelan chuckled. "You shouldn't be in any hurry to enter the Cold Valley."

Niall visibly gulped. "What's on the other side?"

"Nothing you have ever seen before," Cace muttered.

"Are you sure this is what you all want?" Faelan asked. "Lorcan will not hesitate to add you to his collectibles if you're caught. Our Saeculum is nothing compared to the pain you'll feel as your bodies turn to ice."

"We're going," Kellan answered.

"As you say," Faelan said, turning to his son. "Cace, you have an obligation to our bloodline to survive, do you understand me? You are my only heir, and with Mother gone, I am now king. Secure the Cold Valley in my name. Make me proud, my son."

Cace said nothing. His father approached the door and laid his hand flat against its surface. He closed his eyes. The ice around the door started to crack. The door began to shake and the ice shattered. Everyone stepped back as the door opened into howling winds and chaotic flurries. Snow poured into the tunnel. Kellan took a tentative step forward, marveling at the snow-covered trees.

Faelan gave a grand wave of his hand and said, "There you are. Your journey begins. Darragh, my brother, for what it's worth, I do hope you succeed. Our line must live on."

"Thank you, Faelan. I hope to see you soon, but if I do not see you again in this life, I will see you in the life after."

"Come now, Darragh." Faelan tutted. "You and I both know there is no life after this one for us." Darragh nodded sadly. With a flick of his head, he motioned the rescue party through the threshold. They mounted their horses, and they were off.

"How long until we reach it?" Kellan asked. The roaring wind was so loud, he was forced to yell. After traveling for hours, they hadn't covered much ground. The snow cover meant the landscape all looked the same, and the frigid wind made visibility nearly impossible. The group stayed close together. Losing each other in the blizzard would mean freezing to death alone.

"We will not lay eyes on their mountainous home until tomorrow," Darragh answered.

"They don't live underground?" Kellan asked. Cace was the one to answer.

"There isn't exactly a need for them to hide. Not many humans wandering around in these conditions."

"But you said their fortress was filled with humans."

Cace nodded warily. "That it is."

"How do they get them?"

Cace paused before admitting the truth. "There are trades among the clans—food, healing herbs...humans..." Cace stole a glimpse at Kellan, and Kellan glared back, his jaw tight. "As deplorable as it is, it's the way of our kind," Cace explained. He glanced toward Calla with haunted eyes. "No matter how much some of us may want it to be different."

"Aye," Kellan said. "But no creature—human or otherwise—should be subjected to such cruelties. It only takes one, Cace. One voice to challenge others to rethink. It has to start with someone." Cace was not the only one moved by Kellan's convictions. Darragh and Haven seemed to be contemplating Kellan's words, and even Nessa's face showed a semblance of regret.

"Did you see it?" Niall shouted. "There!" He pointed toward the trees, and from the dark shadows, gruesome howls resounded, carried on the wind.

Kellan's blood ran cold. He'd had more than one run-in with these monsters, and he would never forget that sound. The wolves had found them. "Ride!" he shouted.

The wolves burst from the tree line in a solid black line. The horses couldn't maneuver fast enough; their great size and strength became liabilities in the snow. The wolves snarled, pulling back their lips to reveal long, sharp fangs. They easily caught up to the horses, surrounding them.

"We're going to die!" Evelyn screamed. The white-and-brown horse she and Jack rode reared back and sent them sprawling into the snow before vanishing into the woods. One of the wolves followed, and the horse's cries soon echoed around them.

Another wolf descended upon Jack and Evelyn, who could do nothing but cling to one another. With Aileen's arms wrapped tightly around his waist, Liam steered their horse into the wolf's path, cutting it off from its prey. The angry wolf lunged and sank its teeth into Liam's leg. In one swift motion, it yanked Liam from the horse's back and into the snow before disappearing into the woods, leaving a bloody trail in its wake.

"Da!" Kellan screamed. He gripped his reins and tore off after them. His body was pummeled by the frozen tree limbs until he broke through, and the trail opened up. His father lay in the middle of the clearing, the wolf circling him. But Liam was not alone. A hooded figure holding a self-made wooden spear jabbed into the beast's thick, furry hide.

Kellan leaped from his horse's back and tumbled head over heels in the snow before regaining his footing. He unsheathed the dagger Cace had given him and charged, hell-bent on killing the beast. When he reached the stranger's side he swung his knife madly, praying that it would connect. Aileen screamed Kellan's name, but he was unable to tear his eyes away from the black wolf. Darragh and Cace flew from their horses, swords in hand. They joined Kellan and the stranger, trying to push the monster back, but the wolf stood its ground, crouched low and snarling.

Obsidian eyes roamed the four, finally settling their ravenous sight on Kellan and Darragh, as if the beast could sense their weakened state. The powerful animal pounced, sending a burst of white powder into the air and knocking both men down. It towered over them, snapping its fierce jaws so close that the heat from its breath melted the snow that clung to their eyelashes.

Cace rushed to their aid, his usual stride hampered by the snow. Once in range, he shot up off the ground, coiling his body into an elegant flip, and landed on the wolf's back. The wolf writhed and bucked beneath him, its wild movements leading it away from Kellan and Darragh. Cace gripped his sword's hilt with both hands and plunged the sharp blade deep into the meat between the creature's shoulders. He twisted, leaving the wound he had inflicted a gaping hole. The beast's blood steamed, dripping onto the snow with a sizzle. It wasn't until the wolf collapsed that Cace withdrew his steel.

Kellan and Darragh stood up, panting. Darragh approached the hooded man and pointed his sword. "Reveal yourself." The man hesitated a moment before sinking his spear into the snow beside him. He drew himself up, standing tall, and peeled back his snowy hood.

"I think I know you," Kellan said. He tried to remember where he had seen the man.

The man jutted out his chin. "I doubt it. But your friends might—with eyes like those, I'm sure they've seen plenty of my kind."

Kellan was caught off guard by the man's remark and put his hands up, trying to calm him. "We mean you no harm."

"So you say, but that remains to be seen, doesn't it?"

Cace stepped forward, hand over heart. "I promise we'll not hurt you unless you force our hand. Now, your name, please? Mine is Cace."

"Cace? You're Veil's cousin, aren't you?" Kellan's heart began to race.

"You've seen Veil?"

The man's eyes dimmed. "I have..."

"Where?" Kellan asked, taking a step toward him. "Take us to her."

Liam's moans interrupted them. Blood pooled beneath him.

"I'll tell you all I know," the man said. "But first we must attend to his injuries—he's dying."

With the others' help, Kellan lifted Liam up and laid him across the back of Calla's horse. She was their swiftest rider. Niall, who had been quiet since the man revealed his face, offered him a place on his horse. The man grasped Niall's offered hand and slung his leg over the horse's back. He placed his hands securely around Niall's waist.

Niall sucked in a quick breath and coughed. "Where to, *uh*... what's your name?" he stammered.

The man pointed across the clearing to a trail weaving its way through the trees and answered, "Daniel."

31. chapter

Daniel led them to a cave not far from where the wolves had attacked. Off the trail, it was well hidden. Monstrous ice stalactites hung from the ceiling, their tips sharp as thorns. The mouth of the cave was large enough for the horses to find shelter within. Daniel directed them deeper into the frozen cavern until they reached his campsite.

They laid Liam near the circular rock formation that Daniel used as a fire pit. He began striking two stones together, rushing to light a fire to warm Liam, whose complexion rivaled the snow outside. Jack dropped his pack and dug out a lighter. Daniel watched in awe as the flame ignited the tinder and kindling. With Kellan's help, Aileen gently removed Liam's blood-soaked pants, revealing a vicious wound.

"He won't stand a chance if we don't stop the bleeding," said

Daniel.

Kellan's worried eyes landed on Maddy and Aileen, their tear-stained faces frosting over with grief. He turned to look at Haven, who had kneeled down next to him. Suddenly, Haven sprang up and sprinted to his pack. He tore the pack open, hastily digging through the items within. He smiled as he pressed the bog moss into Kellan's hand.

"Here, this will help."

Kellan examined the small green lump in his palm, not at all confident that this unremarkable plant could save his father's life. Daniel snatched the moss from his hand and began packing Liam's wound. Liam howled with pain, but Daniel persisted. The moss created a natural bandage, absorbing the blood and allowing it to clot. Kellan bowed his head, his body slumping forward. Liam would live.

The fire did little to warm their bones. They shivered, their teeth chattered, and their noses turned a raw red. But it was better than nothing. Aileen stroked Liam's hair, careful not to wake him. Kellan watched the slow rise and fall of his father's chest. They had come close to losing him—*too close*. Haven sat to Kellan's left, his arm wrapped around Nessa as she leaned against him, asleep.

"Thank you," Kellan whispered, trying not to wake her.

Haven waved off his gratitude. "Veil is the one who told me about the bog moss. She was always so happy when Dara would teach her new things. She would often share with me...or she used to anyway."

Kellan hadn't spoken much with Haven outside of their training, but he noticed a longing in Haven's voice when he spoke of Veil.

"You love her."

"I do," Haven admitted, closing his eyes. "Not that it matters. I destroyed Veil when I chose Nessa and cut ties." Haven opened his eyes and used his free hand to rub at his hair. "In our world, differences can make you a pariah. When Bidalia and Moira approached my family with the offer to bind with Nessa, I couldn't turn it down."

"But why turn your back on Veil?"

Haven shrugged. "It was the price I had to pay for others to look past this." He pointed to his auburn hair. "It was the only way for my family to regain their pride."

Kellan scoffed. "Doesn't sound like you got a good deal."

Haven picked up a smaller rock, his thumb rubbing the smoothest side. "Veil was the only one who ever truly accepted me the way I am. Maybe it was because she understood, or maybe it was her kind heart, but even with royal blood in her veins, she never looked down on me." Nessa turned her head and nuzzled into Haven's chest.

"And what of her?" Kellan asked.

Haven brushed Nessa's fair hair off her face. "Nessa has a lot of growing up to do, but she is starting to see the truth. She may not be my true mark, but I'm bound to her until death, regardless. I hope we can find common ground."

Kellan couldn't understand the reasons Haven gave for doing what he had done, but he could relate to the rest; he had also treated Veil poorly. He sighed heavily. "Veil deserves so much better than us, doesn't she?"

"No truer words have ever been spoken." Haven chuckled. "But at least you still have a chance to be better for her, to be everything she needs. I lost that chance when I took on these." He lifted his arm until the cloak fell away, exposing the traumatic scars roping his skin and disappearing under the sleeve of his tunic.

"I think we need to reevaluate our plan," Darragh said, effectively ending their conversation. "Daniel, you said you know Veil?"

"I do," Daniel answered, using a small stick to stoke the fire. "She gave me my freedom, sacrificing herself so that I might have time to escape."

Kellan's eyes widened as he finally remembered where he knew Daniel from. "The well," he whispered.

Daniel looked at him sharply. "How do you know of that place?"

"It was the last vision I had of her—you were there."

"Vision?"

It was Niall who answered. "Aye, Kellan's been having dreams—"

"Not dreams," Kellan cut in. "They're more like nightmares, only I know they're real. I can see what she sees and feel what she feels. But I haven't had one since I saw you both in the well."

"If you saw us there, then yes, what you have been seeing is most definitely real," Daniel said, his face tightening with concern. "Do you know why the visions have left you?"

"I have a theory on that," Darragh answered. "Kellan, you said in your last vision Veil was forced to look into someone's eyes." Darragh turned to Cace. "That must have been Lorcan or Colden. I think they clouded her, and that's the reason Kellan hasn't seen her again—she's not herself right now."

"Colden was at the well," Daniel said. "I left at Veil's insistence, but we had planned to leave together. She said it was vital we leave before the ceremony they were preparing for."

Haven shook his head. "Veil made a vow. We witnessed it."

"What does that mean?" Jack broke in.

Darragh didn't spare him a glance. "It means that Veil can't escape. The vow will kill her if she does—she knows that."

Daniel's hand flew to his mouth. "She knew this and she still helped me?"

"So she can't ever leave?" Maddy asked, her chin trembling.

"She can't escape," Jack answered. "You heard what they said. I don't understand why we came if there was no hope of getting her out."

Calla reached for Cace's hand and said, "She only vowed not to escape. She didn't say anything about being rescued. We can carry her out."

"Now the question is, how do we get in to get her out?" Darragh asked, looking toward Daniel.

"I think I know a way," he answered, his eyes focused on the fire. "But you will not like it."

38.
chapter

Liam was left in the safety of Daniel's cave under Aileen and Evelyn's watchful eyes. Maddy, who had become proficient in the skillful art of the bow, stayed behind for protection, and Rory refused to leave her side. Kellan thumped his back in appreciation. Leaving them behind was not a simple task, nor was it easy for them to watch their loved ones go.

Kellan approached his mother, wrapping her in a tight embrace. "If we don't come back, you need to find a way out of here."

Aileen's body tensed, and she pulled back. Her fierce eyes met his. "You will come back to us, you hear me? You all will."

Kellan left her with a small smile, only a slight tilt of the lips, hopeful but guarded. The small rescue party set out on horseback with Daniel in the lead. They needed to find the river that led to the well;

it was their only way in.

The river was difficult to spot under the ice and snow, but once they reached its banks, the frozen river stretched wide and glittered in the afternoon sun.

"Why is it red?" Niall asked. Kellan shuddered as he already knew the answer. He had seen the bodies.

"The Sidhe that call this place home believe their salvation lies within human blood," Daniel explained. "They take it—lots of it—and they discard the bodies into the river when they're finished." Daniel pointed down a path that led across the river. "Come, it's not wise to remain out in the open for long."

Jack's jaw dropped. "You want us to ride these mammoth horses onto the frozen river of death?"

"Time is not an indulgence we can afford at the moment."

"Daniel's right," Darragh said. "We must hurry. Keep your eyes and ears open to danger." He guided his horse to take the first tentative step onto the frozen red river. The rest fell in line behind him as he led the way toward the mountain fortress. Hours passed without incident. The group rode in silence, all their bodies slumping from exhaustion.

"Whoa!" The horse Niall and Daniel rode jerked its head from side to side, refusing to go forward. Its nostrils flared as it began to walk backward. Niall tugged the reins and the horse fought against him, its hind legs kicking out. Daniel slipped from its back. His eyes darted over the ice beneath him, then he scrambled away. A frozen woman floated below the ice, her body carried along by the current. Her weightless light hair drifted away from her face, revealing a missing eye.

The sight sent Niall into a panic. Niall's horse reacted to his alarmed state, rearing and bucking until a loud crack echoed around them. The river swallowed them both, and the current whisked them away under the ice.

"Niall!" Kellan dropped from his horse and rushed toward the hole, only to have Haven and Cace stop him. "Let me go."

"The current has him," Cace said. "We have to spread out." The group scattered and fell to their hands and knees. The ice creaked as they crawled along the cold hard surface.

"I see him!" Nessa screamed. Kellan was the closest and raced over, slipping and barreling into her. More bodies flowed under the ice, their nude forms drifting into one another. Niall's frightened eyes shone alive amongst the frozen dead. He pounded against the ice, quickly growing lethargic from the cold and the lack of air. His time would soon run out. Cace and Haven drew their swords. They lifted them high and swung down, chipping away at the ice.

Kellan followed suit with his knife. "He's going to die!"

"No, he's not," said Calla. She placed her palms flat on the glacial surface with a look of pure concentration. There was a rumbling beneath them. Calla's muscles stiffened, and the ruby water started to churn, bubbling up and out of the hole that Niall had fallen into. "Keep striking the ice!"

Niall stopped fighting, and his body went slack. Shards of ice flew in every direction as they worked to free him, each mighty swing a desperate act. Calla winced as the ice began to splinter. She gritted her teeth, and the ice broke open with a resounding crack. They frantically plunged their arms into the river, struggling against the cold corpses to pull him out. As soon as the frigid air hit Niall's wet face, a pink frost began to spread across everything from his hair to his eyelashes.

"Quick," Kellan said, dragging Niall toward the river bank. "Build a fire."

Kellan stripped himself and Niall down to their underwear. Nessa wrapped the two with as many dry cloaks as she could find while Haven helped Jack with the fire. Niall's normally dark complexion took on a deathly pallor, and hostile tremors overtook his muscles. His skin was icy, and Kellan felt the sting of a thousand tiny icepicks puncturing his body, wherever their bare skin touched. He could only imagine the level of suffering Niall was experiencing.

"You have to stay awake," Kellan ordered, watching Niall's heavy eyelids flutter closed.

"I...I don't know...if I can, mate," Niall slurred.

"You can't leave me to deal with Rory and Connor all on my own," Kellan joked. He rubbed his hands up and down Niall's arms, ignoring the sharp pain.

Niall opened his eyes and shook with stilted laughter. "Aye, I guess it'd be bloody wrong of me to subject you to that misery."

"It would." Kellan chuckled. "Who else is going to help me keep Rory from getting fluthered and going stark naked at the pub again?"

"Ghastly sight, that was. Next time it's your turn to find his knickers."

"Then you'll be the one to get him off the bar and away from the gawkers," Kellan countered. He needed to keep Niall responsive long enough for the combined warmth of the fire and their shared body heat to fight off the hypothermia. It seemed to be working; Niall's color was returning, and his eyes showed more light.

Niall smirked and snickered. "Deal."

39. chapter

The dark stone fortress was well camouflaged. Built straight into the mountainside, its jagged towers blended in with the mountain's peaks. The snow was deep near the foot of the mountain, crunching beneath the horses' hooves. Daniel and Niall shared Calla's horse, with Daniel at the reins and Kellan riding beside them. Ahead of them, Calla rode with Cace, her arms wrapped around him and her head laid against his back, hiding her face. She was devastated over the loss of two of the horses she'd spent her life caring for. Kellan lowered his head, his heart aching as though her pain was his own.

The river narrowed until it was only a few feet wide before disappearing into the abandoned catacomb. As Kellan stared into the dark opening, a chill ran up his spine. "All hope abandon ye who enter here," he whispered.

"*Dante's Inferno*," Niall muttered. He turned and peered into Kellan's frightened eyes. "Remember it said this as well, 'The path to paradise begins in Hell.' We're almost there, Kell... We've almost got Veil." Kellan reached over and took Niall's hand tightly within his own. Niall squeezed his hand in return and said, "Now, let's go get my sister."

The catacombs were narrow, forcing them to leave their horses and their packs. "What about the cold?" Jack asked, not wanting to leave their dry clothing behind.

"When your mind is theirs, you don't pay it too much attention," Daniel explained. "If that is what we wish them to believe, we must act accordingly."

Daniel volunteered to go first, risking his newfound freedom to rescue Veil. Niall gnawed on his lower lip and paced outside the mouth of the catacomb as Daniel disappeared into the darkness, but Daniel was quick to call out that all was clear.

A wretched smell engulfed them. The stench of mold and decay was enough to turn Kellan's stomach, and he fought the urge to vomit. The deeper they traveled, the darker it got, until they were forced to creep at a snail's pace and use their hands to blindly feel their way along the sharp rock wall. The only sounds were the soft rippling of the water flowing past them and their own harsh breathing.

"Look, I think I see a light," Darragh's voice called out. "It's coming from within the water."

"I believe those are from the lanterns," Daniel said. "They line the walls of the well. If that's what it is, there should be some sort of way in."

"I'll have to get into the water." Darragh grunted.

"Uncle, you must be careful," Cace warned. "The well was frequented often when I was last here—and not only by humans and

Sidhe from what I heard."

Darragh eased himself into the water with a soft splash. "I've reached the back wall, but we'll have to go under it to reach whatever is on the other side."

Kellan slipped into the water to follow. It was warmer than it had been outside. He took a deep breath and cautiously made his way toward Darragh's voice. Visibility began to improve thanks to the light beneath the water, but it wasn't near bright enough for Kellan when something bumped into his leg.

"What was that?"

"You honestly do not want to know," said Cace behind him.

Kellan did his best to ignore whatever else was in the water with them, placing his hands on the rock wall to steady himself. In the dim light, he could just make out Darragh's slightly darker silhouette.

"Calm yourself," Darragh whispered. "You will need every ounce of control you possess if there are others on the other side. Let's go."

Around him, Kellan heard everyone suck in a deep breath. The water rippled as they dipped their heads beneath the surface. Kellan forced his eyes open to navigate his way and was overwhelmed by unending crimson. The only reprieve from the monotony was the blurry beams made by the lantern's ambient light. He was thankful that he didn't have far to go. But when he broke the surface on the other side, he immediately wished he hadn't.

Kellan's eyes moved from one corpse to the next. They were piled on top of each other, their bodies naked and twisted. "Why?" he whispered.

"We don't all believe or practice as they do," Darragh answered, averting his eyes. "But there are many of our kind that believe they can take in a human's soul by drinking their blood. The more they consume, the higher their chances of walking through Heaven's gate. It is the possibility of there being nothing beyond this existence that frightens them most of all. If a clan is gifted with a covetable, that only raises their odds of an everlasting life, whether that life be in Hell's fire or in Heaven's light."

"Now is probably not the best time for this," Daniel said. He waded closer to the edge of the pool but stopped to study the bodies. "This isn't right."

"What is it?" Niall asked.

"This... Just all this. There should be someone here, and they never kill so many at once, not unless—"

"The Red Room." Cace gasped.

Daniel met Cace's eyes and nodded. "There wasn't supposed to be a gathering until the binding, but I overheard talk that they were bringing in fresh humans. Veil said this wouldn't happen until the Cold Moon, but it's the only thing I know that could explain this. Is there a chance they would rush the ceremony?"

Cace turned to Darragh. "Uncle, they wouldn't do that, would they? We should have another day."

Darragh shook his head. "Their celebrations have been known to last for days. This could simply be the beginning of what's to come."

Kellan dug his nails into his palms. He had never been more angry than he was listening to Darragh. "You knew this and still waited so long to come to the farm?"

"I was too weak to come any sooner. I wanted to go to her the moment Cace released me, but I couldn't. Lorcan has always been one for theatrics and show. Our histories say the ceremony must take place when the Cold Moon is at its highest, but they say nothing of when the celebrations may begin. I honestly believe he will wait, but if the other clans are already here, we may be too late."

Kellan sloshed through the water, moving rapidly to the shallow end. He ignored the cold air as it hit his wet tunic and marched to the mouth of a darkened tunnel, taking his first step into the black pitch. He turned to Darragh. "The bloody hell we are."

Chapter 40.

Daniel took the lead and guided them through the darkness, away from the sound of lapping water. They reached the end, Daniel and Kellan approaching the opening of the serrated stone entrance, staying as close as they could to the rough rock walls. The stone hallway was massive, and the mysterious whistling of a draft echoed throughout. Without the humid warmth from the well, the bitter chill of the dreary corridor numbed Kellan's body and burned his lungs.

"This is not good," Daniel said. "The halls are never this empty. If they've already locked themselves into the Red Room..."

Kellan's face blanched with fear. "They lock themselves in?"

"Yes," Daniel answered. "Then they release the humans' minds—they enjoy the chase."

Jacked tapped his fingers against his leg impatiently. "What are we waiting for?"

"We have to be smart about this," said Kellan.

"Do I even want to know why they call it that?" Niall asked. "The Red Room?"

"They say it's a sacred color," Daniel explained. "They dress their humans in white and take pride in how fast they can turn them red."

Kellan, sickened by Daniel's words, bowed his head. The honey color of his tunic pulled his attention. "We can't just walk in there—look at us." He gestured to his tunic. "Where are we going to get red clothes?"

Daniel sighed. "I can't get us red, but I do know where we can find white."

"White?"

"It's the only option we have, but we need them to believe that we're all human long enough to get past the guards. We need a distraction."

"Leave that to us." All eyes turned to Nessa and Calla. It was no secret that the two women didn't like each other, but now they wore matching mischievous grins.

The halls were all a stormy gray, with only the icicles hanging from the rock's erose edges and the snow-packed crevices to break up the dullness. Daniel led them into the lower levels where they found rows of empty pallets covered in scraps of blanket. A strong smell of urine and feces permeated in the air.

"That one used to be mine," Daniel said, pointing. "If it wasn't for Veil, I'd still be sleeping there." Niall stepped to Daniel's side and let his fingers graze Daniel's hand with a comforting touch. Daniel's gaze dropped to the floor, a small smile gracing his face.

"If we don't hurry up, there is a chance we'll all be sleeping here—or worse," said Darragh.

Daniel led them to the end of the room and motioned to a pile of white rags. "Choose," he said, with a wave of his arm.

Nessa held up a pair of barely-there underwear, pinched between two of her fingers. "You must be joking."

"Oh, come on, Ness," Cace chuckled. "I've seen you wear less than that back in the barrows."

"Cace, you saw nothing of the sort," she snapped. "Even I have standards as to how much I exhibit. And do not call me Ness."

Daniel shook his head at their bickering. "I suggest we layer what we can, but they'll know something is wrong if we cover ourselves completely. Where we're going, skin is abundant and appreciated." Kellan picked up the top closest to him. The sleeves had been removed and the front slashed. Next he found a pair of linen pants with the barest hint of red stains. Once dressed, Daniel brought them back to the main floor. He guided them through the winding passageway, heading for the Red Room. He stopped and motioned to a connecting hall. "Through here."

Kellan entered the new hall first, the intense, biting temperature stealing his breath. He blinked his stinging eyes and studied his surroundings. The hall was lined with frozen statues. He approached the one closest to him. "What is this?" he whispered.

"Lorcan's collectibles," Cace answered. "We have something similar back in the barrows—a place that Uncle Darragh knows all too well."

Kellan couldn't tear his eyes from a man who appeared to be close to his own age. "Are they dead?"

"No," Cace said, "but I promise you they wish they were." Even as they left the hellish hall, Kellan's thoughts stayed with the poor souls who remained. He questioned the Sidhe's humanity, but Cace was swift to point out that his kind was not human. "That's what makes Veil so special," he said. "If she had been allowed to develop her gifts like the rest of us, there is no telling how powerful she may have become. And she might have stood a chance here."

"She's strong," said Kellan. "So much stronger than anyone gives her credit for."

"We're close," Daniel interrupted. "It's the next hall over. They use the other entrance, so no one usually comes this way. There should be guards dressed in red cloaks standing outside the door. If we see no one, then they have already sealed themselves inside. I never thought I would say this, but we need to run into Sidhe." The group of unlikely companions inched farther down the path, until they could see the archway that marked the entrance of the hallway to the Red Room.

Darragh pushed past Daniel to peer around the corner. He let out a deep breath. "The doors are still passable, but there are three guards between us and it. We need to lure them away." He turned to Calla and Nessa. "I hope you two can pull this off."

Haven pulled Nessa close, and she whispered gentle reassurances into his ear before flipping her blonde hair over her shoulder and turning back to Darragh. "We know what we're doing, Father. Be ready."

Calla winked at Cace, then together she and Nessa stepped through the arch. The men waited, their bodies vibrating from the adrenaline pumping through their veins. With Nessa and Calla out of sight, the waiting dragged on for ages. Finally, they heard Nessa's melodic giggle.

"A little bit closer now," Cace whispered, ready to lunge. He looked to Darragh and Kellan. "Be at the ready. The rest of you, remember—don't look into their eyes." Darragh and Haven already had their swords out, waiting to strike. Kellan held his dagger tight in his hand. "On three," Cace instructed. "One...two...three." Cace grabbed the first red cloak. The three guards were outnumbered and easily restrained after a short scuffle.

Kellan held one in a headlock, straining to keep his hold on the struggling man. "They aren't going to sit here quietly," he said. "What do we do with them?"

The guard let out a creepy chuckle. "You think you can walk into that room and not be noticed?" He gestured toward Cace and the other Sidhe. "No one will ever believe they are human, no matter how much white they wear." Music resonated from down the hall, and the guard grinned. "The celebrations have begun. Soon our clan will rule you all."

"I hate to say it but this disgusting excuse for a Sidhe is right," Cace admitted.

Kellan looked at the guard's red cape. He had an idea. "Take their clothes—you can walk us in."

"Brilliant, Kell!" Niall said.

As they began stripping the guards of their uniforms, the guards intensified their efforts to escape. In the commotion, no one noticed that one had freed his left hand, placing it flat against the cold rock floor. The group understood, too late, when vibrations rumbled beneath their feet.

"Jack, watch out!" Darragh yelled. He lunged toward Jack and shoved him out of the way.

"Uncle Darragh!" Cace shouted. He drove his blade into the guard's neck, but it was too late. Darragh's body hung limp, impaled through the middle by a large stone spike protruding from the floor. Cace raced over, and smashed the base of the stone with the hilt of his sword, catching his uncle's body as it fell. "Hold on, Uncle—Haven, the bog moss!"

Haven shook his head. He answered thickly, "I'm sorry."

Darragh reached out and patted Cace's hand. "It's all right," he whispered. "All is as it should be."

Jack kneeled beside them. His voice was hoarse when he spoke. "Why'd you do that?"

"It's what Maeve would have done," Darragh answered weakly. "Despite what anyone thinks, I loved her and she loved me. I only wish I could join her." Jack held out his hand, and Darragh stared for a short time before he feebly gripped it. They held each other's gaze, and a moment of understanding passed between them. "Save Maeve's daughter." Darragh's head lolled to the side, and a solitary tear flowed across his cheek.

Jack closed Darragh's eyes. "Rest easy, mate. We will."

41. chapter

The door to the Red Room was not like Kellan had imagined. It was not red at all but gold, with depictions of winged angels flying high near the top. Farther down the story changed; the angels' wings were set ablaze, and they fell out of the sky.

"It's the telling of when the first were cast out of Heaven's skies," Cace explained.

"Why were they cast out?" asked Kellan.

"The stories are from long ago, but it is said that it was their vanity and pride." Cace gave Kellan a wry smile. "Heaven is reserved for the altruistic sort."

"Makes sense. No offense."

"None taken," he said. Cace offered his hand to Kellan. "Now, what do you say we get Veil and go home?"

Kellan accepted Cace's hand and shook it. "I'd say that's the best line to ever leave that smart mouth of yours."

Cace grinned. "Indeed. Now, remember those acting skills." He dropped Kellan's hand and stepped up to the golden door. The door had no handles, and Cace turned to Daniel for directions.

"One of you has to place your hand on it," Daniel answered. "Humans can't open it."

Cace cautiously laid his hand against the gold. "Why is it hot?"

"On the other side of this door is a room filled with your kind, all using their abilities at once," Daniel said. "That energy has nowhere else to go."

"At least we won't be cold," Cace muttered before closing his eyes. The door began to shake. It cracked straight down the center, and the halves pulled apart, gradually disappearing into the ragged boulders which held them.

The room behind the door was enormous and carved right out of the mountain, exactly like the rest of the fortress. Instead of gray, however, these walls were red. Thousands of candles flickered along the rockface, dripping thick red wax down the walls like clotted blood. Kellan glanced up and gasped at the large red drapes suspended above their heads. They waved through the air, dancing to the ominous music that played. It was almost beautiful.

Throughout the room, stone tables were piled high with food the color of a raven's wing. Under the food, layers of stains dyed the stone in shades ranging from brilliant red to a lackluster brown. The floor was carpeted in crimson flowers, crushed by the dancing guests. The Sidhe were dressed in scarlet. The only break from all the red were the flashes of white linen—*the humans.*

Cace had spoken of the shapeshifting puca during their training lessons, but Kellan had never seen one until now. The puca had chosen a grotesque goat-like form for that night. They stood on two human legs, and their round bellies sat under protruding ribs. Atop their bony, hunched shoulders was the head of a large-horned goat. Kellan was grateful that the giant wolves were not in attendance as well.

The group lingered in the entrance. Kellan continued to study the room and noticed that no one was paying them any attention. "Why aren't they looking at us?" he asked.

Daniel answered, his body beginning to quake. "It's the euphoria. It happens when their bloodlust mixes with the energy of this evil place. They won't see us until we cross the threshold."

"God have mercy on us all," Niall whispered.

"God abandoned this place long ago, and these acts of abomination are why," Haven replied, his top lip curling up in disgust.

"Now is not the time," Cace said. "If Veil has already been brought in, our time to save her is short. If you're in white, keep your eyes vacant and your heads bowed. For those in red, keep the rest close. And pull up your hoods—remember what my father said about Moira."

It had been decided that Cace, Nessa, and Haven would be the ones to wear the guards' red cloaks as they were the most recognizable. They pulled their hoods up to conceal their faces. The three attached themselves to the others in white, and together they took their first steps into the Red Room.

The heat was heavy, and the contrast from the frigid cold raised sweat to their brows. Dangerous eyes paused to regard them with intrigue. Some of the Sidhe began running their hands over Kellan's white clothing and across his skin. His heart started to pound, pushing his blood through his veins faster and harder. The Sidhe's intrigue grew to excitement, their pulsating bodies hovering closer.

A stick-thin woman with a sparkling, ruby-red headpiece

fastened into her long black hair latched onto Kellan's bicep. "This one smells so good," she said, practically purring. "Why don't you come and play with Morrigan?"

"Hands off if you wish to keep them," Nessa threatened.

Morrigan licked her lips, perusing Kellan's entire form. She delicately ran the tip of the knife she held along his arm. "Surely there is enough of him to share."

Nessa pulled Kellan behind her and snatched the knife from Morrigan's bony fingers. "I'm not in a sharing mood," she snapped.

Morrigan hissed with displeasure but left, taking her delight with another man whose clothing was so saturated with blood that it no longer showed a single speck of white. Kellan shuddered as Morrigan coaxed her nearly lifeless victim over to one of the tables and slashed the man's throat. His body fell limp across the stone slab. More Sidhe joined her, laughing, and together they filled their cups with the dying man's blood. Nessa pulled on Kellan's arm to get him to follow her, moving away from the barbaric scene. Together they weaved their way through the crowd.

"Thank you," he said. Nessa's head was still tucked safely under the hood, but she gave him a slight nod.

"Don't mention it," she replied. "I owe my sister, after all."

"Ah, my friends, it is so good to see you all." All activity stopped as the words echoed around the room. Kellan recognized the voice and the face it belonged to. Lorcan stood on the top step of an expansive crimson stage with a mirror shine. He wore an embroidered long-sleeved tunic, the color of red wine, with a crushed-velvet sash draped over one shoulder. "Thank you for honoring us with your presence. For nineteen years, we have patiently waited, but the time of glory is almost upon us!" The room erupted with applause. Even the puca howled with enthusiasm.

"Yes, my friends, celebrate! Our destiny is finally taking hold, and soon we will possess the power to guarantee our reign—in this life and the one after. The Cold Moon will light the night sky tomorrow, but in honor of my son and my daughter-to-be, we begin the festivities now—seal the doors!" At Lorcan's command, the massive gold doors slammed shut with a deafening boom. The atmosphere in the room changed immediately, filled with hostile anticipation. Lorcan held up his hands. "Before we start the hunt, I'd like to introduce our very own covetable!"

Kellan's knees gave way. Haven, who was behind him, caught him by the arms and held him up. There, at Lorcan's side, stood Veil with her arm tucked into Colden's. With her wild hair sleek and tamed, she looked nothing like herself. She wore a deep red dress. The candlelight caught a shimmering thread of the floral pattern sewn into the transparent bodice, which dropped into a deep V. Her eyelids were ringed in charcoal black, smeared clear to her temples. Her lips were blood red. Her eyes, which had once held so much light, were empty. A grief-stricken whimper escaped Kellan's mouth.

"Kellan, you must calm yourself," Haven said, still gripping Kellan's arms. "She's under the clouding, but we can still do this."

"Look at her," Kellan said breathily. "How do we bring her back from that?"

"You listen to me," Haven hissed. "You have to hold onto hope and fight if she is to have any chance of surviving. Remember, you still have the chance that I do not."

Kellan inhaled a deep stuttering breath and nodded. He searched his hurt heart. His faith in Veil was unshakeable. He knew her strength was undeniable. He would draw on that strength and he would not fail her again. He would fight for her. He would bring her back.

"I'm ready."

Haven released Kellan's arms. "I hope so, for the hunt begins."

Lorcan gave the order. The Sidhe grabbed hold of any human within arm's reach and released them from the clouding, cackling at their disorientation. The humans swiveled their heads, taking in everything from the bloody gore beneath their feet, to the slaughtered bodies that laid on the tables like repulsive centerpieces. The pucas let out a harmonized howl, a spine-chilling sound that broke through the humans' shock and sent them running. Chaos ensued.

"Run!" Cace yelled. He shoved his way through the pandemonium, clearing a path for the others to follow. They had almost made it to the stage when Calla was torn away.

Calla swung her fists at the man that gripped her around the waist, connecting with his nose. He slung her to the ground, kicking her in the ribs over and over until a loud crack, like a snapped branch, could be heard above the mayhem surrounding them. As the man prepared to land another blow, Cace plowed into him, knocking him to the ground. Cace's anger fueled him. He straddled the man's chest and wrapped his hands around his throat. Cace's arms shook as he squeezed. The man struggled against the attack, his eyes bulging. With his hands still tightly wound, Cace raised the man's head and slammed it onto the hard floor until the man's body went slack. Cace didn't realize his hood had been knocked back until it was too late.

"Cace?" The sound of his aunt's screeching voice stilled him. Cace turned his head to find Moira standing on the edge of the havoc. "Lorcan! They're here!"

Cace sprang to his feet. He took hold of Calla and together with the others, they formed a defensive circle. Lorcan's raised hand was all it took for the Sidhe to cease their hunt. The frightened humans froze in confusion.

"Well, it seems we have uninvited guests, my friends. Seize them!"

42. chapter

The fog that filled Veil's mind was dense and dark. The maddening gray blurred her vision while the silken voices kept her disorientated. She was like a bird, trapped in a cage so small that her wings were useless. The claustrophobic feeling left her constricted lungs burning with the overwhelming urge to breathe deep, as though it were a lack of oxygen that kept her lethargic and sent a prickling sensation down her extremities. The sole reprieve from the suffocating darkness were the passing glimpses of life as it occurred around her, like faded flashes of time.

"We know how tired you are," the voices sang. "All is well... Rest easy... Why fight it?"

Why indeed. If living among these monsters, with hearts as cold as their home, was her destiny, then why not embrace the fog and the tranquil sedation it offered. She welcomed the voices as she was washed in the well, the warm water strangely soothing to her tingling skin. She allowed the fog to envelope her like a cocoon as she was primped and painted. She hardly noticed the pain of her wild curls being untangled and straightened.

She hummed along with the melodies in her mind as a revealing deep red gown was pulled over her head, and she was paraded around for all the guests to see. Their hands, clammy from the sweltering heat, pressed against her body in seductive appreciation. She continued to hum, her arm tucked into Colden's, as she was led to Lorcan's side. His words bounced around inside her consciousness, and she hummed even louder to escape them.

"Hunters! The floor is yours!" There were screams, and glimmers of red and white invaded Veil's head. Humans ran hysterically in all directions. The Sidhe gave chase, tackling and slaughtering the innocent. Daggers slashed through soft flesh, ripping and tearing, not satisfied until they scraped against bone. Goblets overflowed into a ruby pond, its waters rising enough to lift the red flowers and they floated past. In her mind, Veil clung to the bars of her cage and begged for it all to stop.

"Well, it seems we have uninvited guests, my friends," came Lorcan's voice. "Seize them!" The hoard descended, dragging them to Lorcan's feet. "Did you fools honestly think that you could make it through here undetected?"

"Takes a fool to know a fool." Veil recognized Cace's voice and the air rushed from her lungs. She followed the sound until she was focused on those kneeling at Lorcan's feet.

Lorcan approached, his demeanor calm. He hovered over Cace then squatted until his eyes were level with Cace's. "With Faelan as your father, one would think you'd have been taught to mind that tongue. He is, after all, so effortlessly complacent." Cace's laugh was sarcastic and overplayed. He stopped to spit in Lorcan's face. Lorcan's lip curled up as he slowly wiped away the saliva. He raised his hand and came down violently against Cace's cheek. "Maybe that'll keep you quiet for a moment." Lorcan stood and clasped his hands behind him. He walked down the line to stand over Kellan. Veil choked on dread, the need to reach Kellan pounding away in her chest. But her wings were still clipped. "The lovestruck one himself. Well, what do you think of my home? I have such lovely décor, do I not?" He waved grandly toward Veil, whose physical form stood prim and proper beside Colden.

Kellan lunged at Lorcan but was knocked back down before he could reach him. "She isn't yours," he spat.

"Pity a vow was wasted on the likes of you," Lorcan said, amused. "You all should have stayed put. Now, let's uncover the rest. Reveal them." He nodded toward the remaining cloaked captives, and their red hoods were yanked off by their handlers.

"Nessa?!" Moira shrieked.

"Oh, Nessa," Lorcan tutted, shaking his head. "Such a shame."

"Please, Lorcan, forgive her," Moira pleaded. "She doesn't understand her actions, my lord!"

Lorcan folded his arms across his chest, one fist coming up to rest under his chin. His eyes wandered the expanse of the Red Room until they stopped on something to his right and a malicious smirk appeared. "Of course, my dearest cousin. Surely our Nessa has just been led astray. I'm quite confident we can manage to bring her back—if she's willing to do one small thing, that is."

Nessa didn't respond, but her mother did. "Anything, my lord, she'll do anything."

"Nessa, rise and return to the good graces of your mother,"

Lorcan ordered. "And would you be so kind as to escort your dear sister to the harp?"

Nessa's eyes widened. She turned toward her companions and then back to Moira. "Mother, please—"

"Do as he says, Nessa. They are nothing but humans. Now, come to me."

Nessa's face went blank. "Tell me, Mother," she said. "Did you feel nothing at all when you killed Grandmother?"

Moira shrugged. "I had a duty and I fulfilled it. Are you satisfied?"

Nessa nodded, her face unreadable. "Quite satisfied, Mother." Moira smiled and held out an inviting hand. Nessa stood and walked toward her mother. She did not stop, even as Cace threw insult after insult at her back, his words slurred from his injured jaw.

Moira embraced Nessa as soon as she was close enough. "That's right, my daughter, your place is by my side."

"My place is with my family," Nessa countered. She pulled the knife she had taken from Morrigan and rammed it deep into her mother's chest. Moira let out a single gurgled scream. With everyone focused on Nessa, Cace and Haven pulled their swords from the concealment of their cloaks. They killed the Sidhe who held them in place, while Kellan and the others attacked their own keepers.

The humans who had survived the hunt were still free of the clouding, and they, too, joined the fight. Veil watched the battle unfold from within her head with blinding flares of vehemence. The Sidhe were outnumbered by the countless humans Lorcan had brought in for the celebration.

"Colden, get her to the harp now," he commanded, wild-eyed and panicked. Colden dragged Veil toward the harp. Her body did as it was directed, but in her mind, she fought, shaking the bars of her prison.

From somewhere in the crowd, Cace yelled, "Stop them! We can't let her play!" Kellan popped up from the ground, soaked in red, and ran for the stairs that led to the stage.

Colden's long, icy fingers gripped Veil's face, wrenching it toward his own until she could see nothing except his piercing eyes. There was no color left in them, only the onyx of his pupils as they swallowed the intense green whole. He shook her face and snarled. "You will play, Veil."

At that moment, Kellan collided with Colden, sending all three of them sprawling to the floor. Veil stood up on shaky legs and followed Colden's command, attempting to make her way to the harp.

"No, Veil!" Kellan shouted. "Fight it!" Kellan's voice reverberated through Veil's mind, but Colden's orders were louder. The muscles of her right leg contracted, lifting her foot to take another step. Her left followed, the involuntary movements jerking her forward.

The two men continued to wrestle. Kellan tried to stand, reaching out for Veil, only to have his feet swiped out from under him. Colden straddled Kellan, his eyes blazing, and landed blow after vicious blow to Kellan's face. With each gruesome strike, Veil felt Kellan's pain. His head was knocked to the side by one ferocious hit, spraying blood across Veil's path. The torment battered her heart. Tears spilled down her cheeks and her body began to tremble. The anguish of her internal struggle dropped her to her knees. But the hellish harp was within reach, and the sight of it compelled her forward.

Veil pushed back against the voices. The more she rebelled against them, the more exhausted she became. With Veil on the losing end of her mental war and nearing surrender, the voices amplified, their mellow tunes no longer serene but shrill and debilitating. Her hands flew to the sides of her head, yanking hair out from the roots, and her fingernails clawed at her ears. The raw sting of scratched skin mingled with the warm wetness of fresh blood, dripping from her self-inflicted wounds down the length of her neck. Her arms spasmed. Her cursed fingers curled, twisting grotesquely. They grazed the dark strings of the ebony harp, that single touch giving life to a solitary musical note. Nefarious and cloaked in alluring lies, it set in motion the maleficent dance and called for the release of the beast.

The shimmering obsidian surface came alive, churning an angry sea. Gloom filled the room, and the bleak haze followed, bringing the unbearable stench of decay with it. Every single human stopped. Their formidable battle cries faded into ominous silence, and their rigid bodies melted into liquid grace. The sinister Sidhe, wide-eyed and breathing harshly, paused, following the lilting movements of their foes with their stares. Sardonic laughter ensued. Without the aid of the humans, Cace, Calla, Haven, and Nessa were easily captured and forced to witness the horror unfolding around them.

Not satisfied with the opening act, the monstrous instrument commanded an encore to feed its hunger. Veil's nimble fingers plucked over and over, the thrumming beat shuddering within her chest. The melody's quick tempo released the haze from the harp in flourishing waves, covering the floor in a heinous blanket.

Still pinned beneath Colden, Kellan's body bucked from the need to join the dance. Viscid veins materialized in the foreboding vapor, pulsing along with the rhythm. Tendrils explored mortal skin, crawling over the humans and slithering across Kellan's face. Kellan's tensed muscles released and all at once the humans crumbled, to lie pliant against the floor. The evil entity thickened, darkening as it grew. At its peak, the tendrils pried open the human's mouths, bringing forth the blood-curdling shrieks. The creature lapped at their lifelines, beckoning their iridescent spirits. It drew the glowing pollen-like particles to the surface of each human's flushed skin and cast them into the air like wishes.

Colden grinned as he studied Kellan's mutilated features. "That looks like it hurts." He smirked, callously flicking at the essence that floated around him. "You really thought love would conquer all, didn't you?" He bent down close to Kellan's ear. "Power is all that matters." The muscles of Kellan's cheek twitched and Colden chuckled. "Oh, you don't believe me? Well let me show you what power can do." He looked up, his gleeful eyes swiftly locating his target. "Veil, eyes on me." At Colden's order, her neck snapped around. "You see, human. Love will always lose to power."

The scraps of Kellan's soul wafted up, riding the air currents to drift over Veil's skin. A final breath, one last kiss, before the descent to Hell's hungry hound waiting below. Veil's sight stayed glued to Colden, but in the space between them, a single glittering grain danced. It sparked a warmth within her, and deep in the darkest part of her mind, another voice rang out.

"You can do this. I know you can."

What started out as weak and temperate transformed to potent and fierce. Veil's heart accelerated, the pulsing power thumping inside her chest. Every nerve fired under her skin, and the flare within her erupted into an inferno. Her self-doubt blazed, allowing her hampered abilities to take root in the ashes. Her bleeding fingers started to shake, and the music stalled. Incapable of summoning souls without the harp's song, the billowing demon retracted its barbs and surged toward Veil. The accursed beast swarmed her senses, intent on bringing her back under.

Veil fought to withdraw her convulsing hands from the harp. Her aching knees gave way, and she crumbled to the ground. The demon hissed with anger and intensified its efforts, determined to take complete control. The voices in Veil's mind matched the demon's pitch, and together they lashed out with a vile screech. The pressure built inside her skull. Blood trickled from her ears. Everything slowed down, and Veil's eyes rolled back in her head. With its victory near, the demon cackled.

"*Faith.*" Dara's voice, though whispered, drowned out the demon. The one word echoed, becoming stronger, and Veil rose to her knees. She pushed a feral scream from her mouth that resonated off the rock walls and banished the evil murk from her mind. In control of her body once more, Veil summoned her power and slammed her maimed hands into the stone floor. The ground shook beneath her palms. The intense energy threw Colden from atop Kellan's abused body, sending him soaring through the air to smash into the rough wall. One last cry belted from Veil's scarlet lips, splintering the stone floor. Pillars of ice erupted from the fractures, encasing Lorcan and his followers inside arctic tombs.

An uneasy silence swallowed the Red Room. Drained of what power it had left, the helpless specter released the vital force it had stolen. Luminous specks fell like snowflakes, each finding its rightful owner. Kellan was among the first to regain himself and used what strength he could gather to make his way to Veil. She closed her eyes and collapsed into his arms. Swaddled against his chest, her eyelashes fluttered, and she gifted him with a tender smile.

"You came," she whispered.

Kellan's watery eyes danced over Veil's face. He lowered his forehead to rest against hers, his eyes falling shut and his lips a breath away from her own. He closed the distance, but not before he whispered back, "I always will."

43. chapter

Veil stood over her father's body. She tried to focus on his face and not on the gruesome injury that stole his life. A myriad of emotions swirled within her. She was ashamed to admit that above all else, she wanted answers—the whole truth from his own mouth. But a callous thief had poached their opportunity and with it Veil's chance at finding closure.

Lost in her thoughts, Veil didn't realize her sister stood beside her until Nessa's hand rested on her shoulder. "I'm sorry."

"He was your father too." Veil's voice revealed no sign of the storm whirling inside her.

Nessa removed the red cloak she still wore. She stepped closer to their father's form and covered him with more care than Veil had ever witnessed from her. "He was," Nessa said, her eyes never leaving the floor. "And you are my sister."

"When has that ever mattered, Nessa?"

Nessa sighed and turned to face Veil with teary eyes, her bottom lip trembling. "It should always have mattered." Nessa closed the space between them and pulled Veil into the first embrace they had ever shared. Veil's body tensed for a moment, but soon her arms clung to Nessa as well.

"Ah, there's that forgiving heart I missed so much." Veil released Nessa and turned around to find Cace watching them, his amusement evident, even under his unkempt hair, swollen jaw, and blood-smeared clothes.

"And good thing for you I still have one too," Veil replied, a small smile playing on her lips. Cace opened his inviting arms. Veil grabbed Nessa's hand and the three held each other in silence. The simple act was all it took for Veil's inner storm to calm. She closed her eyes and soaked up the feeling of serenity; inner peace was not something she was accustomed to. She would never have all the answers she had wished for, but her father had sacrificed his life for another, and a human at that. The selfless deed would have to be enough.

The three kin pulled away from each other a short time later. Veil looked back down the hall toward the Red Room, a place she never wanted to step foot in again. After Veil had bound their enemies, Haven had opened the golden doors. Now, rows of survivors lined the walls, confused and bathed in carnage. Kellan walked out of the Red Room, his arm wrapped around another one of the wounded.

"What will happen to them?" Veil asked.

Cace sighed. "Many of them were brought here from other clans. They could be from anywhere. And that's assuming they can even remember where they are from."

Daniel kneeled next to a person on the floor, carefully attending to their injuries. "Is there nothing we can do for them?"

Cace reached out and took Veil's hand. "I won't lie to you, cousin. I can't guarantee what will happen to the humans once Father takes control of this foul place, but I can give them a choice."

"A choice?"

Cace nodded. "As the new ruler of the barrows, I will offer them sanctuary with us or safe passage back to their realm if that is what they desire. Their memories of this place and our kind will be taken. It's not much, cousin, but it's all I have."

Veil squeezed Cace's hand. "It's a start," she said, smiling once again.

Cace nodded with a smile of his own. "It's a start."

Kellan jogged down the hall toward them, his vigor already beginning to return in the short time since his reunion with Veil. He pulled Veil into his arms, tucked her head against him, and breathed her scent in deep. "We got the survivors out," he said. "Calla wants to know what should be done with the ones that didn't make it...and the harp." Veil's eyes clenched shut, and her grip on Kellan tightened at the mention of the harp. His hands moved along her back, trying to bring what comfort he could.

"I say we seal the room," Nessa answered. "Lock it for good."

"I think Nessa may have the right idea on this one," Cace agreed. Deep down Veil knew that sealing the doors was the most logical solution, but the thought of that monstrous site being the final resting place for the innocent hurt her heart.

"Veil?" Kellan asked.

"I'm all right," she muttered. "I know it's the best plan. It doesn't make it any easier, though."

"No, it doesn't," he said, rubbing his hands up and down her arms. "What about the harp? Can the bloody thing be destroyed?"

Cace bowed his head, giving it a slow and sullen shake. "You can't completely destroy evil. Darkness is real, same as light. The two can't exist without the other. The harp was given as temptation, and it will always tempt. It's up to us not to give in."

Veil stood at the entrance to the Red Room with the others at her side. Inside, the bodies of the slain lay haphazardly across the floor, their murderers encased in an impressive mausoleum of ice. On the stage, above it all, sat the ebony harp.

As if knowing its fate, the harp called out to Veil. Her body stiffened at the intensity of its summons. Entranced by the strength of its command, Veil's eyes glazed over, and she took a single step forward. Mingled with its calls were the panicked voices of her companions. She focused on them and shook her head, clearing away the shadows.

"Close it," she demanded. Haven and Cace immediately laid their hands on the rock walls. The two gold pieces met in the middle with a boom that echoed throughout the fortress. Veil, Calla, and Nessa stepped forward, their hands joining the others against the door. The heat of their combined energy radiated, blowing back their hair. The stone surrounding the door started to shake. It shifted until the gray boulders had completely swallowed the shimmering gold door and the histories it told.

Kellan swept Veil off her feet and into his arms. "Are you ready?" he asked. "The road home is long."

A bittersweet smile pulled at Veil's lips, the toll of her emotions bearing down on her. She closed her eyes, blinking away tears, and whispered, "Home."

Veil's vow to Lorcan burned like a raging fire as Kellan took his first step over the threshold of the fortress with her in his arms. But her heart kept beating and would continue to as long as she was carried out of the Cold Valley. They were overjoyed to find the horses waiting for them outside, and no one more so than Calla. Though there were not enough horses for all to ride, the trek back across the frozen wilderness would be made easier with the help of the large animals. Veil glanced over Kellan's shoulder and frowned. Nessa and Haven stood in the large doorway with a group of humans who had surprisingly decided to stay behind.

"Why do you think they're staying?" Kellan asked.

"For most of them, this is all they have ever known," she answered. Kellan nodded, but he obviously didn't share their opinion.

"Any place would be better than there," he mumbled. They reached Glas, the same clever horse Kellan had ridden into the Cold Valley, and he lifted Veil to place her on the magnificent creature's back.

"Veil!" They turned around to find Haven running their way. The dark-haired Sidhe came to a stop before them, his remorseful eyes cemented to Veil's. She cocked her head to the side, a silent conversation passing between them. Though their bond had been cracked when he had cast her aside, it had never been broken entirely. Veil held out her hand, waiting for him to come to her, and he did. With one innocent touch, regret, understanding, and forgiveness all met.

Promises of "safe travels" and "this is not goodbye" were exchanged with those who stayed behind, and then the group departed. They traveled across the bleak valley, over the frozen red river, and through the frosty forest until they reached a cave. Rory stood guard inside the cave's mouth, his eyes going wide with their arrival. A large smile replaced the look of shock and he ran deeper into the cave, his excited cheers accompanying him. Aileen, Maddy, and Evelyn rushed from the opening soon after, tears of joy streaming down their faces. Evelyn headed toward Jack, and they met halfway, enveloping each other in a secure embrace. Kellan and Niall dismounted, catching Aileen and Maddy as the two women threw themselves into their awaiting arms.

Rory emerged from the cave with Liam holding onto him for support. Liam's injury was significant, but he appeared to be on the mend. His tender eyes shone with happiness and relief at the sight of his family. Kellan and Niall hurried over. A light dusting of snow fell upon their shoulders as they embraced. Caught up in the emotional scene playing out before her, Veil didn't realize that Aileen was beside her until Aileen placed her hand on Veil's knee. Prevented from laying her feet on the ground by the vow, Veil gazed down from Glas' back. Aileen's tears had already begun to frost over, with more still flowing. The last words Aileen had spoken to Veil had been said in anger.

"I'm sorry," Aileen said, her voice hoarse.

Veil's brow wrinkled. "You love your family. I can only hope my mother would have done the same."

"She would have, dear," Aileen said. "But since she can't, I'd be honored to fill in—if you'll allow it?" Veil placed her hand on top of Aileen's, her own eyes brimming with tears. Maddy bounded over and slapped her hand over theirs, breaking the seriousness of their tender moment with laughter. Veil had missed the younger girl's friendship, her quirkiness, and her glowing spirit. Veil didn't believe her smile could get any wider, but then Niall and Daniel approached.

Niall cleared his throat. "Mum, you think we have room for one more?"

Veil gazed at Kellan, who stood behind the others with a

soft smile on his face. No words were spoken between them, but the conversation was crystal clear. Veil tore her eyes from the man she loved and turned to her newest brother. "Welcome to the family, Daniel."

44. chapter

Familiar stars twinkled in the nighttime sky. Veil thought she could watch their bewitching dance for a lifetime. She dug her fingers into the hay beneath her hand, thankful for the feeling of dried grass rather than the chill of ice and snow. She breathed in deeply, letting the earthy smell of grass and soil invade her senses. Even the musky scent of animals made her smile.

Veil sat in the opening of the loft's large window, her legs dangling over the edge. Her head rested against Kellan's shoulder, her other hand entwined with his. A majestic moon hung above, casting its beams over the farm. They enjoyed each other's company in comfortable silence, no words needed to fill the moment. The harmonized tunes of the frogs and crickets were enough. Veil's eyes wandered over the expanse of gorgeous land as she tried to trap the images of her home within her memory.

Their return, and the peaceful year that had followed, had done wonders for the entire McGrath clan. Liam's leg had eventually healed, and he bore the scar with pride. In true Liam fashion, he loved to rehash the elaborate tale of his courageous close call with death. Like in the happier days before Veil was taken, Aileen and Maddy had found their peace in the kitchen, their hands busy with dough and batter. Rory was still Rory, lighthearted and foolhardy, and Daniel had found a home on the farm with Niall. Connor and Farrah never truly understood what the others had gone through, and never would, Lord willing.

Then there was Gavin. The moment his cobalt eyes had landed on Veil, he had thrown his slender arms around her neck. When she had first returned he'd spent most of his waking hours clinging to her, becoming uneasy if she was out of sight, as though she would disappear again if he should even blink. It took him time to trust in her presence. Time was what they had all needed to fully heal.

"Aren't your feet cold?" Kellan asked.

She wiggled her bare toes and giggled. "You've asked me this before," she said, remembering the day he had taken her to Kenmare Bay.

Kellan's free hand came up to rub the back of his neck, a self-conscious laugh escaping his mouth. "Aye, I reckon I have."

He had been back on the farm full-time just shy of a month. It had taken many reassurances, but at Veil's insistence, Kellan had returned to finish his education. Though he had elected to attend university in Killarney instead of in Cork—a compromise he wouldn't relent on. The shorter commute meant he could remain on the farm, allowing him and Veil the time they needed to get to know each other without the influence of Dara's clouding and for their love to take root and grow naturally. Kellan's hard work and devotion to his studies had paid off, a brand new business degree the prize for his efforts. He immediately put it to use with his wood carving skills to open what was sure to be a successful custom furniture trade.

Kellan closed his eyes and took a deep breath. He turned to face Veil and took hold of her scarred hands, his thumbs gliding across her skin. "There's something I need to say," he said, avoiding her eyes. "Or rather, there's something I need to ask."

Veil smiled at his unusual shyness and joked, "Something you've asked me before?"

Kellan's body shook with laughter. He finally raised his eyes to hers and said, "Definitely not something I've asked you before."

Veil's head tilted to the side, her mouth going dry and her heart thumping. "I'll answer anything you ask me, Kellan."

Kellan's eyes searched Veil's. "Are you happy?" The question was not one she had imagined, and it was certainly not something he had asked her before, nor had anyone. Caught off guard, she remained quiet. "Because, I'm happy with you. Not because someone made that choice for me in the beginning, but because I chose you in the end." He flipped Veil's hand over and placed a ring in the center of her palm. The silver band wrapped around a single raw, opaque stone. The ring glittered in the moonlight, revealing the words *Not perfect, but real* inscribed on the inside of the band. Veil's joyful tears collected like dewdrops in her eyelashes as her eyes fluttered closed. Kellan gently wiped her face with the pads of his thumbs. His lips pressed a delicate kiss against her forehead before brushing against hers. "I guess I have one more question to ask you," he whispered. His husky voice sent shivers through her body, goosebumps prickling across her sensitive skin. The connection they shared was, and would always be, unwavering.

"Anything," she said, breathlessly.

The End.

epilogue

The wind blew across the green field, whipping up Veil's wild hair. She sat with her bare feet dipped into the cool water of the shallow stream and tenderly ran her hand over the thriving shamrock patch. Kellan's perfect place—and hers as well. In this spot, Veil had made her choice. She had walked to him in a gown that had belonged to Liam's mother, the blush tulle and sheer embroidered sleeves a perfect blend of her human and Sidhe heritage. Jack had escorted her, squeezing her hand when she nearly cried at the sight of what awaited her. Next to Kellan stood Cace, both men dressed in a deep shade of blue. Calla, Nessa, and Haven were there as well. It had been close to two years since Veil had last seen them.

Her Uncle Faelan had wasted no time settling into his throne in the Cold Valley. As his only heir, Cace was given reign of the barrows and rose to the occasion remarkably well, learning to lead while also keeping his sense of humor. He had already begun to make changes, starting with Calla. They had finally taken the leap to pursue their relationship. That in itself proved that change was possible. Cace kissed Veil's cheek and delicately placed a flower wreath on her head. Then he stepped back, allowing her to close the remaining distance between Kellan and herself.

Niall had officiated the human vows, with Haven taking his place once he had finished. In his gloved hands, he held the silver binding string. Veil's wide eyes instantly searched out Kellan's, which held only love. He did not hesitate to lock his arm with hers, permitting Haven to tie them together. Veil held his gaze, even as the guests and the emerald rolling hills disappeared within the blinding glow. All Veil and Kellan could see was each other. For those who had witnessed Kellan and Veil's love story it must not have been surprising that the little rope melted away painlessly in the end. They had always been each other's true mark.

A sweet voice broke Veil from her memories. "Aunt Ve-Ve!" Gavin shouted. "Look what Lillianna can do!" Now a chattering nine-year-old, Gavin jumped up and down, pointing to a girl with sandy blond hair and unkempt curls. Veil struggled to her feet, laughing along with them as several tiny purple blooms burst from the ground beneath the little girl's outstretched hand.

From the moment Veil's daughter had opened her crystalline eyes, Kellan had encouraged her to be herself, believing in her the same as he had Veil. In no time at all, Lillianna had approached school age, and with her abilities, Veil wasn't sure how the gifted girl would attend. Fortunately for the family, Maddy had gone on to become a teacher, and her classroom would always be a safe place for all the children. While away discovering her passions, Maddy had grown up. She had kept her sunny disposition but left behind the childish fantasies that had once seemed so definite, including Rory. It was now his turn to chase after her.

Veil smiled at the two children, then again when Kellan's familiar strong arms circled around her waist. "What's all the commotion down here? I can hear you lot all the way from the house." Veil peeked over her shoulder to their quaint cottage, nestled against the hill overlooking their perfect place. Kellan had spent almost a year building their enchanting home.

Kellan's furniture endeavor had taken off far more quickly than any of the family could have dreamed. It had taken many long hours sorting orders around the kitchen table, but McGrath's Tailor-Made had become a reputable name known all across Ireland, and they accomplished it all while keeping up the family farm. Veil and Daniel had also ventured into business with their own apothecary, often joining Aileen at the market.

Veil covered Kellan's arms with her own and answered, "Only your daughter entertaining the masses."

"Is she now?" Kellan said, wearing his smirk in his tone. "More and more like her mum every day, I tell you."

"That she is." Veil giggled. "Maybe you'll have more luck with the next?"

Kellan twirled Veil around and smiled, rubbing her bump. "And how is the lad today?"

Veil beamed. "Busy, as usual. Have you thought of a name yet?"

"You know, I think I have," he answered, kissing her brow. "A name in honor of the person that gave me everything—even when I didn't think I wanted it."

"Well," Veil laughed, "what is it?"

Kellan became quiet, lost in thought. Veil reached up and caressed his face, bringing him back to her. Then she waited.

He took a deep breath and said, "Asa."

"Asa," Veil repeated. The single word sounded charmed as it left her lips. "What does it mean?"

"Healer...it means healer."

Acknowledgments

Author, writer, storyteller, or my personal favorite word: weaver. Different words with all the same meaning, and terms that are usually tied to being on one's own. While solitude helps to get the words flowing, this incredible adventure has made me realize just how far from solitary the publishing journey is. I'm not sure the exact words exist to describe how grateful I am to everyone who has supported this book, but I'm going to give it my best go.

To my very own true mark, Richard. Our bond was built on friendship, one that still flourishes, and one which I still adore. Thank you for your unyielding love, constant support, and the witty banter that continues to make me grin (and roll my eyes, of course). I love you, Bear.

To our children, Lillianna and Asa. You two are the reason our hearts beat and why our lives are never short of laughter. Your father and I are so proud of you both. We loved you yesterday, we love you today, and we will love you for all of the tomorrows.

To my publisher, Lost Boys Press. Thank you all for your kindness, your open communication, your constant support, and your honesty. To those who have worked on Those Beneath (Ashley, Dina, Claire, Hannah, Sydney, Chad, Tilly, Anna, Brett). You have added your own unique magic to this book and have made it a special kind of beautiful. I can only hope that every debut author has the remarkable experience you have granted me.

To my editor, Brett Mann. I truly believe you and I were sisters in a previous life. Thank you so much, my friend, for putting up with all of my questions, for blessing this book with your creativity, and for taking a chance on me. It has been such a pleasure working with you, and I hope we will get the opportunity to bring another world to life in the future.

To my dear friend, Ashley White. To be on this journey with you has been incredible. A wild ride that I wouldn't want to take with anyone else. Thank you for being the first to read Those Beneath, for taking me under your wing, and for teaching me so very much along the way. Your talent amazes me and your friendship is priceless. Can't wait to see what your passionate mind creates next.

To the online Writing and Reading Community. Fellow bookish people from around the world who all celebrate when one succeeds and rally together when times are tough. Precious friendships. I hope to meet you all one day in person. May your days be filled with fantastical worlds and glorious emails screaming YES in the subject line.

Last but most certainly not least, to any reader who picks up Those Beneath. Thank you for coming along on this adventure. I hope that by the end you can see the magic within yourself.

Almedia Ryan was born and raised in Southeast Texas, spending most of her early years barefoot and exploring the outdoors. Her love of nature took her to the beautiful state of Montana, where she now lives with her husband, two children, and a spoiled rotten husky named Boulder. She used her education of art and dance to teach art to special needs students and as a performance arts choreographer for public schools. After one too many dance injuries, she left teaching and hung up her dancing shoes so that she could dive back into another passion—writing. *Those Beneath* is Almedia's first fantasy book, inspired by her outdoor adventures, the students she was so blessed to teach, and from the magical stories of folklore told to her by her late father.

lost boys press

www.lostboyspress.com

Also available from Lost Boys Press

Novellas:

A Map to the Stars by Ashley Hutchison
The Garden of the Golden Children by Ashley Hutchison
Marshmallows by Louise Willingham

Full Length:

Ghost River by Chad Ryan
Nothing Special by Dina S.
Those Beneath by Almedia Ryan

Anthologies:

Chimera
Not Meant for Each Other
Heroes
Great Wars
Tales of Somewhere Else by Ashley Hutchison and Dewi
Hargreaves

E-Zines:

Bloom
Storm
Ignite
Moot
Doom

CPSIA information can be obtained
at www.ICGtesting.com
Printed in the USA
BVHW051944270423
663173BV00003B/6